MAD DOG BARKED

When a potential client walks into your office with a unique first edition copy of Edgar Allan Poe's *The Murders in the Rue Morgue* with a letter inside full of disorienting notes, you start asking questions. When this client mentions that his personal secretary has disappeared on his way to find you and then writes an obscenely large check, you have to wonder what the hell is going on. When you ask your new client what exactly he wants you to do and he replies, "Let your conscience be your guide," you know there's going to be trouble....

Scott Porter owns a Florida detective agency that specializes in criminal court cases. When Mr. Edwin Morton Holmes drops the mysterious letter in his lap, Porter isn't sure what he should do with it. Then a thin, hatchet-faced man begins following him, and a guard at Mr. Holmes' estate is found with his head caved in. Almost before Porter can even decide where to start, he's facing not only two dead bodies but the disappearance of his client.

The answer must lie with the letter but Porter is damned if he can figure out what it is. He has other problems, too, with a field agent he isn't sure he can trust, and his attraction to his married assistant, Trudy, who may or may not feel the same way. Things grow even more complicated when the FBI shows up and murder soon becomes the least of his problems....

Mad Dog Barked

by Rick Ollerman

STARK HOUSE

Stark House Press • Eureka California

MAD DOG BARKED

Published by Stark House Press
1315 H Street
Eureka, CA 95501, USA
griffinskye3@sbcglobal.net
www.starkhousepress.com

ISBN-13: 978-1-944520-09-0

Book design by Mark Shepard, SHEPGRAPHICS.COM

Special thanks to Rick Keeney.

First Stark House Press Edition: September 2016

FIRST EDITION

Mad Dog Barked

by Rick Ollerman

To Devin, Meg and Dennis Abraham
for keeping the music going

FIRST HALF

CHAPTER ONE

The jukebox was playing some new white trash song destined to be an anthem for trailer park weddings when I walked in. The two flat screen televisions were each tuned to reality shows with the sound turned blessedly down. "Geeze, will you turn this crap off?" I said to the bartender as I took an empty stool.

"Which crap?"

"All of it," I said, but nodded at the jukebox for emphasis.

"Can't do it. Someone paid for the privilege." Tapping his fingers on the bar to the music, he said, "Don't you know who this is?"

"Some contest loser from a reality show," I said. "Doesn't belong in a bar." I'd been driving fourteen hours straight with nothing but the radio to blot out the highway noise. This same lousy song had played at least once every thirty minutes all the way since Baltimore.

A perky bottle blonde said, "I don't think it belongs in public," as she slid on to the stool next to mine, scooching her seat closer to the counter and closer to me at the same time.

I gave her a quick glance, recognized her. "Neither do you, sweets. Get lost."

She stared at me open-mouthed, like she'd never heard the words before. "Excuse me?" she managed.

"Bourbon," I said to the bartender. "Nothing for the lady."

"I remember you being nicer than this."

"I don't remember you at all," I lied.

That did it. She left in a hurry. Not just her stool, the whole bar. I was lucky she hadn't already been carrying a drink.

Jarod, the bartender, was laughing hard as he freshened my drink. "You've got a way with women, don't you?"

"Only when they let me."

"Who was that one?"

"Another case of bad judgment." I pointed to my glass. "Give me one more when this is done."

"Your judgment was better last week. With that brunette."

"You're a dangerous man, my friend." I winked at him and put a ten spot on the bar. "Here, this ought to buy your silence for a while."

I finished my drink in relative peace. There was a natural ebb and flow to the bar traffic weekday nights, even on a Friday, and Jarod's place wasn't a sports bar, a fern bar, or a boozer joint. He poured a good drink and the atmosphere was casual. You want to eat peanuts and yell at athletes on big screen TVs, you go somewhere else. You want to suck boilermakers and run a tab you never catch up on, same thing. Meet up with someone near the small downtown strip and get a nice, quiet drink, well, here's the place.

After downing my second, it was time to leave. I nodded at Jarod and headed for the door. I'd parked in the lot back of my condo and walked over but it was getting late, my legs were shaky from the drive and all I wanted to do now was get to bed.

There was a scrap of paper, a business card, lying in the entranceway outside and I almost walked by before it clicked that something about it looked familiar. I stooped, picked it up and sure enough, it was one of mine. I flipped it over—nothing on the back. My hand flashed to my wallet, which is where I kept the ones I carried, and it was still in my jacket pocket.

I went back inside, looking closer at everyone at the tables but nobody was looking back. At the bar again I asked Jarod if anyone had been around for me. With a grin, he shook his head no. Smiling at the thought of the blonde, no doubt.

Hmm.

I exited again and turned toward my office, just a few blocks out of the way from my condo. Downtown Sarasota, such as it was, stayed to my left as I headed toward the Gulf. I turned a corner and walked past the small parking lot that came with the lease for my office. It was nearly ten thirty and nothing on this block was open, including my private detective office, but there was a black BMW pulled in to one of my parking spots. It was just in front of the "Employee and Customer Only" sign. As long as it was gone by morning I wasn't going to care.

I unlocked the door and went inside, then kept moving down the hall to my office. The building was empty, which I expected. A lot of what we did was the stuff I considered unsavory, the cheating husband or wife, the questions of dubious paternity. I had a guy who actually liked working these cases so I was happy to let him have at it. We also did a fair amount of background checks for businesses and schools, like credit and employment verifications. The people I had to do that work spent half their time in front of computers and half their time on telephones. That stuff bored the crap out of me.

My own preference was working with defendants or lawyers on criminal court cases. When the district attorney has an array of investigators, police, federal cops and crime labs at his disposal, the defendants were typically outgunned from the start. We were the equalizers, or at least we tried to be. How else could you combat all those public resources?

Our services cost money, though, so most of these clients tended to be either well heeled or high profile, often both. This made us expensive but we went for the facts, all of them, beyond the ones the cops selectively decided to include in their reports. As hired guns we couldn't do anything about the reputation of the profession, we could only try to manage our own. I did my best to be sure my employees were scrupulously honest, no matter where the facts of the case led, but being mercenary by definition, we always put them in the hands of the person writing the checks. After that, they could do with them as they would. We were serving our part in the system. At least for those who could afford us.

I picked up the phone and called my service. No messages. Fine with me. I still just wanted to go home.

As I pushed my chair back the phone rang. I thought about not answering but that seemed silly after making the effort to walk over here just because I'd found a dropped business card. Since it was after hours and I wasn't looking for something to do, all I said was, "Hello?"

"Has my man been to see you?"

The voice was deep, authoritative, something off about it. Foreign? I wondered.

The lack of courtesy was irritating. How did he know I, or anyone, would even be there to take his call? He could have gotten the call service. He should have gotten the call service.

"Who is this?" I asked.

A pause. "My man will explain everything to you. I'm trying to keep out of this as much as possible."

"Let me help," I told him, and hung up. For all I knew he had no idea he was actually talking to me. His assumption that this was so annoyed me. If the phone rang again before I left I was going to let it be.

My condo was the other way, in the direction of the water, but I locked up the office and turned right out the door and walked past the parking lot. Some things just nag at you in this line of work. There was a hatchet-faced man standing on the other side of the BMW, watching me as I passed. I almost stopped to ask if he were looking for me but then I thought, the hell with him. I decided I didn't care enough to slow down. The scene didn't have a happy feeling to it and I knew when I felt like picking a fight with a stranger it was a good time to go home to bed.

Facing off with unknown people at night in quiet places in a state where virtually everyone owns a gun isn't the smartest thing to do. I've got one too, but I don't carry it unless I think I might need it. Taking one out in this town doesn't scare anyone, it just invites them to take out their own. Suddenly It becomes a question of who's faster on the draw and I'm no gunslinger. But if someone does start shooting, it's good to have an answer. Oftentimes having a dumpster to hide behind is the better one.

I didn't mind the car being there before, so I didn't mind it now. I'd walk around the block and head home. The bourbon was the only thing holding me up at this point but I was drowsy. Hatchet-face was staring at me as I passed but I kept going. If he wanted someone to stare back he could invest in a mirror.

Ten minutes later I was in the lobby to my building. I took the elevator up to the eleventh floor, stripped to my shorts, brushed my teeth. Got into bed with the book I was reading. As soon as I was comfortable the phone rang. Because of course it did.

It was the same voice as the one at the office. "Did my man turn up?"

I'd had enough. "Look, who is this? I don't know you. I don't know your man, who that's supposed to be, or how you know how to get hold of me this time of night. You're a bit on the rude side and as far as I know I haven't taken you on as a client. If you've got an issue or have been talking to someone at the office, call the service or call back Monday but I'm going to bed now. You have a good night."

"Wait," he said quickly. "I'd rather not say who this is. Not until I've found my—employee."

"Sorry, haven't seen him. Bye now." I moved to hang up, stopped, then pulled the phone back to my ear. "Out of curiosity," I said, "does your man-employee drive a black BMW?"

Silence on the line. Then: "So you have seen him."

"I didn't say that. I saw his car. It was in my lot a half hour ago."

"Well go get him, man. This may be urgent."

"To you, maybe. Anyway, the car is at my office and I'm at my home. Speaking of which, how did you get this number?"

The caller ignored this. "Can you go to the car, see if you can find my employee? I will pay you to do this. His name is Robbins. Endo Robbins."

"Thin guy, tall, maybe five eleven, face like the business end of a small axe?"

"Heavens no. Endo is maybe half a foot shorter than that and quite rotund. No one would ever think to call him thin."

"Any idea about his skinny friend?"

More hesitation. "Damn. This may be a problem."

"For Endo?"

"For myself. For all of us."

Not for me, I thought.

He sad, "Can you find him?"

"Endo or Hatchet-face?"

"I'd prefer Endo. You likely would, too. The other I don't know personally, I have no idea who he is, but if he comes from where I think he might, my friend Endo could be in some very serious trouble."

I surrendered in the name of commerce. "I'll do it," I said. "But it's on your quarter. I'll go check out his car. How can I reach you?"

"I'll call again." And he hung up.

Silly bastard, I thought. His number's on my phone. I jotted it down on a pad and slipped some fresh clothes on. Thinking about it, I decided to grab my gun from the nightstand drawer and I clipped it to my belt as I went back to the night.

When I arrived back at the office the door was still locked and everything was as secure as I'd expected. Only now the parking lot was empty. On a whim I took the time to walk back to the bar and repeated the description of Endo Robbins to Jarod and asked if it sounded familiar.

He tried, he really did, which was asking a lot of a bartender who saw hundreds of faces a night. In the end he shook his head no. Not knowing if this was helpful or not, I told him thank you and left. Outside the door I looked on the ground, the sidewalk, and the street just off the curb where I'd found my business card but there wasn't anything else to see.

Feeling a little silly, I went back inside. Jarod came over to my end of the bar and I apologized for bothering him.

"No worries, Mr. Porter," he said.

I asked if anyone at all had been looking for me, even during the past few days while I'd been gone, and Jarod said no. "How about another man, thin, pointy face, stares a lot?"

"Tall?"

"Tallish. Just under six feet, thereabouts. Wearing a dark suit."

"There was someone like that in here tonight, a little while ago. Sat at that table in the corner." He pointed. "Ordered a beer but didn't drink it. Stayed about twenty minutes."

"And no sign of the fat guy?"

"Nope. Something wrong?" he asked.

"When isn't there?" I slid him another bill. "Don't drink it all in one place," I told him.

"You got it."

"Oh, was that other guy here the same time I was?"

Jarod said he couldn't be sure, but maybe. Time and faces ran together during working hours. I nodded good night.

Not having anything else to do, I went back home. No new messages. The call history on the phone showed the same man as before had tried calling again, twice. I dialed the number from the display, the same one I'd written down earlier, but no one answered.

Letting go of work, of the night, I stripped again, took out my book, and went to bed for the second time this evening. I fell asleep without finishing a page.

It turned out that at that moment Endo Robbins was on a boat with no running lights near the deep water channel leading out to the Gulf of Mexico, a good twelve miles distant from Sarasota Bay. His body was spread on a piece of canvas on the floor of the boat with a five gallon plastic bucket next to him. On the sun bench in the stern above the inboard/outboard motor were two cinder blocks wrapped with lengths of heavy boat chain.

A tallish man with a pointed face squinted down at him in the darkness, a small pen light in one hand held close to his side. His name was Rico Gallo and he was worn out after everything he'd been through that night. He needed to take care of Robbins, get the boat back to its berth, and get some much needed shuteye. He'd done all he was supposed to do this night, or he would have, after he was finished here.

Gallo knew what he was about and removed the razor sharp filleting knife from its leather sheath on the seat next to him and knelt over the still form of Endo Robbins. It wasn't ready yet. A body dumped in the water will sink unless it's made up of a lot of fat, which is less dense than water. The cinder blocks would help take care of that but they wouldn't be enough.

Rigor mortis was setting in; calcium had stopped moving out of the muscle cells, causing them to stiffen. In about seventy-two hours, enzymes would start breaking down the muscle tissue, allowing it to relax again, and additional chemical reactions would begin. Organelles in the cells would begin to rupture, exuding a chemical similar to hydrogen peroxide. This would start to oxidize everything it touched and gases would be created which would eventually make a submerged body buoyant enough to rise to the surface.

Unless it were weighted down, of course, but sometimes not even then. Depending on how the body was anchored, there were times the force would be enough to pull limbs from sockets as the torso strained upward, away from the sandy floor.

The answer, as Gallo well knew, was to remove enough of the mass where this gaseous exchange occurred in order to keep the body from rising. Deftly he applied the knife and using both hands, he loaded the bucket four times, dumping it over the side with every fill, before rolling what was left of Robbins into a crumpled ball on to the canvas. This he closed up tightly and worked onto the sun bench where he wrapped it closely with the chains. Finally he pushed the two cinder blocks off the stern. The entire package slid off the cushions and hit the water with a splash, disappearing slowly as gravity and water pressure worked to force the trapped air from the wrapping.

Gallo removed his coveralls, knelt over the side, and listened to the bubbles as he washed the bare skin of his arms in water dark as ink. Then he checked them with the pen light. He needed to get away from the channel, get the running lights on, and head home. Tossing the bucket overboard, he moved to the cockpit of the boat and turned the ignition key.

When he finally told me this story, I was very close to suffering a similar fate myself.

CHAPTER TWO

Trudy from the office woke me with a phone call when the sun was already far up in the sky. "Wake up, boss," she said.

I knew better than to argue with her. "What's going on?"

"Someone's here to see you."

"I don't think I care."

"Well, he thinks you should."

"And who the hell is he?"

She said it as though she were announcing titles at a castle ball: "A Mr. Edwin Morton Holmes."

"Never heard of him. Is he cute?"

"Says he talked to you last night."

That at least got me sitting up, and I scratched the sleep out of the corners of my eyes. "Is there a short, roundish guy with him?"

"Nope."

"Tall, sharp-faced gentleman?"

"No, he's all alone."

"Hold on a minute." I set the phone down and stood up, stretching and yawning. I picked the handset up again. "I'm back," I said. "Sorry."

"What's wrong?"

I shook my head. "Beats me. Something's bothering him, though. Why didn't he call me himself? He had my number last night. Kept me up late."

"I get the feeling he's used to having someone do things like that for him."

"Well, that could be his problem. Seems like one of those people of his may have gotten lost yesterday. On the way to find me." I walked out to the kitchen to pour some water.

"I thought you weren't getting back until today."

"Drove through and got in last night. Had a drink at Jarod's, started getting phone calls. What's Mr. Holmes doing now?"

"Standing still as a pole but if he had heat vision I'd be an overcooked barbeque plate. I'm in your office. He can't hear me."

I thought about it. "Looks like money, does he?"

"Oh, yes."

"Well, business is about making some, so I guess I should see him. Describe him to me."

"An inch or two over six feet, thin but trim, grey hair, dark suit, keeps his hands folded in front of him."

Not familiar. "Stand him out front like a cigar store statue, maybe he'll attract more clients with money. Otherwise, ask him if he'll wait half an hour so I can shower and get dressed. I'll hold."

Trudy set the phone down on my desk and I couldn't hear the exchange but when she came back she sounded annoyed. "He's not happy."

Neither was I. "So?"

"He wants to come over to your place. I told him no."

First my phone number, and now my address. "He knows where I live?" I tried to keep the emotion out of my voice.

"Of course not," she snapped. "No one does, right? He asked how to find you."

So he didn't know about my condo. That was something. It still didn't explain how he knew my phone number.

"All right," I said. "I'll be in as soon as I can. If he waits, he waits."

"If he gives me a hard time, I may have to belt him."

"You can shoot him for all I care, just be sure to clean up after yourself."

"He probably has people to do that for him, too."

I laughed. "See you in a bit."

After a three minute shower I threw on some casual clothes and set off on foot. After my trip I didn't have a lot of viable wardrobe choices, at least not clean ones. Before I went in to the office I checked the lot. Trudy's car was there, and Gabe's, as well as two others. One was a Mercedes CL class in polished silver and it wasn't hard to figure whose that was. The other was a black BMW 3-something, I didn't really care. I wasn't a fan-boy car guy. I just knew what I needed for the job.

I went inside and there was the obvious Mr. Edwin Morton Holmes, still standing in our small reception area, looking like he hadn't sat down since he'd arrived.

"Mr. Holmes?" I asked, extending my hand. "Scott Porter."

He shook it with grace as well as a measure of impatience. "It's good to finally meet you, Mr. Porter. May we...." He'd put a slight emphasis on the 'finally.' He gestured toward my office, saving me the trouble of doing it.

"Of course." I did walk ahead of him, though. Didn't know if that meant anything to him or not. I kept moving until I got behind my desk and left him to figure out the set of chairs in front of it. I sat down. He didn't.

I looked at him for a moment, convinced we'd never met. He appeared cool but his forehead was heavily creased. "Look," I told him. "I'm guessing we both have questions. The first thing I'd like to know is why you sent a man to find me last night. And how he knew where I'd be. Most of all I'd like to know how you got my home phone number when nobody has my home phone number." Not strictly true, but close enough.

He nodded and said, "Fair enough but first I must ask you, have you found Endo Robbins?"

That surprised me. "I didn't know I was still looking. Should I be?"

Holmes frowned and thought. "Things are moving too fast already. May I sit?"

Really? "Please."

"Before we go further," he said. "I must admit to being apprehensive. Nervous, actually. Do you carry a gun?"

That's one I hadn't heard before. "Now I'm nervous. Yes, Mr. Holmes, I have a gun. It's real but I won't let you touch it."

He frowned with annoyance. "I just want you to know that you may want to begin carrying it with you."

I could see he meant it. I slid open my lower right desk drawer and took one of the guns out of its snap holster and set it on the corner of the desk, closer to me than to him. I didn't tell him it wasn't loaded. "Better?" I asked.

I didn't think it was but he nodded anyway. "I was thinking about Endo Robbins."

"You sent Robbins to find me last night and haven't heard back. You went looking for him but you had no luck."

"Yes."

"But that is his BMW in the lot, next to your Mercedes?"

"It is."

"Just who is he?"

Holmes waved that away. "It doesn't matter now. I doubt we'll see him again. The presence of his car in your lot is a message."

"Apparently it worked. It got you here."

"Or it failed to keep me away. In any case, it's clear now they know I've come to you. I have people watching this building to be sure they don't come in."

"Then why this?" I asked, gesturing toward my gun.

"I can't speak for the people already inside."

This was getting us nowhere. And insulting my employees wasn't making me warm up to him any. "I'm not going to shoot my staff, Mr. Holmes."

"Of course. I just think you should be prepared."

"Mr. Holmes, I've never shot anyone." This was a lie but it was also none of his business. "If I had to suddenly start now, I'd be tempted to start with you."

"Why do you say that?"

"Let's go with 'just because.'"

"When I leave here I will be on a private jet heading for some place far away. You, on the other hand…."

"Will be doing what, again? Exactly why are you here, Mr. Holmes?"

"We'll get to that."

"Before someone gets hurt," I said, growing very tired of this.

"It's too late. It's already begun."

"What the hell is going on, Mr. Holmes."

"I appreciate your directness, Mr. Porter," he said. "I'll tell you what I know but I'm afraid it's not a lot."

I sat back in my chair with my pen in hand and pulled a legal pad into my lap.

"Are notes really necessary, Mr. Porter? Does the concept of 'off the record' have any context here?"

I shrugged. "I won't know until you start talking, sir. I can always shred the paper."

He studied his hands for a moment until a slight tremor disappeared. "So be it. Let us begin." Holmes took a deep breath, let it out, and said, "Do you know anything about art?" he asked.

"The Dali Museum's up the road a bit but I still haven't figured out the melted bench by the front door. Never been to the Ringling museum here in town."

"How about books?"

"I'm up to number five of Harry Potter."

"I don't—" He stopped. From his case he pulled a slim wooden carton and laid it on my desk.

"What's this?"

"A rather unique first edition copy of Edgar Allan Poe's *The Murders in the Rue Morgue*. Widely regarded as the first true detective novel, it was originally published in two magazine installments prior to appearing solely in book form."

"Should I look?"

"Not necessary. Physical handling, no matter how slight, leaves its traces. This copy was one of the first ever bound between hard covers, I believe, by a man—"

I interrupted him. "Mr. Holmes, why bring me a book you don't want me to touch?"

He made an offhand gesture with his hand. "You may open the traycase if you'd like, and take a look. I had it specially made to fit the book itself. But it's not the book, I think, that is so important. Its provenance is most likely of more interest."

"Provenance?"

He nodded as though he expected this. "Provenance is the record of an artifact's prior ownership. It proves the object is what it is supposed to be by confirming its whereabouts and ownership throughout the path of its existence. Fully documented provenance is often a rare thing, a really trustworthy one even more so."

"And the provenance for this book?"

Holmes shrugged. "Who knows? Sometimes when a collector wants something bad enough the only provenance required is his belief that the article is genuine."

"Is this?" Now I reached forward and lifted the lid of the traycase, essentially a silk-covered box with a lid, revealing a faded blue, gold-stamped cover that looked and smelled like any other old book, giving off a sort of musty vanilla scent. So there was a book in there. I didn't touch it.

"I believe it is, yes."

"How much is it worth?"

"There is no straightforward answer to that question, Mr. Porter. It is, as are most things, worth whatever someone is willing to pay for it."

"Was Endo Robbins willing to pay for it with his life?"

Holmes stared at his lap. "Mr. Robbins has never seen that book. The book is not what killed the poor man."

"So he's killed now, is he? How do you know this?"

"I do not know it, I merely fear it."

"Where did you get the book, Mr. Holmes?"

He reached forward, lifted the box carefully, and returned it to his briefcase. "It was offered to me by mail. I allowed a show of interest, it was brought to my home, an arrangement was made, and it was exchanged for an amount of cash the following day."

"When was this?"

"The week before last."

I dropped the unmarked pad on the desk and pushed back in my chair. "We're not getting anywhere, Mr. Holmes. If you believe Endo Robbins has been murdered, you should be calling the police, not visiting with me. You tell me about a book with presumably questionable 'provenance.' I'm not so smart I can make that all add up, unless this is something about a stolen book. You believe you're in danger and you say you're headed to a private plane and a trip out of the country. What exactly do you want from me?"

We sat quietly for a moment, and then he took a check book from his jacket pocket and began writing. "This is a lot of money, Mr. Porter. What I want is for you to excise me from the consequences of owning that particular volume, including the events of the immediate past and whatever may follow from it."

"I won't do anything illegal, Mr. Holmes." I always said that to clients. At this stage in a case I tried to be optimistic.

"I trust you won't have to." With an arched eyebrow he finished writing and handed me the check.

I took it from him, then tried not to stare at it. "This is, um, quite a lot of money. Just how much trouble are you in, Mr. Holmes?" I laid the check on my desk midway between us, in case he wanted to take it back. I needed to know he was serious.

"Well, I should say that if Endo Robbins, my personal secretary, has come to a bad end merely because he *knew* of the book, or because I sent him to contact a private detective, that my possession of this object might turn out to be a dangerous thing. But I don't necessarily think so."

He went back to his case and pulled out a glassine envelope. "I rather suspect that this letter may have something more to do with it." He laid it on top of the check.

I looked at it, could make out some writing, looked at my potential client, and thought of what was on the paper. "May I?" I asked.

"Mr. Porter," he said. "I leave the letter entirely in your hands. I do not now desire, nor have I ever desired, to even know of its existence. It is merely something I found in my book. I wish nothing more than to be able to forget that I ever laid eyes upon it."

CHAPTER THREE

The letter appeared stiff and somewhat brittle as I gently extracted it from its envelope. The paper was thick and the small, cursive handwriting was as neat and precise as the contents were confused and somewhat disorienting.

It said:

Why did Rosalyn call me to ask how are you doing — very odd
It is Sunday and Elizabeth neither called nor talked to me
Why did Ralph call me — very strange and it seems as if my time
& Tedys here is running out
Things are not right
I feel very scared
They would get me a nice place he said
I am so sad never been so scared if only Don were here
Eban is very restless for the past 3 days too
I pray to join Don every night

Some of the words were smudged and others were faded but that was the best I could make out on first reading. "What does this mean, Mr. Holmes?"

He shrugged, an elegant gesture, as though finally giving me the letter relieved him of his burden. "I have no idea."

I wondered if he was lying. I couldn't tell one way or the other. "Who sold you the book?"

"That I cannot say. I will not say."

"Provenance?"

"Something like that. Any names I could possibly remember would most certainly not be the correct ones anyway."

"So you've done this before?"

"I have bought books before, yes. And art. And other sorts of antiquities. Old things interest me, Mr. Porter." He stood. "I have given you a check. I assume that affords some amount of privilege. You have the letter. The book is of no consequence to anything that happens from this point on."

I stood as well, if only to show my advantage in height. And I put the gun back in my drawer. His eyes followed it the entire way. "What exactly is it you expect me to do?"

He reached in his pocket for a cell phone, dialed a number, then hung up without speaking. "I expect you to deposit that check, sir. Beyond that,

I would suggest you let your conscience be your guide." I heard someone coming through the front door. "It's time for me to leave. I don't expect to be seeing you again." And he turned and walked toward the door.

"One last thing, Mr. Holmes," I called.

He paused, turning only his head.

"Why me?"

A smile. "Why not, my dear man?" And he was escorted by three men out of my office, out my front door, and into his Mercedes which was already rolling before the last door was pulled shut.

I sat back at my desk, looked at the check, then again at the letter. Finally I called, "Trudy!"

She came around the door. "Yes, Scott?"

I handed her the letter. "See if you can type out a copy of this. Handle it with nitrile golves, just in case. Then e-mail me a copy and I'll put the original in the safe."

"Where are you going?"

I picked up the check and felt only a little soiled for doing so. "To the bank," I said. "I've got someone's guilt to deposit. Get hold of Paul if you can and have him come in this afternoon. I'll be back soon."

The check was, as they say, big enough to make me take the job but at the same time, not big enough to make me buy Holmes's story. At least not all of it. I walked downtown to the bank and stood in line for a teller. She took the check, stuck it in a machine, put it in a drawer, and handed me a slip. I asked her when I would know the check had actually cleared. She reached over and pointed out the "Funds Availability Date" on the slip I was holding.

"You can use up to two thousand dollars immediately, but the entire balance won't be available until the check fully clears. That can take up to five business days." She pulled the check itself back out of her drawer. "Since this is drawn on a local bank, it will probably be more like two business days, maybe even less."

I thanked her and left the bank. Two grand was enough for me to start something but if this turned out to be some sort of hoax, that would be about all the time I'd put into it. Holmes with his book, letter and private jet be damned.

Trudy greeted me when I got back and I motioned her into the office with my head. I took a seat behind my desk and she made sure to keep standing, keeping herself behind the two visitor chairs. This had become her usual position when we were alone in my office.

"Close the door," I told her.

Smiling, she said, "I'm not supposed to do that."

"I'll never tell."

"I know," she said. "But I will."

I looked at her, said, "Probably."

She nodded. "Probably."

"You're also not supposed to be alone with me."

"Well, I fudge a little bit here and there. We'd never get any work done, otherwise."

For a moment I wondered, if I really pressed, how much Trudy would actually "fudge." But she wouldn't appreciate the effort. After the one incident of bad timing or bad judgment or even just plain bad choices, our relationship was where it needed to be. We had respect for each other, and if anything that one weekend had clarified our working relationship. It had to be enough, because that was all we could have.

On the other hand, I'd always thought that it was because of that weekend that her husband Tim had started to take the problems in his marriage seriously. He'd done what he had to do to save it. Or so I thought. When I was feeling unusually wicked and thinking of Trudy, I'd give myself a measure of credit for keeping them together. Usually that thought was followed by another shot of booze.

Tim Westland was a sergeant with Sarasota PD in charge of dispatchers and communications. He'd help Trudy when she asked him, which was more often than he'd like, because he knew the requests were ultimately coming from me. Despite his personal feelings, he did it anyway, I think to show his wife that he, too, could rise above the past.

None of us can hide from our own guilt. The best we can do is resolve to regret as little as possible, even if we're lying to ourselves.

Trudy was looking at me as though she knew what I was thinking and I had no doubt that she did. Being away for the past few days and coming back to this new mystery had put me in a weird place.

Before I turned things really uncomfortable, I asked, "What do you make of that letter?"

"Very strange. It makes me feel uneasy when I read it. What's the story?"

I gave her a rundown of what Holmes had said.

"What do you think?" she asked. She had a printout of the letter from Holmes's book and she read it again. "It really is pretty creepy."

"Is it, though? It may not even be real and if it is, it may be too old to mean anything to anyone at this point. Maybe some kid was just scribbling things about her school friends or neighbors." After I said that, it occurred to me that the writing seemed both feminine and young. I had to be sure I wasn't misled by my own unsupported impressions.

"It must have meant something to this Holmes guy."

"That's his story, anyway," I said. "At least that's where we need to start. Can we ask Tim for a hand?"

"Of course we can," she said, but I saw that little thing in her eyes. "Like what?"

I wrote down the license plate number of Holmes's Mercedes. "First, I'd like to find out what we can about our new client, if that's the proper word for him. We can do a workup on his background here, but if Tim could find out if the law knows anything about him, that would be helpful. And if he could check anything international through Interpol, that would be a bonus."

"I'll give him a call and ask him."

"Beautiful," I said, and looking at her, I meant it in several ways, but not so she could tell. "And if you could start the database searches and work up a background for him, that would be good, too."

"What about the Steinkeller case?"

Philip Steinkeller was a real estate broker who had his hand in a number of large commercial development properties. He'd been accused of using unsecured titles as collateral for new ones and been caught up by the law. He thought he had a chance of getting off if he could bury the court in timelines and missing paperwork and his defense attorney had hired us to pull some of the records together. We had, and they showed us Steinkeller was guilty as sin. The question now was how far we kept going with it.

"Have Paul call Steinkeller's attorney—"

"Mr. Schenck," Trudy said.

I nodded. "Have Paul call Schenck and arrange to turn over what we have. Have him be sure to let him know the hole for his client is just getting deeper. There's water seeping in and we're going to drown him if we keep digging."

"You think he'll stop?"

"Anything we give him will be discoverable. Unless his client can point us in a new direction, the prosecution can get access to what we've done so far and that's not going to make Schenck, or especially Steinkeller, a happy camper."

"Okay, got it." She began to walk away. "I'll call Tim and get to work on Holmes. Anything else?"

"Anyone notice when that BMW left the parking lot?" It hadn't been there when I'd returned from the bank.

"No," she said. "You didn't tell us to look."

"Doesn't matter." If anything, I was relieved. With Robbins missing, his car was evidence in my parking lot that I didn't want left behind. "Paul coming in?"

"Should be here before two."

"Perfect."

She nodded and turned toward the door.

"Thank you, Trudy," I called, watching the sway of her skirt. She couldn't see me but she knew what I was looking at.

"No problem, boss."

Boss. Once, though briefly, I'd been something more.

"I like your skirt," I called.

"Stop it."

I sighed and put myself to work. I needed information on Endo Robbins. If there was already a corpse mixed up in this somewhere, I wanted to know first, and I didn't know how far I could really trust Tim Westland. Having him tie us to a body was too much risk. Trudy might have mended fences, and I was happy to have his access to official law enforcement data, but he was breaking rules for us every time he did one of these favors.

For us, I thought. For Trudy, really. I had no doubt he only did what he did to remain in her good graces. She had made it clear she wasn't leaving her job for him. It was part of who she was outside the marriage and she was determined to hold on to it, to prove that she could still be her own person outside of her relationship with her husband. I had no problem asking for his help, and Trudy seemed to enjoy being able to use her own private pipeline to help the business, but I could never be sure Tim Westland wouldn't be looking to bury me if he could.

She'd never said but I was pretty sure Trudy had told him about us. If I were her husband I could only guess how I'd feel about helping out his wife's "boss" after hearing that news. Some things you could never feel good about, I thought, and not just from Tim Westland's point of view.

I fired up the computer on my desk and opened a new spreadsheet. It was based on a template I'd created and I entered the amount of Holmes's check in the appropriate box and read the estimated number of hours he'd paid us to work. From that perspective I'd have to say it was already a good day. In another place on the form, I added perhaps the most critical piece of information from every case: what it was the client wanted. Before I started adding the notes from our conversation, I typed out what Holmes had said when I asked him what that was: "… for you to excise me from the consequences of owning this book, including the immediate past and whatever follows from it."

It was vague, but it was important, for this was the standard by which I was given to measure success. Or at least progress. Edwin Morton Holmes may have a different view, but that was something I wouldn't know for a while yet. Especially if he were on the level.

CHAPTER FOUR

Paul McKay walked into the office before two o'clock and came right to see me. Without asking, he shut the door behind him.

"We've got a new case," I told him.

"So I gather."

"It's a confusing one."

"Private client?"

"It is. A very strange one."

"So he's rich then?"

"The check he wrote says so."

McKay reached out and pulled one of the visitor chairs toward him. "Tell me, tell me, tell me," he said.

I liked Paul McKay a lot. He stood five-ten, went about 160, and was good looking enough to be average. His eyes crinkled when he smiled, he kept up a moderate tan, and he could blend into a crowd without making an effort, which is harder to do on purpose than most people think. Good ones, anyway. He could also turn on the charisma and charm his way into personal situations when he needed to, another critical talent as well as an acquired skill for a private investigator.

I gave him a rundown on the Holmes case and everything the client had told me. I reached into my desk drawer and pushed some buttons, playing him the recorded portion of my meeting with Holmes, the part where he talked about Endo Robbins.

When I stopped the playback, I said, "Apparently this Robbins fellow was looking for me last night. I saw his car parked in our lot. There was another man next to it, and Holmes seemed to think that meant something bad for his secretary. This morning someone took the car."

"Who?"

"At the time I didn't think to pay any attention to it. Now I think I should have."

"Is Trudy talking to Tim about this?"

I shook my head. "Not about Robbins. If he turns up as a corpse, Tim is going to have a problem with how we knew about it first. I'd just as soon turn you loose on Robbins. Trudy's working up a background on Holmes so we can try to get an idea of who really hired us."

"You don't trust him?"

"I'll trust his check when it clears. And what he wants from us is vague enough that there may be enough wiggle room to protect him as well as us should this case turn out to be as funky as it smells."

"What about Gabe? Can I use him?"

An expression formed on my face; I couldn't help it. "Gabe stays where he is. He's got a couple of cases on his desk. Let him wallow with those."

As a professional agency, we didn't turn down cases. Any cases. Basically if a client walked in the door or called on the phone, we were going to say yes, as long as they could pay our fees. The seedy cases, the cheating spouses and the paternity stuff, were the ones Gabe Keller worked, with help when he needed it. He did it because he seemed to genuinely like it, which made him good at it, though I found this attitude vaguely disturbing. Maybe there was something wrong with Gabe, inside, something I didn't want to get too close to. Or maybe not. I kept him where he was as much as possible, on the other side of the building, and gave him as much autonomy as I could. The man just weirded me out.

"Okay," McKay said. "Trudy said you want me to follow through with Schenck on the Steinkeller thing, make sure he doesn't need anything else. He should be set until he works his way through what I had her send over this morning."

"Good. Don't want to make him unhappy. Make that call and get onto this, will you?"

"What is it you want me to do?"

"Ideally, locate Mr. Robbins. Find out what you can about him. Judging by the fact that Holmes sent him to find me last night and that his car was in our lot, I think he was last seen somewhere around here."

"What about the guy you saw that wasn't Robbins?"

"Hopefully he wasn't the one who'd done the last seeing. Him I worry about. He was in Jarod's place on Main Street last night. Jarod said he doesn't remember anything more than that the guy was there." I slid over the business card I'd found in the doorway at the bar. "I think he was looking for me. Or looking me over. I found this there last night."

McKay picked it up and examined it. "One of your cards?"

I nodded. "Dropped by accident or sending a message?"

McKay shook his head, tossed the card back on my desk. "Seems like a lot of work to do when we don't know why we're doing it."

"We're doing it," I said, "because we're getting paid to do it. Besides," I added, "how often do we get the chance to decide what a case is going to look like?"

McKay stared at me and I knew what he was thinking: how much money had Holmes actually paid? He knew I wouldn't tell him and he knew not to ask but I was sure it bothered him. His job he liked; what he thought of me I wasn't always sure.

"What about this letter?"

I handed over the printout. He scanned it quickly, read it again slowly, then gave it back.

"Could be anything."

"Could be."

"Probably is, then. I'll get going. What about you?"

"I'll start poking around."

He gave me a look and turned to leave. I didn't like anyone to know too much about how I spent my time. That was the reason I was the boss. McKay didn't like it, he was much more of a team player than I was, but he knew things were the way I wanted them to be. And twice a month he gave me the opportunity to scrawl my signature across the bottom of his paycheck.

There was one antiquarian bookstore in Sarasota, and as it happened it was also on Main Street, just a few blocks up from Jarod's bar. I took a walk there, enjoying the small but vibrant streets that made up the old downtown area. The new-money ritzy shops were across the bridge at St. Armand's Circle, but here was where you could imagine the department store that was now long gone, the faded silhouettes of old signs and letters still visible above the plate glass windows. A little drug store with soda fountain, small shops with essential things that locals could pick up as they strolled along the street, and the focus of the Friday night cruise.

Now it was furniture stores, art galleries, bars, pubs and restaurants of all different stripes. I won't say it's worse, only different. Still, the faint whiffs of the past hidden by the 1950's architectural style was appealing. A fine contrast to the mirrored glass highrises near the water and a buffer between the ostentatiousness of the new money across the bridge and the old cement block houses east toward the interstate.

The bookstore was on a corner and was filled floor to ceiling with handmade shelves containing books, the way a good bookstore ought to be. These books were old ones, valuable and difficult to find for the specific reader. You wouldn't stop in for the latest New York Times bestsellers here.

I'd been in the store before but never to the back room where they kept the truly rare and valuable stuff. The bearded gentleman behind the counter was reading something ancient, in green boards with no cover printing. He put it down carefully when I stopped in front of him and asked if he could help me.

"I hope so," I told him and handed him a card.

"Investigations?" he said. "Really? What kind?"

"The kind that come with checks attached. Listen, I wonder if you could steer me in the right direction in regards to a book I saw recently."

"Sure. I mean, I can try."

I described first edition of *The Murders in the Rue Morgue* that Holmes had shown me, and watched the interest turn to puzzlement on behalf of Jonathan, the bookseller.

"What's wrong?" I asked.

He stroked his beard like the hippy he thought he was and sat back on his stool. "Are you familiar with the story in the book?"

"I've read it," I said, "though not in a long time."

Jonathan typed some things in the computer on the counter. "It was originally published in a magazine in 1841. It wasn't originally a book."

"Like Dickens' serials?"

"Sort of," Jonathan said. "Poe did print the book as a pamphlet, along with another story, so that volume would have been its first non-magazine appearance. Most experts would probably say that would be the true first edition. Since then, the main story has been printed in so many books it might not be possible to figure out its entire publication history. Guess that's why someone needs a detective."

I smiled because it seemed appropriate.

"Why would it be so difficult?"

He shrugged. "Back then copyright laws weren't what they are today. Bootleg copies could have been printed by just about anybody." He typed some more into his keyboard, played with his mouse.

"The original manuscript was fished out of a wastebasket and later bound and presented to a university, but that couldn't have been what you saw. Perhaps one of the original series of pamphlets had been re-bound? I suppose that could have happened."

"If that were so, how could we tell? Would there be any way of finding out if an item like that even existed?"

"Hmm," said Jonathan, back to stroking his beard. "Difficult. Anyone could have done it any time over the last hundred and sixty some years. You might try checking with the auction houses to see if they've sold anything like that, Sotheby's and the like. Possibly other antiquarian booksellers. I can post a question to an online forum if you'd like."

I thought about that. At this point, it was probably better to let it slide. After all, the point was to keep Holmes out of things—whatever the "things" turned out to be—and calling attention to him by way of ownership of a strange little book didn't make much sense.

"Jonathan," I said, holding out my hand for a shake, "I appreciate your time. If I need any more help, would it be all right if I called on you?"

"No, sure, that would be fine. So, do you want me to post to that forum?"

"Not right now, I think. It probably isn't that important. But I'll let you know if I change my mind." I thanked him again and left the shop, not sure what, if anything, I'd really learned.

This next part of the story I learned a few days later, at the open end of a gun.

CHAPTER FIVE

Rico Gallo was tired. After returning the boat he'd appropriated the night before, he spent a few hours sleeping in his hotel before moving himself into position outside of Edwin Morton Holmes's Longboat Key estate. When Morton came out just after eight o'clock in the morning, Gallo saw the old man didn't seem to be missing his late personal secretary, Endo Robbins. There were four black-suited men with him, all piling into the same Mercedes. Through his binoculars Gallo could see Holmes was carrying a briefcase.

Damn, he thought. Well, if Morton had been alone it would have been too easy.

The four men with Holmes had the look of private security, which meant they could be anybody, from armed services vets with actual soldier skills, or moonlighting and inept steroid-fueled night club bouncers. He couldn't take the chance.

When the silver Mercedes pulled out and away from the electronic gate at the end of the driveway, Gallo casually walked over to his rental car and climbed into the driver's seat. He'd follow Holmes's entourage even though he thought he knew where they were going. That should give him a chance to dump the rental, something he hadn't had time to do last night.

It turned out he was right about where Holmes had been going, directly to the private investigator's office. Parking his car two blocks down the street, he had a distant but clear view of the office entrance when the Mercedes pulled out of the lot and rolled up to the sidewalk in front of the doorway for a few seconds. Gallo knew Holmes was being very, very careful.

Not much for him to do at that point but keep following the party. He got out of the car, leaving the keys under the mat. He took out a cell phone and called the rental agency as he walked. He apologized, he said, but he had to suddenly leave town. Gallo told them where they could find the car and that they could bill him whatever they needed to for the pickup. At this point he had just passed the entrance to Porter's office and quickly stepped into the parking lot.

With the keys he had taken last night, he fired up the BMW and slowly pulled out and headed in the same direction as the Mercedes. The silver car, brightly washed and waxed to perfection, glistened in the morning sun and was such a standout it was easy for Gallo to make up for its headstart. He stayed back enough to reduce the chances of being spotted. Really, though, if they did manage to figure out they were being followed, it wouldn't make much difference to him.

He covered his mouth with the back of his hand and yawned silently. It was a big one, and a tear formed in the corner of one eye. He wiped it a with the back of his hand, then brought it to his mouth and licked the moi, ture off with a slow, sure movement of his tongue. Salty, he thought, though not harsh like the gulf water from last night. This was a smoother, almost pleasant taste.

Gallo watched as the car carrying Edwin Morton Holmes turned off highway 41 into the small road with the big name of Sarasota-Bradenton International Airport on a sign mounted on oversized hurricane-proof stanchions. The silver Mercedes cleared a security gate and headed to a private hangar on the outskirts of the airport property. When a Gulfstream G550 taxied out and the Mercedes didn't, Gallo finally left, having confirmed the lost opportunity to get at Holmes. Still yawning, needing more sleep, he drove back to the house on Longboat Key.

The Holmes estate was surrounded by a seven foot tall stuccoed cinder block fence topped with a decorative but sharpened line of metal spikes. The driveway was controlled by an electric steel gate with a camera and microphone mounted on top of the fence, positioned to get a good shot of any drivers' side windows that pulled up. To make the estate look more appealing there was a well-landscaped collection of trees and bushes along the street-facing side of the fence. Some of the trees were taller than the security spikes and as Gallo well knew that was someone's mistake.

He drove past and left the BMW in the parking lot of a small sandwich shop a quarter of a mile away, then walked back along the street to Holmes's residence. He thought about pushing the button on the intercom to see if anyone was home but he didn't want his face to be caught on security camera. He located the spot he'd scoped out earlier and disappeared behind a clump of banana trees. Smelling sickly sweet, covered with ants and still dripping with the morning dew, he pushed past the heavy stalks with their hanging bunches of fruit and got to a tree, a date palm, growing close to the wall. Quickly and quietly, aware of the traffic zooming past just a dozen yards away along Gulf of Mexico Drive, he used both tree trunk and wall to wedge himself up to a point where he could grab the sharpened tips of the metal spikes. With each hand having a grip and his shoes pressing against the wall, his body bent into a c-shape, Robbins pushed hard off the wall with his feet and pulled himself over the top. There was no way to land gracefully and he flattened a group of plants with his tumbling body as he hit on the other side and rolled.

He stayed there, crouched for several minutes, but there was no movement anywhere. Keeping to the inside border of the fence, he carefully made his way to the house. He hadn't eaten since yesterday afternoon and was thinking maybe there was something good in the refrigerator.

search for Endo Robbins bore fruit when he found the Dorian Robbins, Jr." in one of his computer queries. The ...nced with several other entries, and soon he had all the ...ormation he could get from online sources. This included a telephone number and an address which he wrote down on a pad. He headed for the door, waving to Trudy while she was on the phone.

The address showed Robbins lived in a guest cottage on an estate out on Longboat Key. Traffic was uncharacteristically light and it took McKay about twenty minutes to drive over there. From the street, the main house looked large and excessive but it was difficult to see much as the entire lot appeared to be surrounded by a pretty serious fence; the driveway was protected by an electric gate. McKay drove ahead to the next house, made a right turn into its driveway, and parked. He spoke with the woman who answered the door, identifying himself as an investigator for an insurance company without saying which one, and asked her about her neighbors. He didn't ask if he could ask her questions, he simply came out with them, natural as could be. It was one of his tricks, not to give the subject an opportunity to think about whether they should or shouldn't talk to him. Just two people having a conversation.

The woman told him she only knew the neighbors on the other side of her. She thought a man lived behind the fence but whenever she'd seen him there had always been men in suits around and they always seemed to be on their way out or on their way back in. They acted like bodyguards, it seemed to her, but as she told McKay, but she couldn't know for sure. Why would one of her neighbors need so much protection, she'd always wondered. In a way it made her nervous. And that security gizmo on his driveway was a bit much, if you asked her. This was a nice area, he shouldn't need something like that. None of the rest of the neighbors did.

McKay nodded, agreeable. He asked her about Endo Robbins and showed her an undated picture he'd printed from his computer. She shook her head when he asked her if she recognized the man in the photo.

"I may have seen him," she said. "I'm not sure so I don't want to say. Not much of a picture, is it?" She stared at it some more. "That's not the owner, is it? Looks a bit young to be so uptight. What does he do to be so important he needs all that security?"

McKay told her he didn't actually know, then he thanked her and left. She looked a bit unsure as she stood in her door and waited for McKay to climb into his car. He backed the car around then had to wait a full two minutes at the base of her driveway before there was an opening for him to turn left on to Gulf of Mexico Drive. The woman stood outside her door the whole time. He drove past the estate and tried the house on the other side. This time no one answered the door.

Casually he walked across the front yard to the fence that separated the two properties. With a light running start he jumped into the wall, then kicked himself upwards, barely reaching the base of two of the metal poles that ran along the top. McKay pulled himself up so his chin was level with the top and peered over the wall, between the spikes.

He found himself looking at the side of large house, about thirty yards from the fence. It had a Tudor façade, with the appearance of wide brown beams marking artificial lines across a clean white stucco finish. Behind the house, close to the fence marking the back border of the property, he could see a kidney bean shaped swimming pool with a standalone one-story building on the other side. Robbins was probably living there, he thought.

A side door, almost directly across from McKay, clattered open and a man backed out. He was dragging another man along the ground face up by his armpits. The pair cleared the door and angled toward the back yard. The first man lowered the second to the ground, straightened his back as though it were stiff, then moved to close the door. McKay's biceps were beginning to quiver with fatigue and he wondered how long he'd be able to hold on. With the side door now closed, the first man moved back around the man on the ground, standing over the unmoving figure. He bent down, secured his grip and resumed his dragging, backing along the shale-stoned walk in the direction of the swimming pool. Before McKay was forced to let go of the spikes, he yelled suddenly: "Hey, there! You need a hand with that?"

A thin, lean face whipped toward McKay. Dark, slanted eyes quickly scanned the fence until he identified the source of the voice.

McKay called out again: "Stay there, I'll be right over!"

The man dropped his burden and took off running toward the front of the house.

McKay released his grip and fell backwards when he hit the ground, his arms spent and tingling with lactic acid buildup. Turning quickly, he sprinted to his car, jumped inside, and raced it backwards down the driveway. He stopped just short of the street and threw it in park. There was nothing to see: no man, no getaway car, nothing. The guy could have gone anywhere. He thought about turning around but the chances of spotting the thin, dark-eyed man probably weren't very good.

As for the man on the other side of the fence, McKay had no idea how badly he might be hurt. If he got over the wall, he stood a better chance of finding out what had been going on. Especially if one of the men was Endo Robbins, and finding him was McKay's first responsibility. He put the car back into gear and returned up the driveway.

Leaving the vehicle, he jogged around the neighbor's house to the back and the inevitable pool. Around here there was always a pool. A plastic storage box stood against the side of the house near the pump and filter and McKay grabbed the handle on one of its sides and dragged it over toward the wall. It sounded like there was a pool cleaning hose inside but he didn't stop to take it out. Moving as quickly as he could, he got it back to the spot on the wall where he had been gripping the metal spikes and turned it to the side, lifting it so that it was leaning against the fence's stucco finish, the side of the lid about five feet off the ground. He clambered onto the top of the box and now he was able to stand and grasp two of the spikes easily. He hoisted himself up, carefully pushing off the top of the wall with the toe of one foot, and went over into the other yard.

Landing lightly, he stayed low on the balls of his feet, checking to be sure the first man was still nowhere to be seen. He wasn't. Then McKay ran over to the body on the ground and stood over him. The man was breathing, shallowly but steadily, and a light rumbling seemed to be coming from his throat. McKay felt the back of the man's head, moving his fingers gently through the thick, black hair, until he found the pulpy mass where he'd been hit. The man didn't open his eyes or make a sound other than continue the unsettling rattle of his breathing. McKay could see that whoever this man was, he clearly didn't match the picture he had of Endo Robbins.

McKay was only willing to spend a few minutes there. He whipped a handkerchief out of his back pocket and tried the door knob of the house; it was locked. Evidently it was on a snap lock and he couldn't get in without breaking something. He went back to the unconscious man. Feeling through the man's clothes, he found a ring of keys in the left front pants pocket. McKay worked these free and then decided he was better off looking at the house behind the pool, the one where Endo Robbins supposedly stayed.

He sprinted around the pool and to the door closest to the water's edge. The deadbolt lock slid back with the fourth key he tried.

At first glance, the place was clean and tidy. There was a small kitchen off to one side, a slightly larger living space, then a hallway leading into the bedroom or bedrooms and the presumed bathroom. There was a cordless phone on an end table next to the couch and McKay snatched it up and dialed 911. When the dispatcher answered the call, he said a man had been hurt and was unconscious and needed help immediately. He said all this in heavily accented Spanish. When the dispatcher tried to keep him on the line, McKay simply laid the phone down on the end table, and ran to the back of the house.

As he thought, there were two bedrooms and a bathroom here. The larger bedroom was neat and had the feeling of being used. McKay pulled out several drawers, saw underwear, socks, various shirts; he checked the closet and saw a number of suits and pressed slacks suspended from wooden hangers. On the floor to one side was an empty set of expensive luggage. If Robbins had taken off, he hadn't done so with much planning.

The other bedroom had been used as an office. There were piles of paper sorted on a desk, most of them bills, and a desk calculator sat alongside a ledger book. Out of instinct, McKay grabbed the ledger book and turned to go. He went out the same door he'd used to come in and as soon as stepped outside he could already hear the first siren. He had to get back over the security wall, fast.

The back side of the house was only a few feet from the wall and he dragged a heavy wooden chair from the pool deck over to the house and used it to prop open the same door he'd unlocked. After tucking the ledger into the back of his trousers, McKay stepped on to the wooden chair, then the door knob, and straightened his body until he could steady himself with the top of the door and grab the rain gutter that ran along the edge of the roof. He gripped this with both hands and walked his feet up the door, praying the gutter would hold until he could pull himself on to the top of the roof. This worked and he glanced back toward the house, where he could see the prone man was still on the ground where the other guy had left him. Where both of them had left him. He could also hear the siren and see lights at the end of the driveway. McKay had done all he could.

Staying low, he ran along the edge of the shingled guest house roof and leaped over the back fence, knowing he was going to hit hard on the other side.

He did. Rolling twice he came up dirt stained and limping. The ledger was poking into his low back and he pulled it out and held it in his hand as he walked closely along the back side of the fence toward the house where he'd left his car.

The palms of both hands were raw and stinging; he'd probably scraped them along the shingles when he'd pulled himself onto the pool house roof. He'd do a more thorough inventory after he'd gotten the hell out of there. If the cops had no other way in, they'd soon be checking with the neighbors the same way he'd done and he didn't want them to find him there. As it was, he'd gotten back to his car, turned it around, and made the turn onto Gulf of Mexico Drive just as a uniformed cop walked out of the gated driveway in his direction and gave a half-hearted wave McKay could see from his rear view mirror.

As he drove toward downtown, he took the opportunity to look at the scrapes on his palms and see the dirt ground into the side of his pants. The seam was split open along the left side of his thigh. Fine, he thought. He knew I'd be buying him some new clothes.

And he was right. After he told me his story I told him to go shopping and submit the bills as expenses. It was cheaper in so many ways than trying to pry him out of a police investigation.

CHAPTER SIX

After I'd left the bookstore, I went across the street to pick up a sandwich. I brought it back to my office and two minutes after I sat down at my desk, Trudy came rushing in.

"Miss me already?" I said. "You look lovely, by the way."

"Hush." She handed over a piece of paper. "Tim got me Holmes's address on Longboat Key. And guess what?"

"You're getting a divorce?"

"I told you to stop it. There was a disturbance out there this morning. Possibly a home invasion or a burglary. The police are out there now."

"What happened?"

"Tim said someone from the house phoned it in but when the cops arrived, all they found was an unconscious man. They think he was a caretaker or staff of some sort."

"Why don't they know?"

"Fractured skull. The guy may not wake up."

I took a bite of my sandwich and thought about it. There was no point in going out there with the police on the scene. They'd never let me in, let alone speak to me. If Holmes had been true to his word, he was long gone at this point so this being someone like a caretaker would make sense, but it was no way a sure thing.

"Can your husband get you the name of the victim, anything the police have found out?"

Trudy pointed to the paper she'd given me. "His name's there, near the bottom. I'll figure out where he lives."

"If he was the caretaker, he may have had a room there, Holmes's house. Nice work, Trudy."

"You're welcome, Mr. Porter."

"Mr. Porter who?"

Paul McKay flashed into the room, dirt and grass stains showing on his shirt and the left leg of his khaki trousers. "Guess what?"

"You found Endo Robbins."

McKay pulled up short, looked over at Trudy. "No, but I found someone else. Two someone elses. Neither was Robbins, though."

He told us the story of where he'd gone. Trudy asked him for the address. It belonged to Edwin Holmes.

"That fits," he said, as I took another bite of my sandwich. "You want to take a look at this?"

He held up a ledger book in his hand, then dropped it on my desk next to my lunch. I wiped my fingers on a paper towel and flipped it open.

"This from Holmes?" I asked.

McKay nodded but said, "Not quite. Guest house out back by the pool. I'm guessing that's where Endo Robbins hung his hat."

Trudy said, "Guessing?"

"I didn't have much time, once I'd called the cops. But it fits. Suits in the closet were tailored for a short, round man."

"So who's the guy with the skull fracture?"

"That I do not know. It's the other guy I'm wondering about."

"What other guy?" Trudy said. "Tim didn't say anything about—"

"The guy lammed. I scared him off when I saw him dragging the unconscious guy toward the swimming pool."

I was still skimming ledger entries. They appeared to be a listing of Holmes's expenses as paid out by his secretary, which would have been Endo Robbins. "Think you stopped an accident?"

"People do drown every day," said McKay.

"Oh my God," said Trudy. "That would make it murder."

"It still might be," I said, "if this Flores doesn't pull through." And to McKay, "The man's skull is fractured. Cops think he was the caretaker. You find out anything about him?"

McKay shook his head. "Didn't have time to check. The back of his head was a mess so I called 911 and raced the sirens." He nodded at the ledger book. "How'd I do?"

"Not bad," I told him. "I think it gives us a missing piece. Sit down, you two. We should talk this out." I wrapped the rest of my sandwich in its foil wrapper and used the paper towel again as McKay took a seat in one of the chairs facing my desk. Trudy walked over to the door and closed it first. "Tell us again what happened."

As Trudy sat in the open chair, McKay related what he had seen and done out at Holmes's place. I told him I was jealous he got to have an adventure while all I did was talk to a guy in a bookstore.

"You got a sandwich," he pointed out.

"You can finish it." I shoved it closer to him. "Talk about the man who ran away. In detail. How tall was he, et cetera."

McKay ran through the description and it matched as much as it could to the person I'd seen in our parking lot the night before. It wasn't conclusive, but the odds of two such men running around this case were way too long.

"So where does that leave us?" Trudy asked.

I ran it down, counting on both of them to challenge me on anything I might have missed or was getting wrong. "Mr. Holmes sent his personal secretary, a guy he called Endo Robbins, to find me. It appears the last time he was seen by someone who didn't kill him may have been at Jarod's place, to see if I was there. His car was in our lot, along with the mystery hatchet-faced man. After what just happened at Holmes's house, I don't think we'll be encountering Mr. Robbins in person."

Trudy made a small "oh" sound and McKay shook his head.

"We were hired by Holmes to protect him from the consequences of owning that book."

"And the letter," said McKay.

"The letter may be the thing. I don't see the book figuring in any real way. Otherwise, if you're Holmes, why keep it and drop the letter? In any case, we still don't know what those consequences he was afraid of are. I think the first thing we do is stop looking for Endo Robbins."

"Why should we do that?" Trudy asked.

"Because we might find him."

McKay said, "We're not going to find him."

"Even more reason to stop trying. The problem is, someone else might, some time," I said. "So, other than the disappearance of Robbins, we still need to figure out exactly what it is we need to protect Holmes from."

"And...."

I moved my finger along the open ledger page and stopped at an entry. "This ledger has an entry for several books, including one marked—" I squinted to make out the small, neat handwriting— "*E. A. Poe, 1st ed. Murders on Rue Morgue*." I slid my finger horizontally across the page. "He paid over eighteen grand for it, and it came from someone or something named Rudge."

Trudy said, "So we look for Rudge?"

"We do," I said.

"I think we still need to find out about the book," said McKay. "Like you said, establish its provenance."

I shook my head. "Only to a point," I said. "I want to know about that letter."

"You think that's what this is about?"

"Makes more sense than an old book. The thing may be rare, but if it's only worth eighteen grand, not enough to kill people for, not when you've got the kind of dough Holmes has. Or am I missing something?"

Trudy asked, "What about this man you saw here last night, the one Paul saw out at Holmes's house?"

"Him we may need to find, if only to protect our own skulls," said McKay.

"Let me know if you figure out how to do that. You still got the keys you took off the caretaker?" I asked McKay.

He fished them out of his pocket and dropped them on my desk. "Trudy, can you stay on top of that with Tim, see if the cops come up with fingerprints, DNA or anything?"

"I can try, but at some point he's going to ask what we know and how we know it."

"Which needs to be nothing. Or next to it," I said. "At least for right now. Just ask him. He'll do it to keep you happy. Tell him you'll have to work late with me otherwise."

"Don't be a bastard."

"Some point very soon they're going to figure on three people being at the house. They're going to realize that it's not very likely for someone to smash another man's skull, drag him outside and then phone for help, especially when they find the propped open door to that pool house."

McKay stood up. "I need to get some new clothes, get cleaned up." He stuck his finger through the hole in his slacks.

"Sure," I said. "Then come on back. We'll figure out what to do next."

There was a knock on my door and Trudy stood up and went to it. Gabe Keller was there, pushing his face around the corner. "Got a second, boss?"

"What's up, Gabe?"

"I've got a big one tonight, a separated husband, threatening his wife. She's moving out of the house, wants protection, help with the couch, that sort of thing."

"And?"

"I think I can use six guys. All I have is me and Joey, everyone else is tied up. Can I bring in a couple outsiders?"

"Whatever you need, Gabe. If she's paying, we're playing. Trudy can help with the paperwork."

He nodded at Paul and Trudy, said, "Thanks, boss." He pulled the door shut as he withdrew, having never come all the way into my office. He liked his near-autonomy practically as much as I liked giving it to him.

McKay said, "I know I shouldn't say this, but there's something about that guy...."

"He's good at his job," Trudy said.

I just nodded and pulled my sandwich back. "Let me know what Tim says, Trudy. See you when you get back, Paul."

The two of them left and I moved the ledger aside and picked up what was left of my lunch, already turning into a dripping mess. There were a few things that were nagging at me. I still didn't know why Holmes had come to me, how he had gotten my home phone number, and what the hatchet-faced man was doing hurting people related to Holmes and/or this case. It was one thing taking a job where we were presented with a set of facts that we could pursue. We would set out to find more, verify someone's story, reason things out to a satisfactory conclusion. It was another to have hold of a partial story and find out someone else was also working it, a person with demonstrated violent and anti-social tendencies.

I pushed the intercom on my phone with a relatively clean little finger and asked Steph, our receptionist and Trudy's assistant, if she wouldn't mind bringing me a coke from the fridge. As I sat back in my chair I remembered what Holmes had said about carrying a gun.

CHAPTER SEVEN

Paul McKay came back a short time later, freshly showered and wearing a change of clothes. He kept a modest home in Bradenton, a city just north of Sarasota on the old Tamiami Trail, also known as highway 41. The city had sort of a "left behind" feeling to it but McKay liked being able to sneak up the back way to the Sunshine Skyway Bridge and into St. Pete to see a Rays game when he had the opportunity. He could also head south past the airport through downtown Sarasota and into the office. No rush hour traffic on either the interstate or on any of the east-west feeders to contend with. Smart man.

Trudy had gone to see her husband and brought back some mug shot books. She could only keep them for a couple of hours before they had to be returned but I thought it was worth a shot if I could luck out and find a picture of our hatchet-faced suspect, the man who—I was pretty sure—had killed Endo Robbins. The last we'd heard it wasn't looking too good for Holmes's caretaker, either.

I'd worked my way through the photos but came up empty. So he hadn't been arrested by the Sarasota cops, at least not recently. Didn't say a lot. I called Trudy when I was finished and she came in to take the books back to her husband. She said she'd be back as soon as she could and I refrained from making any smart remarks. She gave me a curious look over her shoulder as she left. I suppose I'd become too predictable. I pulled the ledger Paul McKay had brought back from Holmes's house and tried to determine if any other entries might have relevance to the case.

"Come in, have a seat," I told Paul as he stuck his head into my office a half hour later. "We need to figure out where we're going with this thing." I saw him pressing his palms together, then looking at them closely. "You okay?"

"I'm fine. Just skinned the damned things. It was a bitch to scrub all the shingle dirt out but no big deal." He sat down. "So what's new?"

I told him about going through the ledger and even though I knew more about Edwin Holmes's finances than I cared to, the most promising thing was still the entry for the Poe book and the name "Rudge."

"The thing is," I said, "I would really like to get a handle on this guy with the hatchet face before he comes at one of us."

McKay laid his hands along the smooth wood of the arms of his chair and said, "You think he will?"

"I think he might. If he were after Holmes, he missed him when Holmes flew out of here. If he was after something Holmes had on him—"

"Like the book or the letter...."

I nodded. "He wouldn't know if Holmes still has them or if he left them with us."

McKay took his hands off the arm rests and pressed his palms together again. I could almost feel him trying not to scratch. "You do realize he was dragging the caretaker to the back yard?"

"So?"

"Other than the guest house, the only thing back there is the swimming pool."

"He was making it look like an accident."

"There's another possibility."

"What's that?"

"It could have been a signal. To Holmes."

I thought about that. Holmes would of course find out about what had happened at his house. He had written a big check but this was looking like too much heavy business. If killing the caretaker was sending a message, it could only mean one thing, especially if Robbins was also among the newly dead.

"Scared yet?" McKay asked.

"Thinking about it. You?"

"Well, if you see him standing next to my car in the parking lot and I never come in again, then assume the answer became yes at some point."

We heard the front door open and McKay and I both looked to the door to my office. We were down a hallway about thirty feet from the reception area. I dropped my hand to my lower right desk drawer. Couldn't help it.

Trudy Westland walked in a few seconds later, a bright sheen of perspiration glistening across her forehead. "Hey, guys," she said.

I didn't answer that. I lifted my hand back to my desk top and said, "Tim have anything more on the break-in at Holmes's house?"

"The caretaker, Ernesto Flores, is a documented Mexican immigrant," Trudy said. "He lives in two rooms in the back of the main house."

"How's he doing?"

"He's been in a coma since they got him to Sarasota Memorial. It's not going out to the public yet but it doesn't look good. Skull fracture, cerebral edema."

McKay said, "With the hit in the back of the head he probably didn't see anything anyway."

"Who is this guy?" Trudy asked. "It's freaking me out, knowing he was in our parking lot last night."

"Me, too," I said, adding that it would be nice to know if he were after something on his own or working for someone else.

"What do you think he's doing now?"

"Seems like he was keeping Endo Robbins from looking me up last night. Which could mean he didn't want us to get too close to Edwin Holmes. Beyond that, all we know right now is what Holmes told us."

"And clients never lie," McKay said.

I laughed. "And clients never lie," I said.

Clients always lie.

McKay pointed at the ledger on my desk. "He may even want that."

"Speaking of which." I opened it to the page that held the entry for the Poe book. "Paul, I want you to find this Rudge person, or Rudge place, or whatever this is."

"Got it."

"Work all the angles you can. Find out about the book, anything you can about the letter, and pick up any information about Holmes as well, other possible buyers, everything."

"What do I do?" asked Trudy, anxious to be included.

"Let's see if we can track down our Mr. Holmes. Can you get over to the airport and check out the flight plans? Let's see if we can find where it is our client considers a safe place."

"I'll need to find the N number for his plane. Any IFR or international flight has to have a flight plan on file, and those are all public records."

"Okay, get on that quick as you can, will you? If we can look into it, so can someone else."

"I'll go as soon as we're done."

"What if Hatchet-face decides to come here?" asked McKay.

"Good question."

Trudy said, "Should I hide the silverware in the break room?"

"Leave that for now," I said. "It's only plastic."

"But it's the good plastic."

The timing of her byplay made me wonder if it was in response to my not teasing her when she took the mug shot books out of my office. I threw my pencil at her. She caught it with her left hand and reached forward and rolled it back to me across the desk.

"No, seriously," McKay said, ignoring us. He was used to it. "What do we do?"

"I'll put someone in the waiting area with Steph, talk to her about it. We should be okay." I hoped.

I stood up as if it were time to leave. McKay and Trudy did the same. "We covered with the cops, Trudy?"

"I think so. Tim doesn't know what I wanted the mug books for and the talk about the break-in at Holmes's place was just chit chat."

"Okay," I said. "Keep it that way. If the cops think we know anything about it they'll be all over us."

"Tim wouldn't say anything."

She had more faith in her husband than I did. No matter what she said I certainly wasn't going to underestimate any bad feelings he might still hold for me.

McKay had given in to the itching and was starting to pick at his palms. "What are you going to do?" he asked.

"Same thing I always do."

I never told any of my employees my plans. I never told anyone. Both of them knew this but neither of them liked it. Boss's prerogative. "Be careful out there, you two. Eyes in back of your heads, always."

McKay gave a short wave and left the room. Trudy gave me a mock salute.

"Yes, sir, Mister Porter."

"Stop it. And send Steph in here, will you?"

"Do you need a chaperone?"

"I said stop it, damn it."

"Yes, sir, Mister Porter."

Now she had me on the defensive and I hadn't even seen it coming.

Trudy went out and a minute later our receptionist came in. "You wanted to see me, Scott?"

"Yeah, Steph, come in but shut the door."

She did that and came over rather tentatively, a nervous smile on her lips. I knew what she was thinking.

"You want to sit?" I asked.

"Should I?"

"Doesn't matter. Don't worry, there's nothing wrong. I just want to update you on a situation we've found ourselves in."

The relief remade her features and she quickly took the chair Trudy had just vacated. I told her about Hatchet Face, about how he had been in our parking lot, and that both Paul McKay and I had seen him. He'd slugged the caretaker out at Holmes's place and was probably the last one to see Endo Robbins alive.

"And you think he's coming back here?" Steph asked.

"I don't know," I said. "I just want you to be prepared, is all." I gave her the best description of the man that I could. Steph had two panic buttons wired under her desk. One would sound a siren and set off red flashing lights above the front door. Another was a silent alarm that was sent straight to Sarasota PD. You never knew when an irate spouse, especially from one of Gabe Keller's domestic cases, would take it into his or her mind that the fault with their actions didn't actually lie with themselves.

"If you see this guy, Steph, you start pushing buttons. Do not hesitate, okay? I'll have Al Sutter out there with you in the waiting area, too."

"Got it," she said. "Is that all?"

"That's it," I said, waving an arm toward the door. "Just keep all this to yourself." Steph was still young, in her mid-twenties, tall like Trudy, but with an immaturity that might keep her from being the agent she thought she'd like to be one day. Still, her personality lightened up the place and many clients loved it when hers was the first face they saw when they walked through the door, even though they were quickly handed off to someone else. On the other hand, that someone else was often Trudy. I liked to think we made good first impressions.

Gabe Keller poked his head in the door, just as Steph had opened it to leave. For a second I wondered what he might have heard if he'd been standing in the hall.

"All set for tonight?" I asked him.

"Got it. Just wanted to let you know." He threw a thumbs up around the door frame.

"Good job, Gabe. Tomorrow let me know how it went."

"You got it, boss."

"And look out for yourself, Gabe. I mean it."

"Always do," he said, his usual inexplicable grin plastered across his face.

After Keller left, I shook my head and thought about the man. I'd hired him three years ago when he came out from some private dick's office in Kansas City. I'd checked his references and they told me he'd had no problems with clients and he showed a particular kind of enthusiasm for the work. At the time I took it as a good thing. Now, after all this time with Keller on my payroll, I found he still had his enthusiasm but he was also peculiar in a general, non-specific way. Out of the fifteen or so regular operatives I had working for me, Gabe Keller was probably the last one of them that I would want to go out for a drink with after work. Forget about sitting in a car with him staking some place out.

Like just now at my door, he'd flash that odd expression and grin like an idiot, like someone had just told a joke that only the two of us understood, when the conversation was really no more substantive than what it had just been.

It wasn't that there was anything wrong with his work. He consistently got results and brought good money in to the agency. He was certainly a good earner for the firm but I just didn't want to get any closer to him than I needed. Whenever I thought of this I always attributed it to a weakness on my part. Fine, I'm not a perfect man.

If you had a company filled with commission hungry salesmen, money was always the great motivator. A greedy backstabbing asshole who would do anything for a sale might not be someone you'd want to be around, but they moved product and you were happy to pay them their commissions. You just had to be willing to referee the group of them as they constantly tried to claim influence of their co-workers sales, demanded reimbursements for everything from dry cleaning to windshield wiper blades, and were generally just flat out greedy pains in the ass.

That was sort of how I felt about Keller: he brought in the money working the kinds of cases I didn't have much of a taste for. And if he enjoyed crawling in the pits on his hands and knees I didn't mind as long as his clients paid their bills. But I wasn't about to jello wrestle him in our off hours.

I pulled out a copy of the transcript of the letter from Holmes's book and set it on my desk. It was still disturbing to read, even after studying it as much as I had:

> *Why did Rosalyn call me to ask how are you doing — very odd*
> *It is Sunday and Elizabeth neither called nor talked to me*
> *Why did Ralph call me — very strange and it seems as if my time*
> *& Tedys here is running out*
> *Things are not right*
> *I feel very scared*
> *They would get me a nice place he said*
> *I am so sad never been so scared if only Don were here*
> *Eban is very restless for the past 3 days too*
> *I pray to join Don every night*

If Holmes hadn't thought this thing was so disturbing that he had to get it to me—at the cost of a man's life—and then flee the country, I could almost dismiss it as the jottings of an older lady complaining about living with a family member she didn't like, or staying in a place she'd rather not. I couldn't discount the whole thing as possibly being the ramblings of an unsettled mind.

Still, though, there was a desperation that seemed to come through the words, the paper itself, and we couldn't overlook any possibilities. The unusual names, like "Tedys" and "Eban," might give enough of a handhold to uncover more information. To a lesser degree, "Rosalyn" and "Ralph" weren't exactly on the ten most popular baby names list, either.

...if only Don were here

Why wasn't he? Was he dead? Is the prayer to "join Don every night" a wish for life to be over? Or is whoever wrote the letter a captive somewhere, or a former captive somewhere, wishing for the dashing Don to come and rescue her from her ambiguously dire predicament?

There were too many opportunities for the imagination to carry and I slid the transcript of the letter back into my desk drawer. I'd have Trudy start working on it tomorrow. Maybe the whole thing was some sort of joke? A piece of fiction?

I wasn't feeling completely comortable with sending Trudy out to the airport with Hatchet Face running around but I knew if I'd tried to protect Trudy I'd have needed someone to protect me. She carried mace in her purse, had an emergency alarm on her key chain, and she'd taken any number of self-defense classes. Unless someone was planning on just walking up and shooting her, I had every confidence she could handle herself as well as anybody.

But still, it was Trudy.

If she turned up something on Holmes, that would be a thread to start pulling on, though I didn't have a lot of hope it would actually lead anywhere.

If Holmes had truly left the country, the chances that he'd stayed where the airplane was were probably slim, especially if he had gone into a sort of hiding. All he'd have to do is take a cab away from whatever airport he'd flown to and hire a car and then move on to somewhere else. He'd be effectively disappeared.

Steph called goodnight from the front hallway, and I yelled back. I waited a few minutes then did a walk-through of the office. It had emptied out. Gabe had taken his guys with him, any other business was happening away from the office, and the small building was empty.

From the break room I grabbed a clean rag from under the sink and went outside. Shielding the door with my body as I worked my key in the lock, I wiped down the door handle with the rag, then palmed it and slid it into my front pocket along with my keys.

It was nearly six thirty. Good time for a beer.

I walked down to Jarod's bar and was able to grab a stool at the end of the long counter. Jarod smiled and came at me with a bottle of bourbon but I held my hand up. He raised his eyebrows and I called out, "Beer. Whatever's on tap."

He gave a small shrug and turned back to the bar, taking out a mug and expertly filling it so the foam stopped just shy of cresting the top. "Turning over a new leaf?" he asked as he set it down in front of me.

"Nope," I told him, angling my body so I could check out the room as well as keep an eye on the front door. I gave him a wink. "Surveillance." He laughed and moved on.

I settled in to wait, just to see if something was going to happen. Twelve ounces of beer could be nursed a lot longer than a shot of bourbon. I wasn't really there to drink.

CHAPTER EIGHT

The next morning I was at the office before six, ahead of any staff. The parking lot was empty and I walked around the block and made sure as best I could that there were no parked cars lurking with drivers or passengers holding newspapers over their faces. Or over their laps; you never knew that time of the morning.

I took the dusting powder from my pocket and brushed it lightly onto the handle of my front door. There was a definite set of prints there and I set about carefully lifting them with some clear tape and pressing them onto a white-faced sheet of cardboard. I'd stayed at Jarod's bar most of the evening, pacing myself at around a beer an hour, until I couldn't take it any more and went home. Nothing had happened there but now I knew that sometime during the night somebody had pulled on the handle to my office door. After I'd wiped it clean.

Sure, it could have been anybody; a stew bum walking down the street, some kid goofing as he or she walked into downtown with their friends—anyone. But if a bum had stopped at the door he was more likely to piss in the doorway than grab the handle, and the office wasn't along the normal route for foot traffic to the night life; the line between public parking and the bar and restaurant scene was a few blocks away. So this could be something.

Finished at the door I walked around the corner of the building into the parking lot and looked upwards to where the electric, phone and internet cables ran into the office: nothing was loose, everything looked intact. I hadn't been notified of any alarms going off so this wasn't a surprise. I'd never really thought of hanging a camera out here before—it's just a small parking lot for clients. Most of the employees paid for monthly parking at a public ramp a few blocks away and walked in from there. But maybe if I'd had one I might have been able to see something worthwhile, but I doubted it. Sometimes a parking lot is just a parking lot.

Very often at the start of the case, there was a period of fact gathering and research that needed to be done before you could move on to the action phase. This could be anything depending on what you were actually hired to do. Sometimes there was no action phase, either because the research or knowledge gathering had been the point in and of itself, or else you'd have a client who, after hearing what we had to tell them, decided they didn't wish to take things any further.

With the Holmes case, we had all the earmarks of needing to do something, but I had no idea yet what that would be. We needed more information. But while we were in the process of figuring that out, Hatchet Face was running around already acting out, pursuing goals we didn't understand. I needed to change that dynamic as soon as possible.

I went back to the front door of the building, unlocked it and went inside. I put the fingerprint tapes in a drawer in my desk, locked my office door, went out and secured the door to the building. I thought I'd head over to the Blue Moon for some breakfast and then come back and see what, if anything, had gone wrong during the night. That was the kind of feeling I had. It went well with the mild dehydration headache I'd earned from the night before. I tried not to use the word "hangover" when talking about myself.

Steph walked in with Al Sutter just behind. I called him into my office and gave him a description of the hatchet-faced man and told Al he was now on building security detail.

"What about Gabe's case?" he asked. "I'm still working that Hochstedt settlement."

"That what he was on last night?"

"Yup. Guy never showed, though. The night was a bust."

"Well," I said, "it's up to you if you want to do the after-hours stuff with Gabe. I'll talk to him about it. If you don't want that many hours, I'll have him scare up someone else."

"Okay," Sutter said. "That's it?"

"That's it," I said. "Just wear your gun."

Sutter had been a sheriff's deputy down in Lee County but moved up here when his wife got a job at one of the private hospitals. Lee County, home to the Ten Thousand Islands and the western portion of the Everglades National Park, had never been known for its plethora of job opportunities. At least not legal ones.

Al went out and I called Steph at her desk and asked if Gabe Keller had come in yet. She said he hadn't. I checked my watch and wondered where he was. "Let him know I need to see him when he gets in, will you?"

And then Trudy walked in as I hung up the phone. The first thing I noticed was that she wasn't looking directly at me. She was wearing a tight fitting grey sweater and a knit skirt with a diamond pattern that reminded me of a walking store mannequin, but there were ridges under her eyes that her makeup couldn't hide. Not from me.

I knew I shouldn't ask but I couldn't help myself. "So how's Tim doing?"

"Please," she said. "Don't do this."

"Are you going to sit down?"

She looked over her shoulder at my door, then came around and slowly eased into the chair. It would have been easier if she'd said something first but she seemed content to merely sit.

I stood up slowly. This seemed like a private moment and I was going to close the door despite our strange convention, but without looking up she said, "Please leave it." I lowered myself back to my seat.

"Is it booze or women?" I asked.

"Really, Scott. Don't."

I couldn't remember the last time she'd called me by my first name. Tim Westland may have had a relapse, gone back to the things he'd sworn off, which were the things that had turned Trudy away from him the first time. Or maybe it was the last time. I realized I had no idea how many times Tim had acted against his wife.

That son of a bitch, I thought, but at the same time I felt selfish as I wondered what it would be like to lose the access to Sarasota PD that he gave us. Or gave Trudy. Me he'd back over with his car until there wasn't any more bumping happening. Tim Westland did nothing for *us*, everything he did was for Trudy.

Supposedly. It hit me that it could also be his way of showing his dominance over me, providing something to Trudy that I couldn't.

But that was a crazy thought, wasn't it?

"Trudy—"

"I'm not talking about the past."

"You don't think we need to?"

She sighed and rubbed her brightly painted nails across her forehead. Finally she lifted her chin up and looked me in the eyes.

"No," she said. "Not now. Maybe not ever."

The past for me was a weekend we'd been working together, looking for a runaway girl who'd crossed the border into southern Georgia. The night had started with both of us in different hotel rooms. We went for a walk along the banks of the Chattahoochee and watched the moon come up and light our way along a path that had once been a set of railroad tracks.

"It'll still be there," I said. I meant it to be reassuring and I couldn't tell by what she said next if she knew that or not.

"I thought you wanted to avoid the past, Scott. Or is it just *your* past that's off limits?"

She must really be going through hell, I thought, to have said that to me. I wasn't sure how to respond. Before you can give someone what they need, especially a strong and independent woman like Trudy, they had to be willing to allow you a way in.

Her expression softened in a subtle way. "Do you want to talk about your past?" she asked with a grin. "I'll listen." She leaned forward.

"That's not what I meant."

"I know." She nodded again, this time reaching to her forehead to brush a fallen curl away from her face. "I just wondered if you would if I asked."

I'd never seen her like this before. I was growing more and more uncomfortable but I was an open book to her and it occurred to me she was finally able to see that.

"Are you going to?" I couldn't think of what else to say. "Ask, I mean."

"I've got a license. I could figure you out and you wouldn't even know, couldn't I?"

I didn't reply.

She arched a single, perfect eyebrow. "No?" she asked.

"You could try. I wouldn't stop you."

Now she smiled. More of the tension ebbed from her shoulders. "You wouldn't, would you? I like that about you, Scott, I really do. But you're too good to have left anything for someone to find."

Again I didn't say anything, not sure where she was heading.

"I'd be disappointed if you did, I think."

I leaned forward and put my forearms on the desk. This brought me as close to her as I thought she'd let me get. "Just tell me you're okay, Trudy."

Her hands and eyes went to her lap and she picked up a small notebook from her lap. Then she smiled brightly, unexpectedly, and said, "Of course I am, Porter. We all are."

And just like that the old Trudy was back, sunshine streamed from her hair, and little gleaming sparkles shone from her teeth. Probably rainbows were curling over the building that very minute. She sat up straighter and her energy had returned. But there were still the smudges of purple layered beneath her large green eyes.

For one final second I didn't want to let go of the moment. Just how vulnerable was she right now? Was she reaching out for something or just unable to hold in whatever it was she was going through?

"You could always ask me, Trudy. Anytime."

She answered right away, so quickly that I couldn't tell whether or not she believed me. "I know I could, Porter. But I never would."

I felt the urge to say, *I want you to. Right now, before it's too late.* But it was just this kind of subject, this level of understanding—this was the line we could not cross.

I sat back in my chair, crossed my legs like there was nothing in the world worth worrying about and got back to business. "So what did you get on Holmes?"

The notebook cover was already flipped back and with only a quick glance at a page, she said, "He definitely left town. His plane flew out of Sarasota about an hour after he left here, and his flight plan shows he flew into a small airport outside of Richmond."

"Virginia?"

She nodded. "But I don't know where he went from there yet. I've got a call in to the FBO up at the airport and that should help."

"Bet you a buck the plane's flown on to somewhere else. The problem is, we don't know if Holmes was just making a pit stop or ducking out. He could have driven off or taken a taxi or jumped on a bus to lord knows where."

"Do you really see a man like Holmes taking a taxi anywhere? Or a bus?" She actually laughed a little.

"You're right," I said. "Maybe a limousine, a nice stretch Lincoln. Make sure you check limo services when you try to track down what happened."

"Already doing it," she said. "That all?"

I stared into her eyes and took too long to say anything.

"That's all." She answered herself, got up and walked to the door. She knew me too well. I'd hired her as a receptionist when she and Tim had moved down from Indianapolis. The clients liked her, especially once they started talking to her, and she went on to get her PI license. In six months I made her the office manager and hired her an assistant to serve both as receptionist and to help her with a lot of the routine tasks that she took on as her responsibility. This way she kept her hands in most of our cases and could keep mostly regular hours, which was what she said she wanted. At least it was important to her when she took the job. I found out the reason after she'd told me why her and her husband had left Indianapolis. Seeing her this morning made me wonder about the viability of so-called fresh starts.

"Trudy, wait." I reached down to my desk drawer and took out the tapes I'd pulled with the fingerprints from the front door handle this morning. She came back and stood at the edge of my desk. I hated to do this but I didn't want to stray any further from normalcy. "I also need you to get to Tim and see what he can do with these."

I watched her closely to see how she'd react to my request but everything seemed routine about her response.

She was casual as she picked up the tapes and held them under the light. "Where'd these come from?"

"Some place convenient," I said.

"You are so maddeningly vague sometimes. Actually, you are most of the time."

"You so get me."

"Keep this up and something will get you, believe me."

"Stop flirting with me."

Whatever she'd brought in with her this morning was definitely gone. She gave me one of her scowling looks so I started paging through the papers on my desk. I really didn't know what was showing on my face at that point but my cheeks felt warm.

"What do you want me to tell Tim?"

"Same thing as always, I hope. That it's important to you." I didn't want to tell her it might help keep her safe.

She looked at me with a strange cast to her eyes. "I can do that," she said, and moved toward the door.

"Shut that for me, will you?"

She didn't reply, but she did pull the door closed after her. I felt lousy for putting the firm above her personal life but at that moment, that was all I knew how to do.

Tim Westland wasn't my only contact on the local police force. Oftentimes he was the most valuable, but sometimes he was just the most convenient. In some ways I should probably work at being more discerning about what I asked Trudy to get from him.

I pulled my phone closer to me and dialed the number for Marty Ables, another Sarasota cop, but one I spoke with directly. No one else in the firm knew about him. That was how he wanted it and I was happy to oblige.

"What's up, Marty?"

"Porter, you bastard," he said. "Bad timing to hear from you."

"Why do you think I called?"

"You needed someone's day to ruin. Call you back in five."

We hung up and five minutes later my direct outside line rang. While I was waiting I studied the letter from Holmes's book some more. Ables would have been looking for some place more private than his desk and then calling me from his personal cell phone.

"So what do you need, Porter?"

"I've got a strange one, Marty. Hear me out before you have a fit."

"Oh, god," he said.

"I have six names on a list that I need you to look at."

"Okay," he said, and I could hear paper rustling in the background. "Shoot. We'll talk price later."

"Well, hang on," I said. "All I have is first names."

"I'm sorry, I think you were trying to call the asylum down the street. What the hell are you talking about? We get seventy thousand missing persons in this state every year, Porter. You're trying to give me six *first* names to work with?"

"Bear with me a second, Marty. First of all, they may not even be missing."

"Oh, good thing you called me, then. Something sticky get in your

Rolodex?"

I ignored him. "They could be dead, they could be your neighbors, they may not have anything to do with the state of Florida."

"Seriously, Porter, what jackass put a phone in your hand right now?"

I told him we had a client who'd fled, that he'd left behind a strange letter. Some of the names were too common to do anything with, unless they came up along with a hit on one of the unusual ones.

"But there may not even be a crime here?"

I debated what more I should tell him.

"There are other bodies—"

"Stop," he said. "Stop right there."

His balding head had to be darkening as he combed through the remaining strands of wiry blonde hair with his neatly trimmed fingernails.

"Okay," I said.

"I know you," Ables said. "But I gotta ask: are you on the hook for something here? You, yourself?"

"No," I told him. "Honestly."

"And these bodies—are they local?"

This is where I tried to lead a balanced life. I'd just told him the truth and now I was going to tell him a lie. "They are not."

"Then that's all I need to know. But if I come back with something and have to ask, you should plan now because you are going to tell me."

"Of course I will."

"Seriously. Christ, you're more of a bastard than you were last time you called." I heard him take a breath and say, "So this is a national thing you want me to do?"

"It's probably just pissing in the wind, Marty, but I've got some things I'm trying to get to add up for a client. The odd names on this letter may come up somewhere, and may not. If they do, you could do yourself some good." Without giving him the chance to object any more, I slowly read off the names *Rosalyn, Tedys* and *Eban*, spelling out each one. Then I gave him *Elizabeth, Ralph* and *Don*.

"You know I can't do a lot here, don't you? I can do some database searches on first names, maybe combinations of them, but that's about it."

"But you'd be able to tell if any of these names belonged to open cases, right?"

I could just picture him shaking his head. "Only if they're in VICAP or on milk cartons. Jesus Christ, Porter. I don't know how I can justify any real time—"

"When's that bill due for your country club, the Sara Bay? Why don't you start sending those along to my office for a few months. We'll see if we can't help you nudge that handicap down a point or two."

"Six months?"

"I was thinking two."

"Make it four."

"I'll go three. You spend too much in the nineteenth hole."

"It's a beautiful clubhouse. But done. And you have to know this is thinner than a cockroach in a gum wrapper. Don't wait up for anything."

"You either, sweetie."

I had no idea what I could expect from Ables but I knew it probably wouldn't be much. Unless there was some well-known scandal somewhere in the country that he could turn up that had some mention of an "Eban" or a "Tedys" all I was doing was spending Holmes's money so Marty Ables could cover his greens fees. Regardless, the payoff would keep the man happy and a happy informant is an accessible one. We both knew I was overpaying him but I chalked one part of that up to past favors and another to future interests. It pays to invest.

I slid the copy of the transcript to the side and put my feet up on my desk. My watch told me the day was far younger than it felt. Trudy was at her desk, seeing if she could pick up anything on Holmes. McKay was out looking for this "Rudge" person who had sold the Poe book to Holmes, or so I assumed. I thought of what else the agency had going on and I remembered what Al Sutter had told me about last night's case.

I sat up and punched the extension for Steph's desk. She picked up on the first ring. "Yes, Scott?"

"Did Gabe Keller make it in yet?"

"I still haven't see him this morning," she said.

"Ask Al if he knows anything. I'll hold on." I heard her ask our newly designated security guard if he knew where Keller was.

"Al says—"

"That's all right, Steph," I told her. "I heard him. When Gabe comes in, ask him to see me. Immediately."

"Will do, Scott."

CHAPTER NINE

I wasn't able to find out anything on the name "Tedys." "Teddy" is a nickname for names like "Edward" or "Theodore" but that didn't account for the odd spelling, at least not with the "s" on the end. "Eban" turned out to be a Hebrew name meaning "stone," or "rock." Not much to go on there. I looked at the copy of the letter on my desk. Could the writer have just been a really crappy speller? I kicked back and wondered what the chances were that Marty Ables would be able to come up with anything at all. I knew that with three months of country club dues on the line, I could hold his feet to the fire for a while.

Trudy knocked on the frame of my door and didn't stop as she walked in to my office. "Ernesto Flores just died."

It took me a second. "Holmes's caretaker?"

"That's right. He never regained consciousness so we're not going to be learning anything from him."

"We probably wouldn't have, anyway. Like Paul said, since Hatchet Face got him in the back of the head he probably didn't see anything."

"Unless Flores opened the door for him, and then turned his back. Our guy could have nailed him then."

"Maybe." I shrugged. "Either way, I don't think he could have given us more than what we got from Paul. Probably less. He would have told anything he knew to the police and not spoken to us."

I shouldn't have said that. As soon as I did, I felt as if I'd made an indirect reference to Tim Westland. Trudy was kind enough to let me off the hook by not mentioning it.

"I'm still working on tracking down Holmes from Richmond."

"Good," I said. "I wonder if he knows about Flores. I wonder if this counts against us and his wanting us to insulate him from the problem of owning that book."

"Or the letter."

I often wished I had a window with a nice view of palm trees or a little creek or even a patch of grass with grazing roseate spoonbills or something like that. It just seemed like there were moments that would be suitable for taking a quick look outside and reminding yourself that there were things going on outside these walls that didn't involve this sorry little racket we involved ourselves in. But the boss couldn't afford to think like that.

"It probably is the letter," I said. "Holmes kept the book and left that thing behind. If he were really worried about owning the book he probably wouldn't still be hanging on to it." I slipped out of my chair and knelt in front of my office safe. I worked the combination, pulled open the door, and extracted the original letter in its glassine protector from the top shelf. I'd slid it into a manila envelope from a desk drawer and folded over the flap. Trudy reached out and took it from me.

"Do you think you could find a lab somewhere, maybe at one of the universities, and see if they can tell us anything about the paper that was used? Maybe there's a way to find out how old the thing is from the ink or if there are any peculiarities that could tell us anything."

"How about a graphologist?"

"What's that?"

"A handwriting expert. I think."

"Sure," I said. "Good plan. Maybe they can tell us something about the personality of the letter writer. It would be nice to know if they can identify the same stress we get out of the actual text."

"I know there's a consultant in Tampa we can use. He's been in the paper. I'll get that done right away." Trudy pulled the letter partway out of the envelope. "It's still so... creepy."

"Or worse. Don't forget what Holmes was willing to do to get away from it."

"It doesn't add up, does it, Scott?"

I picked up the empty coffee cup from my desk. "Oh, I don't know," I said. "Not yet. We have pieces, pretty serious ones. One corpse, another presumed, an on the run millionaire—" I paused and looked at Trudy; I hadn't seen her background work on Holmes yet.

"Oh, yes," she said. "You'll get his packet on your desk today."

"Good," I told her. "So we have a running millionaire, a check for too much money, and an unknown man bashing people on the head. That's a pretty good basis for a framework of something."

She pushed the letter back into the envelope. "I guess you're right." She stood there, looking as though she had something else to say. This time I waited her out but it didn't do any good.

"I'll let you know," she said, and turned to leave.

"Thank you, Trudy."

She didn't say anything as I watched the swish of her skirt pass through my door. I had the distinct feeling she knew exactly what I was looking at.

Steph buzzed me from the front a few minutes later and said Gabe Keller had come in. She'd told him I wanted to see him but he had continued on to his office. I thanked her and got up to stretch my legs. May as well take a stroll myself and save him the trip.

I walked out of my office, down the hall, saw Al Sutter reading a magazine while Steph was typing something into her word processor. Trudy, whose desk was behind Steph's, was speaking on the phone. Al looked up as I walked by. "Keep up the good work," I told him.

He looked confused and put the magazine down. I gave him a wink. "You're all good," I told him. "Just giving you a hard time." He smiled back but left the magazine on the chair next to him. I was serious but he didn't seem too sure. My fault. Shouldn't mess with the employees. I knew that but it rarely stopped me.

I took the right turn down the short hallway which led to our small cubicle farm. I went back to the one in the far corner that was Gabe's and rapped my knuckles on the metal frame of one of the dividers. As I looked inside, I was just in time to see Gabe jump at least three inches out of his seat. Quite a feat for a man of his girth.

"Jesus!" he swore.

"Whoah there, Gabe, take it easy. Just checking in."

He finished stuffing something into his backpack then kicked it under his desk. "Sorry, Scott," he said. "Didn't hear you come up."

Okay. "Sutter said your guy didn't show up last night. What happened?"

Gabe swallowed and leaned back in his chair, swiveling it to face me. "Don't know yet," he said, folding his hands across his pot belly. His face and beard were glistening with perspiration and I thought it must have gotten hot outside sooner than it had been earlier in the week. "I've, uh, I've been trying to find out this morning. Hopefully I'll know more soon. By lunch time maybe."

"Have you spoken with the client? What's the name, Hochstedt?"

"I have a call in. Right now I'm planning on going out again tonight."

"Okay," I said, and pulled back from the cube wall. "You need anything from me?"

"No," he said. "No, I'm good. It was just one of those things last night. You know."

I wished I knew what was going on in this guy's mind. I almost asked him if something was wrong but it occurred to me I didn't really want to know. I just needed him to keep bringing in results. "All right, man," I said. "Let me know."

"Sure, Scott. I'll do that. Definitely."

I left him there, and went back to my office. I noticed Al Sutter wasn't reading but the magazine had migrated into his lap. I smiled inwardly. A little fear of the boss was never a bad thing, was it?

Nah.

Trudy came back after lunch and tossed two file folders on my desk.

"What are those?" I asked.

"Profile on Holmes, and the fingerprint results from those tapes you gave me this morning."

"That was fast. Anything good?"

She gestured toward the files while still standing behind the visitor chairs. "See for yourself."

I picked up the two folders, flipped the first one open. It was all background on our client, Edwin Morton Holmes. He'd been a banker, an officer with several institutions listed on his curriculum vitae going back over thirty years. Retired a year ago, had houses in several states. That told me where he got his money from. I closed that, slid it behind the second folder. When I pulled back that cover, I said, "Bingo."

There was a blow up copy of a Massachusetts driver's license with a picture of a man who certainly could have been the man I'd seen in the parking lot two nights ago. "Rico Gallo," I read. I did the math from the birth date. "Thirty seven years old." I looked up at Trudy. "What else is in here?"

"A few arrests, no convictions. Two for trespassing, one for assault. Charges were always dropped."

"Have we heard from McKay lately?"

Trudy said no. "He's still tracking down Rudge. He took a flight up to Boston but I don't know anything more."

I held up the folder she'd compiled on Holmes. "He been found?"

"I'm still trying. What are you thinking?"

I tossed the papers onto my desk. "Holmes wanted us to protect him from something."

"And you think it was Rico Gallo? Then why didn't he just tell us that?"

"I don't think he knew about Gallo specifically. He certainly thought someone was out there, but maybe not exactly who. Or he may have had another reason to keep us in the dark."

"Like what? This guy is a killer, isn't he?"

"Like maybe Holmes himself was into something he thought we wouldn't touch if we knew about it? Who knows? Could be anything. Could be he wrote a big enough check just so he thought he wouldn't have to deal with it."

"Was it?"

I looked her in the eyes, saw that the purple bags had mostly diminished with the passage of the day. "Was what what?"

"Was the check big enough?"

"Yes," I said. "For now. But we still don't know what this is all about, so I'll reserve final judgment."

Trudy turned sideways, propping one gloriously long thigh on the thick back of one of the chairs facing my desk. "But if Holmes is the client, and he isn't paying us to find out about Gallo, why are you so concerned?"

Doing my best not to imagine the form propping up the fabric of that grey skirt, I told her, "Because I'm not going to be treated like an idiot. I'll take his money, I'll do what he asks. But I won't turn away from the hard questions just because they may not be on Holmes's agenda."

She arched an eyebrow at me and my heart jumped when I saw the effect it had on her face. Perfect features don't make for beauty in my book. The right features plus the right flaws—or what some people call flaws—combine to cast a memorable image. Trudy's eyes were a bit small but her cheekbones were high, and when she smiled, a hint of two slightly buck but brilliant white teeth shone through her rich, creamy lips. She could stop me cold with a look like the one she was giving me now. I found it hard to speak. I said my standard "Damn Tim Westland" mantra to myself, then broke myself out of it by saying, "And sometimes I take on my own agenda."

The smiled eased from her face.

"I know you do," she said.

"And that," I said, sitting up and straightening the folders on my desk for an excuse to look away, "is why I say you get me."

"As long as the money lasts."

"Sure," I said. "As long as that." But she knew I was lying.

"I have one more question, Scott."

I could have guessed, but I said, "What's that?"

"Who does Rico Gallo work for? Or is he running on his own?"

"That," I told her, "is what you are going to look into next."

"I should have known."

"Of course you should have. I thought you were better at this stuff."

She stuck her tongue out at me. "Why do you always try to get my goat like we're a pair of eight year olds in a one room school house?"

"Because I can't get anything else."

"Hmm," she said. "You're probably right." She picked the files off my desk and did a little skipping step toward the door. If this is how comfortable she gets after a few hours in the office, doing work, what must really be going on at home with her husband?

I knew I'd feel bad for her if I thought about what was happening between her and Tim but since there wasn't anything I could do about it, I yanked the chain that turned off my desk lamp and headed out the door myself, only I kept on going, all the way out of the office. Al Sutter managed to slide the four month old *Sports Illustrated* down to the seat next to him just as I passed.

"You're doing fine, Al," I said to him as his face turned a first degree burn shade of red. "Watch him, Steph," I called over my shoulder as I stepped through the open door onto the sidewalk. "There may be a swimsuit issue around here I don't know about."

She didn't know how to answer, poor kid. All part of having me for a boss.

CHAPTER TEN

I needed to find a man named Eamon Stanley. This time of day I thought I knew where he'd be but I'd have to head up to Tampa against the steady build of rush hour traffic that was well under way. It seemed like there were very few traffic laws in Florida that people still paid attention to, worse when you got down Miami way. Driving under the influence was one of them, but driving twenty miles an hour over the speed limit in most residential areas wouldn't get you noticed. But do twenty over the speed limit between Sarasota and Tampa and odds are high you will get a ticket. You've made yourself the low hanging fruit.

I settled into the slog and made my way not only through the interminable stoplights on the Bee Line to the freeway entrance, but I coasted along at stop and go speeds north all the way over the Sunshine Skyway Bridge into St. Petersburg. There the traffic finally thinned a bit but the curves going around downtown kept speeds down. Halfway over the Howard Frankland bridge all four lanes fell to a lurching march. For the millionth time I wondered who the hell designed these damn roadways.

Few things in life I hate more than sitting in traffic. Occasionally, though, it gives you relatively quiet time to think, but it only matters if you happen to be in the mood to take advantage of it.

There was a dive bar off Nebraska Avenue, an area where no one looked each other in the eye out of doors. Kind of like Manhattan without the suits or money or tall buildings. Lots of tension, too, the kind that leads to spurious fights on the streets and on the sidewalks, where the losers didn't call the cops or ride in ambulances. The lucky ones maybe crawled away. The luckier ones had friends strong enough to drag them.

I drive an old Chevy Malibu that needed a few bucketfuls of Bondo and a paint job. There was a coat hanger where the antenna used to be, dust on the dashboard and two inches of trash on the floors. I keep a nice Cadillac in the garage beneath my condo building, but that's my weekend car, the vehicle that never sees the light of day while I'm working a case. People who know it's mine are fond of telling me a Caddy was an odd choice for a high end car with all the foreign options available—nobody buys a Caddy anymore unless it's a black SUV with spinning rims, they say—but I grew up next to a family that drove nothing but shiny new Sevilles and Eldorados. The father was a friend of my dad's, and he was a Cadillac dealer. I thought they were cool cars when I was a kid and owning one now was one way of feeling like I'd put something over on my family.

The good thing about the Malibu was that I could park it almost anywhere. I rarely locked it and never kept anything in it worth stealing. I'd learned that lesson long ago. Someone wants to open the door and rifle the glove compartment, have at it. There's nothing to take. If I lock the car, the same thing happens and I'm left with a broken window. It's happened more than once.

I parked in the unpaved shell lot behind Goldy's, as far away from the heaping garbage bags as I could. Just because my car was tramp bait didn't mean I had to entice the dumpster diving crowd. The smell back there was always horrible and many of the homeless used the dumpsters as public restrooms.

I locked my jacket in the car trunk and rolled up the sleeves on my shirt. I was a bit cleaner than the regular clientele but in a place like this, people showed up for as many reasons as there were vices.

When I pushed through the door, a few of the faces propped on bar stools turned a squinting eye toward me, then slowly flickered back to the private spaces between their folded arms and dirty bar space, quietly protecting a glass that hopefully had something in it. The bartender saw me and turned away with deliberate disinterest. Eamon Stanley was at the far end of the bar, holding a stained mug in one hand with two Latina women standing on either side of him. Instead of shoes, one of them stood in bedroom slippers that looked two sizes too small, her callused heels hanging more than an inch over the worn soles.

I had no doubt Stanley knew I was there but he showed no sign until I clapped him on the shoulder and told him I'd buy him a fresh beer. He planted a loud smack on the rear ends of each of his book ends and sent them off, both of them shooting me resentful looks as they tried to figure out who they were going to light on next. Either Stanley had come into some temporary scratch or they were not very good judges of character. Probably a bit of both.

"I don't need anything from you," he said, still without looking at me.

I shoehorned myself between a bald guy on Stanley's left and Stanley himself. The bald guy looked at me but he was careful and decided to settle with inching his stool over just enough to give me room to stand freely. I never turned my head. Attitude dictated how most of these people dealt with you. Some of the rest, they sought out those same attitudes like sharks sniffing out bleeding baby seals. They were the ones looking to make a point. The sadists, the bullies, the ones you didn't push because they lacked the ability to reason—they were the guys too stupid to know stupid they were, and trying to convince them otherwise made their heads hurt and their violence come out.

"Get it from the bartender then." I dropped a twenty on the bar. "Order what you like. We need to talk."

"Kiss my ass."

I brought my right hand up quickly behind Stanley's head and pushed it hard onto the bar surface in front of him. His forehead kissed off the rim of the dirty beer mug and sent it tumbling to the floor behind the bar. The noise made heads turn and I grabbed a handful of bar napkins and started to wipe the spreading puddle of beer as though I were cleaning up after an accident. My body language said "oops" but my voice was low and said something different. "You don't want to play like that, Eamon."

"Christ, you're an asshole," he said, rubbing his forehead and checking his fingers for blood. He tried to get a look at his reflection in the mirror on the wall behind the bar but it was too dirty and the light too dim.

"I'll be anything you want me to be, Eamon. It's all up to you."

He held his hand up and called for Charlie the bartender to bring him another beer. He used my twenty and kept all the change. Charlie probably didn't count on many tips in this joint anyway.

"What do you want?"

"You came down from the northeast, didn't you? Somewhere in New England?"

"Providence," he said. "New England enough."

"And mobbed up enough. I know you try to stay connected." I took out a copy of the picture of Rico Gallo that Trudy had brought me earlier. "Any idea who this is?"

He picked it up and squinted at the details on the copy. "It ain't your mother. Different last name." He put it down on the bar, at the last moment moving it to the side to keep it out of the spilled beer. Little things like that were how you knew you had somebody's interest.

"Yours either. He's from Boston. See if you can find anything out about him, but keep it quiet."

"Then what?"

"I might have a job for you."

This brought out a grin. "How much it worth?"

I slapped him on the shoulder again. "For you, dear, anything."

"Fuckin' don't touch me like that."

"You're right," I said, as I wiped my palm along the side of my pants. "Bad idea. Still, I need you to be ready. This might turn into something quick."

Eamon Stanley swiveled his head on his neck, his long stringy hair barely moving off the back of his collar. "You ain't never gonna let me go, are you?"

This time I leaned against the bar myself, using only my forearms to hold myself up. I looked him square in the face and said in a voice that only he could hear, "I let you get away with your shit once. Once. If it wasn't for me you would either be in a shit hole up in Starke or dead rotting in a ditch somewhere. So no, I ain't never gonna let you go." I stared him down for half a minute, neither of us moving. "But I will pay you well."

He picked up his beer and drained half of it, not bothering to wipe the foam from his upper lip. "You're a son of a bitch. I should just do you and see what happens."

"First," I said very carefully. "You wouldn't like it if you tried. I'm very messy. Second, you might not be able to do it, in which case you really wouldn't like it but in an entirely different way. Think back to what you did to those girls. You've got some of the same body parts."

An ugly, almost wistful expression formed across his mouth.

"See yourself like them, flies and all." I pushed back from the bar. "We good? Be ready for this job."

Stanley's eyes went back to the bar. "Sir, yes sir," he said, as though I'd been dismissed. There wasn't anything more for me to say. He knew I meant what I told him and I knew he'd do what I wanted, even if it might kill him. I'd saved that scumbag's life, but I never got over thinking that it had been a mistake. I could use him now and again but it was exhausting keeping tabs on him, making sure he didn't go back to his old ways. Despite getting away with half a dozen grisly unsolved—as far as the police were concerned—murders, he was now my tool. The problem is, every now and then you have to take your tools out of the drawer if you wanted to keep them sharp. It also meant paying him occasionally and the thought of what he did with the money was not a pleasant one. I didn't need a receipt for sponsoring his vices though it was possible the money kept him from some of his former activities. I didn't really know. There was only one future for a creature like Eamon Stanley. The question was how soon and in what manner it finally found him.

All this was unpleasant but necessary. Otherwise I'd have to take steps to correct what would have been my original mistake with Stanley but I'd already compounded the problem by keeping him a free man. And, of course, in the kind of condition where he could perform a function for me if and when I needed it. He was mine now, ugly as that notion was, and ultimately there would only be one way to get rid of him.

But it wasn't time yet. Rico Gallo was out there.

I motioned Charlie the bartender over and slipped him another twenty. "For the phone messages I'm going to leave for Stanley here." The bill disappeared under Charlie's palm as he gave me a quick nod of the head.

"You'll hear from me, Eamon," I said, and walked out of the bar. "I'll call every day." Three men were standing by the empty gumball machine by the door, its glass cracked and yellowed, and watched me go. One of them looked back to Stanley, then giving up turned around and moved toward a table, his two friends following. Suited me.

I got back into the Malibu, drove north up to Hillsborough Boulevard. I didn't want to brave the bridge over the bay this time of the day again. I really hate sitting in traffic.

Trudy called and asked where I was. I'd holed up in a spaghetti joint in the old warehouse district, close to the extensive projects just north of 275.

"I'm not telling unless you're coming to join me."

She ignored this. "Are you coming back in?"

I wiped my mouth with a paper napkin and said, "Probably not in time to get anything done. What's up?"

"I found Holmes."

"Really?" Finally some good news, I thought. If he wasn't as out of the case as I'd suspected there was likely more we could learn from him. We'd just need a way to get him to talk. "Where is he?"

"Well," she said, drawing it out. "From Richmond a hired car took him north to Alexandria."

I waited but she didn't continue. Something wasn't right. "And?"

Her voice was more serious as she answered. "They found his body this morning. In the bath tub of a hotel. His throat had been cut."

"Christ," I swore. "Which hotel?"

"The Hay-Adams."

"That's in D.C."

"I haven't been able to find how he got there. The car service left him at a restaurant in an area called Old Town."

"I know it." I thought about this for a moment. Three feet off the beaten path of the rich and powerful, Washington, D.C. could be a violent and ugly place, and often was. But Holmes had been one of *them*, albeit a somewhat stale edge of the upper crust. At least that's how he appeared to me. I wondered if Rico Gallo could have been involved. Considering all that he'd been up to down here, it was difficult to see he how he could have tracked Holmes down on his northward flight, let alone meet up with the man himself. That brought disturbing new thoughts to mind.

"Scott?"

"How are you doing?" I asked her. I was still thinking of the purple bags under her eyes this morning.

"I'm good," she said cautiously. "It's not like I knew the client very well or anything like that."

"That's not what I meant."

"I know."

If she wasn't going to give me more than that, I was going to have to pull the trigger myself. "Can you get Tim to call up there, see if he can get copies of what the locals have put together?"

"Oh, god," she said. "Scott, they're going to want to know why Tim and the Sarasota police are interested in their case. It could make some noise. Do you really want that?"

"No," I said. "But I do want to know what Holmes had with him when he was found. Nothing we can do about that. Tim can tell them about the break-in and murder at Holmes's house. That ought to encourage some sort of cooperation."

There was an uncomfortable note to Trudy's voice. "He's not a detective. This could blow up on all of us."

I noticed she didn't say "on him." I told her to never mind. I was thinking I could have Marty Ables make the call. He ought to be able to make that work, though it might cost me another month or two of country club dues. At this rate there wouldn't be a lot of money left out of Holmes's initial check.

"Never mind. You're right, Trudy. I'll check it out myself."

Normally she would have questioned this, but this time she said nothing. "What are you thinking?"

"I want to know if he's lost anything. We know he had the Poe book when he left Florida—did he still have it in D.C.?"

"What would that tell us?"

"No idea. Do you know where his plane went after it dropped Holmes at Richmond?"

"An airport at Lancaster, Pennsylvania. Does that mean anything?"

"Just that I'd like to talk to that pilot. Can you get that set up?"

"I'll try."

"Before the cops?"

"I'll try hard."

"Good girl. I guess I am coming in. It will take me a while, though."

"I'll wait."

I had the sudden thought that she was making the call from the desk in my office. "You don't have to do that."

"I know," she said. "But I'll wait."

Okay. "One more thing. Have you had a chance to look into Gallo?"

"About Gallo? I—I could ask Tim that."

I tried to keep it business as usual. "That would be good."

"I just said so. I'll give him a call."

We hung up but I kept hearing her ask, "About Gallo?", as though she had no other reason to talk to her husband. I pushed back from my table and tried to find my waiter. My watch told me I'd still catch the tail end of rush hour but I couldn't help it now. As for what Trudy was going through at home, I wouldn't allow myself to think about it. It wouldn't be more than a half-assed guess, anyway. She'd grown testy when she'd talked about Tim.

I thumbed through the contact list on my phone until I found the number for Marty Ables. The waiter was heading my way and I tossed my credit card on the table as I highlighted Ables' number and pressed Send.

While I was on my errand to Tampa, a black BMW was parked two blocks away from my office. It moved every hour or so, about twenty minutes before the parking meter would run out, then it would move on and find another space, always within the same two block area. One time, the man inside had gotten out and walked past the glass door of my office. Inside he could see a very large man paging through magazines, slumped in a loose posture on a chair set along the wall. There was also a woman behind the frontmost desk, her eyes focused on the computer screen in front of her. It looked like too big a risk to go inside.

Fine, then. It was around the block and back to the car. He wasn't sure who it would be yet. There was the one from last night, and there was that other woman inside, the one with the desk behind the receptionist's. It was always good to have options, and he knew he had several.

CHAPTER ELEVEN

I got back to the office at about seven thirty. The door was locked, and for a moment I felt foolish that I had overlooked telling Trudy to do that. I was tense as I used my key and walked in. The lights were out and everything seemed quiet, until I heard footsteps coming from my office. I looked to the right down the short corridor and there was Trudy. She had a look on her face that I was hoping was relief.

My keys were still in my hand and I turned and re-locked the door. It gave Trudy a chance to get herself together, if that's what she needed. Normally she'd have gone home by now unless I'd asked her to stay to work on something for a case. This time she'd been the one asking me to come back late. Well, she would either talk about what was on her mind or not. If I'd learned one thing about Trudy Westland it was that pushing her was never a good thing. She'd share if she wanted to. Her terms always.

"What's up?"

"You want to go into your office or talk out here?"

I gestured toward the end of the hall. She'd already gone a good way toward unsettling me. "Sounds like it's more your office tonight. After you."

She turned, the grey sweater and skirt looking a bit less fresh but no less fetching than they did this morning. I followed her into my office, saw papers and folders spread out across my desktop. She walked around the desk and started to gather them up, as if embarrassed she'd left evidence of actual work in my space.

"No, keep them there," I said, and took a seat on one of my own visitor chairs.

"You don't mind?"

"What do you think?"

She hesitated then spread things out again to where they had been. "Sometimes I come in here at night, when I'm here alone. I hope you don't mind."

I just looked at her, wondering how often she stayed late when I didn't know about it. I loved the thought that she was comfortable enough to do that but I also knew the surest way to change that was to pay it attention. "Is this about Gallo?"

"Some of it," she said. Trudy flipped over some papers and gathered them atop an open manila folder. "It seems our pointy-faced friend has done a lot of work for a number of people over the past ten years or so."

"Ten years?"

"That's all I've been able to find so far."

"What kind of work?"

"That's what's interesting. He's been arrested on several occasions but never managed to get himself charged."

"For...."

"That's what makes it more interesting. He's always been released before the arraignment."

"So this is what you thought before, that he's never been charged with anything that stuck?"

"Exactly."

I thought about this. It would seem Gallo had someone with serious juice behind him.

"Does he have a regular lawyer?"

Trudy went through some papers. "Four different arrests: two in Massachusetts, one in Connecticut, and one in Rhode Island. Four different lawyers, including the two incidents in Massachusetts."

"Murder involved in any of this?"

"Assault, battery, conspiracy, racketeering, and on and on, but everything gets dropped pretty quickly, so we don't know how much of this was cops throwing stuff out there and how much was really Gallo."

"Which wouldn't seem to be enough." I thought about my meeting with Eamon Stanley. "What happened in Rhode Island?"

She frowned, paged through more papers. "I don't have details," she said. "Originally arrested on suspicion of murder. Why?"

"Just asking," I said. "Tell me about Holmes."

"I—I haven't heard back from Tim yet about that."

"Okay. That'll keep for now."

"Really?"

Because I had Marty Ables working on it. I'd tossed him a bone, telling him he could link up the burglary of Holmes's house and the murder of the caretaker to Holmes's death in D.C. This should get him some points or favors with someone at Sarasota PD and I was able to save another month of greens fees. I didn't know or care how he linked them up, I just wanted him to get access to information from D.C. about the crime scene. He may not be able to do it himself, but this was probably the best chance I had to learn something quickly.

"So what we know now is that Holmes was probably avoiding Rico Gallo when he sent the missing Endo Robbins to see me. Apparently with good reason. Holmes leaves us a cryptic letter and a big check and jets out of town. A day later he's dead, presumably the precise outcome he was trying to avoid."

"Does this mean we're done?"

"With the case?" I asked, surprised. "No. Gallo is still out there. That letter may mean something—"

"We should hear something back about the paper and ink analysis in the next three days."

"Good," I said, although I was disappointed. "See if you can light a fire under that, though, will you? That may give us the key to what's actually going on."

She looked puzzled. "But if Holmes is dead, and we were hired to—"

"Protect him from the consequences of owning that damn book. Yes, we failed him. But I still want to know why."

I looked into her eyes. She was genuinely curious. The purple lines underscoring her stress were starting to reassert themselves at the end of the day but the eyes themselves were still large and round, a brilliant green color catching the limited glare from the lamp on my desk and reflected it back to me.

"You do realize we no longer have a client."

"Sure we do," I said. "Me. The agency. We can't begin an investigation and let it stop whenever someone takes out one of our clients. We started things moving, and we're not going to let Gallo win just because someone murdered Edwin Holmes."

Her expression told me she didn't buy it.

"Look," I said. "Who hired Gallo?"

"I don't know."

"Who killed Holmes?"

She shook her head.

"What does that paper mean?"

"Scott, I—"

"So we got paid to do what, exactly? We may as well have done nothing as far as Holmes is concerned. That's not what we do. That's not what I do."

"So you're making this about what, then? Vengeance?"

I laughed. "For Holmes? There aren't a lot of clients I've liked less right off the bat. We got involved, for Holmes's money, yes, but that's how we define our business. Things happened, bad things. Maybe we should have been able to get in front of them, maybe not. Holmes kept us in the dark and we started out trailing this thing and haven't caught it by the tail yet. That's not our fault. We've been trying our best. But something's going on, we're part of it, and we don't even know what it is yet."

"You don't think it'll be over now?"

"Because Holmes is gone?"

She nodded.

"I have no idea. Holmes may have been the messenger. He may have been trying to right a wrong, do some damage, could be anything. But whatever it was he'd passed it on to us and I accepted that when I deposited his check. So far we haven't been up to it. Unfortunately for Holmes it cost him dearly. But that's not on us."

Absently she rolled a pencil back and forth across the papers on the desk. I knew she was wondering if I was taking things personally or if there was something else going on. Then she had another idea: "You think this is about the letter?"

I held my hands wide. "I hope so," I told her. "We don't have much left."

She sat back, thinking. "I'll call the university folks tomorrow, get them to move that analysis along faster. I'll do the same for the graphology."

"That would be good." I stifled a yawn and stretched. "In the meantime—"

"Yes, in the meantime."

We sat there, looking across at each other for a good long while. I had the feeling I enjoyed it more than she did.

"You doing okay?" I asked.

This time she didn't blow me off. She looked across my own desk, scanning my face. Her expression never changed. I wasn't sure what she was looking for.

"Day by day," she said.

Whatever that was supposed to mean. "What can I do?"

"This," she said. "This is good."

I didn't say anything. Whatever was going on between us at that moment, I didn't want to break it even though I didn't understand it.

"Just be there for me, okay?"

"Trudy—" I began, and then, "I am, honey. Whatever you need."

We stayed there a bit longer, and of course things began to feel awkward. They always did. I told her I was going to see her home.

"No, Scott, that will just make things...."

"Separate cars, Trudy. No one will know."

"I'm okay, Scott." Her color started to rise, she began to straighten the documents spread across my desk.

"Gallo," I said, cutting her off. "He's still out there."

She stopped moving.

"Oh."

"Yeah," I said. "Leave the papers. They'll be there in the morning."

I followed Trudy to her house at a gated community south of downtown about twenty miles out. She told the guard at the gate that I was just seeing her home but he made me put a guest pass in my window anyway as he noted my license number on a clipboard. As Trudy slowed in front of her driveway, ready to make the turn, I pulled around her and kept going.

Lights had been turned on in the lower level of the house so I knew Tim was there and probably waiting for his wife to come home.

The temptation to just "stop by" was powerful but my respect for Trudy was stronger and I looped around the block and back out toward the gate. I slipped my pass into a box with a slot in the side as the barrier arm rose up toward the sky. I drove off, giving a short wave to the guard in the shack while calling him something nasty he couldn't hear just because I was in that sort of mood.

I hadn't had a chance to go through the file on Holmes that Trudy had put together so I headed north for the office. Traffic was light, the night was quiet and the stars would have shone like the ones in a planetarium dome had the light pollution been reasonable. I drove with the windows down, the air heavy and moist as it filled the car.

When I got back I drove down the street slowly before I parked; nothing looked funny or out of place. I already knew that Gallo had put his hands on the front door handle—probably an idle gesture, just checking the lock—and now since Holmes was dead I figured he was either done with us or about to make himself known, step out of the shadows. I parked on the street two blocks away and walked back. I wanted to keep the Malibu at least a little bit hidden. When it started to feel like it was too well associated with me, I'd pick up another non-descript car to do its job.

As I walked the two blocks, I had the odd feeling that there was something going on behind me. There may have been the scuffle of a shoe on the uneven cement of the sidewalk but the ambient noise from the traffic near the water and even a few blocks away on Main Street made it hard to be sure. Didn't matter. It *might* be real, so I'd treat it that way. I slipped my hand into my right pants pocket and worked my fingers into the knuckledusters I'd taken from the Malibu's glove compartment. If Gallo were out there, he'd already shown he liked to work close. I didn't mind that, either, and brass knuckles were good that way. Guns were for show-offs, and usually the fastest way to draw a crowd.

I stopped on the sidewalk and turned around, half a block away from my front door. There was nothing to see. But I still had the feeling. I took my right hand out of my pocket and let my arm hang freely as I finished the trip.

Nothing happened. I unlocked the door, my head turning freely in both directions up and down the street: more nothing. I locked the door after me when I got in, feeling a bit let down after getting all worked up during the short walk. I had the silly notion of pulling a chair outside to the sidewalk and sitting in front of the door, just to wait and see if anyone would show up. Make it a kind of invitation.

The price of vigilance is feeling stupid when nothing happens, so I took my lumps and walked down the hall to my office. I could smell Trudy's scent in there, and I liked it. I felt like a lecher or a rake but I told myself my first concern was Trudy's safety, followed then by her happiness. In fact, I told myself that about all my employees. Doesn't mean I wasn't fooling anyone.

As I moved around my desk and pulled the chain to turn on the desk lamp, I felt stupid again, for the second time in almost as many minutes. Trudy was the kind of woman a man met only once or twice in his life. Physically attractive, personally magnetic, kind, charismatic, intellectually charming; the more time I spent around her the more I wanted to keep spending time around her. That one weekend we'd had together was magic. But had any of it been real, did it have the meaning I would always ascribe to it? The notion of forbidden fruit was always out there.

The part that bothered me was that voice inside that kept asking, kept insisting on knowing, that if Trudy dropped her husband and suddenly made herself available to me, would I still want her? Would it be the same, or were my feelings tempered by the fact that right now she was, quite certainly, unattainable?

I didn't have an answer, and I didn't like the feel of the question. This is what comes from being afraid at looking at yourself too deeply inside.

Shoving thoughts of Trudy aside, I sat down and pulled out the file on Holmes's life, as opposed to the thin one—so far—on Holmes's death. He was from Boston, born in Cambridge, his father was a lawyer, mother was a rare book curator for the Mugar Memorial Library at Boston University. Holmes had studied economics, world history and literature. I flipped through the pages—Holmes had never had what I considered an actual job. He graduated at age twenty- three and lived with his mother after his father had slowly faded and passed away from early onset Alzheimer's. His mother followed three years later from an illness that was not listed in the file. The only child, Edwin, had inherited the family's assets, which included a large estate as well as a second house, both of which had been several generations in the making, and settled down into the ultra-fashionable Louisburg Square neighborhood in Beacon Hill.

There wasn't a lot more in the file. Millionaire playboy type, without the splashy press and celebrity exposure. He'd been married once when he was twenty eight but it didn't last until he was thirty. From the file it seemed he'd led a quiet, somewhat philanthropical life—there was a list of regular charities he supported—and traveled regularly in his private jet. His net worth was estimated to be somewhere in the eight figure range.

So Holmes had been older and richer and boring. Money may not buy happiness but it seemed personality also made the list. I read a few more pages then gathered them back into their file. Not a lot there to explain why someone would want to kill him; why they actually did kill him. If I took his story at face value, someone was after him because of the Poe book. The letter he'd found in it he had dumped off on me, then took off. All that was fine. It was my business to provide a certain service. In this case that seemed to be taking on the troubles he'd believed himself in by passing them to me along with that letter. The size of his check was a good indicator of the amount of fear he was feeling.

Had it worked, it might have been a good plan. In the end, though, I don't think he'd gotten to me in time and with enough information. I was sorry about that. Before we had gotten our feet steady beneath us, events had moved beyond our influence and left two bodies cold almost as quickly as I'd cashed Holmes's check.

I turned off the light and let the darkness in close for a while. Once a shadow passed beyond my window but with the blinds always pulled all I got was the quick impression of the moving silhouette. Part of me wanted to feel more guilt for Holmes than I did, but we'd both known he hadn't been telling me the whole story. Maybe it would have made a difference if he had, maybe it wouldn't have. The impression I had was that his mind had been made up regarding his own plans before he ever set foot in my office.

Could I have taken the case more seriously? I acted in good faith, set things in motion, and was checking the leads that we had. I couldn't help it that he'd run. Maybe that was a good move, maybe not. But it was something beyond my influence.

Maybe we'd learn more after that letter had been analyzed. I hoped I wasn't just counting on a long shot. Odds were that was the case, though. I stood up, wondering who had killed Holmes if Gallo were still down here. I wished I knew who had hired Gallo or why he was doing—what? It would have helped a lot to know for sure what he was ultimately after. Until I did, I wouldn't know if I had to check under the bed every time I turned off the lights or move on to the next investigation.

This, though, is why I had people like Gabe Keller working the cases he did—so I didn't have to. I'll take the Holmses and the Gallos and he can have the cheaters and the domestic abusers. It may be true when they say a private detective is just one step away from the crimes of his clients. At least as far as the private dicks that have made a career out of it are concerned. The split that I maintained between types of cases was supposed to make me feel better about what I myself did, how I held myself apart. A legend in my own mind kind of thing.

Anyway, I was getting out of there. Maybe a quick stop at Jarod's and then home alone. As soon as I locked up and headed down the street, right hand back in my pocket, I started imagining what Trudy was doing at that moment. Trudy and Tim. Then I forced those thoughts out of my head and walked close to the street edge of the sidewalk, staying in the light as much as possible. I didn't hear any more scuffles.

CHAPTER TWELVE

In the morning I didn't get into the office until just before nine. Al Sutter was inside the door, a large styrofoam cup filled with coffee on the table next to him, a stack of sports magazines set unapologetically on the chair to his right. Good, I thought. He'd finally made a decision for himself.

I said, "Hey, Al," then nodded to Steph, who told me good morning.

"How are you doing?" I asked her.

"Working on reports for Gabe," she said. "Catching up on billings."

"Good on you," I said. Trudy was sitting in the chair behind her desk watching me patiently. "You have something, Trudy?"

"Yes," she said. "You want it out here?"

I made a quick show of thinking about it. As far as I knew no one in the office knew Trudy was anything to me other than a trusted employee.

"Why don't you bring it into my office? I can scrape my face against the walls and try to wake myself up." I turned and walked down the hall. A few seconds later Trudy came in behind me and lingered by the door.

"Open or closed?" she asked.

I was surprised she'd asked. "Close it," I said.

When she'd shut it quietly I told her that the Holmes case needed to be kept on the quiet, especially after her news from yesterday.

She nodded though I wasn't sure she understood my reasons. Didn't matter. She had a small stack of file folders cradled in her arms as she approached my desk, stopping on the other side of my visitor chairs.

"Paul called this morning."

"How's he doing?"

"He said he's got some news. He wants you to call him."

"He know about Holmes?"

She nodded her head. "I think that's what he wants to talk to you about. Part of it, anyway."

"Okay," I said. I wanted to ask her about last night and what happened when she got home, but of course I didn't. She looked better today than yesterday, with a pair of designer jeans and a yellow shirt that may have been just a bit too bright for an indoor office. Made me wonder if the brilliant colors weren't a form of compensating for a certain amount of internal darkness in her life. I'd always wondered if she had many friends outside her marriage, but that wasn't the sort of question you could ask anyone without making it sound like an insult. My gut told me, or perhaps it was my own cynicism, that Tim would not allow for an independent social life. He was too insecure in his marriage. It wouldn't surprise me if he were trying to talk Trudy into having a baby, starting a family. Because that always saves a marriage.

"And I called the university this morning, and got hold of the adjunct professor who has the letter. I told her we really needed her to move things forward quickly. I said it was turning into a criminal case."

"She going to do it?"

"At first she was afraid she might get into trouble and asked if anything she did might end up going to the police. She doesn't want to lose her job by working on a scandal. I told her no, it was nothing like that, but we needed the information to clear a few things up."

"Good girl," I said. "When do we get the results?"

"Hopefully this afternoon."

"Beautiful," I said. "You doing good?"

"Right as rain," she responded, delivering a meaningless answer. Fine, I knew my place. Most of the time, anyway.

Trudy turned and started to leave, then stopped, rubbing her left wrist with her right hand. She looked down at my desktop. "Did I leave my watch in here the other day?"

"You mean yesterday?"

I looked around the desktop but I hadn't been in long enough to mess it up yet. And I'd cleaned up my papers from last night before I'd left. She said, "Yes," as I looked around, pulled out the top drawers, then pushed back in my chair and looked at the floor beneath the desk.

"I don't see it. When's the last time you had it?"

"I thought I put it on my nightstand, the same as I do every night," she said. "But I couldn't find it this morning, thought it might have come off in here somehow."

"If I come across it, I'll let you know."

"Thanks, boss."

"You're welcome. Let me know as soon as you get the results from that letter."

"Will do."

And once again I was transfixed as I watched her walk to my office door. And once again she didn't look back, and I knew with certainty she could read at least one part of my mind.

I dialed Paul McKay's cell phone and he answered on the third ring.

"Paul," I said.

"Hey, I found Rudge."

"And…."

"He manages estate sales, the kind that take place when someone dies and there's no heir or family member who either wants to take all the junk left behind or bother to sell it."

"He's a broker."

The sound of McKay slurping from a coffee cup came over the line, and then, "That's about it. Goes in, prices the goods, takes a slice from the top of the net sales."

"And Holmes got the Poe book from there?"

"Which is the weird part. Rudge said there were something like eighteen hundred books in the library, antiquarian things, a number of them probably worth as much as the book that Holmes wanted, maybe more."

I thought about that. "How many did Holmes buy?"

"Exactly one. Just the Poe."

Which was all that Endo Robbins' ledger had shown. "Any idea why?"

"Nope." I could almost hear McKay shaking his head. "But that's not all. Guess who's estate was up for grabs?"

Clearly I had no way of knowing. "Get stuffed," I told him.

"Joe Calello's."

"Not sure I—"

"Gangster. From—"

"Rhode Island," I finished.

"You know the guy? Out of Providence."

No, I'd never heard of him. But now we have three players out of New England, starting with Holmes and moving on to Rico Gallo and now this Joe Calello. I told McKay I wasn't familiar with the name but the geography wasn't a surprise.

"Okay," I told him. "I need you to find out more about Calello, how he died, all that. But also why would his estate be put up for sale? What did he do for the mob, and if someone was there to take over, why wasn't someone there to take over his estate?"

"What about Holmes?"

"That's the million dollar question. What's the connection there?"

"I have no idea. But he was a banker. Banks deal with money. I hear the mob likes money."

"All right," I said. "Do what you can. Hopefully it will just take you a couple of days. But there is one more thing."

McKay laughed. "I know, I know."

"Seriously, Paul. Keep your head down. Too many bodies have dropped and we still don't have a good idea about what's really going on."

The levity was gone from his voice when he asked me if there was any news about Rico Gallo. "Not yet," I told him. "I'm working on it, though."

"Think he's still down there?"

"I hope so."

"Why?"

"If he left town now we may never know what this was all about."

"That would be bad?"

"It would be… unsatisfying. I'd like to find him and figure it out."

"Well, keep him off my ass and I'll feel better."

If things worked out right, I'd do a lot more. "I'll try," I said.

"All right. Let me get moving. I've got a few things to follow up on here in Boston and then I may make a trip further south. That all right with you?"

"We need the answers. So far this thing is getting bigger, not smaller."

"Okay," he said. "I'll check in tomorrow." He hung up.

I replaced my phone in its cradle, then pulled open my desk drawer to take out the transcript of the mysterious letter. I wanted to read it again. It wasn't there. I must have scooped it up with the papers Trudy had brought me yesterday.

Pulling out the file folder I'd used, I went through each item and was surprised when it wasn't there either. Damn, I thought, annoyed. I'll just make another copy. I turned to my safe and looked at the dial. The mark on the dial was pointing a few notches past one hundred twenty. I always left it on twenty-three.

Someone had tried to get into my safe.

No one had the combination but me. I picked up the phone again and called Trudy at her desk. "Did you take the Holmes letter from my desk?" I asked her.

"Me? No. Why?"

"Did you by any chance try to open my safe?"

"With what? The spoon I bent with my mind? You won't even give *me* the combination."

She knew she was special. "Check your files," I said. "You still have a copy?"

"Hang on." There was a chunk through the receiver as she laid her phone down on her desk. A few seconds later she picked it up again. "My whole folder's gone."

"Mind coming back here?"

She hung up and a few seconds later came through the door, this time shutting it without being asked.

"What's going on?"

"I don't know. Who opened up this morning?"

"Steph, I think. She and Al were both here this morning before I got in."

I gestured to the phone. She dialed Steph and verified.

"She said everything looked normal. Al met her at the door, she unlocked it, turned off the alarm, made a pot of coffee."

"She turned off the alarm?"

"That's what she said."

I was developing a bad feeling deep in my stomach.

"Call her back," I said. "Please."

Trudy picked up the phone again and punched in Steph's extension. "Me, again," she said. "Scott has a question?" The last toward me.

"Ask her about Gabe Keller."

Trudy did, then covered the mouthpiece with her hand. "She says he's still not in. She needs him to complete last week's invoices."

God damn it, I thought to myself. "Tell her he's out for a while, then hang up. We've got to find him."

She spoke a few more lines into the phone and hung up again.

"What are you thinking?"

"Nothing good. Stay in here, will you, and call his numbers? See if you get a hit."

"How about you?"

"I'm going out."

"But where—"

I was already halfway to my door when she stopped her question. I think she knew I wasn't going to answer.

CHAPTER THIRTEEN

On my way out I'd grabbed Al Sutter away from his magazines and asked him to stop outside.

"What can you tell me about the Hochstedt case that Gabe Keller's been working on?"

Al scratched the greying stubble along the left side of his chin. "Well, this guy Hochstedt thinks his wife is fooling around on him. He works as a night manager at the orange juice plant and has odd hours during his night rotation. Same old story, he wants us to get proof of his wife doing the nasty with her boyfriend."

"What's he after, a divorce?"

"He's got some money from an inheritance, doesn't want to see her get it. And he wants the house, the cars, all that. You know, he's angry and hurt and wants to hurt her back."

"Violent?"

"I don't think so. More reptile-like. I think he's playing it cool until we get him the proof. He'll strike then."

I thought about this. "So why is Gabe having so much trouble? Sounds routine as hell."

Here Al looked up and down the street, as though someone else could be listening. "I think there's more than one guy. The wife is a bit of a wild child so it's been hard to set up on her and get the kind of photos or recordings Hochstedt wants."

"Jesus," I said. "What the hell was this girl before she got married?"

"You don't want to know."

"Dancer. Got it. Hochstedt wants his tits back."

"He did pay for them." Al looked a bit uncomfortable. "Is this why— Do you think Gabe got involved with her? I mean, I've seen her, not up close or anything, but—"

"You looking for a lap dance?"

"You know what I mean."

I nodded. "What I don't know is where Gabe is." I thought of my missing letters and the tampering with my safe. "You have any ideas?"

"Nope. Gabe was using the guys to follow the girl and stake out a couple of her favorite places. The problem is those keep changing. That's why we've needed so many guys."

"Yeah, okay," I said. "Do me a favor. Go inside, give the magazines a rest. Use the phone by the door. Call everyone who's worked on this thing. If anyone has an idea where Gabe might be, you call me on my cell and let me know."

"You got it. Where you going?"

I gave him a look. He should know better than to ask.

The Malibu was parked in the lot at my condo and I took off at a fast walk. Behind me I heard a car start but it barely registered. As I turned the corner to head south it struck me that no car had driven by. People with secrets and private investigators operate on instinct. I turned around and looked down the street back toward where I had come from.

Al Sutter was no longer outside the office; he should be inside working the phone by now. I looked at each of the cars parked along the street. My eyesight wasn't good enough to see inside the cars more than a block away but at this time of the morning, the taller buildings were still keeping the rising sun off the windshields, making it a bit easier to see. Most of the cars were empty.

But not all. I saw him in a black BMW, a crouching figure hiding behind the steering wheel. Was this the car I'd heard start up? Judging by the location, it could have been, but it was too warm to see any exhaust and I was too far away to hear if the car was running or not. Same problem with identifying the driver. I couldn't even be sure if it was a man or a woman, but whoever it was seemed to have short hair and gave the impression of being male. I couldn't tell if he was looking at me or not.

I slipped my hand into my right pocket and worked my fingers through the holes on the knuckleduster. I had to be careful when I took the brass knucks out; if my hand was in a fist it wouldn't clear the pocket smoothly. All I needed was enough of a grip so that I could pull the milled metal out and curve my fingers into my palm.

I crossed the street to be on the same side as the BMW and started walking the three quarters of a block toward it. If this was who I thought it was, he might be ready for conversation, or he might be coming for something else.

When I was four car lengths away, he moved quickly inside the car. His arms disappeared below the dash and suddenly the car pulled away from the curb without first starting the engine. This was the car I had heard before.

I stopped and turned as it accelerated past me down the street, not making any turns but heading east toward downtown. There was definitely a man inside, and he never turned his head as he cruised past. I knew I'd seen him before. Those were the same narrow, pointed features that had been in my parking lot two nights ago. The same face, I was sure, that Paul McKay had seen out at Edwin Holmes's house on Longboat Key.

I stood there watching as Rico Gallo disappeared in a car after a right hand turn down Main Street. At least now I was sure he was still in town.

My cell phone rang as I was opening the door of the Malibu. I pulled it from my pocket and looked at the screen: I didn't recognize the number. I thumbed the Talk button and said, "Porter."

"We speak at last."

I knew who it was. Didn't matter that I'd never heard the voice before. It could only have come out of that one face. "Hello, Rico," I said.

"How—" He went quiet and I let him. He can try to work it out for a while. "What exactly did Holmes tell you?"

"About you? Nothing." Keep him wondering. "Nice car, by the way. Had it long?"

"Stop," he said. "Don't talk about things that are not important."

"What do you mean, not important? Personally I prefer the E92 with the turbo package but that damned fuel pump—"

"I asked you to stop. Please. We have to talk."

Actually, I couldn't care less about cars. Necessary pains in the ass as far as I was concerned. I put car lovers on about the same level as people who loved kitchen mixers or stainless steel appliances. "Go ahead," I said. "I do have a few questions for you."

"You do?" He sounded amused. "Like what?"

"Well, I wouldn't mind finding out what you did with Endo Robbins. We never had a chance to actually meet."

"And you won't now."

"Okay," I said slowly. "That answers that one. How about this: what did you want with Edwin Holmes?"

He took his time in answering. "Like you, I had some questions."

"Also like me, I guess you won't be getting your answers."

"I'm not sure. I can find him whenever I want."

Did he not know?

"I hope you do," I told him. "Because Holmes is dead."

Anger sparked his voice as he said, "You son of a bitch. Don't you lie to me."

"I thought you might be more connected than this. And I'm not lying."

Gallo grew silent. I could hear his steady breathing through the phone, along with occasional traffic noises. He was probably still in his car somewhere close. I stood up and turned a slow three-sixty, looking for that black BMW.

"I suppose it doesn't matter," he finally said. "There's another matter you might find more pressing."

"And what would that be?"

"I made a deal with one of your employees. He didn't come through for me. Now there is a different deal to make with you."

"Oh? How's Gabe doing? You keeping him comfortable?"

"You are an annoying and reckless man, Mr. Porter. Keller is alive and reasonably comfortable. The question is what happens to him next."

"What are you thinking?"

"I suspect you know. He was to procure for me a certain letter as well as the information you have collected regarding the Edwin Holmes case. He was only partially successful."

"Yeah," I said, shaking my head. "That sounds exactly like Gabe. And you had him working outside his comfort zone."

"Regardless, I need to know how you'd like him back."

Interesting question. After this betrayal, no, I didn't want him back, either in my company or in my life. Gallo was talking about more than that, though, and if Gabe Keller was going to get out of his current situation still breathing Gallo was going to be sure it would cost me.

I wasn't ready to deal, not yet. And nothing was going to happen to Gabe until Gallo set a timetable for whatever it was he wanted. If I didn't give him that....

"Listen, Rico," I said, placing my thumb on the End button. "I have another call coming in. We'll have to pick this up later." I ended the call without giving him a chance to respond. Then I turned off my phone, left the car, and went upstairs to my condo. I'd make my next call from there.

When Steph picked up the phone I told her to put me through to Trudy right away. When she was on the line, I cut off her greeting and asked, "Did anybody know you were taking Holmes's letter to the university?"

"Well, no, I don't think so. Let me think for a second." I almost held my breath as she considered. "I may have told Steph I was running up to USF but I'm sure I never told her what for. What's going on?"

"This sounds strange, but ask her real quick, will you? I need to be sure."

"Okay," she said. "Hang on."

I could hear her call to Steph across the gap between their desks. Trudy asked her if she remembered when Trudy had left the office to go up to USF in Tampa. Steph said yes but when Trudy asked her if she knew what the trip had been about, Steph sounded confused and said no, was she supposed to?

Trudy but the phone back up to her mouth and said, "You heard that?"

"I did. Just needed to confirm. Can anyone put you at USF with the letter?"

"Only the people at the U. What's going on?"

"Okay, I need you to get up there right now and babysit that thing. I don't care what you need to do. If you can't light a fire under them to get the work done, you need to not allow that letter out of your sight."

"Scott, I can do that, but you really need to let me know what's going on."

"Gabe Keller tried to get the letter from my office last night. Only he didn't know it was already gone."

"But why—"

"Rico Gallo has him."

"Oh," Trudy said. "What does that mean?"

"I think he wants to trade Keller for the letter, but—"

"We have to give it to him. This is Gabe, Scott. He works for us."

I liked the sound of the "us" but I didn't want this to turn into a problem. "Trudy, listen. We need to know about that letter no matter what." I cut off her response. "No, I don't mean at the expense of Gabe's life. Here's the thing. If Gallo can't contact me he can't threaten me. Get it? He can't make a demand unless he finds me."

"So what, you're going to hide?"

"Something like that. My phone's off, and I won't be coming into the office until you get the results of that analysis. Once we know what it can tell us, Gallo can probably have the damn thing and hie his skinny ass on out of town."

"Scott, do you realize how dangerous this could be for Gabe? If Gallo's a killer—"

"He is."

"You can't let anything happen to Gabe, Scott. You can't."

I rubbed my eyes with my fingers and tried to keep the feeling out of my voice. "Trudy, listen. No one wants anything to happen to Gabe less than I do." Lie. "But just because Gallo says he'll let him go doesn't mean he will. Whatever happens you can't forget that."

"You have to try, Scott."

"I will, Trudy. I promise." I wanted to add that Gabe had gotten into bed with Gallo on his own and now he was neck deep in paying off his failure. But I didn't.

She didn't sound convinced. "Okay," she said. "I'll head out."

"Don't be followed," I told her. "Get Al to walk you out to your car. Gallo was driving a black BMW a while ago. Take one of Gabe's guys with you if you want, but this has to look low key. There's no way Gabe knows the combination of my safe." I changed it every month; even if he had scoped it out somehow in the past, I felt reasonably sure he couldn't know what it was now. "As long as Gallo thinks the letter is still locked up in there, he should have no reason to look anywhere else. His main focus should be on finding me."

"Okay, Scott." I could tell she was nervous. "Why don't I leave in about half an hour. It will look like I'm going to lunch. I'll make sure I'm not followed. How will I reach you?"

"You won't," I said. "I'll keep in touch, though."

"Promise me something."

"What's that?"

"No one gets hurt over this thing. Our client is already dead. We don't have to risk anyone else, do we?"

"No, we don't." I hoped I sounded reassuring because to my mind, there was at least one more person who was definitely going to get hurt.

We each hung up and I wondered if I should have been taking this whole case more seriously from the start. I thought I was doing a by the numbers investigation but most cases didn't come with three corpses and a turncoat employee.

It was a fair bet that Gallo knew where I lived. He could have followed me to my condo building any of the past few nights. He also might know my car, especially the Malibu. I needed to get out of there quickly, before he decided he wasn't going to make contact any other way but physically.

I took the stairs twelve floors down to the ground level. I went out through one of the steel emergency door exits. They were exit only and couldn't be used to get back inside. I released the crash bar and guided the door slowly to a quiet close. I looked around—no movement, no black BMW. I walked straight out away from the building to a hedge that separated the property and then turned and walked alongside it to the parking bays and over to the Malibu. I ducked in quickly, started her up and pulled out.

At the parking lot entrance, I looked both right and left along the one way street. It seemed clear. I took a left and drove the wrong direction on the one way. I only had to make it to the corner, which I did just as a large silver SUV turned the corner and had to slam on its brakes. The driver also laid on the horn, which I could have done without, but he was right. I waved in what I thought was an apologetic manner and took off south toward 41. I'd double back and make my way up 301 to Tampa. It was the long way but it would be easier to spot a tail and right now, staying off the grid was my best weapon. I was on my way to find a better one.

CHAPTER FOURTEEN

I pulled into the parking lot at Goldy's Bar in Tampa about forty-five minutes later. As I rounded the corner with the Malibu I saw Eamon Stanley walking toward an old Ford pickup with a sloppy brunette hanging on his left arm. Early in the day for that, I thought. I stopped in front of the pickup, blocking it in, and stepped out of my car.

Stanley turned around and raised an eyebrow, as if giving me one last chance to get out of there without speaking to him. It may have been a wish or a warning but I didn't care either way. He leaned the woman against the hood of his car as if she wouldn't be able to stand any other way and came around the Malibu. He stopped in front of me, about six inches too close.

"I told you I'd get in touch," he said. "Why are you here?"

I looked around. There were a half dozen cars in the lot but no other people. "Who's she?"

"The afternoon's entertainment. Why, want some?"

"We need to talk now."

"What's going on?"

"Things have accelerated a bit. Did you find out anything about Rico Gallo?"

Stanley looked over his shoulder at the woman—she was still there, though now she was leaning face forward with both arms on top of the hood. I couldn't tell if she was going to be sick but I thought she might back up in a hurry with that hot metal against her arms.

"A few things, man. He's a bad news bear. Where he goes people don't tend to follow, you know what I mean? He's a heavy."

"Who does he work for?"

"John Maroni."

I knew the name.

"Head of the Gambino family in New York. He's a hitter."

"What's Gallo doing down here?" Specifically, I was wondering what he wanted with Edwin Morton Holmes.

Stanley gave me a tired expression. His heavy beard gave weight to the look that might have been comical without it. "How the hell would I know that?"

"I was hoping you were good enough." That got me a squint cast from one side of his face. "Never mind. Is he in on the VIP side of things?"

Stanley hawked and spat to the side. I felt the spray but didn't react. "More like an associate, I think. They couldn't make him, he doesn't have the right last name."

"Gallo isn't Italian?"

"It's not really Gallo. It's something like Bronstein or Bronfeld or something."

"Okay," I said. This was getting complicated. "Take this." I pulled a burner from my pocket and handed it to him. "It's disposable," I told him. "Can't trace it. I need you in position tonight."

He took the phone from me. His fingernails were dirty. "I'm gong to need more than a phone."

There was a note of defiance in his voice. He knew I was trusting him but he also knew I didn't know how far I could go. Without taking my eyes from that smug expression that told me he thought he had a firm grip on my balls, I pulled a roll of bills out of my pants pocket. I straightened them out and peeled five of them from the bottom and handed them over. Again came the grubby hand and he accepted the money without breaking his one-sided stare.

Once he had the money tucked away he looked at the woman again, who appeared as though she might have fallen asleep half standing up, half leaning over. "How long I got?"

I kept my disgust in check. "Long enough, I imagine. When you're done, call me here." I handed over a piece of paper with the number of a second burner. "I'll tell you where to be."

Stanley took the paper and slid it into the pocket of his stained work pants along with the money. "Call you in a few hours."

"No more than two," I said. "Things are moving."

"Fuck," he said. "All right, fine. Get out of here. People are going to see us together. I'll call you."

I caught his eyes again and held them. "You do that, Eamon."

"I told you I would."

He spat a second time and went around my car to the woman who jerked to life with a start as if she could suddenly tell he was ready for her. "Easy," he told the girl. "Come on, let's get you into the truck."

I was already climbing into the Malibu. He was right, I didn't want to be seen with him, but for a different reason. Now that I'd given him the burner there was no need for the exposure. I pulled the door shut, started the car, and pulled out onto Nebraska Avenue, heading north. I drove a mile up and found a Winn-Dixie and pulled into the parking lot. A lot of older people were shuffling across the tarmac, pushing their grocery carts out of the lot ahead of them. Someone from the store would make the rounds at the nearby bus stops and retrieve all the abandoned carts by the end of the day.

I pulled out the second burner and dialed the office. Steph answered and as soon as she heard my voice she said, "Trudy needs you, Scott," and put me on hold. The twenty second wait told me Trudy had probably gotten up and made her way into my office. For some reason she wanted privacy.

"Scott!" she said when she picked up. "I've been trying to get hold of you."

I was still enjoying the change from addressing me by my last name. "My phone's off," I said. "What's up?"

"You can't—" I knew she was about to berate me for being out of touch. "Listen," she said. "Gabe called here."

"What?"

"Something's going on, Scott. He sounded scared. He said he needed to talk to you. Right now."

I'm sure he did. "Why are you back in the office?" I asked.

This exasperated her. "I got the letter back from the university. They're all finished. That's not important now."

But it is, I thought. "What does Gabe expect me to do?"

"He gave me a number for you to call." She read it off and I copied it into my notebook. "What's going on, Scott?"

I didn't want to scare her but I needed her to protect that letter. "I told you, he's with Rico Gallo."

"What does that really mean?"

"I'm not sure yet," I said. "Gallo and I had a chat this morning."

"And then what?"

"I hung up on him."

"Hung up—? What the hell is the matter with you, Scott? Gabe's one of us. If you're not out there for all of us, what are we supposed to do? You have to support—"

"Trudy."

She didn't stop. "What if that were Steph?" A pause. "Oh. That's why you have Al—-"

"Trudy."

"What if Gallo had me, Scott? What would you do then? Or are we all the same to you?"

"Jesus, Trudy, will you shut up for one second and listen to me? Gabe went into my office last night. He took the transcripts of the letter I had, he took your folders, and he tried to get into my safe. He didn't know you'd already taken the original to the university."

"You're saying that he's working with Gallo? Scott, that's crazy."

"Is it?"

"But he sounded so scared. He couldn't be faking that. He's one of us."

But I could hear the doubt creeping into her voice.

"I don't know, Trudy. Maybe he's not. He could have been doing double duty for Gallo and Gallo could have changed the terms on him.

Maybe he's being held, maybe he's not. I don't really know yet."

Empty space filled the line. "Does it really matter, Scott? You have to get him back. What you do with him afterwards is up to you but you can't leave him with a man like Gallo."

"I'm working on it, Trudy."

"'Working on it'? Jesus, Scott, would you be working on it the same way if it were me in Gabe's place?"

"You already asked me that." She was making me sad. "It's not the same thing," I said quietly. "It's not the same thing at all."

"Who are you right now?"

That one hurt. "I'll take care of it," I said.

More silence. Then, "Goodbye, Porter." And she hung up.

I wanted to tell her to safeguard that letter but since she had the analysis from USF already it probably wasn't so important anymore. Gallo already had a copy of the text of the letter and whatever the university had to say about it might not mean anything more to him. Probably didn't.

Tossing the burner onto the seat next to me, I started the car and began rolling slowly away from the Winn-Dixie. I had some plans to make.

The next call I made was to Marty Ables. When he answered he wanted to call me back but I wouldn't let him.

"Just tell me," I said. "What did you find about Holmes's death in D.C.?"

Ables lowered his voice and said, "I'll have to be quick. It was homicide. Your boy was strangled, placed in the bathtub, then had his throat cut."

Lovely, I thought. "Any clues? Anything taken from the hotel room?"

"That I don't know. Guy up there promised to send me a copy of the report but he wants something from me first. You come up with anything?"

"Just a name," I said. "Gallo. Rico Gallo. May be a button man from up that way, possibly out of New York by way of Boston. A few priors, nothing sticky. That enough?"

"You know where he is?"

"No idea." I hoped that was a lie.

"Okay," Ables said. "That ought to be enough to keep me in the loop with the D.C. cops. When are you going to tell me what's going on?"

This was the disadvantage of working with Marty Ables. He was happy to accept a little bonus here and there but he still took himself more seriously as a cop than I'd like.

"I don't know much," I said. "When I figure out more, I'll let you know."

There was a rise in background noise on Marty's end and he said, "I'll bet you will. I've got to go. Police business, you know." He hung up before I could thank him, but he knew I'd make it right with a bank draft.

I made a right turn and drove east toward 275. It was the shortest way to the freeway and could even be the quickest, depending on the traffic. I had to get back to Sarasota and do some recon. I'd told Eamon Stanley I'd give him two hours before I called him. That should be enough time to get things set. Rico Gallo and I were in a stalemate, or at least I hoped so, and even though Gabe Keller had got himself stuck in the middle of it at least I could console myself that it had come of his own doing.

Greedy bastard. It was like I said before, money-motivated people could make for good employees, but when it came at the expense of loyalty—which it almost always did—it rarely ended well. It was too early to tell how it would work out for Gabe. I wondered if Gallo had actually paid him.

The gate was open across Holmes's driveway. The only barrier I could see as I drove by was a line of police tape. It made sense that after doing whatever it was they did to get the gate open they'd keep it that way so they wouldn't have to do it again. Most importantly I could see no police car and no one posted to guard the estate.

I turned the car around when I could and looped back, checking the house out again. Not only did the police seem finished with the place for now, if Holmes had any active relatives they seemingly had yet to put in an appearance. Or else the police hadn't given them the okay yet. I thought I should have Trudy check up on that, when I decided it was safe to talk to her again.

Trudy. For one unforgettable moment, brief as that was, had we shared a mistake that showed us how our lives could have been? Or was it a mistake that showed us both we were already what we were supposed to be?

I wanted to call her but it wasn't the time. Instead I found another strip mall and pulled into a parking space. I took out the burner phone and dialed the one I had given Eamon Stanley. He picked up after the third ring and sounded like he'd drunk half a bottle of whiskey and chewed on the glass.

"It's barely two hours," he growled.

"It's close enough." I told him the address where I needed him to be and he cursed me as he told me to wait until he could find something to write with. I closed my eyes and tried to conjure a sense of patience.

"Give it to me again."

I did, two more times, then had him read it back to me to be sure. "Six o'clock," I told him.

"Shit," he said. "That's too soon. I can't there in time. If you want this done right—"

"How much time do you need?"

"At least another half hour. Seven would be good."

"Okay, six thirty." I looked at the time. "Call me when you're set and I'll make the call to this guy's phone. That should give you the distraction."

"Don't need it."

"You'll get it anyway." I thought of Trudy. "And there's another thing."

"Is this one of those deals that just keeps getting better and better? Do I get a set of steak knives, too?"

"There's another guy."

"Are you saying it's two against one, or are you going to get dirty on this?"

"The other guy is one of mine. He works for me. I think."

"The hell does that mean?" As Stanley grew more ornery his voice took on a more sober edge. That was good, I thought.

"I don't know. He could be a prisoner or a hostage. Or he may have gone over to Gallo's side."

There was a loud and sudden gargling sound followed by a sharp expulsion of breath which I took to be one of Stanley's epic mucous discharges. He came back with, "You want 'em both?"

"I can't say yet. I don't know enough about the situation. You'll have to make the call."

"You want *my* conscience to be my guide?"

"You don't have a conscience."

"That's my point. You going to be pissed at me if things don't go a certain way?"

This time I didn't allow myself to consider Trudy. "Do what you need to. I'm saying it would be nice if my guy walked away."

Stanley barked a short, harsh laugh. "You know as well as I do it doesn't always work that way."

"It would be nice, I said."

"Yeah, well I'm not nice, either. I'll call you." And he hung up.

The thing about dealing with people like Eamon Stanley was that you were always walking the knife-edge line between their heavy-handed posturing and whatever true violent tendencies you actually needed. Most people probably wouldn't agree, but there's a place for the Eamon Stanleys of the world, the same way great whites fill a vital notch atop their food chain. I didn't know how to compare having too many Rico Gallos to an over-population of grey seals on Cape Cod so I just slid the burner into my pocket as I got out of the Malibu. There was an Italian restaurant next to a fast food sandwich shop and I went in to have a quick meal before it would be time to move again.

CHAPTER FIFTEEN

A short time later I'd paid for my meal and left the restaurant. The sun was visible through a haze about forty degrees off the western horizon. I pulled my regular cell phone out of my pocket and thumbed it on as I walked back to my car. Halfway there it rang.

I checked the number: it wasn't the office. I pressed the Talk button and said, "Porter."

"You're playing a dangerous game, my friend."

"It takes two, Gallo."

"Why did you shut off your phone?"

I pulled open the door of the Malibu and slid in behind the steering wheel, feeling the waves of heat escape past my sweating forehead. "If I kept talking to you, you would have made demands, I would have told you to go to hell. You'd have made threats, I'd have gotten pissed off. The usual stuff."

A dry chuckle came through the line. "You think things are different now?"

"Well," I said, exhaling loudly. "For one thing, I just had a fine pasta primavera with some very nice fresh-cooked bread, still steaming from the oven. I react better on a full stomach."

"Like I said, you're playing a dangerous game, Porter."

"No," I said. "You are. I'm out enjoying a nice dinner."

"And your man Keller? You think he's enjoying himself?"

"This the time you start telling me what you want?"

"I think I'd like to meet you alone some time, Porter."

"No, see, you skipped the demand and went right to the threat. How does that make me want to talk to you?" Before Gallo could respond, I said, "You're just making me want dessert, maybe some gelato. Call you back in half an hour." And I killed the connection before he had a chance to respond.

I was pissing him off, or so I hoped. The more the better. I still needed to give Stanley more time. If I had been more insistent in Goldy's parking lot he'd have had to choose between doing a job for me and a half passed-out woman. I'd have lost.

As for Gallo, I had the feeling he was used to getting things his way. Vicious people often do, especially those with reputations. Right now I wanted him as distracted as I could get him and having him focused on what he'd like to do to me was as good a way as anything else I could think of. If I was reading him right, he wouldn't forgive the disrespect easily. I just hoped he wasn't too quick to take it out on Gabe Keller.

I was restless and stuffed both my phones into my back pockets and, leaving my car in the parking lot, walked toward the beach, finally taking my life into my hands as I crossed a street filled with traffic that simply assumed the odds were more in favor of someone *else* running me over. I made my way down to the wet, firmer sand carefully, trying to minimize the amount of sand dropping into the sides of my shoes.

What was Gallo after? Holmes was gone, and while Gallo may not have the original letter, he had my copies of what it said. He must know more about what was really going on than I did but I couldn't figure why he was still around.

If he'd take off, like I'd expect a man like him to do at this point, we—my people and I—could move on and hopefully forget all about Rico Gallo and Edwin Holmes. But he didn't seem to want to go anywhere. I still had no idea who he was working for or who had sent him. Could Paul McKay be stirring up enough of a mess up north that Gallo was somehow pushed into coming after me?

Regardless, the man was still a potential danger for everyone working for me. He'd already corrupted Gabe but I'm not sure that would have taken an extraordinary amount of effort. Maybe a nice cup of coffee and some pretty words, I didn't know. I probably shouldn't have kept so much distance from the man but I wasn't going to take the blame for his treachery. My biggest worry was that whoever was pulling Gallo's strings might be willing to engage in a scorched earth policy and eliminate anyone with knowledge of anything to do with Edwin Morton Holmes and whatever secrets he'd been hiding.

All this simply meant I had to stop Gallo. That didn't mean there was a good or easy way to do this. There rarely was. We were operating in that grey no-man's land somewhere between law and order and criminal chaos. Gallo had likely killed Endo Robbins and had certainly done away with Ernesto Flores, Holmes's caretaker, but at the moment he was invisible to the law. Untouchable, out there free to do what he wished.

If I tried to go to the police, my license would disappear, my business would be ruined, and that would only be the beginning of what I'd be facing. The second I hadn't called the cops after McKay had come back from Holmes's estate I'd backed myself into a very tight corner.

To protect Holmes's interests, I'd kept away from the law, settling for foiling whatever it was Gallo had been up to at the estate. Unfortunately it had been too late for Ernesto Flores but nothing I could have done would have prevented that. And what did I really know about the fate of Endo Robbins? In truth, nothing. But if I'd gone to the cops they'd never have believed me.

Their first question would have been why Edwin Holmes had not paid them a visit. Their second would have been why I hadn't.

All this was the past. Gallo was escalating his activities, and prior events and decisions were not so far distant as they should have been at this point. There was no longer an Edwin Holmes to protect but clearly there was still something more going on. How much was I obligated to keep digging into it?

Why not just stop?

In my gut I felt that, at least to a point, I had to do something. I had the money Holmes had paid me, but with Ables' greens fees and McKay's traveling expenses, that wasn't gong to last as far into the future as I'd once hoped.

All these things brought me back to Gabe Keller. If Gallo felt he could just take him because he wanted to, I had to make an effort to get him back, despite his betrayal.

I shook my head and kicked at the sand. Why hadn't Gallo left town? What did he think I had for him?

I needed to be careful as I walked so that the crashing waves didn't run up and soak my shoes. At the same time, I didn't want to take them off because I'd never to be able to get all the sand off my feet when I had to put them back on. As it became more difficult to stay out of the irregular motion I made my way across the drier, powdery sand. There was a footbridge that led over a clump of protected sea oats and back off the beach. I stomped my feet once I was on the weathered boards and succeeded mostly in shooting pain through my knees. I found myself wishing I had a spare pair of socks and shoes in the car.

I trudged back along the Gulf of Mexico Drive, through scraggly patches of sand spurs and St. Augustine grass. There were only periodic stretches of sidewalk and I was surprised when I saw how far I'd actually gone down the beach. It was getting to be time for Stanley to be calling. I began to walk faster.

I started to feel energized with the kind of bottled up fight-or-flight hormones that were building behind an invisible dam in the back of my skull somewhere. This is how I felt when I wasn't sure what was supposed to happen next, be it good or bad. The first time I'd felt this way, really felt this way, I'd ended up killing a man.

I'd been offered a job as a beat rookie in a small police department in another city. A small town, really. I'd thought that would make for a good life, a nice, ordinary career in law enforcement. The kind most cops enjoyed, the career where they'd put in their twenty-five or thirty and never have cause to draw their weapon outside the qualifying range. But when a woman in my building had been having trouble with her husband and when it turned physical she thought she had nowhere to go. She found me, the consoling neighbor, and I did the sensible thing and told her to go to the cops. Because we'd take care of her.

The thought scared her out of her mind but she went anyway. Ultimately her husband appeared and thought the restraining order she'd brought home was a weak joke, just a piece of paper he could rip out of her hands and shove between her teeth and back into her throat.

I was listening at the door when I heard the sounds of her strangling. It was unlocked so I didn't need to kick it open. I just walked in and when the husband turned to me, his face mottled with rage yelling, "Who the fuck are you?", I kept moving and jabbed him in the throat with the knuckles of my right hand. Somewhere in my mind I hoped the wife would be on the phone calling the police.

As her husband stumbled backwards, hands pawing at his neck as he sucked in whatever air he could, I shoved him back into the wall, then spun him around on the rebound. I knocked his hands aside and slid my forearm against his throat and grabbed my own biceps which were locked alongside his head, my other hand palming the oily top of his skull.

He was clawing weakly at my forearm as I could see the wife sitting on the floor, face in her hands. I shouted at her to call the police. She was still gagging a little as she pulled the last of the paper order from her mouth. "Pick up the phone!" I yelled.

Instead she slumped against the opposite wall, in shock, eyes wide with horror. "Call 911!" I tried again, but she'd frozen. Her husband continued to struggle as I tried to talk to the wife, this time in soothing tones. Her eyes were glassy and I wasn't sure she was even seeing me, let alone hearing me. By the time I realized she wasn't gong to help, I noticed her husband had grown still. The smell of his urine filled the room and I released my grip too late and let him slide slowly down to the floor.

His wife jumped up, suddenly come to life, and began savagely kicking her non-responsive husband's body. I heard ribs crack before I finally thought to step forward and hold her back, in shock over what I'd just allowed to happen. The light returned to her eyes as she threw her arms around me and told me, "Thank you," as though whatever had just happened had been done with purpose and intent.

I stood, looking down at her dead husband, imagining how much damage I'd just done to the rest of my life. His wife, now widow, dashed about the apartment stuffing clothes and other belongings into a canvas duffel. She reached behind a cabinet in the small living room and pulled away a large manila envelope that had been taped there and held it out in front of me.

"You see?" she said, the tears and her smile coexisting on her face in some insane combination. "He was a bad man." As if wads of cash were indisputable evidence of an irredeemable life. "How much do you want? You should have some."

I shook my head no and she stood on her toes and kissed my cheek. "Thank you, thank you, thank you," she said as she turned and rushed out of the apartment. I can remember thinking it was at that moment I knew exactly how much I'd just screwed up the rest of my life.

Yes, I'd helped my neighbor, maybe even saved her life, but mine was pretty much over.

I wasn't prepared to accept this, at least not then. If I was going down for this lowlife, I'd make someone have to work for it. I pulled the front door open, wiped the knob with a corner of my shirt. I pulled it shut from the outside and wiped the other knob, too. Then I went to my own place, washed my face, changed my clothes, and went outside. I dropped the clothes I had been wearing into a dumpster around the corner and walked and walked and walked until I calmed down enough to go into an open bar. I spent the rest of the night watching college football, and then a west coast hockey game, until I finally made the trek back to my building.

By rights my life and career should have been over. I'd killed a man. Worse, I'd killed a man and walked away. When I got to the block where I lived the police had cordoned off the street. "You can't come in here right now," I was told.

"Why not?" I'd asked.

They had found the body and were searching the neighboring buildings for the wife. Apparently finding the saliva encrusted restraining order was pointing the finger at her. I didn't think they would find her, not around there; she was savvy, she had money, and most importantly she'd had too much of a headstart.

The next day, after detectives had interviewed me along with the rest of the tenants, I turned down the job with the police and within a week I was on my way to Florida. Like so many lost souls from the Midwest, I ran to sunshine. In my case I ignored Horace Greeley's advice and went southeast and not west.

I'd told the cops I was out all night at a sports bar, watching Baylor play somebody else, followed by the Black Hawks playing somebody else, and then I'd tried to go home. And that was that.

No one ever heard from the wife again, at least not to my knowledge, and I'd never had the guts to go looking myself. The important thing, I thought, was that no one was looking for me.

The burner rang when I was just getting back to my car. Stanley was in position.

"What do you see?" I asked.

"Oh, he's in there," he said. "Fat guy's there, too."

"Does he look okay?"

"How the hell should I know? I've never seen him before. Looks like a fat piece of shit but I'm not a good judge of character."

"Got it," I said. "I'll make the call." By not talking to Gallo and letting him tell me what he wanted—in other words, not allowing him to make his demands—I was, I hoped, buying myself time to assume whatever advantage I could. The danger would come when Gallo believed I was actually taking too long and decided to cut his losses. In this case, that could only mean bad things for Gabe Keller. I thought I should try to avoid that if I could.

I hung up on Stanley and pulled my regular phone out of my other pocket. I pulled up the call log and pressed the entry for Gallo's number.

CHAPTER SIXTEEN

"How was dessert?" he asked, cautious now, some wariness in his voice.

"Lovely. What's Maroni want down here?"

Gallo laughed, a low, throaty chuckle that sounded like it came from a cartoon wolf. "So you've been busy. Why, you want to hire me?"

"Would it do any good? How much would it cost to tell me what you're doing here?"

"I don't do that. Don't ask it again. You're screwing with the wrong people." I heard someone talking in the background. "Your man here makes a lot of noise. Wants to know how much you care about him."

I had moved the Malibu to the public beach parking lot just north from Holmes's place but it would probably take me five minutes to get from there to the house and then out of the car and to the door. Stanley should be getting close to where he was supposed to be.

"Not a hell of a lot. To be really honest, I wasn't that fond of him before he stole from me and tried to get into my safe. I imagine he's worth more to you at this point."

"You think so?"

"Well, not really. You've got all you can out of him and now you're hoping I'm sentimental enough to give you something for him. I just don't want another corpse laying around."

"You called back, didn't you?"

"How else was I supposed to talk to you? You've been following me, but that hasn't gotten you anywhere. I imagine you're on a schedule and you've been falling behind. Recruiting Keller was a good shot in the dark but that's all it was. Now you've got him, you're stuck with him. You're only hoping he's worth something to me. Frankly, that's the wrong horse."

We had a few seconds of silence while Gallo thought about it. "I could do things to him that would make life a bit difficult for you for a while."

This I didn't doubt. "What did you do to Endo Robbins?"

"I could tell you but with your man sitting here the story would possibly upset him."

"But he is dead."

Gallo gave that dry, wolf chuckle again. "The two of you won't ever be shaking hands, if that's what you're asking."

I checked my watch. It was almost time to get moving.

"Where do you see this going?" I asked. "You have a copy of the letter, you must know about Holmes by now, what else—"

"What about Holmes? Where is that prig?"

This was unexpected. Did he really not know? "Someone gave him a new smile, just below his second chin, in a hotel bath tub."

"That— that wasn't me."

"Didn't think it was. You couldn't travel that fast."

"But that means—"

Gallo stopped talking. Through the phone I heard a crash, maybe glass, maybe something else. Shit. I turned the key in the ignition and dropped the car into gear. The dash clock showed me what I was afraid of: Stanley had made his move early.

That son of a bitch. I dropped my phone on the passenger seat so I could use two hands on the wheel as I pulled out of the lot. I had to wait for a few cars to pass; I would have forced my way into the flow but these were Florida drivers—they'd as soon take the fender bender as give up right of way. Take these people out of their cars and they were decent, courteous people. Put them behind the wheel and they were Patton in a tank.

I finally peeled out onto the street and made the two hundred yards south to Holmes's driveway. This time I ripped in front of a pickup truck, his horn blaring behind me as I plowed through the police tape strung across the drive. There were no lights on in the house. I skidded to a stop at the end of the driveway and sprinted to the rear of the building. I could see the edge of the pool and the smaller building that had housed Endo Robbins. Here there was light, a cone of brightness falling through the open front door. I had slipped on a pair of nitrile gloves earlier and I was carrying a small Sig P220 in my hand as I ran along the edge of the pool to the guest house.

I stopped at the edge of the door, the loudest sound being my heavy breathing and the pounding of my heart. I didn't know if my best move would be surprise or stealth but since I didn't have time to reason it out I simply shouted "Gallo!" and kept my body out of the light to the side of the door.

No response.

"Keller!" I tried. "You all right?"

I heard a muffled sound. Could have been a ruse. What the hell had happened to Eamon Stanley? Where was he?

I went in low, around the corner, and rolled behind the first cover I saw, a line of kitchen cabinets. No one shot at me, which was a good thing. I thought I could hear more muffled sounds from one of the back rooms. Staying low, I duck-walked my way in that direction.

Gallo was gone. Gabe Keller was tied to a chair and was flipped onto his side, cushions from the couch covering his head. In the middle of the room, lying on the floor, was Eamon Stanley. The sounds were coming from Keller beneath the piles of upholstery. I let him stay there.

Stanley opened his eyes as I got to him. "Where's Gallo?" I said.

"Fucker's gone," Stanley said, trying to push himself up. I looked around me before I put my gun on the floor between myself and Stanley. His right hand was crossed over his body, blood streaming through his fingers.

"What happened? Why didn't you stick to the plan?"

"Got tired of waiting." He coughed. It sounded wet and full of phlegm but I didn't see any blood spray. "Thought I could take him. While you tried talking him to death."

I was so mad I almost threw an elbow into his face. "You shot?"

He shook his head and flashed an expression that showed he'd made a mistake. "I was too close for his gun. He threw it at me. Never seen that before."

I tried to pull his hand away from his side to get a look at his wound. He wouldn't let me.

"You'll make it worse," he said. "Fucker knows how to wave a knife." He shook his head sadly. "And I thought I was good."

"You can't take a man with a knife when he knows what he's doing."

"You can if you've got a gun!" Stanley roared, then fell into a coughing fit. More blood poured from beneath his fingers. "But he went for that first. Fucker's fast, too fast. Couldn't get to him in time."

I looked around me again. Things were going to have to get cleaned up. Next to the sofa Gabe Keller was still flopping around making noises beneath the cushions. "How about him?" I asked Stanley.

"Whale boy?" he said. "Far as I know, he's good. That Gallo fella clouted him on the head before I came in. Must have tossed those pillows on him to shut him up."

Fine, I thought. He'd keep. "Where's your gun? We need to take it with us."

"Fuck it, I don't know." He turned his head a bit, saw mine. "That's not it. I don't know where it went. Maybe Gallo took it."

"How bad are you hurt?"

Stanley coughed into his hand, spit up the discharge, didn't seem alarmed at what he saw. "I'll live but I got to get stitched. Maybe more, I can't tell."

I picked up my gun and shoved it into my back waistband. As quickly as I could I looked around the little room for the two missing guns, Stanley's and the one he said Gallo had thrown. I couldn't find either.

Keller was kicking harder now, and it was distracting. "Can you hold on?" I asked Stanley.

"You giving me a choice?"

"Just one second." I pulled the cushions from Gabe Keller's head and set them back on the couch. He wasn't gagged, a fact I regretted instantly.

"Scott!" he called, his voice a hoarse croak as I finished putting the couch back together. "He made me do it, Scott! I wanted to warn you, but he—"

"Gabe," I said, moving to stand over him. "Shut the hell up. Say another word and I will kick your teeth so far down your throat you'll be chewing your food in your small intestine."

"But Scott—"

I pressed the toe of my shoe into the side of his jaw. "I mean it, Gabe." He shut up.

"Still good?" I asked Stanley.

He seemed pretty sure I wasn't going to leave him and that mellowed him a bit. Either that or it was the blood loss. "Yeah, but I think we should hurry."

The house was small and it was easy to check. I wanted to find something to protect the Malibu. If we were going to leave blood stains on the seats I was going to have to find a new car. I ran out the front door and behind the house and between the wall along the back edge of the property there was a blue tarp covering what looked like old sheet metal sections from a shed roof. I ripped that off then ran it out to the Malibu and spread it across the back seat.

There was no sign of Gallo, or the black BMW. Since I hadn't seen a car on my way up the driveway he must have had his own escape route already planned.

I went back inside and pulled two large bath towels from a shelf in the bathroom. Stanley didn't want to let go as I forced his arm away from his side. Fresh blood oozed forth but I shoved a towel over the wound and let him clamp it again with his hand. Then I handed him the other towel and told him he should use it to wrap the other one in place if he could. All he managed was a grunt.

His color was getting worse and I didn't want him to pass out on me before I got him to the car. In that case I'd probably have to call an ambulance to save his life and I preferred not to have to do that.

I ducked under Stanley's good arm and forced him to his feet, half dragging, half lifting him along to the car. I pulled the burner phone out of his back pocket and jammed it into mine next to its mate. After I had Stanley laying on the tarp I went back for Gabe Keller. His hands had been zip tied to the back of the chair. I went into the kitchen and found a food prep knife which I used to saw through the nylon.

This was taking too long.

"Go out and get in my car," I told him.

"Scott—"

"Shut the fuck up."

Out he went. Quickly I straightened out the furniture in the room. I pulled a rug from in front of the front door and dropped it over the bloody mess from Stanley's chest. It didn't cover it all, and the blood would soak through it anyway, but after I moved the table on top of it and pushed the two chairs beneath both sides, I hoped it would pass quick muster should the cops come back. If it weren't the original investigators, they may take the new mess for part of the original crime, but if that worked at all it would only be temporary.

I shut off the lights, locked the door from the inside, and pulled it shut. Keller was in the passenger seat of the Malibu. He looked to me as though he might cry.

I climbed in behind the wheel and turned the car around. As I headed down the driveway I asked Stanley in the back seat, "What the hell were you thinking?"

"Fuck off," he said. I wanted to throw a gun at him myself for screwing everything up. We'd lost our best chance at getting to Gallo because Stanley couldn't keep from playing cowboy.

I let it go. No sense arguing with a dying man but even if it would make me feel better, it wasn't something I wanted to do in front of Gabe Keller. The less he knew at this point the better.

As if on cue, Keller tried to talk to me again. "Listen, Scott—"

"Jesus, Gabe. I'm not fucking kidding. I told you to shut up."

"That's not fair," he said. He sounded as though his feelings were hurt. "Gallo's a maniac. The things—"

"Gabe," I said slowly and evenly. "If you speak another word to me in this car as soon as I take care of my friend in the back seat I swear to God there will be another use for that blue tarp back there. And I promise you won't like it."

Keller slumped back in his seat. He wouldn't look at me, which I took to be a good start. "Can I at least say thank you?"

I reached behind me and pulled the little nine mil from behind me and set it in my lap.

At this point I was racing to make the turn to Tamiami Trail and the nearest emergency room, either Doctors Hospital on Bee Ridge Road or Sarasota Memorial, depending on the traffic. I'd figure it out as I went.

"Got your story?" I called back to Stanley.

"Fucking don't worry about my goddamn story," he said, but the bluster was fading along with his strength. We needed to hurry.

CHAPTER SEVENTEEN

We left Eamon Stanley in a wheel chair outside Sarasota Memorial. I kept
the car away from the turnaround in front of the main entrance and sent
Gabe Keller to grab one of the wheel chairs just inside the electric doors.
I didn't want my license plates to be caught on a security camera. They got
to him as Gabe was walking away. Someone called to him to stop but he
just kept walking. Back in my car, I backed away from the entrance and
turned down 41.

"Can I talk now?" Keller asked.

I didn't reply.

"So who was that guy?"

"What guy?" I said. "You've never seen him."

We drove for a few minutes in silence. It was good and I hated to break
it. "Where's your car?"

"It's back— back at my house."

He gave me an address and I headed there, telling him to shut up twice
more before we arrived. I really did want to hit him myself. Once we got
to his driveway, he didn't move. I only gave him five seconds, which was
four too many. I got out of my door, walked around to the passenger side,
pulled it open, then reached in and grabbed him by the arm. I set my feet
and wrenched him out of the car. It wasn't easy. He was a heavy man and
he wasn't helping. If I were strong enough to pull him out all the stress
would go through his shoulder. I was. This just meant he'd feel more pain.
He made "ow" sounds and grabbed his shoulder with his free hand.

When he popped free, still holding his arm, he started to speak again but
I stopped and looked at him. He knew what I was thinking. Slowly he shut
his mouth. Finally.

I walked around the Malibu and got back into the driver's seat and took
off. I hoped never to see Gabe Keller again. As I drove I tossed both burner
phones into my glove compartment. Not only had I failed to find out what
Gallo had been after but he was still on the loose somewhere in my town.
I had learned one thing, though: he hadn't heard about Holmes. I imagined if he had, he probably wouldn't have thought it was safe to hang
around in the dead man's house.

Now it was time to go from one kind of unpleasantness to another. It was
full dark when I pulled into the office parking lot and sure enough there
was just the one car still there: a white mid-sized Toyota sedan. Trudy.

She was already sitting in my office when I went in. Papers from the growing Holmes file were spread out across my desk. She did not say hello.

"Have we heard from Paul lately?"

She gave me a look I couldn't decipher. It was cold, it was distasteful, it was disappointment. It was something more than that, or less. I couldn't really tell.

"He's somewhere in Boston or Rhode Island. He wanted to talk to you and I told him you'd be in tomorrow."

"Good," I said, taking a seat in one of my visitor chairs, keeping my eyes on the desktop.

"Is that yours?" Trudy asked.

I looked up. "Is what?" I didn't know what she was talking about. But then I saw where she was looking. Blood was smeared all over my shirt and jacket. "Shit," I said. I peeled the jacket from my shoulders and took it to the small private bathroom behind the closed door to the left of my desk. Inside there was a rack mounted on the wall. I slid the jacket onto an empty coat hanger and began unbuttoning my shirt. I turned to the sink and scrubbed my hands, arms and neck, and dried off with the towel hanging next to the vanity. There was a fresh shirt on the same rack where I'd left my jacket and I slid that on.

Trudy hadn't said a word. I came out buttoning, then rolled up the sleeves. I left the tails untucked.

"You going to tell me or not?"

"You going to stay mad or not?"

"Depends on what you have to say."

I thought about that. "Could you call the alarm company and have someone come out to change the security code tomorrow? And we're going to need new locks for the doors."

"Is this about Gabe?"

I wanted to spit something out of my mouth. "Don't even mention his name."

"Is he okay?"

What came to mind was better left unsaid. Instead I managed, "He's walking around as well as ever, if that helps you."

"Scott, did you hurt him?"

"No, Trudy, I saved him. But that doesn't mean I ever want him coming back here."

She wanted to ask more but thought better of it.

"Whose blood was that?"

"You don't know the guy."

"Whose blood was that?"

"Trudy," I said, standing up and leaning forward on the outer edge of my desk. "You do not want to know whose blood that is. You may think you do but you absolutely do not. You also do not want to know what happened tonight, or what was supposed to. You do not want to know how sideways things almost went. All you need to know is that Gabe Keller is no longer welcome in this building or in this business and that if he shows his face here it won't leave the same way it came in. You do need to know the rest of us will need new door keys as well as have to memorize a new five digit code for the alarm system."

She sat back in the chair, still with that cool, emotional but in-control gaze, and said, "That's it?"

I stood up and fell back into the chair, exhausted. The tension of the night was draining away and I was about as spent as the first dollar bill.

"What about me?" she asked.

"Trudy, you weren't even there."

There was a pause and I had the feeling I had said the wrong thing without knowing why it was wrong. Suddenly she was gathering the papers on top of my desk into a pair of manila folders without caring how anything was ordered.

"Is that all you need from me, Scott?"

"Yes, that's it," I said, her own toxic emotions affecting me.

She snatched the folders from my desk and started to march out of the office. "Good night, Porter."

That did it. I almost grabbed her arm and stopped her but I didn't. "What the hell is wrong with you?"

She turned on me then, her face opening up, the pieces of what had been there before falling away. "Where did you go?"

I sighed. I didn't want to do this. I couldn't. "To see Gallo."

"Where is he?"

"I don't know."

"I said, where is he?"

"Trudy, it's the God's honest truth, I don't know. He got away from me."

"But you got Gabe."

"Yes."

"And he was working with Gallo."

"Yes."

"What did you do?"

"Trudy—"

"Could you have been hurt?"

"What?" I didn't expect this. "What do you mean—"

"That blood could have been yours. You could have been hurt."

"Trudy, I'm fine—"

"Now you are, aren't you? You always come back fine."

Some of the hellfire was creeping back. "I had to—"

"You ever think about me, Scott? How I'm feeling?"

"What?"

"You heard me." She turned and walked quickly to the door. With her hand on the knob and without turning her head, she said, "You know your problem, Scott Porter?"

I tried something smart for a change and kept quiet.

"You think you're Scott Porter."

When she closed my own door behind her I knew she didn't want me to follow her. Or did she? At that point I wasn't sure what the hell I was supposed to know just then.

I sank into the couch beneath the window that was along the wall opposite my desk. I was planning on spending the night here, until the alarm codes could be changed. After a few minutes I heard the front door open and close and I got up and used my key to turn the dead bolt to the lock position. I went back to my office and brushed my teeth at the sink then headed straight to the couch and settled in, the automatic I'd been carrying all evening pushed between the back padding and one of the cushions.

It didn't take as long to fall asleep as I thought it would, but in my head I kept hearing Trudy say, "You ever think about me, Scott?"

What about her, I thought angrily. What did she expect from me? She was on her way to her home and the bed she shared with her asshole husband. That was her life, not mine.

I rolled onto my side and faced the back of the couch. Was she telling me she cared about me? Then why couldn't she use those words?

Soon I was dancing among unsettled dreams I already knew would be forgotten by morning.

CHAPTER EIGHTEEN

A gentle knock came at the door. I rolled over, not certain what I'd heard. My hand was reaching behind the cushion when the knock came again.

"Hello?" I called, still not fully awake.

"It's Steph," came the bright morning voice. "Would you like some coffee in there?"

"Yeah, um, sure." I pulled out the gun, dropped it into my lap and rubbed my eyes with my other hand. "That would be great, Steph."

I heard her footsteps recede down the hall and I stood up, stretched, feeling and hearing things pop along my spine. Then I opened the door and pulled it halfway open and turned back to the bathroom to brush the night from my teeth. By the time I came out, Steph had left a steaming mug on my desk along with some sort of fruit-filled Danish on a napkin. "God bless you," I muttered as I inhaled the aroma of the coffee deeply, then nearly swallowed the pastry whole as I washed it down with two gulps of the brew. A quick trip back to the bathroom to rinse my fingers and rub them through my hair and I felt ready to go home and clean myself up for real.

The first thing I noticed when I got to the reception area was that Trudy's seat was empty. I glanced at my watch, saw that she wasn't late quite yet. Suddenly it occurred to me that it might be a good idea if I was gone before she got there.

Al Sutter was in the same chair I'd planted him in the past few days, coffee and his own Danish on the end table in the corner. "Morning, Al," I said.

"Morning, boss."

I looked at Steph so that both of them would be listening to me. "Trudy is calling a locksmith this morning to change the locks. The security people will come out, too, so we'll all get new keys as well as a new alarm code."

Sutter raised his eyebrows but Steph just nodded, and made an unnecessary note on a pad.

"And I have a new job for you, Al. If you want it. First, you can be off guard duty." If Gallo didn't come back last night, I couldn't think of any reason why he'd want to now; he'd already taken anything he wanted from the office regarding the Holmes case. He knew I wasn't going to be leaving anything new where he could get at it. "How do you feel about taking over for Gabe Keller?"

"You mean take over as lead on his cases?"

"On your cases. You're the man now. If you want it."

He stood up. "Of course I do." He held his hand out and I shook it. "But what about Gabe?" he asked.

"Gabe Keller doesn't work here anymore." I turned to Steph. "Can you take care of the paperwork?"

She looked shaken but her expression showed she didn't want to ask what had happened. Steph had such a pleasant and ingrained temperament that it was hard for her to turn it off. In her life she'd never had to learn that not everyone deserved or was worthy of her sympathy. That was going to keep her from being the kind of operative she'd always told me she wanted to be. All she said was, "Got it," and made some notes on her pad.

I turned back to Sutter. "So, Al, the first thing to do is get on the Hochstedt case. Figure out where it's at and then let's get that thing closed. Make a list of all the open cases Gabe had going, come up with a plan for each of them—or use Gabe's, your call—and find me later and let's go over what you've got. Good?"

He was smiling. I assume he was already thinking of the bump in pay he'd be drawing but maybe he was just happy to be moving up in the organization. "What if you're not here?"

"You can talk to Trudy." There was a sudden lump in my throat. "She speaks for me."

I patted my pants pockets, felt the keys in my left front. The P220 I'd put back in my desk. "I'm going to run home and change. Be back in a while."

Just like that, business seemed almost back to normal. I wanted some time to let yesterday's events sink back into my subconscious, and to take a nice hot shower and get a full breakfast. When I returned to the office I knew there would be a lot of things that would need to be dealt with. As the door closed behind me and I headed down the sidewalk on the walk to my condo, I thought of Trudy. The office had a hollow feel to it without her at her desk this morning. Or was it just me that seemed that way?

I looked up and down the street for a black BMW or a driver parked behind the wheel of a car. Nothing. My hands deep in my pockets, I shuffled off toward home, feeling my cramped muscles reluctantly stretch as I walked.

Trudy was at her desk when I got back. I hadn't hurried though I'd been feeling a certain anxiety while I had been gone. My phone hadn't rung but when I pulled it out of my back pocket I'd seen that it had either gotten itself turned off or had run out of battery. For the time being I left it that way.

She was wearing a white high-collared blouse, hair and makeup done to perfection. The purple puffiness under her eyes was gone and she nodded in my direction when I walked into the office.

"Good morning, Trudy," I said.

"Morning, Scott. The locksmith should be here any time, and the alarm company will be here before two."

"Perfect. Any word on McKay?"

"He called twenty minutes ago. I said I'd have you call him when you got in."

"Good," I said, then looked down at Steph and gave her a crooked smile. "Al settling in okay?"

"He keeps whistling and everyone keeps telling him to stop."

I smiled. "Good for him." To Trudy, I said, "I'm going to call Paul. Care to join me?"

There was an implicit choice there for her, a chance to distance herself if she wanted, or to stay in the thick of things as much as I'd let her. But after a moment of hesitation—I think—she stood and said, "I'll be right in. Let me get my papers together."

I nodded, turned and headed down the hall to my office. From behind my desk I scooped up the phone and dialed the number to Paul McKay's cell.

"Paul," I said.

Trudy walked in, shut my door halfway, took another step, then turned and shut it quietly the rest of the way.

"How you doing?" he asked.

"Anxious to get caught up on what you've been up to."

"Funny, I was thinking the same thing when I was trying to get hold of you by phone all day yesterday."

"Well, you know," I said, planting myself in my own chair. "It was one of those." With the door closed I punched the button for the speaker.

"And I hear Gabe Keller's gone?"

Trudy sat, several file folders in her hand. "He was working with the enemy," she said.

"Morning again, Trudy. Anyone going to share?"

I sat back while Trudy repeated what I'd told her yesterday. I studied her face, knowing damn well she knew what I was doing but not acknowledging it.

"And where is Gallo now?"

Trudy looked away from me. "No one knows," I said.

"Will he stay gone?" asked Trudy. I had no idea what was going through her head but her tone was all business and that helped me stay focused.

I said, "I have no idea. But let's not get too far ahead of ourselves. Paul, why don't you catch us up?" I pulled a fresh legal pad out of one of my drawers and a ball point pen from another.

"You're not going to like it."

"It can't be any worse up there than what's been going on down here."

"Don't be so sure."

I put my pen down on the pad and folded my hands together. "Well, are you going to share or just titillate with vague warnings?"

Trudy flashed me a look. Over the speaker came the sound of Paul clearing his throat. I couldn't help it, I was growing annoyed. Backlash from the day before, maybe.

"La Cosa Nostra," Paul said. "The New England Mafia and at least one of the Five Families."

"Oh, shit." I picked up the pen again, mostly just to do something. "Not Holmes?"

"I don't think so, but he's clearly connected. I'm just not sure how yet."

"What the hell just happened?"

"The estate where Rudge managed the sale, the one that had the book that Holmes bought? That was owned by Joe Calello. I gave you that before."

I remembered the name but it still didn't mean much to me.

"Calello died in prison. All he had left for family was a son, who's been missing for fifteen years. He may be in hiding, he may be dead. There was no other family, no will. The thing is, the house wasn't in Calello's name. The deed shows someone named Bonnie Solango as the owner, who just happens to be Calello's sister-in-law's first cousin. Seemed to be common knowledge who really owned the place, though. Ms. Solango died last year, and then the house ended up on the market, piece by piece. First the contents, and then the structure. It's still for sale now, if you want to spend one point seven mil for the privilege."

"What privilege?"

"Of living in the house of the man that ran the New England Mafia for almost thirty years."

"New England Mafia?" said Trudy. "That's a thing?"

"A huge thing," McKay said. "A combination of the Boston mob and the syndicate based in Providence, Rhode Island. Calello was so powerful the Five Families in New York would call him in to settle disputes between them. Unless they'd already started shooting, of course."

"So if you're from the area—"

"These are household names. One of the guys Whitey Bulger fed to the FBI was Joe Calello. Helped put him in prison for extortion and racketeering. When he was sent up, Joe's son Anthony took over but he was a far cry from the old man. They called him Junior but it wasn't a compliment. One of the locals here told me two made guys from one of Junior's crew went to New York and talked to Gotti about whacking the boss. That's how much of a putz this guy was. Gotti told them no, you don't want dissatisfied employees taking out the head guys, but word got back to Junior. From then on, the kid almost never left his apartment."

"Think Junior's been playing golf in the witness protection league Thursday mornings in Phoenix somewhere?"

"Maybe. Regardless, people around here don't expect to see Junior again, say ever."

"What did he do, aside from piss off his underlings?"

"This you won't believe. Junior hosted an induction ceremony to make some new guys. He needed more men. In Joe's time, there were almost thirty made guys out there. Since Big Paul Castellano was gunned down in New York in ninety-four, *omerta* has gone out the window. Between the guys in WITSEC and the ones that were after Junior's beanie, there was also an undercover state cop. He bugged the house where the ceremony was happening."

"No wonder Junior disappeared."

"One way or the other," said McKay.

"Wait a minute," said Trudy. "I thought *omerta* was sacrosanct. That's over? How many of these guys have gone into witness protection?"

"The old school 'don't ask, don't tell' defense when they got pinched went out the window once the RICO statutes were passed and a couple of big names, especially Sammy the Bull, flipped. Most of the others started taking the deals and ratted on their friends and got set up in WITSEC. No one knows the number. It's in the dozens, for sure."

"Got it," she said, making notes.

"Boston I understand, I suppose," I said, "but Providence? What the hell's up there? Other than not many people."

"I was looking at that this morning. Aside from being the last colony to join the union, they had a huge influx of Irish immigrants in the 1800's. They in turn were pushed out by—"

"The Italians."

"Exactly. And there are more strip clubs and adult entertainment joints in Providence than in any other New England capital."

"Even New York?" said Trudy.

"New York's not part of New England," I said. She reddened and went back to her pad. "Cash businesses," I said to Paul. "Easier to hide some money."

"Seems that whoever was in charge was either from Providence or Boston. Headquarters was based on the hometown of whoever was boss at the time. Joe Calello ran his operation out of his vending machine company in Providence but took a heavy toll from his capo in North Boston. Calello sold protection along with cigarette and pinball machines, bookmaking, girls. And that was the light stuff."

"Hang on a second, Paul," I said, and scrawled a few notes of my own.

"So how does Holmes tie into this?"

"Well, you see, Scott," McKay said, "I've been up here a whole day—"

"Yeah, okay."

"There is something. So far all I've been talking to are the local press."

"And?"

"Typically the public doesn't find out what's happened inside the mob's inner circles until long after whatever's going on is over, if ever. Guys flip, they tell their stories at trials that take place years after the fact. Looking backwards, we can put together a lot of the pieces. As far as what's going on at this moment...."

"What you're saying is that this may not be the whole story?"

"I'm sure it's not. To get that I've got to find someone on the other side."

I looked over at Trudy. "You got any questions?"

"Paul," she said. "Are you okay?"

"I'm fine, girl. How are you doing?"

"No, I mean, are you safe? Do you need anyone—"

"You want more help, Paul?" I threw in, feeling an absurd need to assert myself. But I knew what the answer would be.

You could hear the embarrassment in his voice when he said, "No, I'm good. We get a couple of guys up here and it's going to look like we've got something going on. Right now I'm just a reporter trying to get a story. The guys that are involved are used to guys like that sniffing around. They don't mind, they just don't say anything they think hasn't been said before. It's the guys on the outside I'm trying to connect to."

"Okay," I said. "Good work. Anything else?"

"Not right now. I assume you want me to stay here?"

"I want you to find a connection between Holmes and Calello that's more than an old book. I don't know if you do that there—"

"—or back in Boston. I know. I'll figure it out and let you know."

"Sooner the better," I said. "Nice job, Paul."

I looked at Trudy, she shook her head, and I told McKay goodbye. He said he'd check in later and hung up.

After I lifted the phone receiver and dropped it back into the cradle to kill the connection, Trudy and I sat there in silence. All traces of the emotion she'd shown the night before were gone. I supposed that was a good thing. I couldn't see how bringing that up would make anything better.

"What have you got?" I asked her.

She pulled a folder out from the one she'd been holding beneath her notepad. "The results from USF on the letter from Holmes's book." Opening the cover, she took out the original paper, still encased in its plastic protector though this time backed with a thin white piece of cardboard, and slid it across my desk. "You can have that one back."

"Thank you."

"And," she said, sliding out a two-page report that was stapled in the upper left hand corner, "here is what they found."

I took the report and looked it over. Trudy sat patiently, hands in her lap, waiting.

"Is there more? What about the graphology?"

"That's it," she said. "Unless you want to chase down a graphologist. You can probably find one next to someone with a crystal ball. Apparently handwriting analysis has been discredited for years."

"Really? I thought if your words slanted to the left you were mean to cats or something."

"Nope. It's become the palm reading or the tarot of forensic document analysis."

"So the big loops for the 'p's' don't mean the writer likes coffee with their eggs?"

Trudy shook her head. "Means nothing. Apparently."

"Hmm," I said, which is what I usually said when I was trying to cover my stupidity but couldn't figure a better way. "This report is useful, though."

"Especially with what Paul just told us."

"Ties the stationery to New England, anyway."

"And gives us an approximate age."

I flipped over to the bottom of the last page. "Twenty to thirty years." I dropped the report onto my desk, over the copy of the original letter. "What do you think?"

"I don't know," she said. "It would appear that Mr. Holmes had an interest in a letter written decades ago that turned up in a house belonging to one of the most effective gangsters in the country."

"Gee, that gets us so much closer to an answer."

"What could be making this letter cause such a ruckus all these years later?"

I sat back in my chair. "If I had to guess, I'd have to put my money on Holmes."

"What do you mean?"

"He sought out the estate sale, found the Poe book—and only the Poe book—and then happened to discover the letter."

"You think he knew it was there?"

"Or looked for it at the estate sale."

She shook her head. "Why didn't he just slip it out of the book, stick it in his pocket?"

"Maybe he wasn't alone. Maybe people were watching."

"Who?"

MAD DOG BARKED

2

I hadn't told her about Gallo's connection to New York. "Who sent Gallo down here? Who killed Holmes?"

She thought about that. "I see your point."

We sat in silence for a while. I was trying to think of the case but with Trudy across from me I kept coming back to the anger she'd shown last night when I'd come back covered with Eamon Stanley's blood. It was suddenly disturbing to think I had absolutely no idea what was going on in her mind.

Finally I said, "Is that an elephant in the room or are you just happy to see me?"

She didn't blink. "What would you like me to do next?"

Asked and answered, I thought. Okay. "I want you to try to do a deep background on Holmes. Follow him back as far as you can, and get me where he was, who he was with and when, and most importantly, any friends and associates."

"Friends and associates?"

"Going back as far as this letter or even beyond. Something hooks this guy to the New England mob," I said. "Which means Holmes knew someone involved."

"Or was part of it himself."

I shook my head. "From what I saw of Edwin Holmes, I would tend to doubt that. He lived too large for the life of a Mafia don. Most of those guys have to hide what they've got or the IRS would be all over them. They have to live modestly, despite whatever bundles of cash they may have kept under their mattress or how many coffee cans of Krugerrands they've buried in the back yard. Holmes was out in the open; private jet, private security, and judging by the size of his retainer to us, a huge checking account."

"What about the Calello house?"

"Could have been legit, could have been in the family since before Calello took over. I'll have Paul check on it. But my guess is he wasn't living like a king himself, at least not openly. That's not what motivates these guys. It's the respect they get from others. They're psychopaths. Snap a finger, someone's life gets ruined. That's what keeps them going. The money is just another way to keep score."

"Okay," she said, standing up and smoothing her skirt. Conversation over. She gathered up her file folders and in a tone I couldn't decipher she said, "I'll get started."

She turned away quickly, almost daring me to call her back. At least that's how it felt. As she opened my door and went out, I choked back all of my usual remarks. Our relationship may have changed and that was not only her choice, it was all I could expect. She was a married woman, after all.

And I was—what? Apparently just her boss.
  Just her boss.
  Really, what else could I be?

CHAPTER NINETEEN

I called McKay back and had a brief conversation. I told him to concentrate on a few things: the history of the Calello house, and as much of a family tree that he could come up with for Joe Calello. If things worked out, Trudy's research into Holmes and McKay's into Calello and the New England Mafia should intersect at some point in the past, and that would hopefully give us the starting point or at least a clue as to what this might really be about.

That was the hope, anyway, and sometimes that's all you get in this business. If anything, this case was taking on the feel of a missing persons case that had gone cold long ago. The more I thought about it, the more I wondered if that's what it had been all along.

Not five minutes after I hung up with McKay, my private outside line rang. Crap, I thought. I wanted some time to sit and absorb what had been going on but that was proving to be an elusive luxury at this point.

It was Marty Ables.

"Hey, Marty," I said. "I was just thinking about missing persons...."

"And I was just thinking about how not to become one. What the hell is going on?"

Great. More shit. "You're going to have to be more specific. They bounce you out of your men's league at the club?"

"We're still on police work, Porter. At the Holmes house. Yesterday. What do you know about it?"

That was fast, I thought. "I don't know anything about it, Marty, or what you're talking about. What's going on?"

He didn't say anything right away. Ables was clearly upset and he'd called me for answers. I almost felt bad I wasn't going to give him any.

"Who killed Edwin Holmes?"

"I have no idea."

"And his secretary, Robbins? Same question."

"Same answer."

"So Robbins is dead?"

He was trying to trap me. "I don't know," I said. "Is that what you're telling me? Where did you find him?"

More silence. "You're a real bastard, Porter. You're telling me you really don't know?"

"I really don't. I could start guessing, Marty, but—"

"No, maybe you don't want to do that, not yet. I don't know the details, homicide is out of my fiefdom, but two detectives were out at the Holmes place this morning."

"About the caretaker's death?"

"I assume. But here's the thing: they found a pile of blood in the guest house back of the swimming pool. The place where this Robbins fellow lived."

Even though I knew better, I asked, "Was it his?"

"They don't know. My first thought was to call my good buddy Scott Porter and see if he was playing me for a puppet fool."

"Marty, I swear, I have no idea whatsoever about what happened to Endo Robbins. None."

"Could he have killed Holmes up in Boston? An argument over salary, lover's quarrel, something like that?"

"Unlikely," I told him. Suddenly I wanted to throw him a bone, though I wouldn't have done it if I thought it would do him any good. "Robbins drove a black BMW, I think. Can you check?"

"Maybe. Probably. Why?"

"I think I've seen it driving around."

"And you didn't think to call anyone?" Meaning the police.

"It's not like I could see the driver. Besides, I don't even know what Robbins looks like."

"Okay," Ables said. "I'll see if I can steer them to the car. They're pretty pissed right now."

"Why?"

"There's a reason they're called homicide *dicks*, Porter. They thought they had a body and an easy suspect. You throw another body in there and they start choking on their clearance rates."

"Yeah, well," I said. "Maybe they'll get lucky with the car." I was pretty sure Gallo would dump it anyway since he knew I'd seen him driving it.

"Maybe," he said. "Okay. Sorry I was a bit hot. Thought you might be holding out on me for a minute."

"Me? Marty—"

"Yeah, I know. You wouldn't do that to me, you son of a bitch."

"Let's not go that far."

"I wouldn't want to, either." I heard him take a deep breath. "All right, Porter, I'll let it go for now. But you better know what the hell you're doing. If you fuck me on this—"

"I know, Marty."

He hung up. I sat back thinking that yes, it would be great if I knew what the hell I was doing. But then I think I'd have to be in a different business.

After I was off the phone with Marty Ables, I opened my safe and put everything I had on the case inside, leaving the dial on the number twenty-three after I'd closed the handle and spun the knob to mix the tumblers. Something Eamon Stanley had said was bothering me. It was about Rico Gallo. He said his real name wasn't Gallo, it wasn't even Italian. It was Bronstein or Bronfeld, something like that, he'd said.

I called McKay yet again on his cell but got his voice mail. I left him a message asking him to look out not only for the name Rico Gallo, but also for the two names Stanley had given me. Maybe Gallo's real identity could shed some light on things. I also mentioned that Gallo hadn't known that Holmes had been murdered, and that I had no idea where he was now. For all I knew Gallo could be headed up that way. I wanted him to be careful.

So far all the bodies had been on the other side of the ledger. I counted my people on one side, everyone else on the other. That made me think of Gabe Keller. He'd made it through his little ordeal, his attempt at double dealing and sleeping with the enemy, but if he was half as smart as I wished he was, he'd know just how lucky he'd been. Gallo hadn't been fooling around. And I still didn't know what I had that he thought he could trade Keller for.

I thought about that for a while. Gallo must have thought Holmes had given me more information than he actually had. He might have thought I'd found out something more once Holmes had gone but some of the larger blanks were just starting to get filled in now.

Maybe.

Or he could have just wanted the original letter by way of controlling the first-hand proof of whatever it was that we still didn't know. It was also possible that he thought he could have traded me Gabe Keller's carcass for the promise of dropping the investigation. If that were so I thought it showed a basic lack of understanding of people on Gallo's part.

The check Holmes had given me was one thing. Bottom line, I worked for money, and Holmes had paid me well. Since he was now dead, what obligation did I really have to continue? He'd wanted me to protect him from something but wouldn't say what specifically that was. Clearly I'd failed. As far as I was concerned I'd have had a better chance if he'd told me the whole truth and then not run away. That was on him. Still, there was more to it than that.

Someone had dropped a shark named Gallo in my local pond. He'd threatened me, one of my guys—even though it was Keller, but still—and I had no idea what he was going to do next. I couldn't necessarily blame him for cutting Eamon Stanley. If Stanley had waited and followed the plan, he should have been okay and we'd have had Gallo under our control for a change. Instead things were even more up in the air.

I wondered how Stanley was doing but I imagined I'd hear one way or the other. The dumb son of a bitch had screwed up the best chance I'd had of getting in front of this thing and I didn't mind if he was feeling some pain for the quality of his efforts.

Bottom line, I wasn't ready to let the case go just yet. I didn't feel we'd done much of anything yet and whatever I felt about my clients and my employees and climate change and the Republican party really didn't make a rat's ass of difference. I'd work the case until I felt we'd either done something worth doing or the money ran out. Possibly then.

Possibly.

This was what I did. If I let other people dictate how I pursued my business then I shouldn't be doing it. We'd keep going. I'd keep going. There was just too much I didn't know.

After checking in with Al Sutter and making sure he was getting a good handle on the loose ends of Gabe Keller's cases, I asked Trudy if there were anything new on the horizon.

"You mean new cases?"

"I do," I said.

"Nothing beyond the telephone stage right now. We have a slew of background checks and a few minor follow-ups but I've been handing those over to Al."

That was good. Sutter hadn't told me that, which I took as a sign of initiative.

"If it looks like he's dropping the ball, let me know," I said quietly.

"Will do." And Trudy turned back to her computer, being the dutiful employee and sending me another non-verbal signal. I wanted to shout at her, Okay, I get it, you can let up now, but I wasn't going to treat her to anything like that.

I told Steph I was going out for lunch and I may or may not be back in the afternoon.

"Okay, Scott," she said. "See you later." The smile on her face made up for a lot of the grey skies clouding the inside of the office. I liked that kid. They should make more like that.

I left the building and decided to walk home. I could make something there, or else go out later. There was some research I wanted to do on the computer and I could do that from the condo just as well as at the office, and with far less tension in the air.

The internet was often a good source of facts that were already known. What I needed was the "secret internet," the one with the stories that hadn't simply been retyped by some lifeless wonk into Wikipedia. Of course there was no such thing so I was forced to make do.

I studied up on the illustrious history of Mr. Joseph Antonio Calello. Born in Sicily, immigrated with his family to Boston when he was seven years old, father moved them up to Providence three years later, opened a butcher shop. At this point the Italians had mostly pushed the Irish aside and were both competing and cooperating on some level for local control. The Federal Hill area where Calello lived became the center for mob activity.

Calello himself seemed to fly mostly under the popular radar until the Mafia's *capo di tuti capi* reform movement hit. This position, the Boss of Bosses, was held by Vito Genovese and made him the most powerful man in what was known as the Commission, the mob's ruling party that started some time around 1931.

All the names and dates and places made my head spin. Where the original Commission was made up of the heads of the five New York families plus the head of the Chicago syndicate, Genovese apparently wanted more for himself, and planned to take out a number of his fellow bosses.

I didn't feel like making the time to wade through an encyclopedia of all the backstabbing and outright murders that were the office politics of La Cosa Nostra. I wasn't sure any of it had a bearing on the Holmes case. When I was finally about to shut it down, I came across something interesting: Calello was said to have been at the infamous Apalachin meeting. He'd been one of the fifty bosses who escaped. The other fifty-eight having been arrested, with less than half facing charges, and the ones that were later convicted ended up freed on appeal a year later.

At the home of "Joe the Barber" Barbara in Apalachin, New York, about two hundred miles outside the city, Genovese had called a summit with bosses from all over the country. At this point in 1957 a cold war had been going on among the Commission members and when a local cop noticed a bunch of fancy cars with out of state plates pulling into Joe the Barber's estate, the authorities first set up roadblocks and then raided the place. The bosses that got away had either taken off on foot through the surrounding woods, expensive suits and all, or were lucky enough to have arrived late and were smart enough to turn back when they saw the blockades.

I tried to find out what happened to Calello. If he'd made it to the house, he must have been one of those that muddied their expensive shoes or had seen the roadblocks in time. He wasn't listed as one of the indicted.

What was interesting was that after this meeting, Hoover and the FBI could no longer go on denying the existing of the Mafia in America. Whether he thought conquering La Cosa Nostra was beyond him or whether he was at that point aware of the fact that a number of his own agents were in bed with the mob will probably never be known.

The other emerging fact that caught my eye were the conspiracy theories, the ones that thought the meeting was a set up from the start, orchestrated by Genovese as a way to further his own ends in the Commission's cold war. He may have been escalating his attacks on the others by using law enforcement to further his own goals.

In a 1958 *New York Times* article about the indictments handed down for "conspiracy to obstruct justice," it was pointed out that none of the bosses from the so-called Jewish Mafia had been present. They may not even have been invited.

Something made me think back to Eamon Stanley and what he had told me about Rico Gallo's real name: it isn't even Gallo. *It's Bronstein or Bronfeld or something.* I wondered if that could be significant.

I pushed away from my computer. The endless parade of names and dates about who did what to whom was making my head hurt. I knew there had always been a mob presence in Florida but for the most part the Mafia had kept it designated as unassigned territory. The different families could work down here, much as they did in Havana prior to the revolution, and that kept out a lot of the violence of the type seen in places like New York, Chicago and Kansas City. But the state didn't "belong" to any one faction.

By now it was early in the afternoon but I went to the kitchen and poured myself a very weak bourbon and water. I still needed to think.

I received two phone calls that evening, one on my cell phone, and one on my private line, the one with the number known to very few people.

The call on the cell was from Gabe Keller. He started out strong and in control but ended up blubbering.

"Scott?" he said when I'd answered. "This is Gabe. Gabe Keller."

I didn't try to keep the surprise out of my voice. "Hello, Gabe. Apparently you were in shock or something last night when I told you I was done with you. Please tell me this is a butt dial call and now you're too embarrassed to admit it."

"Hey, I screwed up, I know that," he said. "My daughter, she's going in to her second year at Miami, Scott. The tuition just went up fourteen percent. I never told you but my wife's job is being downsized, I—"

That was enough. "Shut up, Gabe. Listen to me very carefully. You turned, not just on me but on every person in the agency who worked with and trusted you. You only get to do that once. There are no mulligans, no do overs, no second chances. You screwed me over, Gabe, and that's on me for allowing a weak-assed piece of shit like you in my office in the first place. And you know how I know you're a piece of shit, Gabe?"

"I'm sorry, Scott."

"I didn't ask if you're sorry. I don't care if you're sorry. I asked you if you knew how I know you're a piece of shit."

"Because I took money from that man."

"Oh, okay. I guess that works, too. Goodbye, Gabe. Be a stranger. And lose my number." I hung up.

It would have been nice if that felt good, but it didn't. When you get to the point in life where so many people let you down it's more of a surprise when you spend time with someone who doesn't, something important's been lost. But I wasn't going to worry about it. No matter what else happens the clock never stops ticking.

Since I had the phone in my hand I called Sarasota Memorial and said I was a cousin of Eamon Stanley's and that I'd heard he'd been in an accident the night before. They told me I couldn't speak to him just then. Which was good, since I didn't actually want to speak to him. "Can you just let me know how he's doing? All I know is he had a deep slashing cut to the left side of his chest. They thought the blade cut through skin and muscle and into some of his ribs."

The nurse put me on hold. When she came back she said, "Mr. Stanley's been sewn up and he should be resting comfortably now. The doctor will probably discharge him tomorrow or the day after."

"Okay," I said, ready to hang up. I could only imagine the pain in the ass he was being to the hospital staff.

"We're going to want to go over care instructions with whoever picks him up."

"I hope so," I told her, wondering if it would be that bar hag he'd had out in the parking lot of Goldy's bar in Tampa. I closed the connection. Stanley would be okay. I had thought as much but it was a bit of a relief to know for sure. I didn't need another complication or corpse on my hands. The damned fool.

The second call came later into the night, well after dark. The phone on the kitchen counter rang and I walked over to it. I only knew this time it couldn't be Holmes. I looked at the number of the incoming call and jammed my thumb on the Talk button.

It was Trudy.

"Scott!" she yelled.

"What is it, honey? What's wrong?" I was already moving for my jacket and the P220 I'd brought home with me.

"Remember that watch I couldn't find? I thought maybe I'd left it in your office."

I vaguely remembered her asking me something about it. "Yeah?" I said. "What's going on?"

"It's here, Scott. It's in my house. Wrapped around my bed post."

"And you didn't leave it there?" I wanted to run to the elevators but this was my land line and I couldn't move yet.

"I haven't seen that watch since I left it at the office. I'd have noticed it before now if it was here. And I certainly wouldn't have left it wrapped around my bed post."

"What about Tim? Could he—"

"He's not even here."

"When's he coming back, Trudy?" This was important. She couldn't be alone right now.

"I— I don't know. Maybe late, in the morning." The panic slid out of her voice with the last sentence, replaced by something else.

"You have a gun?"

"In the safe."

"Get it. Sit down in a corner of an upstairs room, away from any windows. I'll be there in twenty."

She sounded relieved or defeated, I couldn't tell which. "Please hurry, Scott."

"I'm on my way."

I went through the same rigamarole with the guard outside Trudy's gated community where I had to stop and get a guest pass for my windshield before he'd lift the wooden barrier from across the entrance. Fortunately Trudy had either called ahead and had me put on some sort of guest list so I didn't have to wait for him to use his telephone. But the process still took a minute and a half I didn't have to spare. The guard kept looking at me as though he wanted to find out what was wrong but he gave a shrug and let it go. His role as a security guard was to hand out or deny passes. Beyond that the only skill he needed was the ability to dial a resident.

When I made it through I raced to Trudy's house, laying tracks in her driveway. All the lights were on in the house. I ran out of the Malibu and pounded on the door. "Trudy!" I called. "It's me!"

She must have heard or seen me pull into the driveway because she was at the front door within three seconds. "Scott!"

I had the feeling she wanted me to hold her but instead she pulled me by the wrist into the house and slammed the door. The neighbors were probably already wondering what was going on.

When she let go of me I turned my hand and grabbed her by the arms. This time I pulled her into my chest. She was stiff at first and then melted into my body, allowing me to hold her tightly. I could feel the heat of her body as well as her heart beating rapidly along with my own. I also felt the sharp weight against my back of the .38 Police Special she held in her right hand.

"You good, Trudy? Everything all right?"

"No, it's just the watch. It freaked me out, Scott. Someone was in my house."

"Where's Tim?"

"Someone was in my house!"

"I know, honey, I know. Where's Tim?"

She pulled away from me then, brushing her hair away from her forehead. The .38 was awkward in her hand and she looked around for somewhere to put it.

"Here," I said, holding out my hand. If something was going to happen, I'd rather have the gun be in my hands than hers. She handed it over and I flipped open the cylinder. The hammer had been resting on an open chamber but the others were filled with unspent cartridges. I pulled open the drawer of a cabinet just inside the hallway and dropped it inside. I still had the P220 in my waistband so we were covered. "Let's make sure the house is secure."

She stuck by my side as I locked the front door, then went through to the kitchen and made sure the sliding doors to the backyard were locked. There was an aluminum bar in the track preventing the doors from being opened more than an inch or two regardless. "Was this here before?"

Trudy nodded. "It's been there all day. We only take it up if we're going to be using the door."

The entrance to the garage was also secure, but it was only by a cheap lock and I looked for signs of tampering. There was nothing but that didn't mean a lot.

There was another set of sliding doors in the guest bedroom but that had the same security bar setup as the one in the kitchen. Next we went along to all the windows, Trudy a step behind me the whole time. We started at the front of the house and worked our way around.

"Here it is," I said. The window above the kitchen sink had been forced, the vinyl around the bottom permanently misshapened by some sort of pry bar. I assumed something else had been used at the top edge and enough pressure applied to separate the latch. Through the glass I saw a tall white vinyl fence separating Trudy's yard from the neighbors.

"He had the best cover here," I said. "Hang on." I lifted the bar from the sliding glass doors, leaned it against the wall, and went outside. The damage was as I suspected. Back in the kitchen I asked Trudy where she kept things like wooden spoons. One hand was covering her mouth but she pointed to a drawer in her center island. I pulled it open and dug around until I found something suitable. I took it over to the sink and jammed the window down as far as it could go and inserted the handle of the spoon along the side of the track. He wouldn't be opening that window again the same way. On the other hand, I thought, he'd already made his point.

We went through the rest of the house room by room, mostly for Trudy's piece of mind. I knew the house would be empty. Trudy couldn't see that anything else was missing or had even been touched. We saved the master bedroom for last.

"There it is," she said, pointing to the bedpost with her watch wrapped around it, the band made from sparkling Black Hills gold that gleamed with pinks and greens in the light from the lamp on the end table.

I sat down on the edge of the bed and after a moment she joined me. We sat about a foot and a half apart. I felt like I was on a mild hallucinogenic when I allowed myself to consider that I was sitting in her bedroom. On her bed.

"I'm sorry, Trudy."

"Was it Rico Gallo?"

I nodded my head. "I think so."

"How did he get my watch? Scott—"

"Gabe Keller."

"What?"

"Keller got in bed with Gallo." As soon as I said the words I felt the irony.

"But that phone call, when Gabe called—"

"Yeah, well, you know what they say about arranged marriages." And then I stopped myself.

"And I was so angry with you." She put both hands to her face and I noticed the professionally manicured nails, covered with clear polish, as she wiped the moisture from her eyes and across her cheeks. "I owe you such an apology, Scott."

"No," I told her. "You don't."

Suddenly she hit me in the arm. "You never tell me what's going on, you bastard. You never tell anyone. You just... you just... do...."

I grabbed her hand before I thought about what I was doing. "Shhh," I said. "Stop, Trudy. You're right, I'm wrong. But you know now."

"You're still not going to change, though, are you? You're still playing the lone crusader when the rest of us—"

"Trudy." She consciously made an effort to still herself as I interrupted her. "You're right, I'm probably not going to change. You wouldn't like me any better if I did, despite what you're saying now." Bullshit, I thought. She'd hate me. "I wouldn't know how to try, anyway. And if I did, it probably wouldn't last long."

"I'm not sure I like you now."

"Oh, hell, you might like me better than you think." Another slip. I really wanted to turn the topic of conversation away from me. "Now tell me, where's Tim?"

That did it. She stood up from the bed and looked for one second as though she thought about leaving the room. Then she stood in place, staring down at her shoes, and finally she held her hands clasped in front of her.

"You know he's, he's had other—"

"I thought he was through with that."

She gave a small laugh. "So did I."

"How long?"

A shrug. "Does it matter? How long, how many, how often. It all comes to the same thing, doesn't it?"

"It's not you, Trudy."

"No, I accept that now. For a long time I wasn't sure. But I've done all that I can, I know it—"

"Some guys really are just dogs, Trudy. They need something to make them feel like the men they always wanted to be. They're not strong enough to actually work at doing it for real."

"Have you ever—?"

"We've all done things we're not proud of. Men grow up with hormones guiding their every move. We shit on the feelings and emotions of the women who are foolish enough to think we see something more in a relationship. Or at least that we see what they do."

"What an awful thing to say, Scott. That's disgusting."

"Well, hopefully we grow out of it. Many of us do. Maybe most of us do."

"But not Tim."

"I don't know him well enough to offer a diagnosis. Really I hardly know him at all. The most I can tell you is that with some guys if the opportunity is there, they're going to take it nine times out of ten. Give a guy like that a position of authority—"

"Like a policeman."

I nodded. "There is opportunity for abuse."

She did a few more things with her hands, gave me a look, then sat down again on the bed, this time a bit closer. The move had probably been unintentional but I was acutely aware of every millimeter.

"What do I do, Scott? What am I supposed to do?"

I should have told her it was none of my business. I should have told her she was a married woman committed to a faithless man and that whatever she might want to happen outside the marriage, she needed to address that situation first. I could have asked her if she still loved him but I was too much of a coward not to be afraid of the answer she might give.

Instead I did the worst thing I could possibly do. I reached over, put my arm around her shoulder, and as she started to lean against me I put my mouth against hers and kissed her, long and slow and gentle, not breaking contact for fear a moment like this would never come again. But she didn't break it either, and after a few seconds her other arm came around and she encircled my neck, scooting her body closer and leaning her weight into mine. We couldn't stop kissing any more than we could stop breathing and eventually we slipped backwards onto the bed.

A very long while later, she pulled back and dabbed at her lips with the cuff of her sleeve. "We are so close, aren't we?"

I said, "Yes," though I wasn't sure what she meant. Not exactly. I felt like an idiot.

"If either one of us—"

"Yes," I said again.

"That's all it would take, isn't it?" She leaned forward to kiss me again and that's when I knew I had to get up.

I rolled her over onto her back again and pushed myself up above her. She had both arms up, above her head, her body open and vulnerable. She seemed as though she were making herself available but I couldn't wrap my mind around the thought.

Now I knew what she was talking about. "We are that close, Trudy." I sat up the rest of the way. "But we can't."

I wanted her to tell me no, to tell me that we could do whatever we wanted. I wanted her to grab me and pull me back down. I wanted her to start removing my clothes as she told me that we could do exactly whatever we wanted, whatever we *really* wanted, and all that actually mattered right now, at this moment, was that the two of us were here. Right here.

On her bed.

But she didn't. She sat up slowly, brushing at her hair with her fingers. "That's why I love you, Scott."

Don't say that, I wanted to answer. Don't ever say that. I didn't want to handle that sort of pain.

Trudy excused herself to go to the restroom down the hall. Carefully I worked the band of her watch away from the bed post. I looked down at the pillows, and imagined the one where she lay her head every night—

Stop it, you ass, I said to myself. Just stop it.

I was waiting downstairs in the living room when Trudy came back down the hall. I thought a change in locale wise. She didn't seem surprised to see me sitting there.

"Found your watch," I said, twirling it on my finger.

She came forward and took it from me gingerly, then slowly worked it over her hand and onto her wrist.

"Thank you, Scott."

"It was easy. I knew where to look."

"No, I mean—thank you."

Up until that moment I still had thoughts of sweeping her up and carrying her back into that bedroom. I knew—I hoped—that she wouldn't resist. I might go back to losing her respect but that could be rebuilt again. At least that's what I always told myself. But I knew I wouldn't do it. Or couldn't.

"You're welcome, Trudy." I didn't know if I was changing the subject or not but I said, "What do we do now? I don't want you here alone."

"Would you tell me the truth if I asked if you thought I was safe?"

I stepped closer and she brought her hands together in front of her. She may not even have realized she'd done it but it was an effective blocking maneuver. I stopped in front of her and said, "He doesn't want to hurt you, Trude. He's just sending a message."

"You're sure?"

"He wanted my attention and he got it. It worked. Now you just have to let it go and let me handle it."

"By doing what?"

"Don't worry about that."

"Oh, is that all?" Her hands moved fast as she plunged them down at her sides, turning both of them into fists. "You're so infuriating. I never know what you're doing, or what you're going to do."

"That's the way I work, Trudy."

"Would you just tell me? Please? Just this one time?"

Maybe I would, if I knew. But I didn't want her knowing anything about me that could hurt either one of us down the line. So I didn't say anything.

"That's what I thought." She moved to a closet and took out a light-weight linen jacket and picked up her purse from a table in the living room. "I think I need to find a hotel."

"Just for the night?" I asked, and wished the words back.

"Just in case," she said. "I don't want Gallo to find me here."

"You could stay at my place," I said, feeling weak.

"Scott—"

"I'll sleep at the office. I've done it before, you know."

"I can't. It— it can't be that way."

What can't, I wanted to ask, but I knew I was already supposed to know.

"Okay. I'll follow you out, though, make sure he's truly gone."

"What's going to happen next?"

"You coming in tomorrow?"

"What else would I do?" The words had a sad sound when she said them.

"We'll figure it out then."

So we left. We were careful not to touch again. The night air helped my chest loosen from the tension left behind in that house. And it had nothing to do with Rico Gallo.

CHAPTER TWENTY

I'd seen Trudy to a Holiday Inn last night and only left her when I was sure no one had followed. Obviously the question of whether or not Gallo was still around had been answered.

It took me a long time to settle down and get myself to sleep once I got back home. Tim Westland was on my mind as I thought about how he was apparently messing around on Trudy again. Or perhaps he'd never stopped; I had no way of knowing. But a desk sergeant in charge of dispatchers had no business working all-night hours, he had regular duty dispatchers that did that. And I knew that if he'd been at work, or anywhere else that he should have been, Trudy would have called him instead of me.

Why would any man cheat on a woman like Trudy, I asked myself. My own theory was that an ass like Tim knew he didn't deserve his own wife and made himself feel big by bedding other women, proving to himself over and over that he was every bit the stud he thought he ought to be. But I believed that somewhere in his head, buried deep, there was a tiny little voice that never quit telling him he wasn't quite good enough, that he'd never be quite good enough, to live up to his own good fortune. Rather than trust in Trudy's choice when she'd decided to give herself to him, the insecure son of a bitch did her like this.

There, that'll be ten cents, please.

If I didn't stop this line of thinking it would eat me alive. Maybe it was all just rationalization. There are always things about the people we know best that we will never find comprehensible. I suppose that's what keeps us interesting as individuals. But why a woman like Trudy, or why any woman, would put up with crap like this....

I was still stifling yawns when I walked into the office a little bit late the next morning. Trudy was at her desk, as though nothing had happened the night before. She did look a bit worn, more so than I felt I did, and on her left wrist was her watch. That made me smile. I'd half expected she'd have thrown the thing down a storm sewer somewhere.

"Morning, ladies," I said. They both answered back as I took a right and headed down the hallway toward my own office. I'd screwed up with Gallo and now I needed to finally come up with answers. Because he was still messing about I knew we'd gotten ourselves involved with something that we not only didn't understand, but something that wasn't going to go away on its own.

I opened my safe and took out a new copy of the transcript of the Holmes letter and laid it on top of my desk. With the new locks and alarm code I wasn't worried about Gabe Keller creeping my office again. Regardless, I was keeping everything locked up in my safe.

> *Why did Rosalyn call me to ask how are you doing — very odd*
> *It is Sunday and Elizabeth neither called nor talked to me*
> *Why did Ralph call me — very strange and it seems as if my time*
> *& Tedys here is running out*
> *Things are not right*
> *I feel very scared*
> *They would get me a nice place he said*
> *I am so sad never been so scared if only Don were here*
> *Eban is very restless for the past 3 days too*
> *I pray to join Don every night*

Clearly I was missing something. With McKay's intel from the northeast, I wondered if there were enough information floating out there to at least come up with a working hypothesis.

I picked up the phone to call him, then thought better of it. I checked my watch and thought I should give him some more time to check in. I knew he was out there, digging away. He didn't need to think I was perching on his shoulder.

Marty Ables called about an hour later. I'd gone back to researching organized crime on the internet. I wanted to learn more about the mob's views on the Sunshine State. I suspected with an economy built on dope that South Florida may not be such neutral territory anymore.

"Still mad at me?" I asked Ables.

"It's early yet. Listen," he said. "The Feds are involving themselves in this Holmes thing now."

Shit, I thought. I said a silent prayer that Eamon Stanley would somehow keep himself out of sight. "Oh, really? What's changed?"

"With the new blood puddle in the guest house at Longboat Key they're bringing in a team to tear the place apart."

I sat up straighter in my chair. "Where you getting this from, Marty? You're still missing persons, aren't you?"

"Buddy of mine is an agent. Turns out he's coming down. He gave me a call, said we should go out for a bump when he's here."

"Down from where? Where's he coming from?"

"Boston."

Edwin Morton Holmes had a house in Boston. Edwin Morton Holmes died in Washington, D.C., heading in that direction after he'd left Florida. Four hundred miles more and he would have made it.

"What's Holmes to your FBI guy?"

"Has to be something, right?"

"You don't know?"

"He didn't say. I didn't ask. I work missing persons, remember?"

"Geeze, you're a frustrating bastard sometimes. Can you ask the guy?"

"Funny you should bring that up, Porter. My friend's name is John Sullivan. Want to meet him?"

I wasn't sure. While I was hesitating, Ables said, "He wants to meet you."

"What are you doing to me, Marty? Really."

"Relax, Scott, relax. We were shooting the shit on the phone, and when he told me why he was coming down, I said I knew someone who had contact with this Holmes guy."

"So he knows about me?"

"What are you, The Shadow? Of course he knows about you. When I told him about your missing persons problem—"

"You gave him those names."

"You're welcome. And now he wants to meet you. Might get you a break on your case."

There was a reason a guy like Marty Ables worked twelve years on missing persons. When a huge majority of his case load ends up being canceled by the person making the complaint, and most of the other miss-ees turned up on their own within a few weeks or months, almost all of his time was spent turning over paper. Actually having to get up and go out into the community to do detective work was an atrophying skill. If a cop like Ables had wanted to do more police work than paperwork he would have transferred out a long time ago.

"Let's hope so," I said slowly. "Did he give you any indication that he could do anything?" It was more likely that since this Sullivan guy had an interest in Holmes and that Holmes was—had been—my client that he wanted to pump me for whatever he could. It was less probable it would work out to be a two-way street but I couldn't afford not to be cooperative.

"That's between you guys. Sully'll be here this afternoon. You're around?"

"I'm not around."

"I'll give you a call when he shows up. We'll meet up somewhere."

"Thanks, Marty," I said, lying through my teeth. "I appreciate the help. But I can't make it tonight."

"You sure know how to show your gratitude."

"You know us private dicks. You public ones get to sit at your desks and work nine to five but I actually have to get my butt out on the street once in a while."

"Get out of it."

"No."

He was fuming but he kept his frustration in check as he said, "Fine, Scott, I'll let John know. Maybe you'll be available tomorrow. You know, because he's the FBI and all."

"I can only try." I hoped the plastic of his cell phone could withstand the amount of stress I was imagining he was placing on its case just then.

"Just trying to do a favor here, Scott."

Yeah, but for who? Me or John Sullivan?

"I appreciate it, Marty."

"Okay, you let me know. I'll try to keep Sully loose. He does have that house to look at. I want to hold up my end of our arrangement."

I knew just the type of graft he was talking about. One of his country club bills had shown up in the mail yesterday. "We'll get something set up. Maybe we can meet at your club." I hung up before he could answer.

When Paul McKay finally called in, the conversation was a short one. "I'm on my way back," he said.

That surprised me. "So soon? What did you find?"

"I'll fill you in when I get there. I'm in a bit of a hurry now."

"You in trouble?"

"I think the wrong people heard I was asking questions. I'm not getting a good feeling about this. I heard some things about Providence but I don't think now is the right time to visit."

If McKay was feeling uneasy about something the smart thing for me to do was listen. I looked at the time. "I've got something tonight I'm not going to be able to get out of. You'll be in the office tomorrow?"

"Bright and early. But I need to get moving now."

"Be good, Paul. See you in the morning."

The case had the feeling of being stalled. In fact the more I thought about it the more I wondered how much it had ever moved in the first place. If Rico Gallo or Bronstein or Bronfeld or whatever his real name was is still around, he was becoming too dangerous for me to just close the file and walk away. He'd corrupted Gabe Keller and threatened Trudy Westland. That wasn't the sort of thing I was going to let go. Ever.

I picked up the phone again and called Sarasota Memorial. When I asked how my cousin was doing they put me on hold again. I thought they were just transferring me to the nurse's station on his floor but instead the same voice came back on the line.

"Let's see, I'm showing that Mr. Stanley checked himself out this morning. Just after ten o'clock."

"That can't be," I said. "I thought I was going to be his ride home. Do you have an idea who was there for him?"

"I wouldn't have any way of knowing that," she said, sounding as though her time on the phone was about done.

"Well, did he have any visitors before he left?" All I could think of was that woman I saw him with in the lot at Goldy's but I doubted any self-respecting hospital would discharge a still-healing patient to someone who looked like she should be committed to the substance abuse wing on sight.

"Again, sir, I can't tell you that."

Meaning she didn't know. I was about to say goodbye when the nurse simply hung up on me. Customer service in health care. I guess I needed to be an insurance company.

So Stanley was gone. I wondered if I should try to find him but I was still pissed off at the man. If he'd only stuck to our plan we most likely would have had Rico Gallo in our hands. I'd have gotten what I wanted from him then. Instead Stanley gets slashed and the cops get more excited and now I have to meet with an FBI guy at some point in the near future. So screw Stanley. I made enough mistakes without making the same ones twice.

There came a light knocking on my door frame. I looked up and there was Trudy, a collection of papers folded in the crook of her right arm. Normally she'd have walked right in, or so I thought, but I was losing my perspective on what normal was with her at this point.

"You have a minute?"

"Of course," I said, neutral, no deflecting humor. I tended to make jokes with her even though I knew she didn't always appreciate it. It was a juvenile sort of way to remind both of us of the things we already knew but couldn't—or wouldn't—talk about in the open.

She left the door open and walked in and sat down across from me. I moved aside the papers I'd been going through and she placed her stack in front of her on the edge of the desk.

"I found out more about Edwin Holmes, like you asked."

"Anything good?"

"His name's not really Edwin Holmes. Or at least it didn't used to be."

I tried replaying his odd touch of accent in my mind but couldn't quite manage it. It had been too long already. "European, then?"

"Well, in England it was still Edwin Morton Holmes. Before he came to the United States in the late eighties."

"Who was he before that?"

"Back in Yugoslavia, his name was, I think, Bojan Zupan, but I have no idea how to pronounce it properly."

"If Yugoslavia still existed that might be relevant."

"And if Holmes or Zupan was still alive. In any case, he was from Slovenia, and that exists as its own country now."

"How did Mr. Zupan get to England? Do we know?"

She shook her head, her eyes down on the papers in front of her. I couldn't tell if she was reluctant to make eye contact or if I was looking for something that wasn't there.

She slid a printout of a scanned image of a passport page across to me. "Look at this."

You could definitely see Holmes in the picture, the high forehead and arched brows, the nose with the bump high on the bridge. He wasn't smiling, either, which made Bojan Zupan look even more like the Edwin Holmes we had known.

"And now this," Trudy said, laying another piece of paper on top of the other. This one was a scan of a British passport with the name Edwin Morton Holmes listed over what was exactly the same picture.

"Interesting," I said. "And there's more?"

She took another piece of paper from her pile but this time kept it so she could read from it. "An Edwin Morton Homes from the city of Leeds, West Yorkshire, in England shows up in New York City in 1994 as an employee of Westchase Bank. From there it's a bit difficult to follow his trajectory inside the company until he becomes an officer some time in 1999."

"Meanwhile his home country is taken apart. Anybody come over with him?"

"I haven't been able to find anyone."

"Does he have family back there, in—"

"It would be Slovenia. And I would have to figure out how to figure that out."

"Okay," I said, thinking. "Holmes had to have people close to him. If he was just worried about his own life, why come to us? Clearly he had enough money to run to where he thought he'd be safe."

"Only he wasn't," Trudy said. "You think he was protecting someone?"

My mind was on those names in that letter, and on the meeting with the FBI agent that was probably going to happen tomorrow no matter what I did. "It's a theory."

"Okay," she said, gathering her materials and standing up. "I'll keep digging. Can Paul help? Since he's close to the area, it might be good if he could visit—"

"Paul's already on his way home. He'll be here tomorrow."

"Oh." She turned and looked over at my still open door, then back at me, and this time her eyes did meet mine. "Is everything okay?"

"Not sure," I told her. "He didn't say much. Here, hang on a second." I turned to my computer and opened a search engine. I typed "private detectives in Slovenia." It returned a number of hits. "Here," I said, rotating my screen toward her. She didn't move closer. I told her what I'd done, told her to hire someone over there. And do it quickly.

"I'll get on it now." She didn't move. I had the impression she was lingering.

"How are you doing I asked?"

"Good," she said. "Good. I think. Still a bit freaked out but Tim told me he'd be in all night."

"So he came home?"

She blinked a few times and straightened the neatened papers she was holding. "He always does. Eventually."

I didn't think I should say anything more. She seemed to be back in control of her marital situation, or at least as much as she had been before last night. She turned to leave.

"We'll stop him, Trudy."

She'd gotten halfway to the door when she stopped and spun around. "Who?" she said, her eyes wide and her shoulders tensing, giving her a sort of frantic look.

"Gallo," I said. "We'll stop him."

"Oh," she said, "him." Her features and posture slumped and she hurried to the door quickly. "That's good."

CHAPTER TWENTY-ONE

"How's everything going, Steph?" I asked as I walked toward the front door.

"Everything's good, Scott. Billings are almost all caught up. Al's got Gabe's cases all straightened out. We're chugging along."

"I didn't know there was anything wrong with them."

Her face reddened. "Just some paperwork things. Al knows about them."

"Oh, he does, does he? Well, that's good. Tell him we should talk later."

"Where are you going?"

"Run a few errands." Behind Steph I saw Trudy's head jerk stiffly away.

"Coming back?" Steph asked.

"Always have," I said, and left.

The drive up to Tampa was as mind-numbing to me as always. The nearly six mile drive just to get to the interstate had enough stoplights to make it feel like a trip five times as long, and from there you could go two ways, either over the Sunshine Skyway bridge into St. Petersburg, or continue straight up 75.

If you went through St. Pete, you still needed to take one of two bridges into Tampa. The Gandy dumped you south of downtown, where the land-locked geography made it difficult to get to anywhere else, and the Howard Frankland brought you in near the airport. All three bridges could choke at various points during the day.

The alternative was to skip all that and go through retirement paradises like Sun City Center, hit I-275 east of Tampa and backtrack into the city from the east. It was a longer route but depending on which rush hour you were closest to, it sometimes made for the best choice.

Goldy's Bar was north and east of the airport and while the bridge traffic may have been tolerable that time of day, it was still a small gamble and for no good reason I made a last minute decision to stay on I-75 and avoid the bridges. I just wasn't in the mood for the possible traffic but, as they say, one never knew.

Heading out Fruitville Road I thought I noticed a car staying a bit too close behind me. It dropped back out of sight and I knew it wasn't a black BMW. Since this was one of three main east-west routes to and from the interstate from Sarasota, a great number of cars heading in the same direction on this road was par for the course. I looked for it once I turned on the freeway but as far as I could see it had disappeared.

Seventy minutes later I turned into the parking lot of Goldy's. Eamon Stanley's truck was parked as usual along the edge of the sandy dirt, beneath the low-hanging branches of a turkey oak. I parked, took one of the burner phones from my glove compartment, and went inside.

He was sitting on a bar stool facing the door as I walked in, just as if he'd been waiting for me. He motioned me over and said something to the bar hag on the stool next to him who reached over, took his drink, and shot me an indifferent yet vaguely hostile look as she pushed past to another place at the other end of the bar.

I sat down and the bartender came right over, but stopped in front of Stanley and not me. "I need another Jack," Stanley said. The bartender looked at me and I shook my head as I pulled a twenty out of my pocket and tossed it onto the damp wood in front of Stanley.

"How are you feeling?" I asked him.

He gave a loud sort of grunt, put his cigarette in his mouth and lifted up his shirt. All I could see was an undershirt of white gauze and bandage with a few rust-colored spots poking through in different places. "Bastard got me from here to here," he said, pointing twice. "Grazed a few ribs but I'll be fine. They gave me some of these, too."

The bartender put his drink on the napkin in front of him but went away without taking the twenty. Stanley pulled out a bottle of prescription meds and poured a couple of capsules into the drink. "Percocets, they called them. Folks around here just call 'em oxy. The old ones you could crush and snort up your nose." He stirred the drink with his index finger then took a healthy swallow. "You sure you don't need anything?" he said, pointing to the bar.

"I'm good," I said. He was more talkative than usual and I chalked that up to the meds. "Listen, Eamon. Why did you jump the gun? If you had waited—"

He waved me off. "Thought I had him off guard. My mistake." He took another drink. "Also, I may have been a little too fucked up."

"I thought you didn't do that stuff when you had a job on."

"Normally I don't. You got to give me more notice, though. I had that chick coming over—"

"Okay, Eamon." Stanley had a combination of sociopathic violence and street cunning that had kept him on the loose and out of a jail cell, and because I had information on him that could dramatically change his lifestyle I had some leverage over him. It wasn't infallible but it had worked before. He just had to be one hundred percent sure I was serious.

"Just wanted to let you know I'm sorry how things turned out for you."

"Hell," he said. "I'm fine. Wouldn't mind a rematch with that son of a bitch what cut me."

"You're in no shape to—"

"I can hold a gun, Porter. And you know I can pull a trigger."

I'd been about to write off the idea I'd had in coming here but maybe I didn't have to. "You really up for another go at this guy?"

"Shit, you gotta ask?" He laid a large, dirty hand across the side of his shirt. "I got something coming to me."

"Can you be straight for tonight?"

"What do you mean?" he said, downing the rest of his opiate-laced drink.

"Lay off that stuff now."

"Fuck you—"

"I mean it. Here," I said, going back to my pocket and pulling out a hundred dollar bill. "Take this now. If you're still good in an hour, call me." I took out the burner and left it on the bar top. "I'm serious. Call me."

"You got a line on Gallo?"

"No, but he's got one on me. When he finds me, I want you there, ready to boogie."

Stanley let out a dry, rasping laugh. "Sounds like a good night to me. What did I ever do to deserve you, Porter?"

Killed two men directly in front of me, I thought. "You've got skills, Eamon. We just need to apply a bit of discipline if we're going to make them useful."

He started to laugh again, then held his side, and stopped. He drained the last of his drink. "Discipline's a damn funny word," he said. His eyes looked a bit droopy. "Hey, ever ask yourself why a woman uses so much damn toilet paper?"

I rapped the counter with my knuckles and said, "Call me in an hour. Actually, make it two hours and from Sarasota. Then we'll see how you're doing." I turned and made my way to the door.

"What, you never wondered?"

The door pulled shut behind me with a bang.

This wasn't the first time I had my doubts if Stanley were up for this. The difference now was that I wouldn't count on him as I had before. I couldn't. If he pulled himself together and could do what I need, at the very least he'd be a warm body that would help me simply outnumber Gallo. And if he couldn't straighten himself out in time? All I could do was hope. But I knew now I couldn't count on him.

CHAPTER TWENTY-TWO

I went back to my condo and took a plastic outdoor chair from my small balcony and carried it all the way down to the office. I left it on the sidewalk outside the door as I went inside and made sure everyone was gone. There was a note on my desk from Al Sutter saying he wanted to go over his new case load but that was the last thing on my mind right now.

Going back out, I locked the door behind me, planted myself on the chair and stretched my legs out in front of me. I wasn't being especially vigilant but I did keep an eye on all the cars that drove by. There was no black BMW of any model anywhere in sight but I reckoned I'd seen the last of that particular car anyway.

My watch told me it was just past six thirty. There was time. I called Trudy at her home and when she answered all I asked was if Tim were there.

"He just walked in," she said.

"Just checking," I told her, and hung up.

My hands were folded across my stomach and for a while I felt like closing my eyes, letting everything go blank, and trying to get rid of some of the constant tension that sitting there in the open made me all too aware of. But it didn't feel right, it certainly didn't feel smart, and I didn't think I could quiet my mind enough to keep my eyes shut no matter what I tried.

I was determined that something was going to give tonight, one way or the other. I couldn't have one guy come into town, mobbed up or not, and have him run roughshod over my business and my employees. He'd already cost me Gabe but I could not allow him to hurt or scare Trudy again. Those were the thoughts that kept me on edge. I forced myself not to constantly look at my watch.

The sun was lowering into the horizon beyond the taller buildings built across Sarasota Bay and with the failing light I began to feel even more vulnerable. Now I did check my watch again. A few minutes before eight. If my thinking was correct, I would have been seen by now, and watched.

I left the chair where it was, knowing I was likely donating it to someone in the homeless community, and walked slowly up the street and turned the corner, heading for Jarod's bar.

The end seat near the waitress station was open and I sat down, waiting for Jarod to come over. "How's it going, Mr. Porter?"

"Oh, not too bad," I said. "Anyone been in for me?"

"Nope," he said. "Not tonight. Bourbon?"

"What is this, a bar?"

As he poured the drink the woman on the stool to my right stood up and left with the man that had been standing on her other side. Jarod slid out a napkin and put my drink on it, the ice making an enticing clinking sound. "Could I get a whiskey over here?" I said, pointing to the newly empty stool.

"What do you need?"

"Cheapest stuff you've got."

He gave me a look but poured a quick shot and put it in front of the empty seat.

"Better add a beer to keep it company, too. Something warm." The bar was crowded, the ambient noise making it difficult to hear conversation clearly from more than a few feet away and I had to raise my voice to make Jarod hear me.

He moved down the bar a few steps and pulled a bottle of Budweiser from a box beneath a drawer. "This do?"

"Perfect."

I sat like that, nursing my bourbon slowly, while the two drinks next to me kept the empty seat warm. Ten minutes later it was filled.

"This is for me, I take it." Rico Gallo slid silently onto the stool and reached for the whiskey. He held it to his nose, sniffed it, and looked at me.

"Drink it," I told him. "I would."

Without taking his eyes off me he downed it in a swallow.

"Any good?" I asked. It was an effort to keep things steady and keep myself seated when a good part of me wanted nothing more than to pummel the man into the floor for what he'd done to Trudy.

"Probably not," he said. "But I could never tell the good stuff from the bad anyway."

Jarod came down and I pointed at my glass. Without any words, he took it away and replaced it with a fresh bourbon.

"You crossed a line."

"I know." He took up the beer bottle but didn't drink. "But I could have done so much more."

"I would have killed you."

"That's so cute that you think so," Gallo said. "We should talk."

"That's why I'm here. To find out what you really want."

He looked at me closely. I'd turned so that we could face each other more directly. If he made a move, I didn't want to be caught unawares. "You know who I am."

"I know Gallo's not your real name. I know you work for the Gambinos under John Maroni. At first I thought you were after Edwin Holmes but then you stuck around after he took off."

"That it?"

"No."

He was wearing a light colored suit, with one button fastened. He chuckled.

"You've been pulled in on suspicion of murder but so far nothing's stuck. You're not Italian or you'd probably have been made by now and not running around like someone else's donkey. This probably pisses you off. Your kind always takes it that way. You're about a hundred pounds too light for that life, anyway, so clearly someone's not passing you the pasta."

His naturally sharp features narrowed even more. "You need to be careful."

"Tell me why you're still here."

Without taking his eyes off mine, Gallo took a pull from the warm beer, made a face despite himself, then put it back on the bar. "Ask me a question."

"You have the letter," I said. "Not the original, but still, you know what it says. If you were after the book it came from, or even Holmes, you would have left town. Especially after I told you Holmes was dead."

He nodded slowly, once, his eyes slow to blink as he kept watch on my face.

"If it's not the letter you want, what else could it be?"

I waited through two long blink cycles. It seemed like he was staring through my eyes. Slowly he picked up the Budweiser and took another slow pull.

"Give me the original," he said.

"So it is the letter. Go to hell."

"Not even for the girl?"

My flinch betrayed me. He knew that meant something. I hadn't expected him to be that direct.

"She doesn't know anything. And her husband's a cop."

Another dry chuckle. "Playing with fire, then, aren't you? But why take a chance? Give me the original letter and I will leave town directly. None of you will ever see me again."

"I've thought about it."

"Of course you have. So will you give it to me?"

What did this case really mean to me anyway? I might be able to get rid of him with this one gesture but I still wanted answers, damn it. He's stacked up too many bodies. "I'll consider it," I said, and I would. "But first you have to tell me why it's so important to you, especially when you already know what it says."

He sat back on the stool, propping one arm on the bar, thinking. "I could take it from you."

I shook my head slowly. "I don't see how."

Gallo frowned. "How much do you know about the men I work for up north? New York and New England."

McKay's rundown came to mind. I started repeating it to Gallo but he slapped the bar and stopped me. "You don't know a thing."

"Fine," I said. "You want the letter, you tell me what I don't know."

He played with the beer bottle again, took another small swig, then set it back down. "It won't do you any good but I can tell you what every soldier on the street knows. I've been watching you. And that stunt at the guest house when I had your man showed me who you were. Would you really have killed me?"

I sipped my bourbon.

"I will have that letter."

"Let's hear it," I said.

He looked around the bar, studying the people seated in the booths and at the tables. Then he made a decision. "Let's go for a drive."

"I'm not getting in a car with you."

A shrug. "Then we walk."

I dropped a bill on the bar and ignored Jarod's questioning glance. Gallo and I walked out of the bar single file, him leading, me in back. On the sidewalk he asked, "Which way to the ocean?"

I nodded toward the bay where there was a long paved walking path along the shore. "Head that way. It's as good a direction as any."

Slowly he turned and I stepped up next to him and we started a slow pace westward, both of us with hands in our pockets, both of us always watching the other.

"You know about the New England Mafia?" he asked.

"Just that there was one."

"Oh, there still is," Gallo said. "These organizations have been around for over a hundred years. They're not going anywhere. Too much money, too much power. As long as that's so, there will always be people to fight over it. On both sides of the law."

"I'm only interested in your side."

Another dry chuckle. "Then you are a fool. It makes no difference. Years ago a very powerful man ran the New England Mafia. He was from Boston but moved to Providence when he was still young. The power shifted back and forth between cities but he was the one always in command. Loansharking was big in those days, bookmaking, and a few other things."

"We talking about Calello?"

He nodded. "All men such as he wear constant targets. From the state police to the FBI to ambitious rivals. It is not always possible to remain free. When Joe Calello died, he'd spent forty six years of his life behind bars. Forty six. And all the while he remained on top."

That meant Calello would have been boss at the time the letter had been written but I didn't know what significance that held.

"Calello's underboss was a man named Nicky Bolano. Traditionally, when the head of the family retires or can no longer function, control would go to the second in command. But Joey C didn't trust Bolano because of some things that had happened in the past."

"What things?"

"It's not important to this story."

"What about Joe Junior? I thought blood relatives usually got consideration."

"They do, they do," Gallo said. "But Junior was no mobster. A second-rate businessman at best. But that's not to say he didn't want the job."

"What happened?"

"Joey C left word with New York that when he went, he didn't want Bolano. He wanted a man named Salvator Acardo. Bolano did not take this well. He showed great disrespect by telling his crew to stay away from Joey C's wake and funeral. He didn't even go himself. A lot of people thought there would be war. New York wasn't happy."

We got to the end of the block. I gestured that we go forward, and we waited for a car to pass and then kept moving.

"The authorities stepped in. They had placed illegal wiretaps in Bolano's lawyer's office and indicted him and his lieutenants on any number of charges. Acardo stepped forward, the way Joey Calello had planned, and for a few months there was peace."

"A few months?"

"Acardo was also arrested. You see, the Feds weren't following the rules. And people had been talking. As they got more of the old-timers off the street, young guys were needed to fill the void. They hadn't been brought up right. They were all about themselves and they didn't know how to keep their mouths shut."

"What about Jewish ones?"

There was a flash of anger but otherwise no response.

"Who finally took over?"

Gallo gave another one of his low chuckles. "The businessman. Everything fell into Junior's lap. New York, out of respect for his father and tradition, allowed this to happen. Two of Junior's lieutenants, though, went to Queens and asked for permission to whack their new boss. They were looking to advance faster than in the old days."

"That's some world you live in, Gallo."

He stopped walking, looked as if he might say something off topic, then turned back to the bay and continued on.

"Gotti told them no, said they had to learn to live with the situation. Once a man like that lays down a decision, it has to be followed."

"Yeah, I know. Or else."

Gallo ignored me. "The only problem was that now so many soldiers had been taken off the streets, Junior's crew was too small. He planned an induction ceremony to bring in new members. But at least one of these was an informant. The FBI had bugged the basement of the house where the meeting was to be held. They taped the whole ceremony. They got everything they had denied had existed for years. Finally the government had irrefutable proof that organized crime in the form of La Cosa Nostra was real."

So far Gallo had confirmed everything McKay had told me from his trip to New England.

"I'll bet that didn't make Junior look good."

"Joey Junior was demoted to soldier by Gotti himself. Control now fell to Carmine Mannolio, old, a man too afraid of his own shadow. He moved back to Providence and rarely left his house. He kept his own operations local, afraid to trust anybody. The Irish ended up taking over Boston but they also paid tribute to Carmine every month."

We crossed the last road before the water at a light, and made our way to the sidewalk that followed the shoreline. We turned south and walked for a few minutes until the traffic noise was lessened. Gallo went on, "Without a strong leader, other factions tried to take more for themselves. It was a very messy time, many walls got painted. Informants were everywhere, allegiances kept shifting, and when Gotti went away to prison, no one knew who to trust."

"Where were you in all this?"

"I'm not important to this story," he said flatly. "Now, you need to tell me what you know about Edwin Holmes."

"You haven't given me what I asked."

"I gave you enough to figure it out."

I thought about this as we walked on, aware of Gallo's impatience. If he wasn't lying, he'd given me a snapshot of the recent history of the New England Mafia. I didn't know why I should care. My interest had been in Edwin Holmes and so far I still had no idea what tied the two together.

"First you tell me why Holmes is a part of all this. He was no gangster."

It was Gallo's turn to hesitate. "You know he was a banker?"

"Of course," I said.

"Do you know how valuable access to a bank can be to the underworld?"

"Be specific."

He stopped and we faced each other. "I hardly think so. There are details of things I cannot go into."

He'd told me about the past and about the players involved, but he hadn't given me any real information as to what they were actually up to. He was sly and I could see his point but I wanted more.

"Holmes wasn't his real name."

Gallo waved his hand. "He was Slovenian. Is this the most interesting material you have?"

I hoped not but I wasn't about to say so.

"Why did Holmes come to you?"

"I have no idea."

"And he did not tell you the significance of the letter in the book?"

"If I knew that...."

"What did he want you to do?"

This was something I'd been wrestling with more and more since Holmes had been killed. It almost seemed as though he thought he'd be safe if he got rid of the document, but then why leave it with me without instructions on what to do with it? I didn't see how that made sense.

"He was a bit vague on that. I think he wanted me to hide it."

"But you do still have it?"

I almost said of course I do, but then I thought about Holmes's secretary. "Holmes sent Endo Robbins to get hold of me, didn't he? He wanted Robbins to give me the letter?"

"Only Robbins didn't carry it with him."

Again he just told me Robbins was dead. "You checked carefully, I imagine."

There was enough light from a passing street lamp that I could see his eyes narrow. He told me the story of what he had done to Robbins on the boat and I felt a chill. "If there had been a letter I would have found it." We took a few more steps. "There's more to it, of course. I believe Holmes had sent his secretary to actually hire you."

"But Gabe Keller got you a copy of the letter. And you're still around. What's so important about the original? Is it in code, is there secret writing I missed, or—"

Then it hit me: I'm an idiot.

"Holmes was killed," I said. "You didn't know that until I told you."

Gallo stopped moving.

"And now you need the original. If you hadn't known Holmes was dead, you would have taken the transcript and gone right back to John Maroni in New York. Isn't that right?"

"What difference does that make to you?" he asked. "You yourself are aware of the contents and you don't need the original for anything. Retaining possession can only cause great pain to yourself and those around you."

"How so?"

"Gabe Keller may not have made such a big impression but really, are you so ready to forget your Trudy Westland?"

I took a step closer to him and he stood his ground. From somewhere to my left another figure stepped into the light from behind a group of bushes.

"Take it easy, Porter," came the familiar growl. At his side he held a matte-finished black handgun against his leg.

"You have good timing for once, Stanley," I said, stepping back. I reached to my back waistband for the P220.

Stanley said, "Hold up there, cowboy. Keep your hands where we can see them."

"*We?*"

Gallo gave a thin-lipped smile and gestured toward Stanley who backed slowly away from the sidewalk. As I began to walk forward, Gallo moved behind me and relieved me of the Sig. "Lift your pant legs, please," he said.

I kept walking and lifted first one then the other. I wasn't carrying anything else.

"Shall we get that letter now?" Gallo said.

CHAPTER TWENTY-THREE

The three of us walked back the way I had come with Gallo. I was more than a little pissed.

"How you doing, Eamon? Any trouble picking us up at the bar?" I asked him.

"Nope," he said, staying close to my right side, with Gallo slightly behind and to my left. "He found you just like you said."

"You mean Gallo here, the man who sliced your ribs and left you to bleed out on the floor of another man's house?"

"Yeah, well, thanks to you I survived."

From behind me, Gallo said, "The man made a better deal. Now shut up."

There wasn't much else I could do. I was unarmed and if I moved on Stanley, Gallo had me covered from behind. If I tried anything on Gallo, I'd be turning my back on Eamon Stanley. My chances were effectively zero either way.

I tried to think of a way out. Once they had what they wanted, they may not kill me. I didn't see the point and they'd have to go to the trouble of either disposing of my remains or put up with McKay and Trudy taking the whole thing public. I was pretty sure the last thing the mob wanted down here was attention. Gallo had gone to great pains to be discreet thus far. I hadn't forgotten that the body of Endo Robbins was never found, and Holmes's caretaker's death had been in the process of being made to look like an accident. But there was nothing that said I couldn't have accidents, too.

Before we got to the office I could drop my keys down a storm sewer. Or I could get us inside and punch in the wrong alarm code. That could keep them from getting the letter but I didn't know if that would do anything to keep me alive or to ensure that Trudy Westland would stay safe. Gallo was too cunning and cold-blooded a bastard.

And if I just gave them the original letter? Would that be so bad? It surely meant more to them than it did to me at that point and it might actually keep me alive. Gallo had to assume I wasn't the only one at my agency who knew about Holmes and I couldn't see him trying to take everyone else out. Without the letter, and without knowing why it was important or how it even related to Holmes, I probably wasn't actually much of a threat.

On the other hand, Rico Gallo was a professional killer. Eamon Stanley did it because he enjoyed it. If Gallo was paying Stanley enough to force his obedience, I might have a chance. Or Gallo might take me out anyway, thinking no one else at my agency would dare to step up and connect my death with the mob, but that seemed weak. The most likely scenario might be for Gallo to have Stanley kill me, and then kill Stanley himself. No one in my office knew anything about Eamon Stanley and Gallo could rid himself of two potential witnesses.

Or a giant meteor could enter the atmosphere and take us all out in the next twenty seconds.

We passed the rest of the way without talking. There didn't seem as if there were anything else to say.

When we got to my office I stopped in front of the door. Stanley was standing to my left side, Gallo was still behind me. "Open it," he said.

I reached into my pocket and took out my keys. The storm sewer option had never seemed all that realistic anyway. They'd have probably cut off my hand and used it as a hook to try to bring them back up.

As I inserted the key into the lock, another man stepped out from around the corner of the building. He must have been waiting in the parking lot. Who the hell was this?

"Porter, is that you?" came the loud, slurring words.

"Who the fuck is that?" said Gallo, squeezing closer. Stanley grabbed my arm.

It took me a minute to place the voice. As he stepped closer into the light, I finally recognized him. There was a sudden sinking feeling in my stomach.

"Get out of here, Tim."

I felt the pressure of Gallo's gun barrel against my spine. "Who?"

"He's a cop," I said, knowing the reluctance of a Mafia man to whack a policeman.

Tim Westland kept coming, seemingly oblivious to the presence of the two men with me. Clearly he'd been drinking. "Are you fucking my wife, Porter?" he asked.

Christ. "No, Tim." I needed to defuse this new situation. "Why don't you go home and talk to Trudy? She can tell you."

He stopped, about twenty feet away. He spread his feet wide and swayed slightly, answering any question about his sobriety.

"Don't you say her name, you son of a bitch. Don't you dare say her name."

Stanley hadn't moved. My keys were hanging from the door lock. Behind me Gallo said, "Get rid of him."

At this point I was trying to save his life. "Where is she now, Tim? Maybe you should go to her."

"I told you not to talk about my wife!" The alcohol in his voice was obvious now. He was not in uniform but a .38 revolver came up in his hand, pointing at the three of us, me in the center. "Don't you talk about my wife!"

Before I could say anything else he squeezed the trigger. I felt Gallo get low behind me. There was a small explosion of brick dust from the wall five feet in front of us as the bullet hit and ricocheted closer. Stanley spun around, grabbing his shoulder. His own gun fell to the ground.

Westland fired again, this time the bullet hit Stanley solidly in the back with a wet, meaty sound. I stepped on Stanley's gun as I heard Gallo take off running down the sidewalk. Another shot, and if I hadn't been dropping and turning, the sound of it whizzing over my head told me Westland would have had me, too. I moved my foot and scooped up Stanley's gun. He was half sitting, half stooping, his bleeding body propped against my office door.

I raised Stanley's gun. "Put it down, Tim! Now!"

"Fuck you!" he screamed and squeezed off two more rounds before I sighted one into his right thigh. He dropped his revolver and fell forward on to his face, his hands covering the burgeoning hole in his quadriceps.

I kept my eye on his gun and moved forward, kicking it aside. He lay there, groaning and bleeding. Doing a lot of bleeding. The wound looked bad. "You son of a bitch," he repeated, his eyes going glassy, either from booze or shock. Either way it wasn't good.

"Take it easy, Tim," I said. "I'm going to call an ambulance."

I could have used my cell phone but I didn't. Instead I picked up Westland's revolver and tucked it in my belt. I had no idea what condition Eamon Stanley was in and I ran back to check. So far the street was empty but it wouldn't stay that way long.

Stanley was on his chest, face turned to the side. I could hear air being forced through the hole in his back, a bloody froth staining his shirt. Quickly I knelt over him, putting his gun in his own hand then pointing it back in Tim Westland's direction and pulling the trigger, roughly aiming for the wall of the building on the other side of the parking lot.

I left the gun with him and unlocked the office door, turning on the lights and tapping the new security code into the alarm system's pad. I ran down the hall to the bathroom and ripped my shirt off, then scrubbed both arms with soap and water up to my elbows. Then I scooped up my shirt and ran back to the front, made the turn and went into my office, again turning on the lights. I turned the dial to my safe and opened it as fast as I could, shoved the shirt deep into the back, then shut it and spun the dial. I'd turn it to twenty-three later.

With the phone on my desk I called 911 and said there'd been gunshots fired outside my office. It looked like two men had been shot. They wanted me to stay on the line because that's what they always do, but I hung up and went to my private bathroom, where I took the last clean shirt from a hanger and slipped it over my head. Then it was back outside to wait for the cops.

When they did a GSR test on Stanley, they'd find he'd fired his gun. If they were suspicious of me the test on my hands and arms would come back negative: I'd washed the gunshot residue off in the sink. I slipped the burner phone out of Stanley's back pocket and put it in mine. Then I took Stanley's gun from his hand and put it on the sidewalk against the building along with Tim Westland's gun. Stanley's breathing out the back trick had almost stopped. I probably would have helped him if I could but I had no idea what to do other than apply pressure but if that was how he was getting air.... It was a bad wound.

I walked up to where Tim Westland was lying in a growing puddle of his own blood. You son of a bitch, I thought. I found myself wishing in a sort of abstract way that he'd bleed faster.

"Tim?" I called his name several times. He didn't seem quite unconscious but he was far from responsive. I thought about putting pressure on his wound and then I said screw it. I'd already changed shirts. I ran back inside, back into my office, and grabbed the blanket that I kept there on those occasional nights when I slept on the couch. The air was loud with sirens now as I rushed back outside and draped the blanket over Westland.

A patrol car screeched to a halt in front of us, with two more just behind. The first cop came out, drew his gun, and shouted at me to stand up slowly. I moved the way he wanted me to and did precisely what he said. His partner came around the car and patted me down, pronouncing me clean.

"Their guns are over there," I said, pointing to where I left them.

"How'd that happen?" the first cop asked.

"I put them there."

An EMT truck pulled up and two first responders jumped down and began pulling boxes of equipment out with them. The cops asked me to sit in the back of their car and I said, "Yes, officer," as they checked out the carnage on the sidewalk.

It was going to be a long night. But at least I was alive. I was pretty sure Stanley wasn't going to make it and as for Tim Westland, I didn't give him much thought at all.

At least until it finally hit me that just fifteen minutes ago I had shot Trudy's husband. He'd left me no choice and I knew it had to be done but at that moment I had no idea what that would come to mean.

SECOND HALF

CHAPTER TWENTY-FOUR

I was sitting in the hospital in a waiting area outside the secure doors of the surgery center. I'd spent too much time with a pair of detectives from the violent crimes unit answering their questions. They didn't know me and I didn't know them. I wasn't sure if that made things easier or not.

There hadn't been much time to come up with a story and at this point whether it hung together or not, I was stuck with it. Changing details now could only jam me up.

When they'd asked me what happened I told them I'd been inside my office, working late, and that the outside door was locked. One minute I heard a pounding on the glass, the next I heard the gunshots. I came out of my office, ran down the hallway to the front door, and saw one man lying on the ground, face down on the sidewalk. It wasn't until I'd unlocked the door and stepped outside that I saw the other man further up the street.

Did I recognize either of the victims?

I didn't think I knew the first man, though I said I didn't get a good look at his face. He hadn't seemed familiar. The other man I identified as Tim Westland, the husband of one of my employees, and a police officer.

Did I have any idea what these two men were doing outside my office at night, well past office hours?

Didn't know that either.

Do you think they were looking for you? Did they have reason to think you'd be there?

I didn't know. Maybe they weren't coming to see me.

Why else would they be there?

No idea. Maybe Tim thought his wife was working late and was coming to see her. Maybe Tim knew the other man or was meeting him there. Could have been bad blood, some sort of argument; I didn't know. Anything could have happened.

If Tim Westland was looking for his wife, why would he come to your office?

She works there. Seems logical.

Did Mrs. Westland often work late hours at your office?

I shrugged. It's happened before. As far as I knew Trudy had always let her husband know when it happened.

And how well did you know Tim Westland?

Me? I've met him a few times but not enough to socialize.

The two detectives looked at their notebooks, looked at each other. I knew there were other questions they were planning on asking but they'd hold off until they got what they could from Tim. Or from Trudy. If they believed I was involved they'd try to trip me up.

They told me they'd had enough for the time being but I knew they'd be checking up on me as much as they could. I wondered if they'd find their way to Marty Ables. Missing persons was a long way from violent crimes and if Marty didn't have a reason to volunteer any information, I hoped he simply wouldn't.

Trudy came rushing in a few minutes after I'd been left alone. The uni that brought her got off at the elevator and then took up position by the door. He'd probably been told to keep an eye on her but that wasn't what I needed right then.

"Scott!" she said, rushing forward and into my arms. I tried to hold her in what looked like a comforting embrace instead of the full-on body crush that seemed so natural. I also wanted to stay like that, feel her heat, her emotion, then look into her eyes and tell her I'd make everything all right. Instead, after a few seconds I pushed her gently away and held her at arms' length in front of me. Damn it! What would a concerned boss and friend say to an employee whose spouse had just been shot?

"Are you okay?" Nothing I could have said wouldn't have sounded as lame. I was lying on too many levels now.

She creased her forehead, searching my eyes. Then, as if she remembered the officer by the elevator door, she stepped back and said, "I—I don't know yet. How are you doing?"

"I'm fine, Trudy."

"They said the bullet hit his femur. That he might lose his leg."

"It's a tough break, sweetheart."

She backed away, completely out of my reach, and turned toward the windows that looked into an empty hallway. At the end of it was a set of electronically controlled doors that required a hospital badge to get open.

"Who was that man? The one that shot him?"

I shook my head.

"You don't know him?"

"No."

"Then why was he—"

"Trudy, why was Tim coming to my office?" And with his gun drawn, I wanted to add.

She sat down in the nearest chair and I walked over to sit next to her. The officer by the elevator hadn't moved, though his eyes were still on us. The rest of the room was empty but I knew the detectives would be back.

"We—we had a talk," she said.

"About what?"

"Jesus, Scott. Married people just talk sometimes, okay? Then he told me he wanted a drink. I went to get him one from the kitchen and then I heard the front door slam. By the time I made up my mind to go after him, it was too late. He was already driving away."

"Did you know he was coming to see me?"

"No!" she said. "I didn't even know where you were! I would have called you if I did."

I lowered my voice so only she could hear, and I sat back so Trudy's head was between my face and the officer's line of sight. "Was he planning on shooting me?"

"What are you talking about, Scott?"

I'd said too much. If that hadn't occurred to her then I didn't want to be the one to put the thought in her head. "The cops are going to want to know why he was coming to my office."

"Did they ask you?"

"I told them I didn't know. That maybe he was looking for you."

"I was at home. The gate guard will know we both were." She turned to look at me. "What should I tell them?"

This was the wrong time to try to concoct a story or coordinate a lie. And probably a very bad idea regardless. No matter what Tim would tell the two detectives, we wouldn't have any idea what it would be until he woke up. He was drunk off his ass when I shot him so I had no idea what that would do to his head. I almost said that to Trudy but then I realized I was supposed to have been in my office at the time of the shooting.

"Tell them the truth," I said. "Always tell them the truth."

She gave me a strange look, and then nodded. I wished I knew what was going on in her mind. She turned away from me and blew her nose gently with a tissue she was already holding. Then she got up and walked to a garbage can by the elevator, dropped it in, and dug another out of her purse as she walked back toward me.

"Have you been in to see him?" she asked.

"No."

The elevator door opened again and the two detectives I'd spoken with walked out. The two of them walked up to Trudy and introduced themselves. "Mrs. Westland, I'm Detective Sergeant Beck, this is Detective Sergeant Morris."

"How do you do," Trudy said.

Beck looked at me and I got the feeling he was asking me to leave. That was fine, and I'd be happy to go, but they were going to have to say the words.

"When was the last time you saw your husband today, Mrs. Westland?"

She glanced at me but I didn't meet her eyes. "Well," she said, "we had coffee this morning before he left for work. Everything was the same as it always was, nothing unusual. Then this evening, he was already home when I got back from work."

Off to her right, Morris was writing things in a notebook.

"Everything all right at home, Mrs. Westland?"

"Um, yes, everything was fine. Why do you ask?"

"What did you talk about when you two were together this evening?"

She blew her nose again. I had the impression she was stalling but I hoped that was just because I knew her so well.

"Nothing out of the ordinary," Trudy answered. "He wasn't in a great mood, so the conversation was a bit strained."

"Not in a great mood?" repeated Beck. "What do you mean by that? Did the two of you argue?"

"No, nothing like that. We never really argue all that much, about anything. We just—talked." She made a motion with her tissue. "And then we didn't."

"Why did he leave the house?" Morris asked.

Trudy turned her head to look at him. "I don't know," she said. "I wasn't aware he'd gone until I heard his car drive away and went to the front window to check."

The two detectives looked at each other. "Why would Sergeant Westland have driven to your office?" asked Beck. "Would he have had a reason to see Mr. Porter?"

"I can't think of one," Trudy said. And if she could she was too cool to show it.

"Could he have gone there to meet anyone else?"

"I—I wouldn't know. I suppose he could have."

"Were your husband and Mr. Porter on good terms, Mrs. Westland?"

"They really didn't know each other all that well," she said. "I mean, they've met before, but I don't think Tim knows Scott any better than I know Tim's supervisor."

Morris kept writing. Beck said, "So you didn't talk a lot about each other's work?"

"No, not really," Trudy said. "I mean, my work is mostly confidential and Tim never seemed that interested in discussing what he did. There were some office politics he'd complain about from time to time, but...."

"We all complain about those," Beck said, a slight grin appearing on his face for the first time. "Have the doctors spoken with you yet?"

"Yes, downstairs," she said. "They told me they'd find me as soon as Tim was out of surgery."

Morris closed his notebook and slid it back into his pocket. Beck turned and looked at me as though wondering why I was still there. "Is there someone we can call for you, Mrs. Westland? Do you need anything from us?"

"No, thank you. I'm fine for now, I think."

He nodded toward the man by the elevator. "Officer Dykstra is going to stay here with you, ma'am. If you need anything, anything at all—"

"I'll be fine," Trudy said. "Thank you. You've been very kind." She looked at Morris. "Both of you."

"Yes, well," he said, looking over at me again. I had the distinct feeling I was about to become a research project down at headquarters. "We try to look after our own." He took a card out of his pocket and handed it to her. "If there's anything else I can do—"

Trudy took the card, glanced at it, then covered it in her hand. "Thank you, Detective."

"Ma'am," he said. He nodded toward his partner and they walked back to the elevator. They said a few words to Officer Dykstra, who bobbed his head up and down, then they pushed the elevator button. The room was quiet until the chime sounded indicating the car had arrived. The doors opened, closed, and the two detectives were gone.

"Scott—"

"You don't have to say anything, Trudy." Our voices were low, and didn't carry to Dykstra.

"Why would that man shoot Tim?"

I looked into her eyes. They were slightly moist with a trace of running mascara.

"I don't know," I said.

She turned and looked at Officer Dykstra. He stared back, expressionless.

"Is he here to watch us?"

"Probably," I said, without looking at him. "At least partially."

"You should go then."

"I'm not going to leave you, Trudy."

"Yes, you are. I don't want anyone talking."

"About what?"

She looked as though she were about to say one thing, then another, and finally changed her mind altogether. "Please go home."

"Trudy—"

"Scott. Really. There are other people here to take care of me."

"Then let them," I said. "Gallo's still out there."

She nodded.

I don't know what I wanted. For her to tell me she was glad the son of a bitch got hurt. For her to say that maybe this would bring things to a head. I wondered if Beck and Morris would investigate Tim and find out he had been cheating on his wife. And I wondered, for the thousandth time, what Tim would tell them when he was finally able.

"Okay," I said, and stood up. I reached over and squeezed her shoulder. She put her hand on mine and said, "Shoo."

"Let me know how Tim's doing," I told her.

She nodded.

When I stepped out of the elevator on the ground floor Beck and Morris were standing there. Whether they were waiting for me or not I didn't know. "The other man, the one that shot Tim Westland? He just died."

I didn't know what I was supposed to say to that. Neither did Beck and Morris I was sure, and that was probably why the ambush. "I hope Sergeant Westland isn't in too much trouble for killing him," I said, and walked out.

I should have been smarter than that I decided as I walked into the heavy humid air. Then I tried to remember where I'd parked my car.

CHAPTER TWENTY-FIVE

I felt like running away. My office was in a small cove of nearly featureless one-story office buildings. We were several blocks south of the feeders into Main Street, which was where all the retail shops were. Those streets offered direct line access to the easy access points across the busy road that fronted the waterfront. I had no doubt people would have heard the shots, or perhaps the echo of the shots, but I couldn't imagine anyone would have been able to accurately pinpoint where they'd come from. So I was fortunate there were no witnesses. At least as far as I'd seen or been told.

It was an ideal location for a private detective's office. Many of our clients would have preferred not to be seen walking into our office, though in truth it wasn't likely anyone who may have been passing by would have cared. When prospective clients came in to see us, there were already too many unwanted notions banging around in their heads.

After I'd left the hospital I drove back to the office with the radio off. There was a patrol car parked by the curb. From the doorway to the side of the building adjacent to the parking lot was a barricade of police tape strung along the sign posts. They formed an irregular line along the street that flapped in the incoming ocean breeze. As I came out of the parking lot I stepped away from the sidewalk and into the street. The cop inside the car was watching me as I held up my hand and stopped three feet away. He rolled his window down, said, "Can I help you?"

"Okay if I go inside my office?" I asked, pointing with my key to the door.

"And you are...."

"I own it."

"Stay outside the tape."

"Yes, sir."

I did as he asked, looking at the fresh blood stains that stood out against the dirty sidewalk. I'd expected it to look a lot worse. Bot Westland's and Stanley's body had given up a lot of the stuff.

I unlocked the door and went inside, relocking behind me, and turned the lights on as I went. I wasn't sure why I did it, other than it seemed less like hiding out that way. In any case, I wanted to be in the office when the staff arrived in the morning. They'd have questions and they should hear the answers from me. At least the ones I was willing to offer.

When I made it to my desk, the only light I turned on was the lamp next to the phone. I turned the dial of my safe so that it stopped at twenty-three, then washed up in my bathroom. I no longer had a blanket to cover me as I laid on the couch but I didn't think I'd miss it tonight. I thought about Trudy.

What had she and her husband been talking about that had driven Tim to come after me with a gun? I wished Trudy would have told me at the hospital but I knew better than to have asked, just as I'd know not to do it now if she walked into the room this minute. Trudy would tell me what Trudy would tell me. That's how she was with her personal life.

Her other personal life.

I forced my thoughts to Gallo. He was in the wind again, only this time I had no idea where he would go or how to draw him out. Would the body count finally drive him back to his masters up north? The bastard had out-maneuvered me with Stanley but that hadn't worked out well for either of them. Gallo still didn't have the original letter and I had a feeling that his boss or bosses might not be so keen to leave it in my possession, but how much longer Gallo could keep himself hidden from the authorities?

At this point I wasn't sure how much of what he'd told me about Holmes or the New England mob's org chart was meaningful, or if it had been strictly a stall tactic until we'd walked to Eamon Stanley's hiding place. I was hoping Paul McKay would have something to add when he showed up.

The last thing I thought about before I closed my eyes was Tim Westland. I'd shot people before, for good reasons and bad, and I wasn't sorry I'd shot Tim. I just didn't know what he'd say when he awoke. I was hoping he was smart enough to see what was laid out for him and take advantage of it, but if he wasn't, I might have some trouble. Probably nothing I couldn't get out of, but enough to seriously hurt my business. Enough to hurt Trudy.

Or would it? If Trudy knew I shot Tim how would she really react? I tried to imagine coming out of this well in her eyes but I didn't know if I could, and I knew I was fooling myself to try.

Let it go, I told myself. I'd had my own adrenaline surge tonight and I was feeling the drain of the aftermath. I rolled over, facing the back of my couch with one arm beneath the pillow, and tried to empty my mind. Eventually that got me to sleep but it didn't keep the nightmares away.

Both Steph and Al Sutter came into my office the next morning, waking me up. I pulled myself into a sitting position and wiped my face with my hands.

"What the hell happened out there?" Sutter said. Steph was holding her arms crossed against her body as she asked, "Are you okay?"

I gave them the same explanation I'd given the cops. It seemed to relax them somewhat.

"How awful," Steph said. "How is Trudy doing?"

"She seemed to be holding up when I left her at the hospital," I said. Suddenly I didn't want to talk about this any more. "Why don't you call her on her phone? If she's at the hospital, tell her you'll bring her some breakfast. Keep her some company."

"I will," she said, and hurried out.

"And you're okay?" Sutter asked.

"I'm fine." I fluttered my hand, remember the P220 that Gallo had made off with. I tried to think if that could be tied to anything for the police. Sutter was still talking and I had to stop him and say, "What? I'm sorry, Al, I was distracted."

"Nothing," he said. "It'll keep." He started backing toward the door. "How about you, you need anything? I'll go put some coffee on...."

"Good idea."

I got up, stashed my pillow in the bathroom and remembered I was wearing my last clean shirt. Fine, so I'd be wrinkled for a while. I'd just finished brushing my teeth and slicking back my hair when Paul McKay came in.

"What's up, man?"

"Sutter fill you in?"

"Just now. You okay?"

"Worried about Trudy a bit, that's all. Shut my door and come back in here, will you?"

He did that and we met at my desk.

"How was the trip?"

McKay scratched along his chin, smiling slightly. "Interesting. At least until I got run out of town."

"What happened?"

"Not a lot, actually. Fortunately I don't think I was there long enough."

McKay was a good man, a good detective, but he wasn't about to put himself out there for someone else's idea of what was worth risking his own health. He worked for his paycheck and because he liked the job. He was diligent, had an eye for detail, and enjoyed connecting dots, as long as he could see them clearly. He wasn't like a private detective in the movies. He wasn't a knight errant, a crusader, he was more like a researcher on the hoof. If he could write worth a damn and if there were still newspapers like there used to be, he would have made a top-notch investigative reporter.

He told me about driving south to Providence from Boston. The first stop he made was at the police headquarters building downtown. He identified himself as a private detective from Florida and wanted to talk to someone about a man named Rico Gallo, or possibly last named Bronstein or Bronfeld. They told him to wait, then brought him back to talk to a detective named Cooperman.

"I had the feeling he wasn't too happy to see me."

"What did he tell you about Gallo?"

"That he'd never heard of him. I told him I thought I'd ask around and he asked me where. I asked him if Federal Hill would be a good starting place, and he blanched."

"Federal Hill was the home of the New England Mafia."

"Still is, I think. Maybe. I don't know. When I left the police station I headed over to Antwells Avenue."

"Find anything?"

"A giant pine cone hanging from an arch. Bakeries. Italian restaurants. And two cars that followed me everywhere I went. I thought lunch might be a good idea so I stopped at a cafe and took a table. Three guys followed me in."

"They say anything?"

"Not a word. They stood behind me while I ordered but didn't get anything for themselves. I took a table by the door and they sat down one over. Through the window I could see three more men leaning against my rental."

"Christ—"

"So I got up, asked for a to-go box. The counterman didn't say a word. He slid my sandwich into a styrofoam container and I took it and left. When I got to the car the men backed away. I got into the driver's seat, started the car, and headed back to interstate 95 headed north. That's when you called. I didn't want them to see me on the phone so I cut it short."

I leaned back in my chair. "I'm sorry about that, Paul. At the time I didn't know—"

"Don't worry about it. Nothing happened. The question is, what do we do now?"

"Let's start with Holmes."

"First tell me this, anything new with Gallo down here?"

"Haven't seen him," I said. "Let's go out to Trudy's desk and find her files."

It took a few minutes but we grabbed everything we could find in the drawers of Trudy's desk, the ones where she kept her work in progress.

"How's she doing?" I asked Steph while we were looking for papers.

"Holding up," Steph said. "It's got to be so hard on her."

What was I supposed to say? I couldn't think of a response that didn't make me feel like a TV weatherman.

Steph made sympathetic sounds and turned to find a tissue somewhere and I hurried down the hall, McKay following behind me.

Back at my desk we spread the material across my desktop and tried to follow her notes from beginning to end. Most of it I already knew but I wanted to give McKay a chance to catch up as well, to maybe make some connections with what he'd learned on his trip.

Toward the end of the stack was a file with an empty tab, which was odd because I was used to Trudy labeling every folder. Inside were papers that showed a number of official letterheads, including one from the Department of Justice. I pulled the file into my lap and started reading. When I was through I pushed it toward McKay. "Look at this, Paul."

He took the folder, paged through it quickly and said, "Money laundering? Mortgage fraud?"

I sat back and turned my imagination loose while he read through the file more closely. It summarized an investigation into Edwin Holmes's bank. Someone at the bank had authorized the buying of existing mortgages of private homes. This was something that happened all the time in the industry. But the rate at which they had been refinanced was nearly one hundred percent. I was far from an expert in banking or finance, but this didn't look right even from my limited viewpoint. I was beginning to see exactly how important Holmes may have been to the New England Mafia, or whichever organization he was answering to.

"Imagine this, Paul," I said, and McKay lowered the file and looked at me. "Holmes's bank, or the part of it that serves as a mortgage company, buys existing mortgages from other banks or legitimate brokers, using mob money. The homes are refinanced and the owners make their payments to the new mortgage owner, Holmes, and that money gets paid back into the hands of the mob."

"Nicely cleaned and laundered."

"And as a steady income, legal on the outside."

"But rotten on the inside." He flipped through the file, stopped at several pages. "Looks like the investigation never took off." He went through some more papers. "She doesn't document how much money we're talking about here."

"She probably didn't get that far yet. But that's not the significant fact."

"Oh?" McKay said. "What is?"

"Why start an investigation into what has to be a major source of the mob's money and then stop it cold?"

"Because they couldn't prove it?"

I shook my head. "Assume it's real. Holmes is—was—real. His bank was—is—real. And Gallo is a known mob associate."

McKay leaned forward in his seat. "You've confirmed this?"

"I've done a little work myself," I said. "But think about it: the bad guys were after Holmes. And they got him."

"That shouldn't stop the investigation."

"It shouldn't," I agreed. "But it would stop Holmes."

"From doing what?"

"From doing the same thing every other real-life gangster does in the modern era: they join Team America and start squealing."

"How would turning rat stop a federal investigation?"

"Two ways," I said, holding up a pair of fingers. "One, the Feds have an asset inside the bank they don't want to expose. And two," I lowered the other finger, "there's a rat inside the G that stopped it."

This time McKay shook his head. "That's a bit of a stretch, isn't it? Would this be a crooked cop, FBI, DoJ, what?"

Paul McKay was a good detective, an excellent operative, but I never thought he had the imagination to break an outside the box case like this on his own. If he had guidance, he'd follow a trail like a crazed bloodhound. But if the trail were too well disguised, he may need a starting point handed to him first. He respected law enforcement a lot more than I did. He'd started out as a cop years ago, but didn't like patrol duty and lacked the patience to deal with the politics. He almost went the FBI route but he didn't want to leave the state and they'd told him that if accepted he'd pretty much have to go wherever they sent him.

His father was still alive, living in a nursing home in Fort Myers, and McKay wasn't ready to take that step. So he'd found me and I always counted myself lucky he had.

"What happened to you when you talked to the cops in Providence?"

"I picked up two carloads of tails." He began to rub his cheek.

"Coincidence."

"Obviously not."

"So now think bigger."

McKay tossed the file back on to the pile. "There's not enough information in there to support that, Scott."

No, but maybe there was something between the lines.

"Do you mind calling Trudy?" I asked.

"You don't want to?"

Um, no. "She's heard enough from me. Call her cell, just check on her, you know. And if she sounds, I don't know...."

"I'm not going to ask her about the file with her husband lying the hospital."

"Yeah, okay," I said. "You're right. But do call on her and make sure she doesn't need anything." The thought of Rico Gallo still out there, possibly growing more and more desperate, was making me tense. As was waiting for the fallout from the shootings of the night before, including whatever the hell it was Tim was going to say when he woke up.

I half-listened to McKay's voice as he spoke. The call lasted about two minutes and when it was done, he hung up my desk phone and said, "She sounds good."

"How's Tim?"

"Still has his leg. Apparently there's another worry about it."

"Is he awake?"

He nodded. "Trudy said they spoke for a few minutes. The doctors came in and she was asked to step outside for a minute. I got her in the waiting room."

I pictured the small, octagonal-shaped room outside the security doors that led into the intensive care unit. I tried to imagine what was going through Trudy's mind but I couldn't do it. My own was too full of Gallo and Holmes and vague feelings of guillotine blades chopping through my neck.

"What do you—" McKay said, but was cut off by the intercom sound on my phone.

Steph's voice came through, speaking rapidly. "Scott, there're some people coming to see you."

I was about to ask "Who?" when my door came open and in walked Marty Ables followed by two men in dark suits. I'd forgotten about the visit from the FBI that Ables had arranged.

"Don't let the door stand in your way, Marty," I said, standing. I extended my hand and he grabbed it firmly.

"Yeah, you know, we were in the neighborhood." He looked down at McKay. "It's Paul, isn't it?"

McKay stood, saying, "Paul McKay. Good to meet you."

"Marty Ables, Sarasota PD. This is Special Agent John Sullivan—"

A heavyset man in his early forties stepped forward. His face was fleshy, and his whole body seemed a little bit too packed into his suit to be entirely comfortable, especially in the Florida heat and humidity. A heavy hand reached toward McKay and they shook. Then the meaty hand came my way and I grabbed it with authority and said, "Scott Porter."

He nodded and stepped back as Ables said, "And this is Special Agent Dan Fitzwater."

We did the round of handshakes again. I stayed on my feet and gestured toward the couch, the only seating that would accommodate all the new arrivals.

"No, that's okay," said Sullivan. "We'll stand."

"Whatever you'd like," I said. Assholes. I deliberately took my chair and motioned Paul McKay to sit back in his. This was probably going to be it for the Holmes case. I didn't care who was doing what to who fourteen states away in the northeastern part of the country. I needed to find a way to get Gallo gone. He either had to give it up at this point, or make another run at the letter, possibly through me directly, or even through Trudy again though she was surrounded by cops at the hospital.

These two Feebs were welcome to the mess. I'd been paid. Then I could deal with what could ultimately turn into my biggest headache: the story Tim Westland would tell when he started talking. Shooting a police office never went over well, but shooting one and lying about it would bury me.

Special Agent Fitzwater said, "Perhaps you could give us a rundown on what you were doing for Edwin Holmes."

I gave Paul a "let me do the talking" look and started laying out the case, from the first phone calls to my home to Holmes's visit, and to his leaving on his private plane. Both agents had notebooks and pens in hand and each took several pages of notes. I wondered why one of them didn't listen and the other take the notes maybe that's how they were training them in FBI school these days.

"What happened to the book?" Fitzwater asked.

"Holmes took it with him."

"And the letter?"

Before I could stop him, McKay slid a copy of the transcription from the piles of paper on my desk and held it up for Sullivan to grab. He read through the copy twice, then handed it over to Fitzwater. "What about the original?"

"It's here, in my safe," I said and got off my chair and knelt in front of it. My mind was still at least half on McKay's conversation with Trudy. *He said they'd spoken alone for a few minutes, before the doctors came in.* What had Tim been telling her? What was he about to tell the cops?

I was working the dial first to the right, then spinning it back to the left, when Sullivan's voice registered, saying something about how relieved we'd feel if we didn't have the letter when Gallo comes back. Too true, I thought, working the dial back to the right.

When Gallo comes back.

I went past the third number and had to spin the dial and reset the tumblers so I could start again. "Shit," I said, rubbing my eyes. "Long night."

Slowly I began turning the dial again. I felt Sullivan step closer to my desk. *When Gallo comes back.* Was he talking about last night? That would make the most sense. When Gallo had been here before, there'd been no mention of the letter. That document hadn't become important to me until Gabe Keller had tried to steal it. But last night was different.

The thing is, how would the agents know Gallo had been here?

I made it to the final number, turned the handle, and pulled open the safe door, just far enough to allow both of my arms to reach inside. Covering the opening with my body, I pulled a stack of papers from the upper shelf inside the safe onto the floor in front of me. I heard or felt the advancing of the agents and I quickly fanned through the papers then jammed them back onto the shelf. I pushed myself away, shutting the door and spinning the knob as Sullivan hung over my shoulder.

"It's not here," I said. "Paul, check Trudy's files. Maybe she has it in one of her folders."

His eyebrows rose a quarter inch but he immediately bent forward and began gathering the manila folders to him and looking inside each one.

"What's going on?" asked Fitzwater.

"With everything that's been happening," I said, "I guess I thought I had the original when Trudy must have taken it for her research."

Sullivan's eyes weren't leaving my face. Paul McKay said, "I don't see it here."

"Look, Porter—" said Sullivan.

I cut him off. "Oh, wait a minute. I brought a box of pending case files home with me last night. After what happened out front, I wasn't sure if we were going to be allowed to open the office today." That seemed plausible. After all, there were still forty yards of police tape and a patrol car out front. "I must have stuck it in there."

Sullivan made a show of looking at his watch. "You're not the only reason we came to town, Porter. I need to see that letter. Now."

There's that good old federal authority. "Really?" I said. "Why don't you stop acting like I have to give it to you?" He started to say something but I held up my hand, cutting him off. "But I'm happy to be rid of the thing."

"The transcript isn't good enough?" asked McKay, trying to placate the agent.

"No," Sullivan said. "It isn't."

It wouldn't be, I thought. And both of us knew why.

Fitzwater stepped up and in a much less aggressive tone asked what it would take to actually get our hands on the letter.

"A quick walk over to my condo," I said. "If you gentlemen would like to wait here for me—"

"No, we wouldn't," said Sullivan, looking at his watch again. Probably for show, I thought. "Why don't we come with you? Then we can get out of your hair that much quicker."

"Fine," I said. I was hoping he would suggest that. "Paul, why don't you come along too, just in case the agents have more questions on the way."

"That's all right with me," he said, smiling. He probably hoped he could leave a good impression on at least one of them. He knew I wasn't doing a good job of it.

I gestured toward the door and our little group headed toward the exit, Agent Fitzwater in front, then Ables, followed by Sullivan, and finally McKay. I was last and as we went out, I shut the door behind me. Fitzwater and Sullivan were already to the lobby when I said to McKay, "I'm just going to run to the bathroom and then tuck Trudy's files into a desk drawer.

Keep these guys here."

"Scott," McKay said. "I can't just—"

"I need one minute, Paul. One." I turned and hurried down the hallway back to my office. I opened the door and shut it behind me. My phone was in my hand before it had closed.

I dialed Trudy's cell phone, praying she was still stuck out in the waiting room. She answered on the second ring.

"Hello, Scott." She sounded exhausted.

"Trudy, listen. I have two FBI agents here. They want Holmes's original letter. I can't give it to them."

"Why—"

"No time, Trudy. They can't even know we're talking. I need you to get down here and get it out of my safe."

"But I don't even know—"

I spat out the combination. "You got it?"

She repeated it to herself and I knew she was writing it down. "But I can't leave now. Tim—"

"Is with the doctors and will probably need to rest for a while after they're through with him." I heard McKay's voice and then footsteps coming down the hallway. I turned the door lock and headed off toward my private bathroom.

"Trudy, I really need you to do this. The whole case may depend on it."

"Scott—"

"Please, Trudy."

"Can't you get Steph? Someone else?"

"I can't trust anyone else with this, Trudy."

"Only me." I heard a long sigh. "Right now then?" she said, surrendering.

"That a girl," I told her. "Yes, right now. I can probably give you half an hour to forty-five minutes. Can you make it?"

"That's awfully tight, Scott."

The knocking had started on my outer door. Trudy could hear it through the phone.

"What's that noise?"

"They want to get going. I have to hang up."

"I'm on my way."

"I'm counting on you, girl."

She hesitated and then said, "I know." Then, "One thing, Scott. Tim was awake this morning." Then she hung up.

What the hell did that mean?

I ran into the bathroom, flushed the toilet, then ran the sink over my hands and patted them on my shirt.

"Hold on!" I shouted.

The pounding on the door subsided. I walked across the room, unlocked the door and there was Sullivan, looking at me strangely. "What are you working at, Porter?"

I pressed another wet handprint into my light green shirt and said, "I drink a lot of coffee, Agent Sullivan. I needed to go to the bathroom. That's just something I like to do in private."

He looked behind me into my office but I pushed past and said, "Let's get going. I know we all have better things to do."

I went outside the door and waited to the left of the police tape until the other four men had piled out of the building.

"How far is your place?" asked Fitzwater.

"A few blocks," I said. "Not far. We should walk it. There's not a lot of guest parking and if there are no spots it'll take longer finding a place to park and walk back then it would to just hoof it in the first place."

"That what you think?" Sullivan said to McKay.

"I don't know," he said. "I've never been there."

"This way," I said, stepping into the street to go around the cordoned area. First I had to get everyone out of there so Trudy could get to my safe. I'd figure out the rest on the way. Or so I hoped.

Marty Ables moved up and walked next to me. Keeping his voice low, he said, "What are doing, Scott?"

"What do you mean, Marty? I'm trying to get these guys their letter."

"You're fucking them around, man. You don't think they know that?"

"Relax, Marty. They'll get their letter and then they'll be on their way. Everyone will be happy."

"No one's happy." Ables looked behind him. McKay was trying to make small talk with the two FBI men but only Fitzwater was answering. Sullivan was behind the group, hands stuck into his front pockets. "It's the Federal Bureau of Investigation, Scott. You can't screw around with these guys."

"Screw around? Me?" That was me impersonating sincerity. "Come on, Marty. My client is dead. This thing is over for me."

We turned a corner and walked on in silence for a long minute. "I don't think I trust you right now, Scott."

"That's up to you, Marty."

"I think you're keeping secrets."

"I'm always keeping secrets."

"From the freaking FBI?"

I didn't answer. We walked along the block. Eventually Ables said, "After this, Scott, I don't think I can help you anymore."

"That's up to you, Marty."

We walked the rest of the way in blessed silence. I needed time to think but it seemed that everywhere I turned there was always a crowd forming.

CHAPTER TWENTY-SIX

A yellow sedan was parked facing out in one of the visitor spaces in the small parking lot near my condo entrance. The car looked familiar and I thought of my drive yesterday when I thought briefly I may have been followed on the way to the interstate. The sun was bouncing off the windshield and I couldn't identify whoever it was behind the wheel.

As our little group crossed the last street the driver gave two brief honks on his horn and a white-sleeved arm emerged from the window and made a gesturing motion. I looked around at Ables, McKay, and the Feds but no one showed any sign of recognition. I turned back to the car as the driver gave another tap on the horn.

I jogged ahead through the parking lot then walked up to the car. Gabe Keller was inside.

"How many times do I need to say it, Gabe?" I said.

"Hey, Scott." With his fleshy cheeks and sweat-stained collar he gave the nervous impression of an over-sized adolescent behind the wheel of his big brother's make out car. "You okay?"

"What are you doing here?"

I looked behind me. My little letter posse had stopped on the short sidewalk leading to the front door and was standing there, watching me.

"I've been following you a little," Keller said. "You know, in case you needed anything. And after last night—"

"What did you see?"

"Nothing, Scott, nothing. I wasn't there. Well, I was, but after, when the cops had turned up."

There was an awkward silence while I tried to decide if he was telling the truth. How could I know? If he'd seen what I had done with Eamon Stanley's gun—

"Gabe," I said carefully. "I told you we were done and I meant it. You screwed me over. You—"

"I know what I did," he said, interrupting. "That's in the past now, though. Really. I want to get back in, Scott. I miss the work. And I've never been fired before."

Or never been caught. "Go away, Gabe." I nodded toward the men waiting for me. I saw Sullivan slipping his notebook back into his pocket. "I've got to go." I dropped something into his lap and pushed away from his window.

"Scott—"

I held up a finger and cut him off. "I've got my own troubles here. Get out of here, Gabe. Now."

I backed away from the window and heard Keller start to say something else but it turned into a mutter as he started the car. The tires squealed as he pulled out of the space too fast then hung a hard right onto the street, heading northeast. Just keep going, I thought.

McKay started speaking as I came up to the impatient group. "Was that Gabe Kell—"

"Doesn't matter, Paul," I said.

"Who was that?" asked Fitzwater.

"Used to work with us," said McKay. "He's the one that went into our office with Rico—"

"Really, Paul, it's over. He's gone. Come on," I said, trying hard to end the discussion.

"Maybe your friend knows where Gallo is now," Sullivan said.

"I don't think so," I said, turning toward the door. "I think those two are pretty much done with each other."

"Why do you say that?"

"I don't know," I said. "I just do."

My keys were in my hand as I opened the glass security door and held it open until the four of them were inside. It was a small air conditioned lobby with an empty desk situated in one corner. Packages left for the tenants were piled on the floor next to it. Directly across the door was a bank of three elevators.

"Okay," I said, jangling my keys. "I'll be right down. Should just take a minute." I pushed the Up button and stood there, feeling awkward.

"Wait a minute, Porter," said Sullivan, stepping forward. "Why don't we all go?"

I squared my shoulders to him. He was a few inches shorter than me but probably fifteen pounds heavier. "I wouldn't want you to see the mess. The maid doesn't come till Friday."

McKay tried to keep the peace. "Agent Sullivan, Scott is a very private person. I've known him for six years and this is the first time I know of that he's even shown anyone where he lives."

"That's right, Paul," I said. "I'm going to have to find a new house now."

Agent Fitzwater stepped forward and said, "We can wait here, Mr. Porter. That's not a problem. It won't take long, will it?"

"Shouldn't," I said. "It's just one piece of paper." I noticed Marty Ables was keeping silent.

Sullivan still wasn't giving up. "I'm going with you. I could use a drink of water after that walk. This Florida weather's a bit different from what we get in Massachusetts."

"Good idea," I told him. I pointed to the drinking fountain set in the wall down from the elevator doors. "You don't want to get heat stroke. Paul,

why don't you come up with me. Agent Sullivan's right. Two sets of hands
might be better than one."

The elevator doors opened and I stepped in, holding them long enough
for the frowning McKay to move forward. Sullivan was moving slowly to
the drinking fountain and Fitzwater was watching him. Ables was exam-
ining his shoes.

When the doors closed Paul McKay turned to me and said, "What the
hell is going on, Scott?"

The elevator took us smoothly and quietly to the eleventh floor. When
the doors opened I pointed to the left and we moved down the hall to my
unit on the corner.

"Remember our discussion of what happened to you in Providence?"

That stopped him short. I walked the rest of the way to my door and slid
my key into the lock.

"You're saying that those guys are connected to that?"

"One or both," I said as we walked inside and let the door swing shut.

McKay looked around my place, caught himself, then lowered himself
onto a bar stool in front of the kitchen pass-through. "Are you going to
tell me about it, or what?"

"I want to, Paul. I can't do it yet, though. Not until I know more."

"But you just met these guys."

"Exactly. Which is why I need time."

I think if he didn't know me as well as he did he would have kept arguing. "I'm going to shut up and let you be the boss now," he said, clearly
not liking it. "But I'll only go so far. Do you actually have the letter?"

"It's not here, Paul. And if it was I couldn't give it to them."

"Why the hell not? Even if they are bad, they're still the FBI. They already
have the transcription. What are they going to get from the letter they don't
already have?"

"Who wrote that letter, Paul?"

"I have no idea."

"And neither do they. That's how I'm trying to keep it."

"Okay, boss. I'm not happy but you're forcing me to trust you. Right up
until they want to throw me in a federal prison. But I don't like this at all.
I'm on very uncomfortable ground here."

"Got it," I said. "That makes two of us. Now we have to figure out what
to tell them when we go back downstairs."

"You have any ideas?"

"Not many." I went around and into the kitchen. "You want anything?"

He shook his head. I pulled a clean glass out of a cupboard and filled it
with water from the tap, took a swallow.

"Marty Ables is pretty pissed," I said.

"What's the deal there?"

I downed the rest of the water and set the cup on the countertop. "We had an arrangement of sorts. But he doesn't like my actions in regards to his two friends down there any more than you do."

"You were using him like Tim Westland?"

"He was compensated. All his choice."

"This could get us all in some pretty deep shit, Scott."

"I hope not, Paul. I'm not trying to involve you in this. Well, that part of it, anyway."

"How do you know these guy aren't right? What makes them bent?"

I wanted to tell him about Sullivan's remark about "Gallo coming back" and what that had to mean but then he really would be in the middle of it. For his own good, I didn't want to put that on him.

"You're not going to tell me, are you?" McKay asked.

"I don't think it would be a good idea."

"Damn it, Scott," he said, standing up. "As long as I've known you you've always done your own thing. No one knows where you go half the time or what you're doing. The thing is, you usually get results. But right now I'm not sure whether you're acting like a good guy or a bad guy."

I'm not too sure, either, I thought, remembering shooting Tim Westland in the leg last night. And not regretting it. "It's just the way things are, Paul. I don't have anything else to tell you."

"So what do you expect from me?"

"Well," I said. "We'll go back down there, tell them it's not here."

"And then?"

"We go back to the office."

He thought about this. "They'll want to see what's inside your safe."

I shrugged. "They've seen where I live. No one sees where I live. They might as well see what's in the safe."

"Then why did you—"

"Don't ask, Paul. You can't afford to know the answers."

"This isn't what I signed up for, Scott. I thought we were friends as well as co-workers."

"I still think that."

I watched McKay's face as he struggled with what I was telling him.

"Just to be clear, you're asking me to blindly trust you?"

"I am," I said.

"And if you're wrong?"

"Then I won't bring you down with me. That's what this is about. That's all I can promise."

He thought about this for another minute. I didn't move, not wanting to break his concentration. "Is Endo Robbins dead?"

"Gallo said as much, yes."

"You spoke with Gallo? When—"

I stopped him with a look. He went back to his original thought. "Then there was Ernesto Flores. And what about that stuff outside the office last night? Was all that related?"

"Part of it," I said. "Tim Westland was an accident."

"So you know the guy who was killed?"

"Paul—"

"Why did Tim shoot him?"

"Tim was trying to shoot me."

"What? Why?"

I didn't answer that. "Gallo was there, too."

"This is too much, Scott. Way too much." He leaned forward, pressing his forearms against the counter. I waited for him. "Tell me you know what you're doing."

"One can only hope."

"Jesus, you can be an asshole." He ran a hand through his hair then wiped it against his trouser leg. "Okay, let's go face the music. I'll try not to contradict anything you say."

"Thank you, Paul."

"Just get this right, Scott."

"I don't have much of a choice."

The elevator ride down seemed to take twice as long as it had going up. When we reached the lobby Sullivan immediately asked, "You get it?"

I shook my head. "I don't understand it," I said. "Paul, are you sure you didn't miss it in any of Trudy's files?"

"You saw me look," he said. I thought I saw a bit of a pout cross his face.

"Well, it's got to be somewhere." Marty Ables looked embarrassed and I felt bad for him. Agent Fitzwater was studying my face and Sullivan looked like he wanted to go for his gun. We filed out of the small lobby and started back for my office. Sullivan began talking about federal search and seizure warrants and I let him talk, not answering the first few times he looked for a response from me.

"Look, I can't believe I'm saying this but you're welcome to search the office," I finally told him. "I only hope it's still there."

Sullivan said, "What do you mean?"

"Gallo got in once, didn't he? I thought we had everything locked down after that. Maybe I missed something."

When we got back to the office I opened my safe and stood back as Sullivan emptied its contents into a pile on the floor. He and Fitzwater went through the papers I had in there, counted the small bundle of bills I kept in cash to the tune of a few thousand dollars, not enough to worry anyone over, then went through the papers again. They shook out my dirty shirt from last night but aside from a raised eyebrow didn't comment.

"Not there?" I asked.

"Anywhere else we can look?" Fitzwater asked.

"Wherever you'd like," I told him.

"We're taking it all," Sullivan said.

"No, you're not. You can look at anything you'd like, but you're not taking anything with you. For that you'll need your warrant."

Sullivan looked away and sat at my desk and went through the files we had on the Holmes case. Fortunately I didn't file my notes and there was none of what Gallo had told me about the goings on of the New England Mafia. And Paul hadn't yet typed up his report on what had gone on during his trip to Boston and Rhode Island.

"This isn't a hell of a lot," Sullivan said, finally.

"But it is what we have."

He realized that one of them should have stayed behind while the rest of us went to my condo. Anything could have happened here, and he knew I wasn't going to give it away. Sullivan looked like he trying to figure a way to threaten me that might actually work. I just matched his stare.

Fitzwater stepped forward, looked at Marty Ables. "Perhaps we've done all we can here, gentleman. Mr. Porter, thank you for your cooperation. If that letter turns up, I'd greatly appreciate it if you'd let me know." He held out a card.

"Immediately," I said.

Sullivan stood and headed for the door. "Let's get out to the Holmes place," he said. "That can't be too far." And he was gone.

Marty Ables pushed himself off the couch, looked at me, shook his head, then followed the federal man out.

Fitzwater shook my hand first, then Paul McKay's, and said, "Hang on to that card."

"I will," I said.

"I mean it. I can help." He turned and left.

Finally they were gone.

McKay sat himself down in his usual chair, looking over the mess of files left behind. "They didn't try too hard to be tidy."

"I'll take care of it."

"So," he said, leaning back. "Where is the letter?"

I shook my head from side to side, slowly. "Why don't you go grab some lunch, Paul?" I waved my hand over the loose piles of paper covering my desk. "I've got some cleaning up to do."

He stood, hesitated, and said, "Watch yourself, Scott. There are too many bodies in this one."

I gave him a nod. He left. He was right, there were too many bodies in this case. Unfortunately I had a feeling that unless I was very careful there would be more.

As I pulled the papers into recognizable piles the thought occurred to me that if Rico Gallo really was in with the FBI guys, his next move might be to make a run at my condo. Something to think about, I thought as I kept working. There was a reason no one was supposed to know where I lived.

Too late now, I said to myself as I began forming little stacks out of loose pieces of paper. Not sure how I could have avoided that trip anyway.

CHAPTER TWENTY-SEVEN

I thought I had three main avenues to worry about. Gallo had told me about the power struggle in the New England Mafia. I believed that the FBI was compromised, and simple internet research showed me it's happened before. There's no such thing as Superman. What I didn't know was if one or both of these two FBI agents, Sullivan and Fitzwater, were not on the level. The power structure working against me was one of the worry areas.

Despite who was part of it, they clearly wanted the letter. They knew the same thing I did: the handwriting of the letter would tell them who wrote it. It was the only value the letter had left. Whether it would provide them a tool for revenge, blackmail, or possibly the continuation of a massive bank fraud operation, I didn't know.

It seemed to me that if Gallo wanted the original of the letter, and the FBI wanted the original of the letter, then they were either working with each other, thereby confirming the crooked cop theory, or they were working against each other, which could mean either a classic good guys vs. bad guys scenario, or just straight out bad vs. bad. Pick your poison.

But Sullivan had known Gallo had been at my office last night. How could that be, unless they were working the thing together?

Right now I had Gallo and Sullivan on Team Mafia. Agent Fitzwater could go either way; I didn't have enough information yet. Assuming I was correct, it stood to reason that Gallo would stand down until he communicated with Sullivan, but that could happen any time with a phone call. It was possible I'd introduced a doubt in Sullivan's mind when I suggested that since Gallo had been in the office before, when he had bought off Gabe Keller, that he may have been more successful on a return trip. At best it could sow confusion or distrust between the two, but it was little more than a blind shot in the dark. Nothing I could count on.

When Sullivan and Gallo got together it was likely that out of the two of them, Gallo would make another try for the letter. That could be through me at my condo, or worse, he could make good on his threat and go after Trudy, but the number of cops around her now should discourage that.

Whatever the case, I needed to get to her before anyone figured out this morning's deception. When I had ducked back into my office, it wouldn't take a genius to guess that I'd made a phone call. The question then was how long until they figured out who I was most likely to have called. Sullivan could even conceivably justify pulling my cell phone records.

I took out my phone and called Trudy. She answered on the first ring.

"Everything go okay?" I asked her. "Where are you?"

"I'm back at the hospital," she said, the heavy tones still weighing in her voice. "I have the letter. What would you like me to do with it?"

I wanted to ask her what was wrong besides the obvious but like ninety percent of the time a man asked a woman that question, I really didn't want to hear the answer. At least not the honest one.

I settled for asking how Tim was doing.

"Fine. He's doing fine."

Okay. Clearly the wrong question.

"Would you mind terribly if I came out there and got the letter from you?"

"Sure, Scott, that would be okay," she said. "Call me when you get here. I'll meet you at the main entrance."

"All right, Trudy. I really appreciate what you did."

"I'll see you when you get here."

I left the rest of the mess as it was and hurried out of my office. I needed to get that letter under my control before anyone beat me to it. In the reception area, Steph was talking to Al Sutter.

"Everything under control?" I asked.

Sutter said, "All good. I called in the extra guys and I think we have everything covered." He hesitated for a moment and looked at Steph before he went on. "I could use your help to make sure we're doing everything the right way."

"What do you mean?"

Steph jumped in with, "He's not sure how to code his reports for billing."

"Can't you help him with that?"

She looked at her desk. "I've never really done it myself. I've seen enough of them, though. I could try, if you like."

"Do you mind, Al?" I asked. I figured he might like the extra time working with Steph.

"If that's what you want."

"Sorry," I said. "It may not be ideal but too many other things are happening right now." I moved to the door. "Not sure when I'll be back. When Paul's done with lunch, get him to help you guys out. He'll know what to do."

"That would be a big help," said Sutter.

With one hand holding the door open, I stopped and called back to Steph: "When all those guys left earlier, did anybody say anything to you?"

"Um, yeah, one of the FBI agents wanted to know if anyone had been here while you guys were gone."

"What did you tell him?"

Steph knew enough to be shrewd. "You mean about Trudy? Nothing. It was none of his business."

I gave her a big smile. "You're on your way, kid. Good move."

"I'm not going to get in any trouble, am I?"

"I don't see how," I said, and I left, hoping it was true.

I didn't have to call Trudy when I got to the hospital. As I walked up to the entrance I could see her standing just inside the glass doors, waiting. She came right out when she saw me, an envelope in her hand. I'd been careful to be sure I wasn't followed but even so I took the envelope and slipped it quickly into my back waistband and under my jacket.

"It's good to see you, Trudy. How are you—"

Her right hand flew out from her side and slapped me across the side of my face, hard.

"You shot my husband."

I took a step back but she took a bigger one forward and cut loose again. My head hurt and my face was stinging. She knew how to hit.

"Trudy—"

She swung with her left. I hoped that meant her right was tired. I caught her wrist and felt the trembling strength. Slowly she eased back and pulled her arm away, crossing it with her right. She began pacing back and forth.

I looked around. People were looking but no one was stopping. Happy Florida. There was a plastic coated metal bench alongside the semi-circular turnaround in front of the hospital entrance. "Let's go over here," I said, turning my back and hoping she'd follow.

She did. We stood by the bench, further from the door and less likely to draw extra attention.

"You shot Tim," she said again, less angry this time, more sad.

"He tell you that?"

"Yes," she said.

"He tell anybody else?"

"Stop worrying about your own ass, Scott."

"I'm not, Trudy. I'm worried about his."

"What are you talking about? Did you shoot him, or didn't you?"

"Yes, Trudy, I shot your husband. In the leg. To stop him."

"What are you talking about? Stop him from doing what?"

"From killing me. Did he tell you that part?"

She looked shaken. "No, he didn't."

"I was out in front of the office with two other men. One was the man Tim hit, a man named Eamon Stanley."

"Who else was there?"

"Rico Gallo."

That got her to stop pacing. She sucked in a breath and stopped to look at me. "What did you have Tim doing?"

"Nothing, Trudy. You know better than that. No one from the office talked to Tim but you. I steered clear. One hundred percent. We weren't exactly best buds, you know."

"Then why was he at the office last night, Scott? Why?"

I gave her a moment, then asked gently, "You really need me to answer that?"

"You think he was coming after you? Why would you say that?"

"He came around the corner just as I was about to unlock the door to the office. He'd been waiting for me, Trudy. He must have known or guessed it was my car in the lot. He stepped onto the sidewalk, his gun already drawn. He started yelling things and then began pulling the trigger. One of his rounds got Stanley in the back and he went down."

"What happened to Gallo?"

"He pulled the gun away from my spine and took off."

"He pulled— What was going on?"

"Nothing good. Tim probably saved my ass."

"And so you shot him in the leg."

"To keep him from killing me."

"You live a hell of a life, Scott Porter."

"I picked up Stanley's gun and fired once, hitting Tim in the leg. That put him down and gave me a chance to get in front of the situation."

"And Tim doesn't get booked for attempted murder." She looked away, watching the traffic grind past on the busy roadway in front of the hospital. "He told the detectives he doesn't remember what happened. They know he was drunk. He told them he was going by the office to get something for me but he doesn't remember what it was anymore. They're trying to figure out who this Stanley guy was."

"He was a bum," I said. "But a sadistic one. He killed two men outside of a bar in Orlando two years ago for buying a drink for a hooker he was trying to negotiate a discount with."

"So you knew him?"

"In a way. He was helping Gallo. But that's not for the police."

"They were after the letter."

"They were."

She stopped all of her moving and fidgeting and stood facing me. "I'm sorry I hit you," she said at last.

I smiled. It hurt and my jaw gave a little click when I spoke. "It's okay, Trudy." I was wondering just why she had been so upset. Was it more for

Tim's sake or mine. Again, I knew better than to ask.

"How's his leg?"

"He's not out of the woods yet. We won't know for a few days. The bullet shattered his femur."

Part of me wished it would have clipped his femoral artery while it was in there. "That's too bad," I said, realizing how lacking it sounded coming from me.

"Well," she said, "we'll deal with it."

I wondered if I were included in that "we."

"There is one more thing," I told her. "Until these guys get this letter, or give up on it—"

"Wait, 'guys'?"

"It's not the time, Trudy. I just don't want you to be alone."

"Tim's brother is here. He's offered to stay at the house with me while all this is going on."

Dylan Westland was a Tampa cop. That should work, I thought.

"Okay," I said. "But be careful. And talk to no one. Not even the FBI."

"The FBI? What FBI?"

"Another unknown. Just play dumb when they talk to you." I realized what I said and held out my hand, palm up. "Poor choice of words, Trudy. But if you can keep Tim on the right story it will be easier all the way around. But you have to be careful. I need to find Gallo. Don't be caught alone anywhere, especially at home."

She nodded and said, "I'll see what I can do." She looked into my eyes. "I should get back." She turned, took a few steps, then stopped. "He really doesn't like you, you know."

"I had a feeling."

Then she did something that surprised me. She came back, reached up and instead of slapping me laid her hand gently along the side of my face. "I really am sorry I hit you."

I started to lean closer, to bring myself nearer to her, and for just a moment she seemed to be doing the same. But she straightened suddenly, pulled her hand away and said, "Let me know what's going on when you can."

"I will."

With a wan smile, she turned and left. As I did too often in this hell of a life she said I lived, I watched the woman of my dreams walk away toward another man, one I was fairly sure she didn't even love.

She was right. It was a hell of a life. She'd always been right.

CHAPTER TWENTY-EIGHT

Now that I had the original of the Holmes letter back, I needed to figure out what to do with it. Again I tried my best to be sure I hadn't picked up a tail from the hospital but the early afternoon traffic was so thick there wasn't anything I could do to be positive. Assuming there were no electronic devices involved I could use it to my advantage, and with a few detours along my way I thought I was clean.

I was on my way to the post office on Ringling Boulevard. I paid for six months' rent on the smallest sized post office box they had available, then bought a large envelope and postage and mailed the original Holmes letter to myself. Instead of taking the key to the box, I asked if I could come back and pick it up later. The clerk gave me a funny look but said, sure, that they'd leave it there with a note. But I'd have to show ID, he said. Perfect. Today's post office, always ready to serve.

I thanked the man, dropped the receipt he had given me into the recycle bin by the door and went out into the sunshine.

The letter was secure where no one should be able to find it. Trudy should be reasonably safe as long as she was careful. Now I had to turn my attention to Gallo and Sullivan and Fitzwater. One way or another I had to find a way out of this. I just hoped it worked out better for me than it had for my client, Edwin Morton Holmes.

I was never told what the FBI had found or not found when they went to the Holmes house on Longboat Key. My next contact with them came with a loud knocking on my door that night as I was sitting down with a takeout pizza and a bottle of beer. I thought it may have been a rare contact with a neighbor since no one had pushed the security button from downstairs but when I opened my front door I understood immediately.

Sullivan was there, a folded piece of paper held in one thick, meaty fist.

"You know what this is?"

"I can guess."

"You got a problem with it?"

"You're an idiot. But come in anyway."

Behind Sullivan were half a dozen Sarasota PD cops, most of whom I at least knew by sight. Following that group was Special Agent Fitzwater. As Sullivan deployed his borrowed troops, I indicated my small kitchen table and said, "May I?"

Fitzwater said, "Go ahead."

"Grab a slice," I said, sitting down. "There's beer in the fridge, if you'd like."

"That would just piss off Sullivan."

"One can hope."

He didn't take the pizza or beer but he did take the chair across from me. "They going to find anything?"

"What do you think?"

"I doubt it."

"You doubt correctly."

"Do you have the letter?"

I took a large bite of a piece, barely catching a mass of dripping cheese and a mushroom before it separated from the still hot crust, and cooled it off with a swig from the beer bottle.

"Still missing," I said after swallowing.

Sullivan was in my bedroom with two of the cops, two of the others were in the guest bedroom and the last was working on the master bath. I figured Fitzwater was supposed to be babysitting me and keeping me out of the way.

"I need to try again," Fitzwater said.

"Go ahead," I said, still working on the pizza.

"Sullivan will do everything he can to get that letter."

"That's up to him."

Fitzwater looked uncomfortable. He looked around him, made sure we weren't being overheard, then lowered his voice. "I'm not sure you're getting this. He will do everything he can to get that letter."

I met Fitzwater's eyes. "Is that warrant legal or did he just flash a blank piece of paper at me?"

"The warrant's real. He's got another one for your office, but I'm not supposed to tell you that."

"I figured that already."

"I bet you did. Anyway"—he looked around again—"that may not be all he's planning."

I put down my food and wiped my fingers and mouth with a paper towel. "What are you telling me?"

"You need to be careful."

"By giving him the letter."

"That would be one way," Fitzwater said.

"If I had it."

"I suspect Sullivan may not stop with the warrants."

"What else can he do?"

Fitzwater sat back in his chair, sighed, said, "You might not be as intelligent as I thought you were."

"I have that same thought every now and then. You aren't playing bad-special-agent, good-special-agent, are you?"

He just shook his head, reached forward for my beer and helped himself to a long pull. He stifled a belch and slid the bottle back over to my side of the table.

"Why does Sullivan want that letter so bad?"

"This isn't the place," Fitzwater said.

"Sure it is." We could hear the sounds of the men moving through the other rooms of my condo. "Tell me."

"Maybe he was sent here to get it."

"By your boss?"

He actually laughed. "No, not my boss."

"I see," I said. "So what are you doing here, keeping an eye on your partner?"

"First, he's not my partner. Second, no comment."

I leaned forward and lowered my voice. "Fell into a mud puddle, did he?"

"Meaning?"

"He's a dirty."

Fitzwater looked pained. "Maybe you are sharper than a marble. Keep proving it. Try to stay off his bad side."

"I'm already there. Doesn't look like I'm leaving. Who does he work for?"

"I would have thought you could figure that out yourself."

"Well," I said, picking up another pizza slice from the box. "With the current unrest in the New England mob, I figure it's either Junior trying to stay on top of the garbage heap with the money from the mortgage scheme, someone lower playing King of the Mountain, or possibly someone trying to settle an old score of some sort that I know nothing about."

Fitzwater stood up, walked down the hall. I heard him ask Sullivan, "Anything?"

"Not yet," came the answer. "Keep an eye on that bum out there. I don't trust him out of our sight."

Two of the cops made their way into the living room. Fitzwater sat down in the chair across from me again.

"We need to meet, away from...."

"I got you," I said. "You know where to find me."

"Give me a good number," Fitzwater said. He took a pen out of his pocket and shot it across the table.

I picked it up, wrote the number of the burner I'd been using on the paper towel, and pushed both paper and pen across the table. None of this was going to be linked to my regular phone.

One of the cops came into the kitchen. I knew him but not enough to remember his name. "I have to start in here," he said. He looked a bit embarrassed.

"No problem, mon," I said. "Try to keep it neat if you can."

"Yes, sir," he said, and went to the first cupboard over the pantry.

The call came just after eleven that night. Fitzwater's voice was loud and clear over the burner. "Sullivan's just left. Can we meet?"

"Where are you at?"

"Hampton Inn, off the interstate and Bee Line Road."

I was going to have him meet me at Jarod's bar but then I thought of Gallo and how he knew that could be a good place to find me. I was sure Fitzwater wanted to keep our meeting just between the two of us, but even so, I wanted something public.

I described to him a bowling alley that was open late a little north and east of downtown, about halfway between where both of us were.

"Half an hour," he said.

"Forty five minutes." I told him I had to walk back to the office to get the Malibu. It was still in the lot at the office.

"See you," he said, and hung up.

I'd been waiting for the call and was actually already sitting in the Malibu next to a shuttered Chinese restaurant across the street from Bob's Bowl. If any surprises showed up ahead of Special Agent Fitzwater, I'd know.

It was twenty minutes before Fitzwater arrived, which was still early. He may have had the same idea I had. I gave him another fifteen then drove across the street and parked within clear sight of the entrance. The agent was standing near a row of ancient vending machines, the kind with the mechanical pull levers they don't make anymore, near the device they use for polishing balls. I nodded and walked past him to the lounge.

"Come here a lot?" he asked as he fell in beside me.

"Only on league nights," I told him. "Team America should join."

He looked at me sharply. "Why do you say that?"

I pulled open the door and held it for him. "Isn't that what you call it when you get organized crime figures testifying for the G? You know, on their way to the witness protection program."

We entered the dim interior of the bar area, still with that unique smell of wax, polish and shoe spray filling the air. Only now it had beer, too. Sporadic collisions between balls and pins could still be heard over the piped-in music. I hadn't answered Fitzwater as I led him to one of the small tables at the side of the bar counter.

"How about a beer?" I asked.

"Coke," he said.

I stood up, went to the bar, came back with two Cokes.

"What's on your mind?" I asked.

Fitzwater took a sip of his soft drink, put it down on the napkin, pushed it away. "We have to stop this shit. Someone's going to get hurt."

"Oh, you mean other than Endo Robbins, Ernesto Flores and Edwin Holmes."

"And Eamon Stanley," Fitzwater said. "I know you two had a history."

"I'm not the only one," I said.

"What do you mean?"

"Rico Gallo."

The FBI agent looked surprised, then sat back, thinking. "The other night, in front of your office—"

"Gallo and Stanley. They were setting an example for your buddy Sullivan."

"The letter?"

I nodded.

"Would they have gotten it?"

"Probably," I said.

"How did that cop get involved?"

"He's not involved. That was just dumb luck. For me, anyway. He's not part of this."

"Still, he was there for a reason. A dispatcher with a gun drawn—"

"He's not part of this."

Fitzwater let it go. Smart man. I wasn't bringing Trudy into the conversation. She was none of his business.

Eventually he said, "I really need to know what you do about all this."

"What I know?" I said. "In all likelihood, very little. I can suppose a whole lot, however. I'm usually pretty good at that."

"You mentioned Team America."

"Do Italians make good bowlers?"

"Knock that shit off. We don't have a lot of time."

"Where's Sullivan?"

"I don't know. He took off twenty minutes before I called you."

"Think about following him?"

"Too much risk. He already suspects why I'm here. He's not stupid. But I don't want to give him cause for too much concern."

"Because he's dirty."

"Stop saying that."

"Then enjoy your Coke. I still have a condo to straighten out." I pushed my chair back. I fully intended to leave. I had my own priorities right now, and sitting here with Special Agent Fitzwater didn't help me get Gallo the hell out of town or keep Trudy Westland safe.

"Sit down, sit down," Fitzwater said.

I gave him a long look and sat. "You sure?"

"Yes."

"Then tell me."

"Before the Bureau pivoted to focus on terrorism, they placed a lot of emphasis on cultivating informers in position to provide information on organized crime. In the eighties and nineties the thought was that the Mafia was the primary target—"

"The New England Mafia."

"In this case, yes. But New York and Chicago, too. It's just that New England presented its own problems."

"Such as?"

Fitzwater sat back, took a long drink of Coke, surveyed the lounge and bowling alley, doing a good job of appearing casual. Then he said, "Careers were made on bringing in informants. If you couldn't do that, you were shipped out and held back. But if you could bring someone in, someone who knew things, and then one or two of his friends—"

"Commendations and promotions."

"It's what makes the Bureau go round. But the whole system is like politics. Ideals are one thing, but you can't use them to buy a new boat in Boston Harbor."

"The rats all look alike."

"And they're all rats, now. There aren't many left who'll stand a prison sentence and not give up names. The sentences under RICO are too severe and the government gives too good a deal. Omerta is dead. So what's better than squealing from prison?"

"Not going there in the first place."

"You got it. There are a few guys like Sullivan, especially if they came up in the neighborhoods, you know, that had ties with the same guys we were after, that figured getting dope on a Mafia deal was more important than shutting down something local."

"Local?"

"In Boston you have a pretty strong Irish mob presence."

"So Sullivan would get an Irishman to give up something on the Mafia and in exchange the Irishman would get a pass?"

"If only," Fitzwater said. He took another swallow from his Coke glass, his eyes scanning the room again. "Sullivan's contacts would get registered as informers for the Bureau. That meant they were supposed to stop committing their own crimes."

It was starting to make sense. "But they didn't. Their price for ratting out their rivals was a measure of autonomy."

Fitzwater nodded. "And worse. The new informers were so 'grateful' for their new relationship money and gifts began to change hands."

"So your own agents were in on the take." I laughed, then drank some of my own soda. "You ended up with good guys and bad guys working both sides of the fence."

"That's what happened, yes."

"Jesus, how can you guys tell anyone apart?"

"And now...."

"For starters, neither side can afford to get busted."

"That's right. They look too much alike. Guys like Sullivan, and there aren't many, but he has friends in the State Police as well as the local cops, keep their status by helping break up the Italians. Meanwhile, his Irish friends take up the vacated territory."

"And he shares in the profits."

"That's what we think."

Something wasn't adding up to me. "Gallo works for the Italians, doesn't he?"

"I should be surprised that you said that, but I'm not. How do you know?"

"Actually, he told me. That was right before my own man Stanley jumped me and the two of them took me back to my office."

"Gallo made him a better offer."

"Probably came with a hot shower. I should have upped my game. In any case, how does all this put Gallo and Sullivan together?"

"This is what concerns me right now," Fitzwater said. "What makes you think they're working together?"

"I'm not, exactly," I said. "But when Marty Ables brought the two of you to my office, Sullivan made a comment about Gallo coming *back* to my office."

"So?"

"That means he knew Gallo'd been there the night before."

"Couldn't the police—"

"They didn't know. When Tim Westland came around the corner shooting, Gallo had a gun in my back. Eamon Stanley went down and Gallo took off. No one saw him."

"You don't think Sullivan could have been watching?"

I thought back to when I'd picked up Stanley's gun and shot Tim in his leg. "No," I said. "Sullivan would have said something about it."

"What could—"

"He could have jammed me up. Let's just leave it at that. So if he's not talking to Gallo, I don't see any way he could know he'd been there."

Fitzwater picked up his glass, twirled it around, making the ice cubes click. "I'll have to think about this."

"Tell me something else."

"What?"

"Who killed Holmes? And don't give me that 'I can't tell you' bullshit. Not if you want to keep me talking."

"We don't know—"

"Stop it."

He held up a hand. "We don't know, but…."

"But what?"

"John Sullivan called in sick the day before Holmes was killed. Missed two days."

"Oh shit."

Fitzwater started spinning his Coke glass on its paper coaster. "We haven't been able to establish his whereabouts anywhere in Boston."

"Is that your FBI way of saying that you haven't looked in Washington, D.C.?"

"Let's just call this off limits for right now."

"If you—"

"Like the actual location of Holmes's original letter."

I shut up. "As you like," I said. I nodded at the bar. "Another Coke?"

"I need that letter."

I thought about it. "Not yet," I said. "People I care about aren't safe."

"They'd be safer if I had the letter and you didn't."

"Maybe," I said. "Either way there are rats, informants, whatever you want to call them, involved. Last I heard, the mob doesn't have a statute of limitations on vengeance."

He smiled. "They actually get better at it when they let some time pass." Fitzwater sat back, silent, thinking. I didn't interrupt. "How about a Xerox copy at least? Leave me something for when you get two to the back of the head."

I smiled. "Don't forget about a shank in the liver. I'll think about it. You want that Coke, or not?"

"No, I'm good." He checked his watch. "One more thing, though."

"What's that?"

"What makes you trust me?"

"Sullivan was easy. You could go either way. I'm still trying to figure everyone out."

"So you're saying you don't trust me?"

I got up to leave, tossed two dollar bills on the table for the bus boy or whoever cleaned up in this joint. "You don't see that letter anywhere, do you?"

Before he could reply, I added, "But it figures best that way."

CHAPTER TWENTY-NINE

Gallo called the office late the next morning, shortly after I'd arrived. When Steph passed him through and I answered, the first thing he said was, "How did we get here?"

I pushed away from my desk and pushed back in my chair. "Seems to me it started about the time you came to town, don't you?"

"Holmes gets no blame?"

"You're all a bunch of crooks, Gallo," I said. "Listen, if I'd have known Holmes was mobbed up, I wouldn't have taken his money."

"So you say."

I thought about that. "You're right. That's what I say but who knows what mood I would have been in if everyone had started this thing by telling the truth. Maybe what the guy really wanted was help going straight."

"Did he say that?"

"Actually, no."

Gallo chuckled. "You tell fancy stories," he said. "I hope you keep talking fast because you don't have as much time left as you think."

"Oh, I think I have a pretty good idea. I know your reinforcements are here. But you have to also know there are a lot of cops around. Good ones, even," I added.

"What do you mean?"

"Just that anything you do right now would be messy. Too many bodies are around, too many people know something's up. And frankly I just don't think your friends are that good."

"My god," he said, laughing. "You really are a funny guy. Or maybe just really, really stupid."

I gave a little laugh, too, sharing in the spirit. "You may be right, Gallo," I said. "But if this whole thing came to light right now, who do you think would get the rubber hose and spotlights?"

"I've got friends."

"Friends who need scapegoats. And who better than the guy who's actually killed—"

"I didn't do Holmes. You said you knew that."

"I did, but I'm not sure you'd want me testifying on your behalf. And if you can't prove your whereabouts, who do you think is going to be held accountable for Holmes's little accident?"

Gallo stayed quiet for a moment. "It's a hell of a life, isn't it?"

"I've always thought so. You want an alibi, though, you let me know. Maybe I'll change my mind."

He knew what I was getting at. "I'm not a rat," he said.

"And I'm not the G. Up to this point you haven't hurt me. You haven't even scared me a little." Except for the threats against Trudy but I wasn't going to put any emphasis there. "You've disrupted my staff but hey, that comes with the job. One of my employee's husband got himself shot—"

"You know that wasn't me, either."

"Well, he was a cop that was either trying to prevent the commission of a felony by yourself and the late Eamon Stanley, or he was just a drunk son of a bitch who happened to be the wrong cop in the wrong place."

"You got pencils in your mouth, Porter?"

"I'm just saying that things can go in different directions here, now, this one time."

"You trying to help me?"

"I might be."

"Then give me that letter. I'll blow town and you'll never see me again."

That was certainly an option. On the other hand, the cops weren't walking away from the murder of Ernesto Flores or Eamon Stanley. A guy like Marty Ables was already smelling rotten eggs and now that the FBI was involved, such as they were, the most likely person to have their life run over in all this was still me. And there was always the question as to what would happen if Gallo's masters finally procured that letter. They'd been willing to kill to get it, what would they be capable of once they had it? These were things I'd need to know first.

"Well, that's a moot point. The letter's gone."

"I'll bet we can find it. Together."

"You're not hearing me. You already did. Your boyfriend didn't tell you?"

Gallo stayed silent on the line. Finally, "I'm going to enjoy dulling my knife against the flats of your ribs."

"Suit yourself, Gallo. But I think you may be out of pals."

"What does that mean?"

"Someone has the letter. And it ain't the cops. Not the ones I know, anyway."

"Then help me get it back."

"Why the hell— no, how the hell could I do that?"

"I told you, I'd leave town."

"You're leaving anyway."

"You're not hearing me. Not without that letter. And you're going to help me get it."

"I'll think about it," I said. "It might be possible. But I'm not doing it blind. Consider what I said. Lay low, for a while. I may be able to do something for you if it's in my best interest."

And I hung up. I didn't let him bluster on about why he called but I left him with something to think about. I imagine he was dialing his buddy Special Agent John Sullivan at that moment, asking if he had the letter. Next I had to figure a way to exploit what I'd just done. I didn't even know if it would stick.

There was a knock on my door.

"Come in," I called.

Paul McKay walked in, a bit slowly, not with his usual bouncy step.

"What's wrong?" I asked.

"That obvious?"

"I'm a detective. Sit down."

He did. I already knew what was on his mind, so I told him.

"You're right," he said. "But I can't lie to the FBI, Scott. I can't do it."

I nodded my head. McKay was a good man, and I probably needed him if I was going to see this thing through the right way. But not if I couldn't trust him. So I told him about my meeting the night before with Special Agent Fitzwater.

"So he told you Sullivan was dirty? Just like that?"

"I already knew."

He shook his head back and forth slowly. "I need a vacation."

That might be best for everyone, I thought. When push came to shove, though, I was still hoping I could count on him. I told him about Sullivan knowing that Gallo had been at the shooting in front of the office.

"So?"

"How could he have known that, Paul?"

McKay sat back, chewing his lip. "Shit."

"Yup."

"So what are we going to do?"

He used the right pronoun. I hoped that meant he would be with me on this.

"I'm working on that. It's going to be a bit tricky."

"I won't do anything illegal."

That made one of us.

"You shouldn't either," he added.

"Paul, I'm just trying to get out from under this so no one else gets hurt."

"What happens if you give it all to that other agent, Fitzwater?"

I shook my head. "I don't know yet. That might turn out to be the easiest thing."

"So what's stopping you?"

"Oh, the usual. What happens if Sullivan's got wider influence? What happens if they can come back on me with obstructing their investigation? How about if they try to pin the Flores murder on us?"

There were a lot of things he could have said, and each of them spent a split second running across his features. "Part of this is on you, you know."

"I don't deny. But we've got all these loose pieces of string now that have to be tied up."

McKay nodded slowly. "You need me right now?"

"I have some figuring to do."

"How about I help Steph and Al with Keller's billing?"

"That would be great, Paul."

He nodded again and turned and left my office. I just hoped he didn't let his tendency toward FBI-worship make him do anything stupid.

CHAPTER THIRTY

I had done something to the relationship between Gallo and Sullivan, but I only wished I knew what it was. Gallo should be knocked a bit off balance—I hoped—and he might step back from working with Sullivan, at least temporarily. The fact that they were both crooks should still be to my advantage. It was a good bet there wasn't a lot of trust between the two of them to begin with.

I picked up the phone and called Marty Ables. I got him at his desk.

"I thought I made it clear our relationship was over," he said.

"I know, you did. It's me, not you, I get it. I'm trying to make something right here."

"Why are you calling me?"

Because I didn't want to call the two douchebags who were investigating the Eamon Stanley/Tim Westland shootings. "Trying to throw you a bone, Marty. A big juicy one. It still has meat on it."

"Put it back in the soup. Not interested."

"Marty, wait." I needed to stop him before he hung up. "There's another body."

"God damn it, Porter! You know the number to homicide. Use it."

"It's more like they know mine. Listen, Marty, just for a minute. If you don't want it, fine. I'll figure something else out."

"Jesus, Scott, why are you always playing with shit that can only get you hurt?" He sighed, and I could imagine him running his fingers backwards through his thinning hair. "Okay, where is it?"

"No idea."

"Goodbye, Scott."

"Hang the fuck on, Marty." I was starting to get pissed. "Just listen for a minute." I told him about Rico Gallo, about who he worked for, and what he had done to Ernesto Flores.

"Wait, wait, wait," he said. "How do you know all this?"

So I told him about Gallo recruiting Gabe Keller to go after the letter.

"Does Gallo have it now?"

"I don't think so," I said.

"Then where—"

"You don't want to ask me that right now, Marty."

"Do you remember the two FBI agents I brought into your office yesterday, Scott? Is there anything worthwhile rattling around in your head this morning? Didn't they make any sort of impression? I heard they tossed your office and your home."

"Let's stick to murder first. I think Gallo was looking for the letter. That's why he went out to Holmes's place, and that's why he caved in the back of Flores' head."

"Why haven't you—"

"But there's more. Who lived in that house back by the pool?"

"That was Holmes's secretary or someone, wasn't it?"

"A fat little guy named Endo Robbins. Look him up."

"Where is he?"

"Gallo wouldn't tell me."

"You think he's dead."

"That Gallo did tell me."

Ables was quiet for a moment, spinning his mental wheels. When three cherries didn't come up he said, "Here's what I'm going to do. I'm going to get my lieutenant—"

"No, you're not."

"Fuck you, Scott. This is bigger than whatever it is you're playing at. I'm not going down because you're busy screwing over your clients."

Which wasn't at all what I was doing but it wasn't something to argue about. It didn't hurt me for him to think that's what was going on. "You attribute this to me and I deny everything."

"Then why the hell are you even telling me this?"

"You're the cop, Marty, not me. I just thought I could give you something to make up for the hard feelings yesterday. If you don't want it or can't use it, just forget I said anything."

"I can't do that, Scott—"

"Thanks for taking my call, Marty." And I hung up.

I sat back in my chair, trying to see the future. If Ables took it to someone in house, he'd have to give me up and risk me denying everything. But his friend was in town, Special Agent John Sullivan. Who else could advise him on the proper course of action if not a member of the hallowed and sanctified FBI?

At least that was what I was counting on. Sow a little discord between Gallo and Sullivan and see what happens. I played with a letter opener on my desktop and wished I really could see into the future. On the other hand, I was reasonably sure I wouldn't have liked it. The present was just too messy.

I was flapping my butterfly wings and waiting for the hurricane. I just hoped I'd remembered to close the cellar doors.

I was trying to figure who I'd hear from first—Gallo, Sullivan or Ables—when my cell phone rang. Time to find out, I thought, scooping it off my desktop. I looked at the incoming name.

It was Trudy.

Without realizing I'd been tight, I felt my body relax as I pushed the Talk button and said hello.

"Scott," Trudy said, and just her saying my name made me feel better about what was going on around me. Then I felt guilty I hadn't thought about her at all for the past hour while I was trying to puzzle out a plan.

"What's up, lady?"

"It– it's Tim," she said.

"He's still going to be okay, right?" I wasn't sure I knew how I wanted her to answer. Shame on me. Instead I felt even worse when she told me about the blood clots.

"Oh, Trudy," I said. "How serious is it?"

"They don't know yet," she said. "They've removed the ones they found in his leg and put some sort of filters in his veins. And of course he's on blood thinners. Apparently whatever's happening is more complicated than they'd like. He might need more surgery but they have to wait to see if the clots stop forming."

In a strange way I almost wished Tim would just pop up and be better so Trudy could come back to the office, so that she could continue with her life, and that her life might—

"What's that?"

"I said I need to get out of here. Will you come and get me?"

I checked my watch and saw that it was nearly eleven thirty.

"Of course, sweetheart. I'll be right over."

"Thank you, Scott."

I should have hung up but instead I said, "I miss you."

There was a long beat on the line before she finally said, "I miss you, too." Then she broke the connection.

Adrenaline surged through my veins but I stayed where I was. Regardless of this artificial high I had to be sure I wasn't overlooking anything with Gallo and Sullivan, especially if Trudy was no longer keeping her distance. I should have asked her where Dylan Westland was.

I took a step toward my desk and my landline phone when it rang as I was picking it up. It was another outside call. "This is Porter," I said.

It was Fitzwater.

"What the hell did you do?"

"And good morning to you, Special Agent," I said. "I take it you've got news."

"Sullivan took a phone call fifteen minutes ago and blasted out of here like something out of Cape Canaveral. I started to go with him and he told me he had a personal emergency to take care of."

"And you thought of me?"

"We're from out of town, asshole. What other emergency could there be?"

"Gallo called me this morning," I said.

"Shit," Fitzwater said. "What did that bastard want?"

"He didn't say."

There was real anger in Fitzwater's voice as he swore again. "Bullshit, Porter. Look, if you're too stupid to know when someone's trying to help you—"

"I know, I know," I said. "Maybe it's time we saw other people."

"Damn it—"

"Gallo didn't tell me what he wanted because I didn't give him a chance. That's the god's honest truth. You happy?"

"You talked about what, then? The weather? Sports?"

This time I chuckled. "Nothing that juicy," I said. "But I may have let slip that Sullivan has the letter."

Dead silence. The only sounds on the phone came from Fitzwater's breathing.

"If I didn't know any better, I wouldn't believe you."

"You think that's where Sullivan went?"

"To find Gallo?" Fitzwater asked. "Why the hell didn't you let me in on this little stunt? I could be on Sullivan's tail right now. Maybe we could have gotten—"

"Nothing, and you know it. How long's he been playing for the other side?"

No answer.

"That's right," I said. "And he's too smart to let you catch him now."

"How does this help us?"

"I have no idea."

"I hate amateurs," he said. "You know who I mean. I hoped you might be better than this."

"Don't tell me I've disappointed you, Fitzwater. No, please, anything but that."

"Watch your ass," he said just before he hung up.

"Someone ought to," I muttered as I cradled the phone. I turned to leave, then stopped and went around my desk and took the burner out of my drawer. I dialed a number from memory and when the other voice answered, I only needed a few seconds to tell him what I needed.

Then I was off to see Trudy.

CHAPTER THIRTY-ONE

Trudy was already outside the hospital entrance this time as I pulled around to let her in to the Caddy. She opened the passenger door and said, "I'm sorry, Scott. I can't leave right now."

I did my best to keep the disappointment off my face and she did her best not to show me she noticed. "Come inside," she said. "We can grab a bite."

I nodded and told her I'd be right back. She shut the door and I drove down the small incline and turned right into the massive parking lot until I found a visitor's space. Then I walked back to the front door and she was still there, only now she stepped forward and embraced me, fully, actually giving me a kiss on the cheek.

What the hell did all this mean? I had no words.

"Come inside," she said. "Let's find a table in the cafeteria."

I let her lead me deeper into the air-conditioned hospital and kept following her down a short hall and to the cafeteria. We mixed in with the line and the smell of the food more than the sight of it made me hungry. I ordered a cheeseburger as Trudy built a salad and ladled herself a bowl of soup into a styrofoam container. This was good. We were close, but too far for talk.

But that didn't last. I was confused about the affection she had volunteered, although it beat the hell out of the last time I was here and having those wonderful little hands slap my face fire engine red.

A corner booth suitable for six was open and we slid into it anyway, from opposite sides, and met in the middle. "What's going on, Trudy?"

She was clearly troubled and I wondered if she had told me everything that was going on with Tim.

"I don't want to talk about that now," she said. "Let's talk about what's going on out there—" she waved her hand at the windows— "for a while."

"We could," I said. I was so very aware of how close she was sitting next to me. We were just inches apart— "You know," I told her, "when we were at your house, if either one of us—"

She reached out and placed her finger across my lips. "Don't, Scott. Not here. Not now."

More public contact. My head was swimming. I could smell lotion on her finger and I pulled back and picked up my burger to keep my hands busy.

"Okay, then," I said. "What do you want to talk about?" I couldn't taste my food.

"Now you've got me thinking about what was going on that night," she said.

"I'm sorry."

"No, that's all right. Tell me what's new with Gallo."

Talking work was good. Talking work was not talking about her marriage, or her husband, us, or other things that might have been. I caught her up on everything that had been going on with Gallo, told her about Sullivan and the phone calls this morning. When I was through she sat back against the padded bench seat and looked at me with an expression I couldn't identify, not even in her eyes.

"What's going to happen?" she asked.

I shrugged my shoulders. "I really don't know. It would be nice if the two baddies took care of each other for us."

"Sounds too easy."

"Who knows?" I said. "Anything could happen."

"But probably not."

"No, probably not."

She spun a plastic spoon around in her soup. So far she hadn't eaten anything. "I don't want this," she said. I assumed she meant the food. "What did you do with the letter?"

I looked around automatically but of course no one was there, not in earshot. And not anyone that would care. I told her about renting the post office box and having them hold the key for me. There was no reason not to. I trusted Trudy like no other.

She started to say something but a person in purple hospital scrubs came up to our booth and said, "Excuse me, Mrs. Westland?"

Trudy almost seemed relieved at the interruption. "Yes, Doctor?"

"I'm just the PA," he said. "Doctor Ramadhi would like to see you upstairs, if he could."

She had already started sliding out around the edges of the table. "I'll be right up," she said.

The physician's assistant nodded and walked away. Trudy stood and said, "I'm sorry, Scott." Suddenly she seemed very sad.

What the hell, I thought. I'd shot her husband and he's upstairs in a sterile room throwing blood clots in his shattered leg. This was only... food.

"It's okay, Trudy. You want—" I gestured at her uneaten lunch.

"Toss it for me, will you?"

"Of course."

"Then come back and take me to dinner. I still need to get out of this place."

This shocked me, but I said, "Seven o'clock?"

"Six," she said.

"I'll be here."

Again she was waiting outside the hospital for me but she had somehow found the means or time to change clothes. She was wearing long-legged designer jeans and a light sweater that were the kind of casual clothes that made most men look twice at women in supermarkets, the kind of women that could be attractive without even trying.

I pulled through the turnaround and she had climbed into the seat almost before I had stopped moving.

"How's Tim?" I asked.

She reached over and grabbed my hand and squeezed it hard. "The same," she said. "Just drive." She didn't let go.

"Trudy—"

"It's fine, Scott. His brother's up there with him. I just need to get out of here."

"You're sure? We—"

"You liked it when I slapped you?" She turned in her seat to face me.

I moved my foot off the brake and said, "Roger that. Where to?"

She gave my hand a lighter squeeze and said, "Something to eat that's not hospital food. And music, not to be confused with Muzak. That would be good."

"We can do that," I said.

She let go of my hand altogether and fluffed at her hair with her fingers, then slumped back into her seat, her eyes closed against the declining light of the afternoon. I wanted to stare at her face, study her, try to figure out what was going on inside her head, or maybe I just wanted to enjoy looking at her. There was too much traffic to do anything other than wish that thought away, but it wasn't easy.

Eyes front, I drove south, thinking about nice but not *too nice* restaurants, but all I could think of were seafood places with no music. There was a place in Venice, south of Sarasota, but it was almost an hour away. Traffic would be with us, though, and Trudy would have distance as well as time separating her from the problems at the hospital.

As if reading my mind, she asked, "You know where we're going?"

"I do," I said.

"Good." She snuggled down further into her seat. "Just one rule. No talking about this case."

"What about—"

"Him, either."

"That's two—"

"Shut up."

Everything suited me just fine. I drove, she drifted, and if only in a temporary sense, we literally left our worries behind us. Regardless, though, we both knew this was always going to be a round trip.

We had some wine, maybe a bit too much, some nice steaks, and in the restaurant's lounge we sat close together on a small couch. Had I been there with someone else, I would have called it a love seat. As it was, there was a three piece jazz combo with a female singer that was no Ella but knew how to sing for her money. We sat through two and a half sets. At one point Trudy asked me to request "Autumn Leaves."

It was one of the best nights of my life, and it felt like I wasn't even trying.

"I'm cold," Trudy said, leaning into me. I was, too, with the over air-conditioned air blowing over us. I asked her if she wanted to leave and I was sorry when she said yes.

In the car I had the strongest sense that I didn't want the night to end, and I said so.

"Just drive," she said, her hand once again in mine. The combo had done "Autumn Leaves" as a ballad, just like Cannonball Adderley and Miles Davis, only with words, and she hummed the melody off and on for a while. I could have listened to it all night.

It was almost painful to see the sign that said we had re-entered Sarasota's city limits. I broke the silence with, "Where to now?"

"Get off here," she said, then, "Turn left." After a mile she said, "Left again." She continued with one word directions, guiding us away from the freeway and deeper into the city. There was no other conversation until it became clear where we were going. The only question I had was why.

I pulled my hand free of hers and reached for a sheet of paper from the seat behind us. "Is this pass still good?"

"If not," she said, "I know the guard," and she laid her head on my shoulder.

I was filled with the scent of her hair, the comfort and warmth of her weight against mine. Until that moment, I wouldn't have thought a woman could still make me feel light-headed but I would have been wrong. I wouldn't have thought I would have been scared, either, but I would have been wrong about that, too.

I was all too aware that some mistakes are too tempting not to repeat. But by the time you recognize that what you're doing really shouldn't be happening, it's almost always too late. Whatever it is has become a decision.

Full speed ahead. Damn the torpedoes. Run away. Whatever. We all make choices. The ones that we regret? We only know those for what they are after the damage is done.

CHAPTER THIRTY-TWO

I spent the night.

She was the first one to awake and when I felt her body shift and start to slide away, I tightened my grip around her middle and pulled her back toward me. Just the sight of her bare back excited me. She resisted at first, but only a little, and then allowed herself to come to me. She rolled over and I kissed her forehead, then her cheeks, and lifted my leg over her hips. As she relaxed onto her back, she smiled lazily and said, "Again?"

"Shhh," I told her. "And good morning." My hands were gently moving along the sides of her body, my mouth working its way toward hers, when she turned her head and looked at the clock on the table.

"I can't, Scott."

"I know better."

"No, I have to be at the hospital. Dylan might come back, and the doctors—"

I pushed my way off her and lay back, staring up at the ceiling. The reminder of—what? Real life?—was sobering.

"I love you." I said it without looking at her.

"You always have."

As Trudy leaned forward and kissed me tenderly on the cheek, I was hoping to hear her say something else. It didn't matter that I knew it was too much too ask, not from a woman like her, not at a time like this. Life is long, I told myself, and she didn't have to say anything at all. Not really. Both of us to knew last night was anything but casual.

"I'll give you a ride in."

"Don't talk dirty. And of course you will, my car's still there."

"You do a good impression of me." It made me feel good to say that. What an idiot. "How much time do we have?"

"Just enough for a shower." Trudy got out of the other side of the bed, absolutely gorgeous and unashamedly naked. "Coming?"

A little voice in the back of my head was screaming at me that this was too comfortable and that this wasn't my house, my bed, or my shower. But the little voices, despite carrying the biggest messages, are the easiest ones to quash. "After you," I said. I was used to her watching her walk away from me, only this time things were… better.

Eventually I made it home. I'd dropped Trudy off at the hospital in time for her meeting with Tim's doctors, exhausted from the night before. I called Steph and told her I wouldn't be in until later and to let the place burn down if it came to that. Then I turned off my cell phone, unplugged the land line, curled up on my sofa and took a nap.

I was still hearing the buzzing noises of a fairy tale life when I awoke two hours later. I took another shower, this time a quick one. I put on some fresh clothes and walked over to the office. As I moved through the door, Steph gave me a strange look and waved a pink slip of paper at me.

"Keep it," I told her.

"Nope," she said. "It's the cops."

The message was from Marty Ables. Something inside me tightened up a bit as I felt the old pressures of the Holmes case start to creep back into my bones. I couldn't think of what Ables would have to say.

I trudged down the short hall to my office and shut the door behind me. Sitting on the edge of the desk as though it meant I was still living in last night's dream world, I dialed the number on the message slip. He answered on the second ring.

"Well, you've done it now," he said.

"Probably more than once, and better than you."

"Stop messing around. I planted that little seed with Sullivan about Endo Robbins being dead. According to you."

"And?"

"And now he wants to look at you for it."

Sure he does, I thought. "How do you know this guy anyway, Marty?"

"Sullivan?" he said. "We both grew up in Prospect Park. The Jersey one, not Brooklyn."

"Wouldn't want to make that mistake."

"Fuck you. We went to high school in Manchester, he was a year ahead but we played on the same football and basketball teams. Mostly he hung with my brother."

"You guys keep in touch?"

"Hell, no. But he's a good guy. Seen him a few times over the years but not for a long while. Heard he was with the Feds but I had no idea he was coming down here until just before he showed up."

The only reason for Sullivan to say what he had would be if he thought Ables was going to pass it on and hope I felt the squeeze. I wondered how far he would take it if he thought he could investigate me and make it official. If Gallo was as thorough with the corpse as he'd led me to believe, Sullivan was a lumpy bag full of shit. But if Gallo had something he could give to Sullivan to use against me, anything might happen.

"Why are you warning me, Marty?"

"Because—again—I'm telling you we're through. If anyone thinks I had a hand in helping you with any of this—"

"You did."

"Well, if anyone else thinks so I'm coming out there and strapping a dead body around your neck for every cop, special agent and cadaver dog to use to drag your ass off to a hole in the ground somewhere. You can get tattooed with ball point pens and make new friends in the shower for all I care. We clear?"

He was sounding tough, at least for him, and I was starting to get angry. I wanted to tell him something to put him in his place, as much for spoiling my mood as for what he was telling me. The smart thing, though, would be to let it all go. Sometimes even I can muster that much self-control.

"We're clear, Marty. Thanks for—"

The line went dead. Prick, I thought. I replaced the phone on the cradle and folded my arms across my chest.

Did my plan with Gallo and Sullivan backfire? They were supposed to go at each other, not team up against me, but that was always a bit of a longshot anyway.

Screw it. I was tired of the case, tired of the letter, Sullivan, Fitzwater, Gallo, Ables—all of it. Like a school kid, all I wanted to do was be with Trudy, which suddenly didn't seem as impossible as it had the day before. Demonstrating all the restraint of a hormonal teenager, male, I picked up the phone and called Trudy's cell. I wanted to get the hell out of the office before I heard anything else I'd rather ignore.

"Scott," she said when she answered. Her voice had that sharpness back in it, and I felt a twinge in my stomach as I wondered if that were the sound of regret from last night or something to do with Tim.

"How are you?" I asked.

"Tired of this stack of old gossip rags that have been keeping me company. Where are you?"

"At the office," I said, "but not for long."

"Oh? What's up?"

"Nothing, it's just me. I'm not in the mood." I knew I should ask her about Tim but I didn't cross that line just yet, not until I knew how much things had changed between all of us. What I really wanted to do was go get this woman and take her far away somewhere, anywhere, and not have to think or worry about this stupid case any longer.

I couldn't do it, I knew. People would start to notice, if they hadn't already, and I had no idea if last night's episode was a beginning, an ending, or something apart, a bubble that's already burst.

"Go, then," she said, the peculiar quality still in her voice. "You're the boss. Go do something fun."

Unlikely, I thought. She hadn't said anything about last night so I wasn't about to, either. I was starting to feel depressed.

"That's right, I am," I said. "Sometimes I wonder if you guys notice." I tried to stay light but the phone was weighing heavy in my hand. "I'll go grab a bite or something. Just wanted to check on you."

"Thank you, Scott. I appreciate it."

Jesus, that sounds formal. "Steph's at the door," I lied. "Let me go. If you need anything…."

"I'll let you know."

"Okay, Trudy. Talk to you later." This time I slammed the phone back on its unit, then flung the whole thing off my desk with a backhanded swipe. The hell with it, I thought. What was I expecting, anyway? Being with Trudy last night didn't make her any less married.

The next thing I wanted to do was punch a new door through the wall and get out of here without anyone seeing me. Too noisy, I told myself. Instead I went to the bathroom, splashed cool water onto my face, then toweled off and straightened out my desk. As I picked up the phone I had serous thoughts about my maturity level but knew that as an adult, everybody had long ago stopped caring. I could act as rotten as I pleased, especially to my own phone, and no one would say a thing.

They could think all the nasty little things they wanted.

It was a small blessing that Steph was on the phone as I walked through the small lobby. Al Sutter called my name as I reached the door but I didn't stop or turn around as I pushed my way through. I turned right on the sidewalk, hoping Al would leave me be. He did.

I pulled the burner out of my back pocket and made one more call. Then I hung up and walked the short distance back to my condo, got in the Malibu, and drove off. I resisted the urge to lay rubber in the parking lot and leave a year's worth of tire on the pavement as I headed for the water and what I hoped could be a calming drive along the Gulf of Mexico. I wasn't feeling quite rational but I knew down inside it was my own fault. No one to blame but me.

The radio was blaring oldies music from the sixties and I hit the switches to roll down all four windows. The hell with Trudy, I thought. The hell with all of it.

Too bad I didn't mean it.

Driving up the coast only went so far heading north. It doesn't take an awfully long time before you end up at the bridge and then to St. Petersburg and suddenly you're in a city again. The ocean's out there, it always is, but if you want to stay close to it you'll have to do it in a crowd.

I headed north anyway, mostly because that was the direction I happened to take when I hit 41. Ables. Sullivan. Gallo. I tried to force myself to think about the case, tried to guess at what may or may not have happened between Gallo and Sullivan. If I had been able to plant a big enough seed of doubt with Gallo, I was still hoping he could end the Sullivan problem. With a big piece like that off the board, we'd be back to me and Gallo and despite his getting the drop on me once, I still liked those odds.

But I couldn't keep my focus on those threads. The pictures in my mind, the scenarios I tried to figure out, all of them blurred at the edges as thoughts of Trudy and what had been our second night together, an event I'd never thought would have been repeated, pushed everything else out of the way. Was that a night of total honesty for the both of us? Or just more lies for everyone, including Tim?

I wondered if she'd ever tell him, then decided that after he'd tried to kill me, probably not.

I pulled over in the shell covered parking lot of a seafood joint almost in the middle of nowhere off highway 19. As I rolled to a halt I realized I'd been gripping my cell phone in my hand. I wanted to call Trudy but I couldn't. I wouldn't. I'd already done it this morning and I still didn't know what to make of her odd response, like she was living her life in a vacuum.

There was something cold to drink in the restaurant, and I wanted it, but I didn't get out of the car. Once again I looked at my phone on the seat, its black screen empty, vacant and mocking.

I wouldn't call her.

I backed the car around and turned right on 19, heading back the way I'd come. That fact was immaterial, I just wasn't done driving.

And then Trudy called me. I thought about not answering but of course I did. It was like kicking the doctor after a tap on the patellar tendon—quick and beyond your control.

"Trudy," I said, and waited. It didn't take long.

"Can you come to the hospital?"

"What's wrong?"

"Just come," she said. "Please, Scott. I need you here."

I should have thought about it, should have tried to do what was right or what was best for everyone. Turns out none of that mattered. I couldn't tell the difference anyway. Trudy called and I went. Simple as that.

I don't know how long it took me to get there but I knew I drove too fast. I was lucky to avoid getting pulled over. When I got to the hospital I whipped into the visitors' lot, took the first spot I found and jogged up to the front door. Trudy wasn't there so I signed in, took the proffered badge and rode the elevator to the fifth floor, Tim's home since the shooting.

And there she was, in the waiting room, sitting in a plastic covered armchair, facing a corner of the room. I could see her through the glass but as soon as I opened the door she turned and faced me. She didn't get up.

"Tim had a stroke," she said.

I stopped two feet away from her and knelt down so I wasn't towering over her.

"How is he?"

"They don't know yet. They can't tell yet but they'll know more when the swelling goes down." She sniffed and dabbed at her nose with a wad of Kleenex clutched in her hand.

"He'll be okay, Trudy," I said, feeling as hollow as the words. "He's young, strong."

She patted her perky little nose, red with crying, again and turned and looked me in the eye. At no time did I have the feeling that she wanted to reach out for me. Oddly enough, I found I didn't want her to.

"And they took his leg."

"They— Wait, they did what?"

"The doctors said they weren't stopping the clots from forming and the filters weren't catching them but then they found— they found gangrene. If they didn't take the leg off he could have died—"

She broke down into a silent cry. I looked around for more tissues and saw a box on a desk across the room. I stood and took it from the desk, and an older lady said to me, "Those are for everyone."

"I know," I said, gently. "They'll be right over here."

The old woman turned back to the silent television set as if she had never seen me in the first place, staring at the closed-captioning scrolling across the screen. I set the tissue box next to Trudy's lap and resumed my kneeling position.

"What has Tim said?"

This brought new sobs and I knew I'd blurted out the wrong thing. "He doesn't know yet. He was still unconscious from the stroke. The– the doctors didn't think they should wait."

This time I was close to reaching for her hand, but I resisted. "You can't blame yourself, Trudy. You're just looking out for him."

"Really, Scott? Is that what I'm doing?"

I couldn't blame her for her resentment. Tim had put himself in front of that bullet by trying to kill me. I could have done worse to him but I tried to put him down as easily as I could without pushing him after Eamon Stanley on his way to hell. It hadn't worked out.

But then I slept with his wife. Was she feeling the guilt of being with me, the shame of caring for a man who had been unfaithful, something else? I told myself I had no part of her pain but I knew I was lying. Maybe I just didn't know what she wanted me to do.

For the first time I had the thought that they had both cheated on the other. What did that make them?

"What do you need from me?"

More tears. More tissues.

"I'm sorry, Trudy. I wish I could tell you how much—"

She looked around, making sure no one else could hear. "I'm not blaming you, Scott."

"You can't blame yourself, either."

"How can you know that?"

This stunned me. I felt as though we'd suddenly become strangers, aloof and apart from one another.

"I know he tried to kill you, Scott. You were only trying to save yourself."

Her words made me feel weak. "I was trying to stop him, Trudy. I wasn't trying to cripple him."

The door opened behind me but I didn't turn around until Trudy began to straighten and stand up. A doctor I hadn't seen before was walking over. I didn't know if Trudy wanted me to stay or go. Before the doctor could speak I said, "Maybe we should talk about this later."

She looked at me, again with that detached, almost vacant look. The color in her eyes was dull despite the sparkle of her tears. "Yes, okay, Scott. Let me call you."

I reached out and squeezed her upper arm, a concession that I had no idea how to handle the situation. I wasn't even sure what it was.

I nodded at the doctor as I passed him on my way out of the waiting room. The old lady who had been on Kleenex monitoring duty gave me a disapproving look as I crossed between her and the television screen. My mind held unkind thoughts.

CHAPTER THIRTY-THREE

I must have been in something close to shock as I drove away from the hospital. I didn't remember getting to the car, starting it up, leaving the parking lot, anything. Not even navigating the thick flow of traffic heading south in the general direction of the office.

Hubris gets all of us every time. Your one chance is to be in charge of exactly nothing. Don't start a business. Hire no one. Don't take a partner, don't fall in love, or worse, let someone fall in love with you. As soon as you feel good about something, or you taste a glimmer of success, you think it's something you can do, or worse, something you deserve to do. Maybe even something you're good at. And then life will invariably rise up and smack your nose flat against your face.

Did I love Trudy? I thought I did, I knew I did, but I couldn't separate it from the fact that I could never have her, not really, not long term. She was married. Didn't matter how much of a creep he was. That only made her safe for me to love her.

I couldn't believe she loved me back, not really. Why would she? She spent all her non-working time with the man she had chosen to marry. Yes, he turned out to be a lying bastard, but she stayed with him. Oh, she always stayed. She had a bit of fun with me—two times now—but as soon as I thought of those occasions I could almost taste the bitterness rise in my mouth.

Maybe Trudy didn't love anybody. If she loved Tim she wouldn't have given herself to me, however temporarily, would she? That thought used to make me feel good. But if she did love me, she'd had ample excuse to leave that piece of shit Tim.

Maybe it wasn't just Tim Westland and it wasn't just me. Maybe there had been others she'd been with since she'd been married. Maybe she wore her morals like one of her coordinated outfits she displayed in the office. One day they looked like one thing, the next the other, but always oh so fine.

Shit. I wasn't being fair. I slammed the steering wheel with my palm wondering if these damn things ever break. What the hell were they made of anyway? I was aware of my anger and in some corner of my mind I knew I probably shouldn't be driving. But I didn't care.

I saw a fast food chicken place and felt hunger. There was a fitness center on the corner and I suddenly wanted to work out.

My mind was spinning away from me on the end of a light string. Let it go too far and it would float away, carried by the wind, landing somewhere else. Anywhere else. Probably in a tree or wrapped in power lines.

I almost ran over someone crossing the road at a crosswalk. I tried to force myself to calm down but after thousands of years I didn't think anyone had come up with meditation techniques that powerful.

Why was Tim in the hospital? Because he'd tried to kill me? Was that really what he was going to do? Maybe he was trying to scare me, pistol whip me, steal my wallet, how could I really know?

But I did shoot him. With purpose, with malice, and with intent. Could I have drilled one through his forehead, or his heart? Or his gut, making him suffer as he slowly bled out? I knew the answer and it wasn't reassuring.

Maybe Trudy did love me. Maybe she was an idiot. I deserved all the love and care of a cactus. Get too close and I'll sting you bad.

When the light turned green I pulled into some parking lot and pounded on my steering wheel until sweat was streaming from my face and both hands had grown numb.

Jesus, what the hell did it take to break one of these damned things?

The radio was on but I never heard it. I only became aware when I heard the ringtone of my phone chirping away from my back pocket. I made an angry stab at the power switch on the radio then reached behind me to pull out the cell. Looking through the windshield I realized I didn't remember where I was.

I didn't look who was calling. I couldn't think, I didn't want to interpret. Pushing the Talk button I held the phone up to my ear and said only, "What?"

"You screwed the pooch bad, Porter. Really bad."

It took me a second. The voice on the other end was angry but it was a different kind of angry than what I had been feeling. Suddenly it clicked.

"The fuck do you want?"

"Fuck you, too. Last chance, asshole. I want the letter. Now. I'm done screwing with you."

"Gallo, you do not want to talk to me right now. You do not want to threaten, plead, buy me a drink or kiss me behind the ear." I stopped before I went on a full-on rant. "No, wait. I would like to see you, you son of a bitch. I'd like to see you real bad right about now."

"You really think you're coming out of this okay?"

"You have no idea." I hung up.

It was odd, I thought, that as the seconds passed since I'd ended the call and tossed the phone on the seat next to me the world seemed to regain some clarity around me. I recognized a shopping mall to my left and knew there would be a ballroom dance studio up ahead on the right. I started driving again and there was. I knew where I was at and I made my way into the left lane preparing to make a turn at the next light.

Gallo, Sullivan and the letter all came back to more prominent positions in my consciousness, pushing Trudy and the hospital and Tim Westland literally behind me. Maybe my plan to pit Gallo and Sullivan against each other was working after all. I had to think about it but it was still hard to remember everything that had been going on, everything I had known before....

Before I'd gone off with Trudy. That was just a trap for me now. More dangerous creatures were out there and one of them had just called me on the phone. He was a threat. Sullivan was another. I could focus on a threat.

What good is caring for something you can't touch? No one loves a cactus.

The phone rang again and this time I actually smiled. I was headed back toward the office and the wet hazy sunshine couldn't take the sharp edge off what I was seeing now. The voice on the phone belonged to Steph.

"Hey, girl," I said. "What's going on?"

"You okay, Scott?"

I think I grinned. I didn't know. Either way my face hurt. "I'm fine. What do you need?"

She sounded uncertain but she didn't ask again. "Special Agent Fitzwater called. He wants you to meet him."

"He say when?"

"Soon as you can."

Fine. I was going to be a two thousand pound shark. I was going to make something happen. "What's his number?"

"He said he didn't want you to call."

Because of Sullivan, I thought. The two of them must be together now. "Where and when?"

"Oscar Scherer State Park. Three o'clock."

That was a huge park, fourteen hundred acres, that was filled with old-growth vegetation and looked as much like Old Florida as you could find anymore on the Gulf coast. And it was far enough from the bigger cities to be mostly empty of tourists. And like locals everywhere, Floridians ignored their own attractions.

The park was large enough that the sparse visitors could get themselves lost among the twists and turns of the paths that wound through the trees, on foot or by bike or whatever, as they made their way to the dunes along the beach. These were almost always virtually empty—the public beaches in either direction took in all the crowds.

"Thank you, Steph."

"Are you—"

But I was already hanging up. My cheeks were still hurting so I thought I was probably still grinning. I worked the burner phone out of my other pocket and dialed the usual number. The man who answered wanted to be chatty but I didn't.

"Shut up," I said without sounding mean. "You know our deal."

I got off the phone less than a minute later. I really needed to stop smiling, get this rictus off my face before something else inside malfunctioned. I had to get clear.

I turned the car again, and started toward the interstate. The park was in the in-between nowhere south of Sarasota but north of Venice. I was ready to be there now, so I went. It was time to make things simple.

CHAPTER THIRTY-FOUR

Early afternoon, bright sunshine, the parking lot of the Oscar Scherer state park that I had pulled into had two other cars in it. Floridians couldn't stand the heat unless they were either drunk or it was a weekend. Tourists loved it either way, until the bugs came out, but other than the sand fleas, you just didn't want to be caught DEET-less around twilight time. I walked onto the paved trail that led to a shaded playground area. Empty, as expected. I was tempted to look up Fitzwater's number in my cell phone's call log but if something had gone wrong and he was still with Sullivan, that could ruin everything.

The heat was sobering after whatever it was I had been going through in the air conditioned car. Somewhere during the trip down I had begun to feel more like myself, whatever that meant. All I really knew was that I didn't have to like it, but as with all of us, I had my whole life ahead for self-loathing. In the meantime there was a case to wrap up.

I slowly walked along the paved path toward the gulf. Palmetto palms at sloppy angles leaned every which way, interspersed with Australian pines and patchy spots of tall grass that filled the wild spaces on either side of the trail. Giant spider webs between the trees caught the occasional sun rays that found a clear line through the foliage.

After a while the path started to rise as I crested a line of dunes. The trees fell away and sea oats dotted the rolling white sand. No one was in sight. I took out my phone to make sure I had reception. Three bars. Score one for modern technology, but let the shrinking Florida wilderness take another hit in the shorts.

Gingerly I walked down toward the firm sand at the water's edge, and I just walked. My mind was pretty wrung out at that point, a wasted muscle pushed past its normal endurance. Fitzwater would call or find me when he could. In the meantime I passed a few people walking, like myself, but no one made eye contact. People were here for privacy at this point and the presence of another human was felt as a violation to most. I made sure I didn't look back.

There was a wooden bridge up ahead that crossed over the sea oats, which were a protected plant, at least until a developer was allowed to buy them up and bulldozed them for a subdivision. They'd call it something like "Sea Oat Estates" and sell to northerners whose only experience with oats of any kind were in their children's cereal bowls.

I crossed over, away from the beach and back into the windy paths beneath and among the last of the untainted wilds of Florida. I'd been here enough that parking where I had and taking that bridge had given me my bearings. Still my phone never rang.

So I made a call, this one to Steph, who said she no one had tried to reach me. Before I could stop myself I asked if she'd heard from Trudy but the answer again was no. I wasn't surprised. She said she'd call me and I felt foolish for asking Steph. Apparently thoughts of Trudy hadn't subsided as deeply as I'd thought.

Partially as a distraction, I began to wonder if something had gone wrong with Sullivan. Whether I'd succeeded at creating a rift between Gallo and Sullivan was almost immaterial at this point: it had either worked or it hadn't. The big fault with the plan was that I had no real way of knowing which way the thing had gone until one of them told me.

My watch said I'd been there for over an hour already. I started thinking about how long it would take me to get back to my car from where I was, and even how to get back to my car, so that I could get to Trudy when she called.

Trudy again. When she called.

Screw it. No Fitzwater, no phone call. I thought I'd walk ahead on the path and see where it led by way of taking me back to my car. Since it was heading away from the beach it had to be either taking me toward a parking lot, perhaps even the one where I'd left the Malibu, or on a circuitous nature hike that ought to at some point connect with other trails. Somewhere along the way a map should make an appearance.

The path was a paved macadam and I wondered what kind of machines they had to use to do the paving. They must have been smaller than what was used on a city street. What kind of maintenance did they have to do? Did the roots from the indigenous trees here raise up parts of the—

I didn't really hear anything until I felt the crunch at the side of my head. I was still conscious as I crumpled to the ground in what felt like a slow-motion banana roll but I couldn't control my legs. When my eyes could focus I realized I was looking at a pair of shoes. Not mine, I thought, ridiculously. Then it came to me with the same force as the blackjack: Rico Gallo.

He stood above me and as I reached around my back for the P220 that used to be tucked under my shirt he merely chuckled, stepped over me, and showed me the weapon in his own hand.

"Having a bad day, Porter?"

Oh boy, did I have a comeback but while my jaw opened my tongue didn't feel like moving just then.

"See how wishes come true? I told you I wanted to meet you alone some time and boom, here you are."

I tried to roll so I could push myself up but it ended with me flat on my back again. In one hand he still held the sap he'd slugged me with and in the other he was twirling my gun.

"No, no, don't get up. Take a minute. We've got all the time in the world."

Which made me want to get up even more, and faster, and I would have if I could. After a few seconds my legs were starting to work better and I was able to roll over again and get myself to my hands and knees.

"You're doing good, Porter, you're doing good. I know how to use this thing." He tossed the blackjack a foot or two in the air and caught it, then slipped it into his front pocket. I didn't see the Sig anymore, either.

"Here, let me help."

"Faugh yoo."

He laughed, said, "No, seriously. We should get off this trail. Someone might ride over us with a bicycle." And he chuckled again.

I let him lift me off the trail. It wasn't as though I could fight him off yet anyway, and the more I moved the more control seemed to seep back into my limbs. At this point what I needed most was time. And however much I had at that point was whatever Gallo was willing to give me. I started to hope we could have a long chat about Holmes's letter.

I felt his hands in my armpits as he helped me stagger to my feet. He supported my weight as I half walked, half stumbled where he led, off the path and into the trees. I bounced off rough pine bark and sharp palm points as we made our way to a clearing that was a little lighter than the surrounding area due to an open window to the sky above. He must have spent some time finding this spot, I thought. Before spying on me walking the beach.

I was better but still not recovered enough to try to take him physically. And I knew what he could do with his knife which I saw was the only thing he was holding.

Sitting on the ground, forearms resting on my knees, I looked up at him. He was all business, looking like whatever was going on here wasn't any different from anything else he'd done dozens of times before. I was sure it wasn't.

I reached up and felt the knot in the fascia and temporalis above my ear. It felt like a potato waiting for harvest.

"You're not Fitzwater," I said, finding my tongue.

"And you're too easy." He laughed, gloating.

"He okay?"

Gallo shrugged. "No idea. He's Sullivan's to worry about."

"What do you want?"

"You know what I want. First, I have to tell you, my friend, you scream, you die."

"I sort of took that as a given."

"Good. Not that I took you for the screaming type. If it matters, I don't normally have to sneak up on people."

"I guess you don't need to when we walk right into it."

He chuckled again. His worries were mostly over, and he knew it. "It helped you were so distracted. Woman trouble?"

"Don't you—"

"Relax, cowboy. All I want is one thing."

"The letter."

"Of course."

"What about your boy Sullivan?"

"I got some news about that zook. I get the letter, I go home. He doesn't."

"That supposed to make me happy?"

"Frankly, I don't really care. This is it for me. Last chance. Ask yourself, sport, what good does that letter really do you? Why should you care what happens to it?"

I watched the knife flitter casually in his hand as he twisted the handle, the highly polished blade catching glints of the lowering sunlight.

He was right. If I just gave him the letter, Gallo would more than likely kill me, but maybe not. There might be a way to work it so that I could get myself free once we got to the post office. Assuming we got that far. I didn't think he looked enough like the picture on my driver's license to get past the clerk but as long as he could sign my name, would they really care?

My head was aching as I thought about it. If Gallo did get the letter and went away, would that be such a bad thing? I may or may not have a future with Trudy, but suddenly I sure as hell wanted to see her through Tim's recovery, whether she wanted me around or not. We could figure things out afterward. That was more important to me than anything that might happen in New England, regardless of what the mob was up to.

The real question seemed to be whether I could convince Gallo he needed me to get the letter from the post office. He'd have to keep me alive for the time being, no matter what it was he'd been planning.

"Okay, Gallo," I said. "This is too funny."

"What is?"

"You can have the letter. I'm done."

"No more games, Porter."

"I'm serious. I don't want it. What the hell for? My client's dead, his cash is in my bank, and I don't have any more fucks to give about what you and Sullivan or any of you assholes do to each other."

He stared at me. I knew he wouldn't believe me easily.

"And I hear Sullivan may try to pin Endo Robbins' murder on me."

I could tell by his expression that I'd surprised him.

"Robbins was you though, wasn't it?"

"I wasn't given a choice."

"Anything in it?"

He shook his head.

"Tell me where he is."

"You'll really give me the letter?"

"I'll have to take you to it."

Gallo stepped forward, bringing up the knife.

"No, no, hold it," I said, showing him a palm, not even trying to defend myself or get away. "It's in a post office box but I had them hold the key." I told him just what I'd done, and how. "I thought it was perfect. There's no way anyone but me can get into that box."

I could tell he was thinking.

"We go together. I sign for the key, open the box, the letter is yours. You just have to do one thing."

This wasn't easy for him. He'd had his mind made up before he slugged me. "What do you want?"

"Just get Sullivan off my back."

"I already told you he wouldn't be going home."

Now I saw what he meant. "Where's Robbins?"

Gallo made a careless gesture toward the sea. "Where do you think? It's too fucking easy down here."

"Okay, then," I told him, making eye contact. "My car or yours?"

CHAPTER THIRTY-FIVE

Something made Gallo turn.

Damn, I swore and kicked at the side of his knee, not quite ready, connecting just enough to drop him to one side. Gabe Keller was behind him, swinging a piece of driftwood and connecting with the side of Gallo's head, in much the same way Gallo had clubbed me. Only harder. And with a bigger stick.

Gallo fell forward and I scrambled out of his way, remembering that damned knife. I needn't have worried. Keller had been aiming lower but my kick had changed where Gallo's head had been.

As he went down he was still spinning. His feet were caught up in the loose sand and he fell awkwardly, almost spiraling into the ground. I made it to my feet and didn't see the knife again until I rolled him over. It was sticking out of his abdomen, just below his rib cage.

At first I wasn't going to touch it but on second thought I slid it out and wiped it clean on his pants leg. Then I reached into his pants pocket and took my gun back, along with an even smaller .22 automatic. I also took his wallet and his cell phone. These I'd take care of later.

Keller was staring down at Gallo's still face as he dropped the driftwood and collapsed onto his knees. A second later he was vomiting down his shirt front.

Gallo's eyes started blinking and his jaw began working up and down. Just before he died he said something like, "You suck... the shit... out of a cat's ass." He coughed twice, weakly and not enough to discharge anything from his throat, and then it was over.

It wasn't difficult being on my feet now. Keller had emptied himself out but had now started to cry. I felt sorry for the son of a bitch. He'd fucked me over and then tried his best to make it up but the reality was that he never had a chance. That day at my condo, when I'd brought the FBI agents and Paul McKay over to my place ostensibly to look for the letter, Keller had been waiting. He'd been planning to beg his way back into my good graces but it wouldn't have worked. What saved him at the time was that Sullivan had slipped up and so I dropped the second burner phone, the one that I had originally picked up for Eamon Stanley, into Keller's lap. I'd been calling him on it, letting him know where I was going and how I planned to get there, in case he picked up Gallo, or even Sullivan, following me.

Now look at the poor slob. This wasn't what he wanted. Whatever that was he'd thrown it away a long time ago.

In the end it worked out for me, I suppose. There was a better than even chance that Gallo would either have killed me outright or tried once he'd gotten hold of the letter. As it was, he was off the board but now I wondered if Gabe Keller would become an issue. Not only did I not want him around, he was now a first-time murderer, and with his state of mind I had no idea what he would do next. Taking someone's life wasn't easy in the best circumstances. Or the worst.

"You all right, Gabe?" I asked. I reached forward to touch his shoulder but stopped myself. I couldn't bring myself to do it.

"You– you used me," he said.

"I use everybody, Gabe. That's what I pay them for."

He wiped at his eyes with a dirty sleeve and seemed to notice the mess on his shirt for the first time. The smell was actually growing stronger as the minutes passed.

"You weren't paying me."

"Let's not, Gabe. You wanted something, I showed you a way. Neither of us saw this coming."

"Didn't you?" He tried to look me in the eye but I didn't bother staring him down. Gallo's eyes were stuck open and I watched as a large black fly landed just beneath the left one.

"The question is, what do you want to do now, Gabe?"

"What– what do you mean?"

"You just killed this guy, Gabe. Look at him." I nudged Gallo's body with my foot. "You're a murderer now. A killer. I wouldn't have thought you had it in you."

Keller pushed himself onto his feet, dripping. "I just saved your life! Don't forget, he kidnapped me! He would have killed me except—"

"That's right, Gabe. He would have killed you. Except I saved your ass. Now what do you want to do about it?"

"I don't– I don't understand—"

I pulled out my cell phone. "You want me to call the cops? I'll tell them anything you want me to, that it was self-defense, an accident. You tell me what to say and I'm there for you, man. All the way."

"I was trying to help you," he said, tears still dripping down those chubby cheeks.

"And now I'm trying to help you. How do you want me to do that?"

Keller turned his back as the full reality of what had happened in the clearing settled in. He nearly fell backwards into a tree, then used it to rotate around, still leaning his back against the trunk. "I'm going to jail. I'm going to jail."

"Is that what you want, Keller?"

"What? Um, no...."

"Then get out of town. Now. No one's looking for this asshole and no one's looking for you. This piece of shit has killed more people than you've kissed ass and you've done the world a favor."

"Yeah, but—"

"But it doesn't mean they won't hang you for it. You know where he parked?"

Keller nodded dumbly.

I got down next to Gallo's body and dug out a set of keys from his pants pocket.

"Take these."

Keller just looked at my outstretched hand.

"Take them now." I pulled his arm toward me and forced the keys into his palm. "Get in Gallo's car now, right now, and drive down to Fort Myers. It's a rental and someone will find it eventually and the car company will get it back. You come back in two weeks, no, make it three. Live off your credit cards. I'll make them good when you get back."

"Maybe I won't come back."

I won't miss you, you treacherous fat fuck. "That's up to you, Gabe. If you want out of this situation, you've got to go. Send me the bill no matter what you do."

Keller pushed away from the tree, walked shakily over to Gallo's corpse.

"Thanks for having my back, Gabe."

"I should never have listened to him." He drew his foot back and drove it into the body's side. Keller kicked him hard but the body barely moved in the sand.

He drew back his foot to do it again and I reached across the space above Gallo and shoved him back while he was off balance. "That's enough. You need to get going."

"What about—"

"I got it."

Finally, without another word Keller traipsed back through the sand, disappearing among the trees and out of sight within seconds. I wondered what it was that Keller had wished Gallo hadn't told him but none of that mattered now. Gallo was gone and I didn't have to see that slug Keller anymore. I was grateful he'd been there but I didn't forgive easily. Somehow it seemed to balance the books, his killing the man who had given him the opportunity to screw me over.

Love me like a cactus, asshole.

Using the discarded driftwood, I dug as much of a grave out of the soft sand as I could. I managed only about a two foot indentation as the rounded grains kept falling back in on themselves. Before I rolled Gallo into his grave and covered him up, I pulled out his wallet and his phone. I was sure he'd be found quickly, the question was by what sort of animal. Regardless, I thought, both Keller and I should be reasonably safe.

The sun was just inches over the far waters when I found my way back to the Malibu. I knew now the discord I'd sown between Gallo and Sullivan had been real, I just didn't know anything about Sullivan's activities. Whatever they were, I knew sure as hell he had to be up to something I wouldn't like. I was starting to feel annoyed that the real Fitzwater hadn't called me but again, if he were staying close to his partner that might be the best thing for all of us.

The problem was, for the rest of this to get wrapped up once and for all, I had to find out what he was doing. The dash clock told me that I had been at the park for nearly four hours. The nodule above my right ear had gone down somewhat but now I couldn't stand to touch it at all.

I needed to get home and get cleaned up. Trudy had said she'd call and I knew she would. I wanted to be ready.

CHAPTER THIRTY-SIX

I was showered and clean, feeling fresh in the air-conditioned space of my condo. Other than the soft spot on my skull I was feeling up to seeing Trudy again. But she still hadn't called.

Something with Tim again? I wondered. But no, that hadn't stopped her from reaching out before. I felt an extra chill. Gallo was gone. Could Sullivan—

I grabbed my phone and broke my own promise and dialed Trudy's number. It rang until it went to voice mail. Three minutes later I did it again, then again.

This is ridiculous, I told myself, then grabbed my keys off the table and rode the elevator down to the garage and the Cadillac. The Malibu was starting to carry a stench but I took the things I'd placed in the glove compartment into the Cadillac's. Until this thing was over I was keeping everything in one place.

The first stop was to the hospital. It took me almost twenty minutes to get there but Trudy was gone. Tim was sleeping, resting comfortably or whatever the hell it was they said, but Trudy had left hours ago. Tim's brother Dylan was napping on the reclining chair-thing they had in the room but I didn't want to see him.

She wouldn't have gone to the office. The only reason for her to have done that would have been to see me and she would have called my cell phone first. I couldn't think of what else to do so I drove to her house. Another twenty minutes, but when the guard tried Trudy's home he couldn't reach her either. Nothing I could say would get him to let me pass. He wouldn't even tell me if she was home but he must have known she wasn't or he wouldn't have kept trying to call her more than once like he did. He just wanted to get rid of me.

I backed out of the entrance to her gated community and pulled ahead onto the shoulder past the gate and dialed Fitzwater. Before I could say anything, he started with, "What the hell have you done?"

"What are you talking about? Look, I can't find Trudy—"

"Sullivan has the letter."

"That's impossible. Where is that asshole, anyway? I'm worried he might be looking for—"

"Yeah, you said. And it's not impossible. What did you fucking do?"

"You don't want to know what I did. Will you listen to me for one second?"

"Will you tell me how Sullivan got the letter?"

"You're serious?" I asked. Sullivan couldn't have the letter. There was no way he could even have found where to look for the letter.

I thought about Gallo: could he have been wearing a wire when he had me down in the clearing? I thought about it but I would have found it when I buried his body. His cell phone? I still had it in my pocket next to my burner, though its time was about up. I double-checked: Gallo's phone was turned off. It couldn't have been recording anything.

Keller was in the area when I told Gallo about the post office box but we weren't speaking that loudly and I didn't think there was any way Keller could have been close enough to hear what I'd been saying. Plus, he wouldn't have had time to do anything with the information if he did have it.

"Meet me at your goddamned bowling alley," Fitzwater said, and hung up.

Shit.

This time I pulled straight into the parking lot of the alley. I could see Fitzwater's company loaner off to the side and I turned and parked at the other end of the lot. He was waiting for me in the lounge, the same place we'd sat before. There was an untouched beer stein in front of him.

I took the seat opposite and for a moment the FBI man just glared at me. Then he said, "You drinking?"

"Don't know yet."

"Then you are," he said, pushing his beer over to my side of the table. "Have mine."

"Thanks," I said, but I didn't touch it. "What the hell's going on?"

Fitzwater made a show of looking at his watch. "I imagine Sullivan has that goddamned letter by now."

I shook my head. "You're wrong," I said. "He can't have it. He can't even know where it is. What makes—"

"This afternoon at approximately 3:30 p.m. Special Agent John Sullivan applied for and received an emergency federal warrant to open a post office box at the Ringling Avenue—"

"Yeah, I know where it is."

"So," Fitzwater said, deadly calm. "What did you do? I thought we had an understanding."

"We did. We do. Let me think about this for a second."

In my head I ran over everything I'd done earlier. Yes, I'd told Gallo but he died immediately afterward. Keller couldn't have heard it, I was positive, and even if he had he wouldn't have had time to do anything about it.

"Could Gabe Keller have been working with Sullivan?" It was a long-shot but it was the only thing I could come up with.

"The putz that used to work for you? He still involved somehow?"

"I don't think so. He *might* have heard me say—" I stopped myself. If I told Fitzwater I'd been in contact with Gallo there would be more explaining to do.

"So Keller knew about the letter?"

"That's just it, it's virtually impossible that he could have. And if he did, he wouldn't have been able to do anything about it...." Not without being able to talk a post office clerk into thinking that he was me. And I did the math in my head: he couldn't have even tried until after 3:30 p.m., the time when Sullivan applied for his warrant. Which meant not only that Sullivan knew about the post office prior to that time, but that he couldn't have gotten the information from Gabe Keller regardless of whether he knew it or not.

"No," I said to Fitzwater. "It couldn't have been Keller. I'm positive."

Fitzwater wasn't getting any happier. "You better drink that beer, son," he said. "You might start making more sense."

I did reach forward and grab the handle. I pulled the cheap draft to my lips and took a small swallow. And then I almost spit it up as I realized there was one other person who knew where that letter was.

Trudy.

"What?" Fitzwater said, leaning forward.

"I don't believe it," I said slowly. "I can't believe it."

"Tell me and I'll help you believe it."

So I did, slowly. I told him about seeing Trudy last night, taking her away from the hospital and out for dinner. I left out the part about where I'd spent the night but his manner suggested he took that for granted.

"And you told her about the letter."

"I told her about everything. I always do." This sounded pathetic even as I heard myself say it. It wasn't even strictly true, it was more an idealized statement of how I wished things could be, not what they'd ever actually been.

"So why the hell would this woman of yours say anything to Sullivan?"

There was only one reason I could think of.

"Can I ask you a stupid question?"

Fitzwater laughed, resigned to the downturn of events. "What the hell. As long as you don't mind a stupid answer."

"I realize you have no reason to trust me but I'm going to ask you to tell me the truth."

"Because that's worked out so well already."

"You haven't really told me anything other than what I'd already figured out," I said. "I'm asking for more than that."

He reached across the table and took his beer back. After a long swallow where I could see most of his anger had disappeared, he said, "Keep talking."

So I told him about what really happened that night in front of my office, with Stanley double-crossing me and Gallo holding a gun to my back.

"So when you told me they could have gotten the letter—"

"This is what I was talking about. Then Tim Westland happened. He came around the corner shooting. He took Stanley down and Gallo was off like a prom dress."

"And Westland was there why? What was his interest?"

"I think he wanted to kill me."

Fitzwater laughed hard, drank more beer, almost choked. "That I can understand." He wiped his mouth with a cocktail napkin. "So you took him out with a shot in the leg, blamed it on the dead guy?"

I nodded.

"Classic. This Trudy know what happened? What really happened?"

"She does now."

"Fuck," he said, leaning back in his seat. He looked around, making sure the lounge was still empty enough for our conversation to remain unheard. "So she's screwing you over by telling Sullivan where to get that letter." He shook his head. "You fucking peckerwood."

"No," I said. "That's not it." I couldn't believe that.

"You are a peckerwood."

"Up yours." Then I did think about telling Fitzwater about my night with Trudy but that was still none of his business. Besides, he might not find it as exculpatory as I did and I didn't need to lose my temper on this man.

I took the beer back and finished it. "I've got it," I said.

Fitzwater leaned forward on his elbows, hands crossed in front of him. "I surely hope so, because this shit is clear as that shit you just poured down your throat."

"What if Sullivan knew what happened that night in front of my office?"

"And how would he know that?"

"Gallo. They were working together to some degree, weren't they? Gallo took off but it wasn't until after Westland came around the corner shooting."

"What do the locals think happened?"

"That I was being held up, that Tim Westland saved my ass."

"Ah, the accidental hero. But that wasn't it."

"The accidental fuck up. He was drunk, but he wanted my ass dead on the sidewalk."

"So Gallo tells this to Sullivan, who then goes to Westland's wife, tells her the world of shit he was about to rain down on her husband—indictments, prison, the whole FBI special—"

"And Trudy gives him what he wanted."

"To save her husband." He thought about all this. "So where does that leave you?"

"With Trudy?" I hadn't a clue, but I thought that explained her most recent behavior. "That's none of your business."

"Okay," he said. "You're right. Better still, I don't care. What was it you wanted to ask me?"

"Now that he has it, what's Sullivan going to do with the letter?"

"No comment."

"So we didn't actually have a deal?"

Fitzwater smiled like an ad for a dentist.

"Look," I said. "You know he's dirty but you haven't moved on him."

"Which means what to you now?"

"So pull your head out. That means either you don't have something that will stick or you think that he'll lead you to something bigger."

Fitzwater raised his eyebrows, considering. "And?" he said.

"What do you mean 'and'?"

The Special Agent said nothing.

"There are more."

Fitzwater nodded slowly.

"Sullivan's not the only bad egg in the carton. You want them all."

"That's my job," said Fitzwater. "Get the bad ones out."

"Behind bars?"

"If possible."

"Okay," I said, thinking. "The only thing the letter can tell you is the person who wrote it. The handwriting gives you that."

"The message could mean anything."

I explained to Fitzwater what Gallo had told me about the hierarchy of the New England mob. "Any of that true?"

"In essence, yes. As far as we know right now."

"I'm guessing whoever brings home that letter has the leverage to keep the money from the mortgage scam flowing."

Fitzwater twirled the beer stein on its coaster.

"Holmes must have stopped cooperating. What was that about?"

"You want another beer?" Fitzwater asked. "I want another beer." He pushed himself back from the table and walked up to the bar.

So he was willing to listen to me and I hoped he would straighten me out if I went wrong somewhere. The only reason he'd do that much was if he thought I might come up with a way to help him. He came back with a single beer and set it down on the coaster in front of him. Bastard.

"You got to Holmes," I said.

That set him back slightly. "We had conversations," he said.

"And Sullivan found out. Or someone above him who passed the information down. That's what you think?"

Fitzwater took a slow drink from the beer stein and smacked his lips.

"Okay," I said. "The Feebs stink on ice. The rest of the world already knows that." As Fitzwater pushed the beer aside, I held up my hand. "I know, I know, but you do a hell of a job on counter-terrorism." And I reached forward and helped myself to some of the same lousy brew as before.

"Sullivan snuck out of Boston and killed Holmes in D.C.," I said. "Now he's got the letter. What's more valuable to you, the letter, or the person on the other end?"

"Where's Rico Gallo? His minders are going to want to know."

I feigned surprise. "Why ask me?"

"Because the two of you have been dancing around each other this whole time. If you haven't seen him you've talked to him. I may need him."

I pulled my cell phone out of my pocket and dropped it on the table between us. "Help yourself."

He didn't even look at it.

"So you're not talking?"

"And neither is Gallo."

The FBI man stared at my face and it was difficult to remain clear and neutral. I wasn't sure how well I did.

"He's off the table?"

"As far as I know."

"For how long?"

"He's off the table."

This time Fitzwater took the beer and drained a third of it in a gulp. "Anything I need to know?"

"You already know it."

"Okay," he said. "No more Gallo. That means Sullivan's alone."

"What will he do with the letter? Can you get it from him?"

"It's going to be too late. He's probably taken a picture of it with his phone and e-mailed it on to whoever is pulling his strings."

"Then why are you guys still here?"

"You're thinking the letter gives him a way to negotiate himself upwards?"

I shrugged. "Are you up on the phone?" Dumb question. I realized it as I said it. If the Feds suspected corruption in the ranks, the good ones couldn't risk letting the bad ones know they were being looked at with a phone tap. "Never mind," I said, waving it away.

Fitzwater finished the beer, looking very, very unhappy.

"What do we do?"

"We either give the pooch a cigarette this morning because we have surely screwed the hell out of it, or we come up with some dangerously free thinking and find a way to get this thing back on track."

I pulled out a piece of folded paper and tossed it across the table.

"What's this?"

"Transcript of the letter. Doesn't show the handwriting but it still should make sense to someone."

Fitzwater unfolded it quickly and read through it, then did it again.

"These names are garbage," he said.

"I figured."

"But they relate somehow. I might see—" He pulled his own cell phone out of his jacket pocket and said, "You mind?"

"Be right back." I got up, left the lounge, found the men's room. I gave him plenty of time while I thought about Sullivan and the letter. And Trudy. How the hell could she have done that to me? To us? Revenge for crippling her husband? What? If only the bastard had stayed home that night....

I went back to the lounge. The bartender looked up so I walked over and bought a courtesy beer, leaving him a five buck tip. There was a pair of rowdies in one corner and Fitzwater was just hanging up his phone.

"Good news?" I said.

"Fuck off."

"I just gave you that letter."

"You mean the one you could have given us before." He reached for the new beer but I picked it up first and drained the first half.

"Okay," he said. "The names she used tells us something. We might be able to figure out who this is."

"She?"

"Don't push. If this works, it will take some time. We'll have to start with the people Holmes worked with, the ones who might know what was going on internally in regards to the mob."

"That can't be many people."

"It could be no one."

"But you have a suspicion."

"Call it a hunch. It's not the same thing in this case."

This time I let him grab the beer.

"The important thing is the information may not mean much to Sullivan yet. Or whoever it is he's working with."

"They'll find out you've got it," I said.

"Of course they will. But we may have a bit of time."

"What are you going to do?"

"I'd answer that but I'd have to shoot your badge first."

So I was back out. Fair enough. I'd never wanted to be in. But I did want to help stop Sullivan if I could.

"Any chance of getting Sullivan for Holmes?"

Fitzwater shook his head. "Not without tipping off the people we're after. And even so, they tell me it's no slam dunk."

I looked at him until he realized I had something serious to say.

"What?"

"Do you even want Sullivan stopped?"

"By stopped—"

"You heard me."

Fitzwater slowly reached forward, picked up the beer, drank the last of it away, then set it down and stood up.

"No," he said. "I didn't."

CHAPTER THIRTY-SEVEN

I drove away from the bowling alley asking myself, why would Sullivan still be in town if he had the letter he'd been after for so long? He must have been or Fitzwater would have been sitting next to him on the next plane out of here.

Loose ends, I thought. There's Gallo, who seemed to have been in competition for the letter with Sullivan, with each of their sides standing to benefit. It must have all been a matter of who got to control the money from the laundering scheme now that Holmes had been removed.

I could think of two other possibilities. One of them was me. The other was Trudy.

The Gallo angle would take care of itself once Sullivan realized they'd lost contact. The only thing was he couldn't be sure why that had happened. There might be something to work with there.

Trudy had done her part. I'd find out more when I got to her. I tried calling her again but still got no answer. For the hell of it I drove up to the guard house at her gated community. The man recognized me and he was over being courteous to me.

"You coming back again?" he said.

"Is she in?"

"Maybe she never left."

I felt like getting out and ripping his ears off. "Any visitors?"

"Look, bud," he said, drawing up all hundred and fifty pounds of himself, including the scraggly hair above his lip. "I could call the cops."

"Do it, then," I said. "Here." I scrawled Marty Ables name and number on a page from the notebook in my glove compartment and held it out my window toward him. It was clear he didn't want to take it but he slowly reached forward and read the words.

"Call him," I said.

"I don't really—"

"Call the fucker," I said, "or call Mrs. Westland. Look, all I want to know is if she's safe. I don't need to see her, I don't need her to come out. I just need you to ask her if everything's okay. Can you do that?"

"I'm not supposed to—"

The knot on my head was throbbing and I didn't have much patience left. That's when I tended to do really stupid and illogical things. "She was involved with the police earlier today. And the FBI. Did you know her husband is in the hospital?"

"Mr. Westland? Is he okay?"

"No, he could explode any minute. Just call his wife and ask her if she is okay, or if she needs any help."

The punk guard turned around and went into the shack. I resisted the urge to get out and follow him inside. He'd probably tase me.

He came back a short minute later and said to me, "She doesn't want to see you."

"She doesn't even know I'm out here."

"Is your name Porter?"

Fine. "Never mind. What else did she say?"

"That she's okay and that no one should worry."

"That's all?"

"Yes, sir."

"One more thing, then," I said. "And no goddamned lip or I'm going to get out of this car and take over your job for the next fifteen or twenty minutes. You understand?"

"Hey, man, I've done what you wanted—"

"Has she had any visitors?"

"Look, I can't—"

I started to open my car door.

"No," the guard said quickly, stepping back. "No visitors."

I tossed him a business card. "You call me on that cell number if she gets any, you understand?"

He surrendered. "Yes, sir."

"And I don't care who it is. If a car comes to see her, I need to know about it. This is about her safety."

"I guess I can do that."

"Good, that's what your job's all about, isn't it?" I said. I fished in my front pocket for some money, found a fifty, held it out the window. "For your trouble."

"No, I don't—"

"Take the fucking money."

He did. I backed out and pulled away, thinking Trudy was probably safe. If Sullivan was interested in her, he probably wouldn't have let her go after she'd told him about the post office box. If anything, he'd probably want her where she wouldn't be missed and he could find her if he wanted to. So far, so good.

I pulled over into a shopping center down two miles down the road and wondered how I could speak to Trudy short of wearing a black turtleneck and going over the wall surrounding her neighborhood. Gallo's phone was still in the glove box. I took it out, turned it on. The charge was low so I plugged it into a cigarette lighter charger, hoping the thing would come up without a password.

It did. Now I had to ask myself how much of an asshole I was prepared to be. And if it would even work.

Fuck it. I dialed her number. It rang for a long time. Just before her machine would have picked up, Trudy's voice came on the line.

"It's over," she said. "You can't hurt me now."

"They can always hurt you, Trudy."

"What—"

"It's me. Please, just listen—"

"But the phone number— How are you doing this?"

"None of this matters, Trudy. None of it."

She choked back some sobs and I could hear her falling backwards onto her sofa. "Oh, Scott. You shouldn't have called. You should– you should probably never see me again."

"It doesn't matter, Trudy."

"Stop saying that! You don't know what—"

"I know everything, Trudy." And I explained it to her until she believed me.

"Then how can you— How can you even want to talk to me?"

"Can you hear me, Trudy?"

"Yes, Scott, of course...."

"I love you, Trudy."

"Damn it, Scott. Sullivan said he wouldn't hurt you. He said if I gave him that letter he wouldn't go after Tim for attempted murder and the dozen other charges he said he could file. That would have finished him. He said you'd be out of it, too, Scott. No one—"

"None of that matters."

"What did you say before?"

"I love you, Trudy."

There was a loud inhale, a long pause, and then she said, "I love you, too."

Oh my god. "I never thought I'd hear you say—"

"It's true, damn you, and you know it. It's been true for such a long time."

"Then why—" I started, but stopped. I couldn't bring myself to mention her husband's name. But she did.

"Tim hates you, Scott, hates you with an incredible passion. He was only helping you—helping us—with your work because he was afraid of what I might do if he stopped."

"But the women, Trudy, his cheating. Didn't you—"

She sighed. "Does any of that matter when it's already over?"

"You stayed though, Trudy. You could have left him any time, but you didn't."

Now she gave a bitter laugh. "I wanted him to go to counseling, you know that? I wanted him to try to... stop. But he wouldn't do it. And he knew I wasn't ready yet. To give up. He used to tease me—"

"About—"

"Us, Scott. He suspected, but he didn't *know*. And until he did, he wasn't going to ruin me, to ruin you."

I couldn't believe this. "You can't be telling me you stayed with that asshole all these months because of me?" I wanted to put my head through my own windshield.

"Oh, Scott. He said he could do all sorts of things to your license, maybe get you thrown in jail. He'd make it a scandal with my parents, Scott, and they're so old, so proud I'd married a policeman...."

I knew Trudy's father had been a cop down in Fort Myers, and his father a sheriff in Jefferson Country before that.

"It's all over now, Trudy. It has to be."

She sniffled again. "I— I know it, Scott. You should see him since they removed his leg. He's not the same man, and I don't mean to make a joke of it."

I wanted to make a different joke, ask if he were a better man. Take off some of the rottenness, what you had left ought to be an improvement.

"I can only imagine," I said.

"No, you can't. I thought he'd be bitter, full of hatred, even more so than before. But he knows he screwed up, Scott. He knows he made this happen. All by himself."

Then he knew I could have killed him instead of just planting a slug in his leg, but I wasn't going to say that. Right now I was wondering if it would have been easier if I had.

"He's broken, Scott. He knows he's done being a cop and that's all he's ever known. If he's awake right now he's sitting in that ugly white hospital bed, wearing that stupid flowered gown, crying his eyes out like a child. I couldn't stay, I couldn't watch that anymore. I couldn't pretend in front of the doctors, his brother."

I gave her some time. The silences on the phone were actually comfortable ones; I felt as connected to her as if I were sitting close to her in her living room.

"So what's next, Trudy?"

"I'm leaving him."

My heart choked in my chest, or did something that physically I hurt. I took a breath and it still hurt. I tried a longer, shallower inhale and it was better, the pain not as sharp.

"You're not going to say anything?" she asked.

I had been about to, but I thought better of it.

"Do you want me to?"

That's a hell of a thing to ask. "You need to do what's best for you, Trudy.

You can't leave Tim because of me. You have to do it for yourself."

"You can be such an asshole, Porter. I know all that. Get it?"

And I thought I did, but I couldn't come up with the words to say so.

"Are you done now, Scott? Are we done now? With this whole Holmes business?"

"Um," I said, swallowing hard. The stabbing in my chest had shrunk to only a slight ache. "Yeah, not quite. I still need to do something there."

"Really, Scott? Even if I asked you not to?"

I knew what she was saying, what she was offering. Something new, something different. But I thought of my conversation with Special Agent Fitzwater and knew I couldn't just blow him off. He knew too much about me now, or suspected. Maybe I would anyway, maybe if Trudy hadn't given Sullivan the letter, but I felt responsible and I didn't think it would take much to finish everything off. But....

"You're not asking, are you?" I said.

After a second: "No. I guess not."

"Then you get some rest, Trudy, okay? I think you're safe now. This should all be over in a few hours anyway. You just take care of you."

The same sort of tension that had been in her voice when she thought she was taking a call from Gallo was back in her voice. "You're going to—"

"Don't ask, Trudy."

"You still have it, Scott, don't you? That part of you that goes off and never tells the rest of us what you're doing, where you're—"

"I can stop, Trudy."

"Really?"

I was still thinking about my answer when she let me off the hook.

"You better," she said, and hung up.

I thumbed the End button on Gallo's phone and stared at it in my palm. Well, I thought. Didn't see that one coming.

All I wanted to do now was put Holmes and Sullivan and the whole mess behind me as fast as I could.

CHAPTER THIRTY-EIGHT

I sat in that same parking lot mulling things over. When I finally managed to stop replaying Trudy's words over and over in my head, I took up Gallo's gun, ejected the magazine, then pried each bullet out and reloaded it. It was time. I only hoped this worked. I took Gallo's phone and dialed Sullivan. As soon as I heard him pick up, I pushed the End button.

Within a minute, the phone rang back, just as I thought it would.

Of course it was Sullivan, though it wasn't his name that appeared on the caller ID.

I made note of the number. It was different than the one I'd called. He was being as careful as I thought he would be, at least when it came to leaving a trail that could connect him to Rico Gallo.

After a few rings, the phone kicked into voice mail. I waited another thirty seconds and then started texting.

Me: "U THERE?"

Him: "WHO'S THIS?"

"U KNOW. U HAVE LETTER. ME TOO"

"SO?"

"I HAD IT FIRST"

There was a bit of a wait until the familiar chime came.

"ANSWER UR PHONE"

"NO," I typed. "PORTER WATCHING. DON'T WANT HIM TO SEE ME TALKING"

Another pause.

"WHAT DO U WANT?"

This is where I hoped I had him figured. "WE CAN CUT OURSELVES IN"

"CRAZY SHIT. U KNOW WHO I WORK FOR"

"AND U KNOW WHO I WORK FOR. I KNOW WHO WROTE THE LETTER"

"HOW"

"HANDWRITING. SAME WAY YOUR BOSSES ARE GOING TO FIND OUT"

"SO?"

"FED EX CAME TODAY. WITH NEW LETTER. HAD HER CHANGE SOME OF THE NAMES. NY WON'T IDENTIFY"

"WHY?"

"MONEY KEEPS FLOWING, WITH 2 NEW SLICES OFF TOP"

"ME AND U?"

"WE CAN GET RICH"

Sullivan was thinking about the 31 foot cabin cruiser he'd bought last year but was forced to resell immediately. His bosses didn't want him to draw undue attention. And he still lived in the crappy little house his in-laws had loaned Joanie and him the down payment for twenty-three years ago. He was thinking of the place on Summit Hill that he coveted, looking down on the rest of his neighbors, being the man on top, quite literally. I'm sure he was thinking of a whole bunch of other crap, too, and I was just waiting for him to give in.

"WE NEED EACH OTHER TO DO THIS"

"YES. WE BOTH HAVE LETTERS. WE HAVE TO TURN IN THE SAME ONES TO NY SO THEY'LL BUY IT. EASY"

"PORTER?"

"WE TAKE HIM OUT"

"WHEN?"

"RIGHT NOW. WE HAVE TO MOVE BEFORE MY GUYS SEND 'HELP.' CAN U COME?"

"WHERE"

I texted him the name Oscar Scherer State Park and then the location of the parking lot closest to the trail where I'd left the real Gallo's body. That took a few minutes and my thumbs were getting tired. I wasn't used to doing this.

"I CAN FIND IT"

"I CANT STRING P ALONG MUCH LONGER. HOUR?"

Another wait before the chime. "OK"

"I WILL LOOK FOR YOU"

"OK"

"BE THERE"

"I SAID I WOULD"

And that was that.

I started the Caddy and got it moving. I called Fitzwater on my own phone and told him what was going on.

"Wait," he said. "How do you know Gallo's going to be there, too?"

"Because I told him I was through, that he could have the letter."

"You asshole," Fitzwater said. "Hasn't it occurred to you Sullivan's already told him *he* has it? Or are you playing the lottery here?"

"Stop calling me an asshole, asshole. I told Gallo I'd give him everything I had, including a Xerox of the original. In effect, he'll have everything Sullivan does. More, if that matters to anyone."

"Jesus Christ," Fitzwater said. "What do you expect to happen now? A shootout at the Palm Beach Corral?"

"That's on the other coast," I said. "Florida's a peninsula, dumbass. No,

I expect you to get down here and take them both in. Sullivan will have the letter and I'll try to get everything on tape."

"Florida's a two-party consent state."

This meant that all parties to a conversation had to approve of its being recorded, which made some of the things I did in my business damned inconvenient. Or illegal. "Are you trying to talk me out of it? At least you'll have them speaking in their own words. Play the recording back in the right ears—"

"Which would still be illegal."

"If you don't—"

"Fuck off. I know what you mean. Tell me where to be."

I did. And I told him he had to hustle because everyone else was already on the way.

"You should have called me first, damn it," anger in his voice.

"I was finishing my beer," I said. "Relax. You get there in time, you make your case. You'll get everything you want."

"You know I will."

"So get moving."

"I'm already driving."

CHAPTER THIRTY-NINE

There was enough light to see by, but not much more. I pulled my car deep into the shadows at the end of the parking lot furthest from the trailhead. I loaded my pockets with the things I'd taken from Gallo—his gun, knife and cell phone—then walked over along the edge of the pavement. I knew it wouldn't be too difficult to find Gallo's corpse. Once you got on the trail, there were two large bends about sixty yards in, then a relatively straight section with a bench just before another large curve. The clearing where Keller had saved my ass was inside that area.

I wasn't sure how this was going to go down. Sullivan was going to be suspicious when he saw me but I needed to get him to give me some leeway and the only way I could think to do that was a bit on the morbid side. Actually, it was a lot on the morbid side.

I made my way up the trail and found the bench that marked the start of that final curve. I pushed my way through the brush holding a dead palm frond in front of me to take out the spiders and their webs. I must have made a god-awful noise but I couldn't help it. I knew Gallo wouldn't spook.

The clearing was to my left but even knowing that I almost missed it in the dark. I didn't want to use a flashlight until I was deep enough in so that the odds of being spotted before I was ready were greatly reduced.

I found the lump in the sand that should have been where I'd left the body of Rico Gallo. Oh, it was still there, but it was mostly uncovered already. Using the light I saw the sand was dotted with tiny feet and claws of various shapes and sizes. All it took was one pass with the light over the exposed face to know I didn't want to look at that again. There wasn't much I could do about the smell.

I put the flash back in my pocket then knelt in front of Gallo's corpse and slid my arms beneath his arms, facing toward his feet. I held my breath as I pulled him out of the pit I'd dug such a short time ago. Rigor was already passing and the body was pliable in only the way a—

I wasn't going to dwell on it. I pulled him toward me and over to the edge of the clearing where I propped him against the bole of some palm I couldn't identify in the dark. The important thing was that I was able to keep him in something like a sitting position.

I took my flashlight out and found the spider-brush I'd been using and made my way back to the trail. I found the bench and sat down after carefully making sure the recording app on my phone was set and the brightness of the screen turned all the way down.

Now it was waiting time but it didn't take long. Within twenty minutes I heard the heavy, cautious steps coming up the trail.

"Sullivan," I called, softly.

The steps stopped and in a moment he said, "Gallo?"

I flicked on the flashlight. "It's me. Porter." I wiggled the beam across the trail.

"The fuck you doing here?"

"Waiting for you?"

"Why?"

"Because you scare the hell out of Gallo. Why do you think?"

He came closer and I could see him standing at the bend but I kept the light off him. "Where is he?"

"Back here," I said. "He told me he texted you."

Sullivan thought about this. He was being careful. "He told me you were watching him."

"I was. But that was before we arrived at our own little deal."

He tried to walk quietly but he couldn't leave the trail without rustling the vegetation. The sand on the tarmac beneath his soles was impossible to stifle. There was a gun in his hand as he came forward into the light.

I put pressure on a spot on my smart phone's screen in my jacket pocket. "You don't need the gun," I told him.

"I don't know that yet," he said. "Why are you here?"

"Good question. I'm here to end this thing so that everybody's happy."

"Let me see your hands."

I held them up, careful to keep the flashlight beam away from his face. I didn't want him any jumpier than necessary.

"I need to see Gallo."

"You will," I said, motioning with my head. "He's waiting. I'm earning my part here. He wants to make sure there's a deal before he faces you alone in the middle of a deserted state park."

"What do you know about any deal?"

"Lower the gun and I'll tell you."

He did, but he didn't put it away. "I knew you were a crooked son of a bitch when I met you." He said this with the disgust and revulsion that only those already bent beyond recovery can manage.

"Well," I said, "we all have secrets. Here's what I know." And I recounted the conversation I'd had with Gallo, the one he used as a distraction until he had me set up with Eamon Stanley. The late Eamon Stanley.

"You still don't know anything."

"I know a bit more than the mob's current org chart. I know that letter listed in code the names of the principals in Holmes's mortgage scam. I know those are names for the people who are getting the money."

"Who wrote the letter?"

I shrugged, but he may not have been able to see it. "Gallo knows. All he told me was it's a woman he knows. I don't need any more. When I gave him a Xerox of the letter he recognized the handwriting right away."

"That son of a bitch! He told me—"

"He told you he didn't know who wrote the letter, didn't he?"

Sullivan didn't answer. I hoped that meant I was correct. I went on.

"Gallo got hold of her. Today she sent him a new letter, overnight express."

"What for?"

"It changes some of the names. Enough so that Gallo thinks he can spin the scheme a different way."

"Why would he do that?"

"Because with the changes he made you guys get a piece of the pie. Isn't that what you want?"

"You don't get to know what I want."

"Stop talking so tough, Sullivan. You're just another dirty cop out to get what he can for himself."

"You—"

"Stop it. I don't care. Not even a little. You killed Holmes and your boyfriend back there in the woods threatened my woman. I want you gone. I got paid by Holmes. There's nothing left in any of this for me. I just want you boys out of my state."

"I haven't killed anyone." In the flashlight I could see him looking around him. Part of him had to be thinking that if there was anyone listening he wasn't going to admit to any murders. "If what you said was true you wouldn't be sitting here."

"Well, it's true that I'm looking for a bit of a negotiating fee from yourself and Gallo."

"You're more of a bum than I thought you were."

"Sure, but I set all of this up. See, it only works if you go back to your dirty bosses with the same letter that Gallo turns in. And that has to happen soon, like tomorrow, because you've already told them you have it, haven't you?"

Tiny wheels were spinning inside Sullivan's head. I was just hoping they were coming up dollar signs.

"Take me to Gallo."

"I want twenty grand."

"You're an idiot. If this works out the way you say, I can give it to you. Once."

Bullshit, I thought. "And so will Gallo. That's my end. One time only payment."

"You're damn right it is. If you fuck with me I'll pin so much shit on you—"

"Stop embarrassing yourself. I know what you can do. Why do you think I want out? I can't beat the Feds."

"You're right."

"Especially the crooked ones."

"Yeah? How long did it take you to figure you couldn't make that letter work for yourself?"

"Funny, I thought I was."

He started forward and I took that as a good time to get up myself and lead him to Gallo. As I turned into the trees he said, "My gun is pointing at your back."

"I assumed," I said, without turning around. "If you pointed it at your dick you'd fall over."

His reply was lost in the palmetto frond I snapped back into his face. I kept the flashlight beam on the ground immediately in front of me and stopped at the edge of the clearing.

"What are you doing?"

"Gallo's not going to let you know where he is until he knows you're on board."

"How do I do that?"

"First, put away your gun. Second, tell him."

"He's here."

"He is."

I gave Sullivan time to think about it. Since I had the light on in front of us, he should figure that Gallo would be able to see him and not the other way around. He also knew he could get me any time he wanted. "Give me your gun," he said.

I was going to leave it in the car but I thought this way was easier. I eased it out of my back pocket and held it behind me. It was gone in a moment.

"If Gallo wanted to shoot you, he would have done it already. I could have, too, if you think about it."

He ignored me. "Why doesn't he say anything?"

"He's not giving away his position until he knows you won't be doing the shooting."

"I don't like this," he said, but he knew the logic was sound and he reached to his hip and inserted his pistol. "Why do you keep speaking for him? Gallo?" he called. "You see that? No guns. Where the hell are you?"

I moved the light slowly across the surface of the clearing. "It's good, Gallo. He's agreed," I called.

I was beginning to get nervous. Where the hell was Fitzwater? Normally I felt cooler in situations like this but part of me couldn't forget my earlier conversation with Trudy and it was distracting as hell. I had to keep myself focused.

Another flashlight snapped on to my left.

"Jesus," I said. "You took your time." I was worried Sullivan might try to run but as I turned two large hands shoved me hard into the sand that had recently been part of a grave.

"He's right here, Fitzwater. You've got him. And there's—"

"Shut up," Fitzwater said. "Where's Gallo?"

I used my own light to pass over the dead man's sand-covered shoes.

"Come here," Fitzwater said.

I wasn't sure who he was talking to, but I pushed myself up and walked forward. I heard Sullivan coming, too.

"Do I need to search him?" Fitzwater asked me. Sullivan was off to my right, still behind me. I assumed his gun was in his hand and pointed at Sullivan.

"This is what he had." I took Gallo's gun, knife and phone out of my jacket pocket and held them out to Fitzwater. He dropped the knife and phone onto the sand in front of the body but kept the gun.

"Does he have the letter?" asked Sullivan.

I stepped back, but not too far. "You're welcome to check." I shined my light on the ruined face again just to share the effect.

Fitzwater said, "There's no letter, is there, Porter?"

"You know there's not."

"So Sullivan has the only one?"

"He has the original. There was no Xerox. We figured the letter was in a code or cipher of some sort, so we were more concerned with the text. If we needed an actual copy, we could have made one any time."

"But you didn't," said Sullivan.

"I just said that."

"Where's the letter, John?" asked Fitzwater.

Sullivan patted his chest, where his breast pocket would be. "It's here."

Fitzwater brought the gun up and fired once into his partner's stomach.

"What the—"

Fitzwater stepped forward but I stopped him. "You don't want to make too much noise," I said. "Sometimes you get park rangers down here after dark."

"They'd have a hard time finding us," the agent said but he stepped back anyway. I shone my light on Sullivan's body. Fitzwater knew what he was doing. Sullivan wasn't getting up again, at least not unless a surgical team appearing onsite within the next minute or so.

"Hand me the letter," Fitzwater said.

I knelt down and worked it free from Sullivan's pocket and handed it up to Fitzwater. He shook it open and glanced at it. "This is it?"

"That's it," I said. "An awful lot to kill two people for, isn't it?"
Fitzwater looked up at me. "Two?"

"Your partner here is one, but you did Holmes in D.C., didn't you?"
A crooked little grin appeared on his face. "What makes you think that?"

"Any number of things," I said, as I started to stand.

"You're fine down there," said Fitzwater. "Like what?"

I stayed where I was, crouching. "It didn't really add up," I told him. "I showed you the transcript of the letter at the bowling alley. You said the names were garbage."

"So?"

"How the hell would you know that?"

"That's thin gruel, my friend."

"Well, you are standing there with a gun pointed at my eye. And you had your partner here on an awfully long leash if he were really a dirty cop you were supposed to watch."

"Nothing you can prove."

"Do I get a chance to try?"

"I don't think so, no."

"One question," I said. "Was Sullivan—" and I laid my hand on the dying man's chest—"really dirty?"

"He played at it," Fitzwater said. "I wasn't quite sure if he meant it or not. Doesn't matter now though, does it?"

"I suppose not. Can I get up now?"

"No," he said, and fired, point blank range, at my face.

I slid my hand into Sullivan's jacket pocket and pulled out the P220 before Fitzwater had a chance to react and pull his service weapon. I fired the Sig four times before he dropped to his feet. Once or twice would have been enough, but I knew he'd understand. You shot till they dropped.

"I only put one round in Gallo's gun," I said. "Asshole."

Sullivan had gone quiet but Fitzwater's mouth was still moving. Whatever he was trying to say, I wasn't interested. I reached into his pocket and took out Gallo's cell phone and knife, wiped them down, put them back. And I took Holmes's letter back. Whoever wrote it was safe enough from this thing, and hopefully they'd get the hell out of Dodge since they surely already knew Holmes had been killed because of it. But I didn't care much either way.

Someone else will sort this mess out. Shame about my little gun, though. It was about to find a new home in the Gulf of Mexico.

I turned off my flashlight and did my best to make a clean path back through to the macadam. No one seemed to have been around to hear anything, which was what I expected. If someone had been around, it would have been almost impossible to pinpoint the source unless they'd been almost right on top of us. And if that were the case, we'd have heard them moving around, talking or doing something, but there was nothing.

Like I said, the park was a beautiful place, but it was much harder to get to than the public beaches both up and down the coast, so even with the swelling cities, towns and subdivisions of a constantly exploding population, it was still possible to find little jewels of what Florida used to be.

And probably should be still, but this was as corrupt a state as any when it came to land development. Law enforcement, too, I thought as I made the pavement, switched off my light and headed toward the car. The gun would have to wait for one of those public beaches a few miles up the coast. Just to stay safe I wanted out of there as soon as possible.

CHAPTER FORTY

It was the birds that did it. Turkey vultures and other carrion birds didn't usually cloud the skies that close to the beach and as they circled around a particular clearing in the Oscar Scherer State Park, they were certainly noticed. As were the bodies of three men, two of which the authorities identified quickly. The third one took them a while longer.

I had gone back to Sarasota after first stripping down to my shorts at a public beach and walking out to a drop-off about forty yards out. I tossed my gun as far as I could out into the waves, thinking I was deep enough that storms and rough waves wouldn't carry the gun back to shore.

When I made it back to my condo I found I was exhausted. There was a message on my machine from Detectives Beck and Morris asking me to come in the next morning. Fine by me. I took a steaming hot shower, washing salt water, gunshot residue, and any other sort of trace evidence I might have on my body. My clothes and even my shoes went into the over/under washer in my closet.

The next morning I went in to give another statement to the cops regarding the Tim Westland shooting. I was a bit surprised to learn about the seriousness of his stroke—Trudy hadn't gone into details. Apparently with the paralysis along his right side, they were resolved to take one last statement from me and call it a day. Since things were actually worse for Tim than I'd thought I wondered how Trudy was handling things. But it didn't matter any more, did it? Not really.

The detectives and I shook hands all around and I left the headquarters building, resisting the urge to call the office. Paul McKay was there and he could handle anything that came up. I found a florist and went in and bought an arrangement for Trudy. I figured if I was going to the hospital I could give her the flowers openly, especially with the cops backing off, and if anyone thought it strange I was giving flowers to another man's wife, well, we could always pretend I'd brought them for Tim. It felt a bit strange but I was past caring. I just wanted to see Trudy again and I didn't want to go empty-handed.

She was sitting at his bedside when I walked in. She turned to look at me but didn't get up. She looked at the flowers and said, "Those should be for Tim."

"But they're not. Although you can share if you'd like." I walked around the bed and placed them on a table by the window. "He's sleeping?" I wanted to be sure before I said anything inappropriate.

She nodded and said, "His brother went home today."

"Really? He coming back?"

"I'm sure. Work things...."

Now I could see the lines beneath Trudy's eyes, the sagging cheeks.

"What's wrong?" I asked. I tried not to look at the asymmetry beneath the covers where both Tim's legs should have been.

"It's the stroke," she said. "He can't speak very well, and he's lost most of the use of his right side."

I studied his face. He looked thinner than I'd ever seen him, and much less of an ass with his face completely at rest.

"How long has he been out?" I asked, not knowing if that was a stupid question.

Trudy nodded. "He just closed his eyes a few minutes ago. The physical therapists try to get him doing some exercises twice a day but they mostly just seem to wear him out."

I walked back around the bed and squeezed her shoulder. "I'm sorry this is so hard on you."

She put her hand on top of mine and said, "We should go for a walk."

"Beautiful," I said. "The sun is shining and the air is steaming but there's a sea breeze so it's nice out there. Come on," and I reached for her hand. It felt so right when she took it, in public, for the first time with the two of us—together.

As we left the room she squeezed it tightly and pressed her shoulder into my side. If anyone looked at us strangely, I didn't notice. And I certainly didn't care. It was a new day in so many respects.

We made it outside and crossed the parking lot, not saying anything to each other, just walking slowly, almost swaying, lost in each other's company. There was a small garden back of the hospital and we slowly made our way there.

It was empty. I'm sure it wouldn't stay that way but with how transplanted Floridians loved their air conditioning I wasn't surprised.

"I love you, Scott. I love you with all my heart."

I guided her to a bench and sat her down, then leaned over her and gave her a tender and passionate kiss that must have lasted for hours. Her hands rubbed across my chest then encircled my back and pulled me closer and closer until I finally had to grip the back of the bench to keep from falling on top of her.

And it was wonderful.

When we finally stopped the kiss, I said, "I love you, too. You know, I've been hinting at it for years."

She punched me in the arm as I settled next to her, very close, on the bench. "Yeah, I noticed. You should stop now."

"You always say that."

"You never stop."

"I never will."

Her face grew serious and all I could think of was how much I wanted to lean in and kiss her all over again.

"None of this is easy," she said.

"I know it, honey, but we'll get through it."

"I— I don't know."

"What do we need to talk about? Tim? His insurance will pay for the care he needs, he'll get most if not all of his pension, he'll be okay, Trudy. It's a tragedy what happened but we don't need to go into that again. I don't mean to be insensitive. Whatever he tried to do to me wasn't ever as bad as what he'd been doing to you all those years."

"He only did to me what I let him," she said.

"Why do you say that?" I asked. "We're here, together. We're going to be happy. You don't need to feel sorry for yourself anymore."

She acted like she hadn't heard me. "Who knows why people stay in situations like that? You don't want to fail, you didn't go into the marriage on a whim so you shouldn't get divorced easily. Maybe he'll stop, you tell yourself. Maybe things will get back to what they were at the beginning. Maybe I need to do something different, be different. Pick one. Pick several."

"But it's over now," I said.

"It is, Scott. You've seen him, if just for a minute. He's not the same man he was. He may never be again. You should see him try to eat, part of his mouth working and chewing and the other part just... slack, loose. I'm ashamed to say it but it's ugly, Scott. It's just... ugly."

My arm was still around her and I pulled her tight and kissed her temple gently.

"It'll be okay, Trudy."

"But it won't, don't you see? Yes, he tried to kill you and part me wishes you had— you had—"

"Don't say it, honey."

"But you didn't, and it was one thing when he lost the leg. He could get a prosthetic, he may even have been able to work again. But the stroke, Scott—"

"We'll get him what he needs, Trudy. We will. Together we can make sure—"

"There is no together, Scott."

The heat of the day vanished, and my spine turned chilly and hard.

"You said you were leaving him."

"And I was, Scott. I meant everything I said. I wasn't toying with you. I wanted to be with you, to melt with you, to share life with you, be everything with you."

"Then we'll do it, Trudy. I want all those things, too."

"I believe you are the love of my life."

I wanted to say the same thing back to her but I'd never thought in terms like that and I actually didn't know how to reply. I didn't want to be as foolish and exuberant as I felt and parrot her words back to her. Instead I said, "I love you more than I've ever loved anyone, Trudy. What more do we need?"

"Nothing, Scott. In a better world, not one damned thing more. But that man up there—"

"The one that tried to kill me." I couldn't stop the bitterness.

"And the one that cheated on me," she said, keeping even. "He's there because of what both of us did. Not just because of you, but because of the two of us."

"That's insane, Trudy. I'm the one that shot him."

"He came after you because of me, Scott, because of how I feel about you. He knew all about it. How could I hide something like that? And he couldn't take it anymore. I've always wondered if that's why he started cheating in the first place...."

I pulled my arm back and got to my feet, shading her face from the sun with my body. "That's crazy talk. Tim cheated because he could, because he put on that uniform and that gave him a ticket to pick up a certain kind of woman, the kind that would make him feel like he was bigger than he was for a little while. And when that stopped working, he took all his bullshit, all his guilt, and put it on me and tried to do something about it, drunk like a coward and shooting his gun."

Trudy put her face in her hands and started to cry.

"That's the sort of man that's lying in that bed up there, honey. He may be injured, maybe he'll never be the same man he was, but he's not your responsibility any more. He made his choices, and they were selfish ones. Tell me just once where he considered you in all of that. Tell me!"

I was being cruel now but I couldn't stop. The more she cried the more I feared what was coming.

"This is our chance, Trudy. This is *our* chance. You've done all you can for that man, both before and after I shot him."

More sobbing.

"You told me you were leaving him. You were going to be with me."

She didn't look up.

"You told me I was the love of your life." This seemed like a dirty trick, saying this back to her this way.

"Trudy, come with me. Come with me now."

"I want to, Scott. You'll never know how much I do."

"Then isn't that the reason to do it? Right now. We'll figure everything else out later." It felt imperative that I get her away from this place now, this very moment. I had to break the grip her guilt, or whatever it was she was feeling, had on her.

"I can't, Scott," she said. "You saw him. He's not the same man."

"He never was the same man," I said, feeling like a brute.

"I can't leave him like this. I just can't."

"You can, Trudy. I'll help you."

"That's the whole problem," she said, dabbing at her eyes with her sleeves. "I don't think you can."

"We need to try. Together."

"You saw him up there."

"Trudy—"

"I love you."

I didn't know what more I could say, what else I could do. Ridiculous images flooded through my mind like flash pictures: what if I hadn't shot him? Or what if I'd killed him instead? What if I'd told the truth about what happened and he were rotting in jail right now? Would that have freed Trudy from her obligations? Would she be taking my arm right now, would we be starting a new life together, finally, as one?

"I— I love you, too." Then, "Don't you dare forget me."

I hadn't realized I'd already begun walking away.

"Scott?" she called. "Don't you forget me."

I wanted to stop, I wanted to ask her one more time, beg her if necessary, but there was no part of me that thought there was any possibility of her changing her mind. I did know her that well.

So I kept walking, with Trudy behind me crying into her hands, her crippled homicidal cheating "husband" lying upstairs trying to figure out what the hell he'd done to screw up his own life so badly. At least I hoped that's what he was doing, if he were still capable. I didn't know or care how much brainpower he could muster at that moment but I'd have given a lot to know that he could feel sorry for himself. It made me angry that he would be spared the self pity of losing his wife.

You won, you bastard, I thought. After all the shit that you pulled, shit that could have put you in the ground or behind bars, and you still ended up with the girl.

My girl.

I would have kept walking but there was no place to go, not really. The area was a mecca for cars and bad driving so I made my way back to the Cadillac. I wanted to sit for a while and let my mind fill with blankness but the car was an oven and once I started it for its air conditioning, I couldn't stop the urge to put it into gear and just drive away.

And just drive away.

Also by Rick Ollerman...

"You want grim, you want fast-paced, you want in-your-face moments you'll find them here. But you'll also find nuanced characters and a style that serves the story, yes, but is capable of giving us real resonance and even a kind of ugly beauty. I not only enjoyed them, I admired them." —Ed Gorman, author of the Sam McCain series

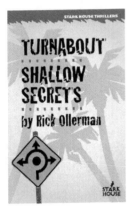

TURNABOUT/SHALLOW SECRETS

"Rick Ollerman's *Shallow Secrets* and *Turnabout* are just the sort of thrillers I like: filled with tough, unsentimental prose, surprising plot twists, compelling characters, and pure, powerful storytelling."
—James Reasoner, author of *Dancing With Dead Men*

"All the slam-bang anyone might want."
—Booklist

Rick Ollerman **Turnabout / Shallow Secrets**
978-1-933586-47-2 $19.95

TRUTH ALWAYS KILLS

"Highly recommended as an excellent piece of contemporary noir, and fully establishes Ollerman as an author to be reckoned with."
—Alan Cranis, *Bookgasm*

"What makes this novel a winner is Ollerman's storytelling chops and his vividly memorable characters. Highly recommended."
—*Deadly Pleasures*

Rick Ollerman **Truth Always Kills**
978-1-933586-82-3 $17.95

Stark House Press

1315 H Street, Eureka, CA 95501 · 707-498-3135
griffinskye3@sbcglobal.net · www.starkhousepress.com